For

Cathy,

FROM

Reba Wilton

8/1/09

Seeds of Temptation

REBA WILTON

TULSA

LIBRARY OF CONGRESS CATALOGING-IN-PUBLICATION DATA

Seeds of Temptation | Reba Wilton

ISBN 13: 978-09798345-2-3
ISBN 10: 0-9798345-2-X

Library of Congress #2008936319

Cover and interior design by Müllerhaus Publishing Group.

Published in the United States by:

Müllerhaus Publishing Group
5200 S Yale Ave | Suite 501
Tulsa, Oklahoma | 74135
mullerhaus.net

Printed in the United States of America.

9 8 7 6 5 4 3 2 1

To the loving memory of my mother
who died when I was fourteen.

The world is filled with the dead and crying,

As plague smites both the living and dying

While the mourners hope for another breath,

The first dreaded symptom means certain death.

An orchid transplanted in desert sun,

Has nowhere to hide and nowhere to run.

They die suddenly with nothing to do.

Will all humankind meet their Waterloo?

Prologue | Plague and Panic

Some are doomed to die from disease... JEREMIAH 15: 2

Has God abandoned humankind? Currently over forty million people have died worldwide and the death rate is still climbing. Authorities claim this devastating plague—which kills men and women differently—isn't contagious. Funeral homes, casket makers, cemeteries, and florists are thriving while medical examiners and research doctors struggle to find clues to the cause...

Dr. Alex Mueller finished reading the story in the *Atlanta Journal-Constitution* as he waited for the news conference to begin. All too soon a camera operator whistled, motioning for him to take his position on the podium. With the stench of fear permeating the air, he reluctantly walked to the front of the conference room as cameras flashed and shutters clicked wildly. He looked at the reporters who were either extremely brave or desperate for a story, with only their thin cotton masks to protect them from the most deadly plague in recorded history. Unlike everyone around him, he hadn't donned a mask since he didn't believe they could stop the senseless deaths.

A crew member signaled only two minutes remained until airtime. As he glanced at the cameras, each second seemed to take an eternity and his stomach knotted. How could they expect him or anyone else to have answers about a plague with an unknown cause and such a strange pattern of death?

Alex dreaded public speeches. Pesky stomach butterflies and occasional spells of stuttering always nagged him, but today his stage fright was soaring toward a new peak. With the tension thick in the room and the press conference being aired on national news, Alex could feel his knees begin to tremble and his jaw tighten as he stood in front of the small, wooden podium. Shy, with a photographic memory, he'd maintained the physical appearance of a teenage boy whose shoulders never broadened and muscles never toned. He personified the ultimate, forty-two-year-old nerd. Mousy-brown hair danced in every direction around the sharp angles of his narrow face and his thick, round glasses sat slightly tilted upon his long, pointed nose. Acting as Chief of the Atlanta Department of Health for over ten years hadn't improved his bashfulness or overcome his Woody-Allen looks.

As a camera operator counted down the last ten seconds, Alex's anticipation peaked. Soft groans accompanied a low murmur that engulfed the room. The frightened reporters seemed on the verge of becoming an angry mob.

Finally, they signaled that they were on the air. Alex cleared his throat and began, "I know you're here today for explanations of the cause and cure for the plague ravaging our world. I personally don't have the answers you seek, but we're going to allow you to question Dr. Cleta Worthington in a moment. Dr. Worthington is a friend and colleague who's conducted an enormous amount of research on the plague, and therefore, she's the most knowledgeable regarding it. Dr. Worthington worked several years at the Atlanta Center for Disease Control as the chief microbiologist. She also spent ten years as the supervisor of the microbiology lab at one of our most reputable pharmaceutical facilities, Clayton Research Center." With a quick nod in her direction, he said, "Dr. Worthington."

The crowd collectively grumbled as Dr. Worthington approached the podium and straightened her notes. A dynamic woman in her late thirties, her husky build prevented her from being a raving beauty. Even so, she was far from unattractive. Unlike Dr. Mueller, she typically considered public speaking a breeze; but she, too, was uncomfortable under these circumstances.

After nervously clearing her throat, she began, "First of all, I'd like to say that I've studied this pandemic for many months now, but I'm not alone. Doctors and scientists have industriously contributed from all over the world, trying to find a cause. We assembled at the CDC earlier this week to discuss our collective findings. We have some bad news and some good news. The bad news is we don't have a cure yet because we currently are unable to determine the precise cause."

A visible wave of frustration moved across the crowd as the reporters collectively moaned.

Raising her hands, she continued in a calm voice, "Wait! Please, let me explain. We've failed to diagnose the cause of the plague because, based on all our research, it cannot be identified as any known bacterial, viral, fungal, or parasitical pathogen. Since there isn't any existing evidence the source is a germ—no cause, no cure. We've performed numerous blood tests on many of the victims—all with unremarkable results except a slightly elevated white blood count in a small percentage of cases. This is normally associated with infections or organ transplants—neither of which were found. Therefore, the good news is, whatever the enigmatic plague is, it doesn't appear to be contagious—or at least not contagious in a known method. Nevertheless, I can assure you our diligence will continue until we find an explanation and a remedy. Now, I'll answer all the questions time will allow." She pointed to an attractive middle-aged woman in the back of the room, "You first, ma'am."

The reporter stood to ask, "Since the first reported cases of the plague were in the heartland of the United States, is there any chance this plague was engineered by terrorists?"

"There isn't any evidence remotely tying any terrorist organization to the plague. After 9-11 and during the war in Iraq, the world experienced a disease known as SARS or Severe Acute Respiratory Syndrome. This disease was questioned as a possible terrorist attempt to cause the deaths of more innocent people, but we now know that a previously unknown member of the coronavirus is the source of SARS. The common cold is an example of this strain of viruses. Unlike SARS, the nature of this plague is still unknown and doesn't seem contagious."

A small, heavyset man—resembling a troll more than a reporter—was just one of the many people to raise his hand. She pointed to him, maybe out of pity, or solely because he stood out in the crowd. Adjusting his black, horned-rim glasses, his deep voice bellowed through his thin cotton mask, "If the plague isn't contagious, why are so many people dropping dead like flies? This morning the world's cumulative death toll estimation from the plague is over forty million with the hardest hit being third-world countries. Can you explain why so many people are dead?"

Dr. Worthington replied, "I'm sorry. We don't have an answer yet. We're working as fast as humanly possible to discover the nature of the illness. Next question, please."

This time she selected a pretty, young African-American from the back row. The charming reporter stood and spoke in a soft voice. "Is it true the plague doesn't seem to affect the very young or the elderly? And if so, is it possible the plague has been created by scientists in laboratories as an effort to reduce the world population by eliminating a percentage of those capable of breeding?"

The question hit a raw nerve with Dr. Worthington. She became lost in thought as the crowd muttered. The possibility that this could be a man-made catastrophe had crossed her mind more than once. She remembered all too well the scandal when vials of dangerous pathogens went missing from the Clayton Research Center. Was the Clayton family capable of trying to control the world's population? She was almost certain the answer was yes.

Regaining her focus, she replied, "It's true this disease rarely kills anyone under twelve or over seventy-five. Whether the disease is man-made or not has yet to be determined. Next question please."

This time she selected a handsome, middle-aged man on the front row, who asked, "Is it true the plague kills males and females differently? And if so, is there any credence to the speculation about space aliens or death angels from heaven selecting the victims to complete an apocalyptic quest?"

The audience went wild, groaning, and mumbling with heightened discontent.

Dr. Worthington, beginning to lose patience with the mob-like group, shouted, "Please—everyone settle down! You're acting like children. You need to remember I'm not the enemy. I didn't cause the plague, but I am working extremely hard to find its cause and cure. I want to stop this epidemic as much as you want it stopped, but I can only give you the answers I have."

When the room grew quiet, she calmly said, "Sometimes the first noticeable symptom is sudden death, with the cause being uterine and or vaginal hemorrhage in women and cerebral hemorrhage in men. So far, we haven't been able to explain this gender difference. Logic dictates that the tabloid trash about aliens or death angels is simply untrue. And last, but certainly not least, before someone asks about the bizarre patterns of death, we also cannot explain why the plague typically kills either the husband or the wife, but rarely both. We know the exception to this 'one or the other rule' is extremely rare. Because the plague manifests itself with this strange pattern of death, it has been coined the Spouse Killer..."

* * * * *

The television screen faded to black as Alex Mueller took the VCR remote from Cleta Worthington's hand and ejected the videotape. "Please," he pleaded, "It's been three days. We don't need to watch the tape again. I'm telling you for the last time, the press conference went as well as you could have expected under the circumstances. You couldn't give them answers you didn't have!"

"I know," she replied. "I also know someone from Clayton Research Center is connected to the plague. I'm just not certain how—or who—but I'm almost positive the source of the Spouse Killer will eventually be traced there."

"I thought you liked Dr. Pamela Barnes. You seemed happy to see her at the last conference. Isn't she connected to the Clayton Research Center?"

"Yes, by marriage. I've always liked Pam and Roulett Barnes—it's their husbands, Kirk and Jack, I don't trust and never did. I could be wrong, but I don't think old John-George Clayton is culpable, other than for hiring his grandsons, Jack and Kirk Barnes. My gut instinct tells me that one or maybe both of them are responsible for the Spouse Killer."

Sitting on her sofa sipping wine, Alex was hesitant to mention his suspicions about her persistent attempts to connect Clayton Research Center with the Spouse Killer. Since he'd always based their relationship on honesty, he asked, "Do you think maybe you resent everyone from Clayton Research Center because they unjustly fired you?"

Barely missing the colorful fruit tray, she slammed her glass on the table. "They didn't fire me—they just didn't renew my contract!"

Alex knew to smooth her ruffled feathers or he'd be kicked out of her nest. "I'm sorry. I didn't mean to upset you. You told me the reason they didn't renew your contract was that the board accused you of stealing vials of dangerous pathogens from the lab. Isn't that true?"

She snapped, "The board didn't exactly accuse me of stealing them. They simply blamed me because the vials were missing. I was the only individual who had the two keys needed to enter the biohazard level-four lab. I explained that I wasn't responsible for the missing vials and that the only other people with access to the level-four lab were John-George Clayton and his two grandsons. They had identical biohazard keys that couldn't be duplicated. The only way to enter the level-four lab was with two keys in the two locks, turned at the same time. Obviously, since I was the only person with access who wasn't a member of the Clayton family, I was the primary suspect and their scapegoat."

"So you think someone from the Clayton family—or maybe two of them together—stole the vials?" he asked.

"It *had* to be one of them because I didn't do it!" Changing the topic, she pointed to the tray of fresh strawberries, blueberries and sliced cantaloupe. "You should have some fruit with your cheese and crackers. The way you eat, you're lucky you haven't had a heart attack."

Alex replied, "Okay. Just promise me that you'll stop worrying about that conference and the Claytons. I hoped we could have a nice relaxing evening together.

Let's forget about the Spouse Killer, at least for this evening."

"You know the name Spouse Killer isn't always accurate. In fact, it would be more politically correct to call it the Significant-Other-Killer."

"I know. Please, just drink your wine and relax."

"All right," she said as she took another sip.

"I think we should unwind, drink, and forget about everything else."

"Oh, I can already read tomorrow's headlines, *Alex Mueller, Chief of the Atlanta Health Department, arrested for DUI.*"

"Maybe I should stay over tonight, so we'll be assured that won't happen," he teased.

"In the interest of protecting your flawless reputation, the guest bedroom has clean sheets."

"The guestroom wasn't exactly what I had in mind..."

"Are you trying to get me drunk and take advantage of me?" she asked, gazing at him over the rim of her glass.

Smiling back, he replied playfully, "That's right. Drink up!"

"So you think you want to go to *No-Man's Land*, huh?"

"What do you mean?"

She replied, "Since my last sexual experience was over ten years ago, I call that part of me *No-Man's Land*. In fact, I'm not certain the hole isn't gone, completely grown together. You know the old saying, *if you don't use it, you lose it.*"

Pouring her another glass of wine, he said, "*No-Man's Land* sounds like an adventure to me."

"Do you have protection?" she asked, blushing.

"Sure, if I haven't worn it out by carrying it around waiting for you to be in the mood."

"Well excuse me, I'm not a mind reader—this is the first time you've shown an intimate interest in me."

"I have to confess I don't only have one condom...They're cheaper by the dozen. I guess, I'm an eternal optimist!"

Taking his hand, she led him to the bedroom. For hours they explored each other's bodies, reveling in the exhilaration of newfound love. Finally, they drifted into a deep, sated slumber.

* * * * *

Early the next morning before dawn, Cleta jerked awake, startled by the presence of another person in her bed. Divorced for over ten years, it had been too long since she had shared her bed with a man and she realized it would take a while to adjust. She cuddled next to Alex, closed her eyes again, and wondered why he'd waited so long to express his true feelings.

She'd met Alex shortly after his divorce a little more than three years ago and felt an attraction to him, but considered their relationship strictly platonic. They'd often discussed their failed marriages over dinner and drinks, consoling one another for allowing their devotion to their jobs to ruin their marriages, and agreeing they would never find a mate who'd understand their compulsive drives to work. They had become close friends over the years, but career commitments left neither the time nor the energy for a serious relationship. It occurred to her that it had taken a world crisis to bring them together.

She shivered, her nakedness leaving her much cooler than her usual flannel nightgown. She moved closer to Alex and noticed that he felt cool, too. Pulling the blanket from the foot of the bed, she lovingly draped it across him, while thinking how wonderful it was, despite the circumstances, to be with him at last.

Her thoughts drifted as she wondered how their lives would change. Would Alex back away at the prospect of a serious commitment? Would he propose? If so, was he ready? Was she? Cleta began envisioning his proposal and imagined herself at the altar in a wedding gown surrounded by beautiful flowers and candles. The chapel seemed dark as she visualized herself smiling softly and whispering, "I do." A feeling of doubt crossed her mind and she realized she was standing alone. Another chill swept through her already shivering body. Why was her heart screaming that something was wrong when her mind felt everything was finally great?

Careful not to disturb Alex, she quietly put on a robe and left the room. The sun had not yet touched the horizon, so the house was still dark. When she reached the hall, she flipped on the light and checked the thermostat, which showed a brisk sixty-two degrees. Since the weather had been unseasonably warm, the heat was off. For the first time this season, she turned on the heat and padded to the kitchen for a drink of water as the odor of burning lint, dust and things that accumulated in the furnace over the spring and summer floated in the air.

As the water filled her glass, she began to feel queasy. She decided it was probably from last night's wine and quickly downed half a glass of water. The feeling reminded her of college, when she occasionally attended parties hoping to meet a nice guy. With an extremely heavy class load she dated very little, and the few guys she did go out with all seemed to be the "jump-you, hump-you and dump-you" type. She took her grades very seriously and rarely drank; but when she did, it always made her sick. How silly it was, she thought to herself, for her to be standing in her kitchen justifying that last glass of wine while the love of her life lay naked in her bed. Alex's lovemaking was better than her wildest expectations. Thinking about it made her hunger for him. She quickly took another sip of water and returned to her room.

Still cold, she kept her robe on, slipped under the covers, and put her arm around Alex's waist. Snuggling as close as possible, she whispered into his ear, hoping to wake him and arouse him once more. She began caressing him, awaiting his response to her urges, but only heard a soft gurgling sound. After listening for a few seconds, she suddenly sensed something was definitely wrong. Leaning closer, a familiar odor assaulted her senses. Her heart pounded wildly as she jumped out of bed. Turning on the light, she gasped as she saw what she had already smelled—blood—trickling from Alex's nostrils, eyes, and ears. Cleta realized the gurgling sound was Alex drowning in his own blood.

"Oh my God, Alex, Alex, wake up!" she pleaded, her voice trembling, "Please Alex, talk to me!"

She tilted his head back and wiped the blood from his mouth with her fingers before checking his pulse. It was faint. He was suffering from hemorrhagic shock. She begged, "Oh Alex, I'm losing you! Please hold on; please don't leave me."

Grabbing the phone, she dialed 911.

The operator asked, "Fire, police, or medical?"

"I need an ambulance! My friend is hemorrhaging and he's unconscious—1214 South Magnolia Road. Hurry!"

"Okay ma'am, I need you to calm down. Where is your friend bleeding?"

"His nose, eyes, ears and mouth. Oh my God, please hurry!"

"Ma'am I've already dispatched an ambulance, they are en route and only minutes away, but I need you to stay on the line and give me some more information. Was he shot?"

"No, but I think he's dying. He's drowning in his own blood."

"Does he have a pulse?"

"No, I can't feel one. He had a faint pulse when I found him, but he doesn't now. I thought he was sleeping—he was asleep—I think he's dying! He's not breathing! Where are they? Why are they taking so long?"

"They're on their way, stay with me ma'am. I need you to help him breathe until they arrive."

"CPR...Hold on..." She put down the phone and began alternately breathing for Alex and compressing his chest. After a few minutes, she realized her efforts were in vain. "He's not responding. Why aren't the paramedics here?"

"They're on the way. Ma'am, cover him with a blanket and put something under his legs to raise them higher than his head..." before the operator could finish, the doorbell rang.

"They're here. I need to let them in." Following her lead, the paramedics rushed to the bedroom. She knew that no one had survived the Spouse Killer, but she desperately hoped Alex would be the first. As the paramedics worked frantically to bring Alex's motionless body back to life, she shivered.

The young paramedics had responded to so many Spouse Killer calls that they realized the situation was hopeless. Even so, they worked diligently to save Alex. After shocking him several times to attempt to restart his heart, they announced that he was gone. Glancing at Cleta, one softly said, "I'm sorry ma'am. There was nothing we could do."

"No, he can't be dead!" she cried. Following them to her driveway, she watched in disbelief as they loaded Alex's lifeless body into the ambulance. As it drove away without flashing lights or a siren, she made a vow. She would try for the rest of her life, if necessary, to prove the Clayton Research Center had cost her Alex's love.

Chapter 1 | Feelings of Doom

Dark and hopeless days... AMOS 5:20

Two years earlier in Petrolia, Oklahoma

Roulett Barnes wasn't an ordinary woman, but neither was life in the Clayton family. In spite of the wealth, she desperately worked to balance her life's losses and gains on the tightrope of sanity. As though teetering on a high wire without a safety net, she constantly felt that she could fall at any moment into a pit of despair. Roulett realized as a child that she was different for many reasons, but the most compelling were her recurring dreams and accurate premonitions.

An overwhelming feeling of impending doom overshadowed everything else that Thursday morning. At the kitchen table, in between bites of oatmeal her husband, Jack, asked, "Did you buy a dress for the Christmas party?"

"No, not yet. You know how much I hate going to Joyce and Lou's house. Maybe I'll be lucky and catch the flu or something," she replied, barely touching her breakfast.

"I guess I already knew what you'd say before I asked," he said with a sigh.

"Then why did you bother?"

"So I can nag you until you buy a new dress. No matter how much you hate it, we have to go to that party. Look on the positive side: it'll be four more years before the party will be at Joyce and Lou's house again. Next year the party will be at Mom and Dad's; at our house the following year; and at Pam and Kirk's after that. Besides, we always have fun with Lou in spite of Joyce," he added.

"You know your mother feels the same way I do about her."

"I realize that, Roulett. Mom will be there trying her best to have a good time, so I would appreciate it if you'd try to do the same..."

"Well, I just don't understand why Joyce acts so snooty! I mean, I could understand your mother being a snob. After all, her dad owns most of this town. But she isn't. Your mother is kind, sweet, and pleasant under any circumstance. She once told me that she learned how to treat others from her mother-in-law, Bertha. Bertha always said she liked her jewelry fake and her friends real—now that's character! Joyce has only had money since she married Lou—she's just a poor girl who married well."

"Married well? Sounds a lot like you," he muttered.

Roulett wasn't going to let him win. After a brief hesitation, she replied, "Yeah, I guess you could say it sounds a lot like me—or maybe like your dad." With a smug expression, she poured Jack another cup of coffee and raised her own cup in a mock toast to her victory.

Realizing his defeat, he nodded and smiled. "You better call the kids down for breakfast or they won't have time to eat."

Roulett used the intercom to yell, "Michael! Tammy! You're going to be late if you don't come down here! You know the new bus driver is never late. Hurry!"

Michael and Tammy scurried downstairs a few moments later. Michael, Jack and Roulett's first child, was almost ten years old. His hair and eyes were brown like his mother's, but he had inherited his father's height. Although Tammy was two years younger, she seemed five years older. She had her father's light hair and blue-green eyes, but her face had the same shape as her mother. Neither short nor tall, she was a typical, beautiful child.

Roulett put bowls of oatmeal on the table and asked, "Would either of you like a banana? You need to eat more fruit."

Tammy replied politely, "No, thanks. We don't have time."

Michael didn't stop eating long enough to answer. He'd just shoved the last bite in his mouth when they heard the bus. Grabbing their backpacks, they rushed outside calling quick goodbyes.

With his head buried in the newspaper, Jack asked, "What's for dinner tonight, honey?"

"I probably won't have time to cook tonight if I have to shop for that darn dress," Roulett grumbled, disgusted with herself for bringing up the subject again.

"Most women love to shop and spend money. Why don't you?"

"I have a horrible feeling about this party that I can't seem to shake. It's as if a dark cloud comes over me every time I think about it. I can't help it."

"I'm sorry you feel that way, but you do have to go even if you don't buy a new dress.

Heck, you can wear the one you wore last year if you want. I simply thought since this is a party...you'd want a new one. But whatever the case, I still need you to be there with me." Jack hugged her tightly as he said, "You're a gorgeous woman with a hot body. I like showing you off. I want you to dazzle them! So what do you say?"

Relaxing in his arms, she replied, "All right, I'll go look today. I'm not going to promise to buy one, but I'll look."

"Good," he said, as he pecked her on the cheek. He folded his newspaper and shoved it into his briefcase. As he opened the door to the garage, he turned around, "So, what about dinner?"

"How about pot roast? I can leave it in the oven while I'm shopping."

"Sounds great, I won't be late," he yelled over the sound of the garage door.

Alone with her thoughts, Roulett began loading the breakfast dishes into the dishwasher. The dreadful gloom settled over her again. Her ominous feelings toward the Christmas party seemed to go much deeper than not wanting to contend with Joyce Gordon for an evening. In her mind, avoiding the party meant averting a catastrophe. Somehow, she knew the party would change her life forever.

* * * * *

During his morning commute, Jack thought Roulett was being ridiculous about the annual Christmas party. Jack and Lou had been best friends since the day they met. Although sixteen years had passed, he recalled the day he'd hired Lou as if it were just yesterday...

The afternoon sun was beginning to peer defiantly through the thin metal blinds, spreading its stubborn rays across most of Jack's mahogany desk. He took another sip of cold coffee as he leaned back in his black leather chair to adjust the blinds. His 2:30 interview should be arriving any moment. With his elbows propped carelessly on the desktop and his head slightly tilted, he rubbed his hand across his barely stubbled cheek and chin while wondering if his grandfather had ever faced a similar medley of situations. It had been a stressful few years for Jack since he'd been appointed the new vice president of the Clayton Research Center.

When his predecessor retired, his grandfather, John-George Clayton, took the opportunity to bring more Clayton blood to the scene. Jack had just graduated from the University of Tulsa with his Masters degree in Business Administration and Management. Since Jack wanted to climb the corporate ladder on his own merits, he was hesitant about joining his father's organization so near the top. John-George had insisted that starting near the highest rung would prove much more challenging than he anticipated. It seemed hard to believe at the time, but after several years, Jack agreed wholeheartedly. Although well-received in his new position, if for no other reason than his name, he was too green to understand the art of delegation and good business leadership. Many late nights followed as he worked diligently through the stacks of paperwork on his desk.

After only three years on the job his grandfather retired and promoted Jack to president. He accepted his new position, determined to improve the managerial staff. He tackled a long-needed and enormous restructuring of management, adding several new positions. For two months, he'd been juggling his already hectic schedule while interviewing candidates. His days were riddled with phone conferences, luncheons, and meetings, while his evenings were consumed poring over the volumes of résumés. That day he was interviewing applicants for the Pharmaceutical Lab Supervisor position. He grabbed his notebook and looked at the next candidate's résumé. "Dr. Louis Gordon. Maybe, just maybe, he'll be the one."

He barely had time to glimpse at the credentials listed neatly on the résumé before his secretary buzzed him to announce Dr. Gordon's arrival.

"Send him in," Jack replied, a bit hoarse from hours of interviews.

Dr. Louis Gordon stepped inside, took a hurried glance at his surroundings, and confidently approached the desk.

"You must be Dr. Gordon," welcomed Jack, shaking the man's hand while motioning with the other for him to take a seat.

"Oh please, call me Lou. Even though it's been a few months, it still sounds strange to me to hear my name with doctor in front of it," he said with a light chuckle.

Lou was an intelligent-looking man in his late twenties, with dark curly brown hair and bright blue eyes. His long body showed early signs of a thickening waistline. He wore a pale blue button-down oxford with a navy sports coat, khakis, and tan alligator boots. Jack noted that he was the first applicant to skip wearing a tie.

"I tell you, Lou," Jack began, easing into his chair a bit, "I'm going to handle this interview a little differently than most. I've spent many days over the past few weeks filling various positions and I can see that you are clearly qualified for the job. So, instead of inundating you with a bunch of questions, I'm going to cut right to the chase. Tell me why you think you should be the one I hire."

Lou leaned forward and said, "I'm very qualified to handle the position. I think I would be the best man for the job because—I believe, given the opportunity," he paused for a few seconds before continuing, "I will portray and share the same vision that appears so obvious in that man right there." Lou pointed to a portrait of John-

George Clayton, founder of Clayton Research Center and Jack's grandfather, hanging on the wall.

Jack smiled, remembering once again why he had hired Lou on the spot. Like it or not, Roulett would soon be attending the Christmas party at Lou's house.

Chapter 2 | The Hospital

Our lives are like grass. We grow and flourish like wild flowers until the wind blows and we are gone, never seen again...

PSALMS 103: 15, 16

That night after dinner, the phone rang while Roulett was cleaning the kitchen. She called, "Can someone answer that? My hands are wet!" After the fourth ring, she grabbed it herself. "Barnes' residence."

A gravelly voice asked, "Is Jack there?"

"Yes. May I ask who's calling?"

"This is Ned—Ned Dobbs. I nit to tawk to Jack."

Roulett realized she should've recognized his hillbilly drawl. He didn't want to talk to her, knowing her negative opinion of him and his family. Ned had been John-George's caretaker for the last ten years—a position that had become increasingly profitable as John-George's mental faculties began slipping.

Jack's brother, Kirk, and Roulett argued repeatedly about John-George's caretakers. Roulett called them his *lack-of-care-takers.* His poor health concerned Roulett while Kirk maintained the situation was adequate, especially since it didn't cost the family any extra money. Considering John-George Clayton's wealth, she felt he deserved better.

She'd had a similar argument with Kirk over the care of John-George's wife, Florence, a year earlier. She wanted the family to hire a nurse for Florence when she became ill, but Kirk argued repeatedly that his grandparents were both adults capable of making their own decisions. He had insisted Florence would be fine in a few days, but she died shortly thereafter. In Roulett's opinion, Kirk's neglect directly contributed to Florence's death.

Roulett said, "I'll put you on hold while I find Jack." After unsuccessfully trying the intercom, she finally found Jack napping in the den on his recliner. Nudging him, she said, "Wake up, honey, Ned wants to talk to you."

Jack rubbed his eyes as he asked, "How long have I been asleep?"

"About fifteen minutes, I think."

"I wonder what Ned wants."

Roulett handed Jack the phone and suggested, "Here, ask him."

Jack yawned, then asked, "What's up, Ned?"

"I gist wanted to let ya know we're here in the horspital in Barteesville with yar granpa John-George. The doc thanks it wuz a stroke. Irene called the ambuelance after Ah found ya granpa passed out. I rode in the ambuelance with him and Irene brung the cawer to town. The ambuelance driver 'cided to take him here 'stead of Tulsey. We is in the mergencee room now. They won't let us saye him yit," said Ned.

Jack asked, "Have you called Mom?"

"No, I thank ya shud tell Marie."

"I'll call her from the car. We'll be right there. Thanks for calling, Ned."

Roulett asked, "What's wrong?"

"Grandfather John-George is in the emergency room in Bartlesville. Ned said the doctor thinks he had a stroke. Tell the kids to grab their coats and meet me in the car. We'll leave the kids with Betty, so Mom and Dad can go with us."

Roulett and the children hurried down the stairs and met Jack in the car. After explaining the situation to his mother on the cell phone, she replied, "Well I guess I can't say I'm surprised. You know his health has been failing for years. Listen, Sam and I have had a long day and I feel like I might be coming down with something. I don't want to expose Dad to anything when he's already down, so we'll just stay with the children and you can call us when you arrive to let us know how he's doing." She did not even try to hide her lack of concern for her ailing father.

"Sure, Mom, we'll call you as soon as we know something," Jack said, disappointed by her indifference.

The three-mile drive to her ranch seemed like a hundred miles.

Tammy asked, "Is Grandfather going to die?"

Roulett replied, "Honey, we don't know yet. We'll just have to wait and see."

Marie greeted them at the door and repeated again, "Call to let me know how he's doing. I'm sure I'll feel better tomorrow and should be able to visit him in the morning."

The trip to Bartlesville seemed endless, with a light drizzle only adding to the gloom. Roulett leaned her head against the headrest and closed her eyes to avoid the occasional glare of oncoming headlights. The windshield wipers' steady rhythm was painfully familiar—*swish-swoosh, swish-swoosh*. It rained the entire day of her mother's funeral and for a full two days afterward as well. She could still remember riding in that big, black limousine, with its wipers beating with her broken heart. As tears flowed freely down her cheeks, the sky cried steadily outside, and she thought to herself, *Mama wouldn't have needed to water her garden today*. At thirteen her world had been shaken to the very core. She was no stranger to death. Her father, a classic drunk, had choked to death on his own vomit when she was seven. His entire life he'd struggled to avoid the reality of the world around him and at thirty-eight he accomplished his goal. At eight, her paternal grandfather died of pneumonia in the same hospital. She barely knew him, but could still smell the stench of death from his hospital room during her forced visit. Her maternal grandmother died when she was ten. Since her grandmother had always seemed to go out of her way to be less kind to her than she was to her other grandchildren, Roulett had been indifferent. Nevertheless, her mama's premature death was too much.

At thirteen, she felt powerless, forced to create a new life without her parents. There were other family members—Aunt Frieda took her in shortly after her mama's death. She meant well, but she was a bit of a religious nut. Sunday after Sunday she would drag Roulett to church to soak in the "Hellfire and Brimstone" preaching of Rev. Isaac Hail. However, only a few Sundays and sermons later, Roulett was unequivocally convinced that she, through her own sin and disobedience to God, was the cause of her personal losses and misfortune. Certain she was directly responsible for her parents' deaths, she always wondered if they would have lived longer if she'd been a better little girl and prayed more. With all good intentions, Aunt Frieda and her church family created a mental bomb, ticking away. Roulett retreated to the darkest, innermost part of herself, finding refuge in her room in bed, where she was sure, in her constant state of prayer that her severed soul could cause no harm to others or herself. She remained there the entire summer after her mother's death only leaving when forced to bathe, eat, and attend church. It was during that period of solitude she chose to read the entire Book of Revelation, a decision that only further complicated her already overwhelming guilt and paranoia. Nevertheless, when fall arrived and the new school year began, Aunt Frieda evicted her from her bed and her state of recluse—resembling her lost mother's womb—and forced her to attend the eighth grade.

Teetering on the brink of a complete nervous breakdown, she struggled to establish a balance among her overly sensitive conscience, her under-nourished social skills, and her newly discovered sexuality. While stumbling through puberty, she eventually found comfort in alcohol which led to a lifetime struggle. Now riding to the same hospital that held nothing but terrible memories, she longed for a drink to ease the pain. Thankfully, her children had been born in Tulsa. She reached to rub her temples, suddenly sick at the thought of John-George dying. Feeling helpless, she began to pray.

After pleading with God for John-George's life, she opened her eyes to see they had just arrived at the ER parking lot. Jack drove around several times before locating a space a long way from the entrance.

"I'm sorry. I should've let you out at the door," he said.

"That's all right. I'm not made of sugar—I won't melt."

They ran to avoid the rain, which was coming down hard. Once inside, the emergency room receptionist asked them to wait there for a few minutes while they transferred John-George to a private room. They both breathed a sigh of relief that he was well enough to leave the emergency area.

Finally, after a thirty-five minute wait, the receptionist gave them John-George's room number and directed them to the elevators. Much to their surprise, Kirk was already in the hospital room when they arrived. Ned had apparently called Kirk first—more confirmation of Roulett's conspiracy theory.

Jack asked Kirk, "How long has Grandfather been here?"

He replied, "About three hours. He's doing much better now." Jack didn't say anything else about it, but she instinctively knew he felt Ned should have notified them at the same time.

John-George's condition didn't seem critical but he looked tired and several years older. Roulett reached for his hand and he met hers not with his right hand, as he normally would have, but with his left.

Answering the question already forming in her mind, Kirk said, "He's partially paralyzed on his right side. The doctor says his mobility should improve over the next few days."

John-George looked at Roulett and tried to speak, "Oofed eeea."

Unable to make out his words, Roulett said, "We're so glad you're all right Grandfather, but you need to rest now...doctor's orders!" She squeezed his hand and then reached to pull his blanket to cover him better. "I'll be back tomorrow and you can talk to me then. For now, you rest."

Kirk said, "His speech should improve in a few days, too."

Roulett started for the door. "I'm going to the waiting room to call Marie. Jack, I'll meet you outside."

Chapter 3 | Why are there no Umbrellas?

When I woke from the dream I was greatly disturbed and pale with fright, but I told no one of the vision... Daniel 7: 28

A large group of people stood in a long line—so long, Roulett couldn't see where it began or ended. *What are they waiting for?* she wondered. Dressed in long white robes with cumbersome gold ropes tied about their waists, they waited in the pouring rain. *Must be some kind of a cult or something. Will the rain ever stop? Where are their umbrellas?* So many people getting soaked to the skin making their robes seem transparent. They appeared to be mostly women. She stepped closer to observe what they were waiting for and then she heard screams and moans all around her but she couldn't distinguish the source. As she moved closer, she saw that the people were weeping and wringing their hands in agony. Her heart began to race and she tried to yell but she couldn't hear herself. Another desperate try produced no sound.

Suddenly, a distant, loud buzzing startled her, making her jump with fear. It was the alarm clock. She tried to sit up in bed, but she was shaking uncontrollably and her limbs felt like wet noodles. Reaching for the snooze button, she tugged at her nightgown, which was cold, damp with sweat, and clinging to her body. Beside her, Jack stirred.

At the breakfast table over coffee, Roulett told Jack she'd had a nightmare, although she didn't share the details.

"Oh honey, it's simply your subconscious reacting to last night. You were upset and worried about Grandfather. You need extra rest today, that's all."

With her head throbbing, Roulett decided not to cook breakfast like she normally did in the winter months. Instead, she took out several boxes of cereal and the milk. Then she strategically placed the basket of fruit in the center of the breakfast table, hoping the children would eat some with their cereal. Once she knew the children were up and around, she took her shower and dressed so she would be ready when they finished their breakfast.

After everyone was gone, she quickly made herself a screwdriver—it's orange juice, so it's a breakfast drink, she rationalized. Deciding to heed Jack's advice, she retreated to her bedroom and set the alarm for noon, with plans to straighten the house and visit Grandfather in the hospital before the kids came home from school.

Later, with her headache dulled but not whipped completely, she headed for the kitchen. She wrapped a piece of bread around a slice of leftover roast and called it lunch, the first real food she'd consumed for the day. While still eating her so-called sandwich, she began clearing the table and cleaning the kitchen from breakfast. Afterward, she shuffled through the house, making beds and straightening each room. It was almost two o'clock when the phone rang.

"Hi honey, it's me. Would like to go out for Mexican food tonight before we visit the hospital?" Jack asked.

"That sounds like a great idea. After last night, I could use a margarita," she replied, thankful she wasn't going to have to fuss with dinner.

"I'll meet you at Mom's house about 4:30."

"Great, I'll see you then."

She slapped on some lipstick, straightened her hair, and headed out the door.

When she arrived at the hospital, she stopped by the nurses' station to ask how John-George was doing. The nurse told her they'd stabilized his blood pressure and he'd had a good night, with visible signs of improvement already.

"Good, what about his diet, any restrictions?"

"Just a low sodium diet, but he hasn't eaten much since he's been here. Maybe you'll have better luck," the nurse said with a smile.

A few moments later, Roulett entered his room holding a frozen vanilla yogurt from the cafeteria. A little crooked smile lit his face as soon as he saw her.

"Hey Grandfather, are they feeding you anything in this place?" she asked.

John-George shook his head and tried to make a face.

Bending to give him a hug, she said, "I brought you some frozen yogurt." She fed him spoonful after spoonful of yogurt while chattering away about how much she enjoyed being part of his family and how thankful she was for all the wonderful memories of their time together. He nodded and tried to speak occasionally, but his speech was too slurred to understand. After feeding him, she read the newspaper aloud until it was time for her to leave. She hugged him again and straightened his covers.

"You just rest. Jack and I will be back to visit this evening," she promised on her way out of the room.

On the way home she decided to take Michael and Tammy to the ranch to feed and ride their horses after school. *No time today to shop for a new dress,* she thought, *maybe tomorrow?* They tried to tend to the horses at least five days per week if weather permitted. It was a sunny, unseasonably warm day with the temperature gauge on the side of the barn registering almost sixty—a perfect day for riding.

After the children rode off on their horses, Roulett went into the clubhouse for a drink. When she emerged with a drink in hand, she saw a car pulling in the driveway. She thought she recognized the beautiful African-American woman driving the car.

She rolled down her window to ask, "Is this where Marie Barnes lives?"

Roulett, suddenly realizing who she was, asked, "Hollie?"

Hollie replied, "Yes?"

"I'm Roulett Bar…No, you knew me as Roulett King...from Kelly High!"

"Oh, Roulett. Yes, I should've recognized you. You look the same as you did in high school, but I wasn't expecting to see you here. Am I at the right place?"

"You certainly are. Park your car and I'll show you where Marie is."

She parked and Roulett showed her the way to Marie's house. Hollie said, "This is a beautiful place! I've known Marie all these years, but I've never been here before. Do you work here?"

"No. I married Jack Barnes fifteen years ago—he's Marie's oldest son."

"Oh, I see. You did very well for yourself. Is Kirk his dad?"

Roulett replied with a chuckle, "No, Kirk is his brother. Why?"

"My brother, Quinn, talks about Kirk all the time."

They reached the house, so Roulett opened the door for Hollie and called, "Marie, I have someone who wants to see you."

Marie emerged from the kitchen, smiling as she approached.

Extending her hand, Hollie said, "Hi, I'm Hollie—Harvey Jordan's daughter."

"My goodness," Marie replied, holding Hollie's hand. "I haven't seen you since you were about six. You were only a little girl then, but now, well look at you, you're all grown up. Here, have a seat. Would you like something to drink?"

"No, thank you, I had a late lunch."

"Well, if you'll excuse me, I need to go back to the clubhouse to check on the children. It was so nice to see you again, Hollie," Roulett said.

"Do you two know each other?"

"We went to high school together," they replied in unison.

"Kelly High School—We had the same history class our senior year," Hollie added.

"Yes, we both had Mrs. Simms," Roulett said, grimacing.

"Oh, don't remind me of that witch. Another word suits her better, but to be polite I won't say it. We all despised her. She gave pop-quizzes over material we hadn't even covered!"

"We did have some good times together at school, just not in her class," Roulett said.

"Yeah, we sure did. You know we should get together and catch up on old times. I'd really like to talk to you some more."

"Let's do that. Why don't you meet me here at noon tomorrow and I'll treat you to lunch? Afterward, I'll show you the ranch."

"That sounds great to me!" Hollie replied. "I'll see you tomorrow."

"Great. Marie, we're going to go out for Mexican food tonight before we go to the hospital. Would you and Sam like to join us?"

"Since I didn't go to the hospital this morning, Sam and I thought we would go this evening around six. Why don't you eat and then drop the kids off before you go to the hospital, unless you were planning to take them."

"I was going to let them decide if they want to go. If they don't, we'll bring them over after we eat."

"That'll be fine," Marie said.

Roulett noticed the children returning from their ride as she walked back to the clubhouse. Michael was rattling about something to Tammy, but they were still too far away for Roulett to hear. Tammy, as usual, was listening intently, clinging to his every word. Once they were close enough, Roulett walked with them to the barn to help them unsaddle and clean up.

"Hey, do you guys want to go see Grandfather in the hospital this evening?" she asked.

Tammy nodded, more out of politeness than eagerness, as Michael asked, "Can he talk yet?"

"He's trying and he is getting better, but he's still very hard to understand. I tell you what, if you would be more comfortable, as soon as he can speak more clearly, we'll make a special trip for you both to visit him. How's that for a deal?"

They both nodded.

"Tonight we'll drop you off here again and you can play foosball in the clubhouse or watch a movie if you want. And, by the way, Dad's taking us for Mexican food tonight," she added with enthusiasm.

Suddenly much more chipper, they both said, "Yea, all right!"

Later that same evening, Jack and Roulett arrived at the hospital just in time to see Ned and Irene. They'd been visiting John-George and were about to leave, except Ned couldn't stop talking to the nurse. He was telling her some ridiculous story when Jack and Roulett came into Grandfather's room.

"If ya chaw on a snake, then ya'll never looz your tayth," he rambled to the nurse as he let out a snort and a goofy laugh exposing his completely toothless head.

Roulett couldn't help but roll her eyes. However, after only a short visit with Grandfather, a nurse came back into the room and asked them to step out because she needed to give him a sponge bath and draw some blood. They chose to say their goodbyes and leave early, knowing John-George was too tired to enjoy their company since he'd been shuffled from place to place, having tests all day.

On the way back to the ranch, Roulett asked, "Do you have any idea what happened to cause the friction between your mom and her father?"

Jack replied, "No, that's been a family mystery for a long time. Kirk and I both have asked Mom for years why she is so cold and distant to him. She always answers, 'Different people have different ways of showing their love,' but Kirk and I both know there's something she isn't telling us."

"Did you ever ask Grandfather about it?"

"No, it's rather like accentuating the negative, he doesn't need a reminder of the way she treats him. Mom creates enough pain for him. Besides, you know how men are, we don't talk about such things."

"It doesn't make any sense to me. Grandfather has always been so good to your mom and dad. They were given the ranch and a steady income for a lifetime—neither of them have ever needed to work. So why the conflict?"

"That's true, but we don't know if Grandfather did that because of generosity or out of guilt."

"I never considered Grandfather being guilty of anything except maybe being too gullible in his old age."

"Maybe Mom blames him for her mother's death because she died from a miscarriage," Jack said.

"No, I can't see your mom thinking so illogically for all these years. It doesn't make sense. There has to be more to this than we know."

"Mom always said there were problems between Grandfather and his own father, Great-Grandfather Roy. She never knew what caused the tension, not even after Grandfather Roy died. Mom thought the problem must have started before she was born or when she was very young because she couldn't remember a time when there was peace between them. So maybe it runs in the family."

"Which part? The part about being angry with your father or the part about not telling anyone why?" asked Roulett.

"Maybe both..."

"I can believe that."

"Did I ever tell you the story about Roy's Grandmother Edith?"

"No, I don't think so."

"As the story's told, my great-great-great grandmother, Edith Clayton, claimed that she saw an angel shortly before her death. This was supposed to have happened in England somewhere around 1890."

"That's really interesting, but many people claim to see angels or deceased family members shortly before their deaths."

"Oh, but there's more! Edith said the raven-haired angel proclaimed that one day her descendants would hold the fate of all humankind in their hands—which means it runs in my bloodline," Jack said.

"Yeah, like I'm going to believe that," scoffed Roulett.

"I'm just telling you what I heard..."

"I believe that being a wee bit crazy runs in your family. Is this the same grandmother who owned the so-called 'cursed' diamond?" she asked, making invisible quotation marks with her fingers.

"No, that was Rebecca from the next generation. Her husband, Edward, was the first Clayton from our family to come to America. He was my grandfather Roy's father and the first Clayton to become a diamond broker. Before him they were silver and goldsmiths, making mostly jewelry and watches. Apparently Edward brought the diamond home as a gift for Rebecca when he returned from one of his many African diamond-purchasing trips. Edward told Rebecca that he'd traded something ridiculously unequal in value for the diamond because a superstitious medicine man thought it was cursed. Rebecca lost a premature son shortly after receiving the diamond, making her believe the story about the diamond was true," Jack said.

"I can understand why she felt that way although it's not rational. Does your family still have the diamond?"

"I have no idea—it may still be in the family, but I've never seen or heard about it."

"Did Roy have any siblings who could've inherited the diamond?"

"No, Roy had two sisters. Shortly after their marriages, they both tragically died in childbirth and neither baby survived."

"Wow! I remember your mother saying that Clayton men are tough on their wives! John-George has outlived all three of his wives and his father Roy outlived two of his three wives. That makes Dorothy the only survivor of six wives. I'm beginning to think that being a Clayton female is extremely dangerous."

"After losing two wives, Roy and John-George both married much younger women. Even that didn't work for Grandfather John-George."

"Which only proves my theory that being a Clayton female by blood or marriage is hazardous to one's health."

"My mother survived being a Clayton female before marrying Dad and becoming a Barnes," Jack added.

"But the odds weren't in her favor," replied Roulett. "Besides, I always wondered how she ended up with Sam. She was a beautiful woman from a wealthy family and Sam wasn't handsome and he was dirt poor."

"Well, at least I learned from my ancestors' mistakes and married a younger, beautiful woman the *first* time," Jack replied with a wink.

"I don't know if you learned or were just extremely lucky when you met me!"

"Actually, I think you were the lucky one. I was the most eligible bachelor in Petrolia—one of the top three in the state of Oklahoma because of my family status and the fact that I'm drop dead gorgeous."

"I'm not so sure that I would've thought I was so lucky if I'd known the mortality rates of the Clayton females in the past."

"Aren't you glad that I'm a Barnes instead of Clayton?" he asked.

Roulett gently punched Jack in the shoulder as she replied, "As difficult as you are, I would say that you have plenty of Clayton blood running through your stubborn veins!"

"Let's not play pick on Jack. We still haven't uncovered the problem between Grandfather and Mom that may've started with Grandfather Roy."

"But Grandfather seems to have a good relationship with Roy's widow, Dorothy."

"That's true. Grandfather John-George and Dorothy became close after she and her son Charles moved here, but that may have been because they were so close in age. Dorothy's only a year older than her stepson John-George. So it's unlikely their conflict had anything to do with Dorothy—it must've been something prior to Roy and Dorothy's marriage."

"I'll bet it's the curse of the diamond!" Roulett said with a smile as they pulled into the driveway.

Chapter 4 | Hollie & Roulett at the Ranch

Some friendships are fleeting, but some friends are more loyal than brothers. PROVERBS 18: 24

As Hollie stepped into Roulett's new red Cadillac the next day, Roulett asked, "Are you married?"

Hollie replied, "Not any more—it's a long story. I'll explain it over lunch. So, where are we going?"

"How about Hamilton's? I think they have the best salads in town."

"Sounds great to me. I didn't have breakfast this morning, so I'm starving. When did you get this car? It's beautiful!"

"Thanks! My husband bought it for me for Christmas last year."

"It certainly makes my twelve-year-old Ford look like a piece of junk," Hollie said.

"I've driven a Cadillac ever since Jack and I were married. I think that if God dropped a car from heaven it would be the Cadillac. I'll tell Jack how much you like it," Roulett said, as she pulled into Hamilton's parking lot.

Inside, seated at a small table by the window, they had only begun scanning the menus when a young waitress approached the table.

"What can I get you ladies today?" she asked.

"Gosh, what do you recommend, Roulett? I've never been here before."

"I usually order their chicken Caesar salad. It's wonderful—they serve it with fresh garlic and cheese sourdough toast."

"Oh, that sounds delicious! I'd like iced tea with a lemon wedge, too."

"And I'll have the same," Roulett said, handing the menu to the waitress.

"So, Hollie...Wow! I can't believe this—it's been so long. You disappeared our senior year and I haven't seen you since. What happened? Where'd you go?" Roulett asked.

"I got pregnant and married—in that order."

"Oh my, who did you marry?"

"A guy named Truman Fouler. He's six years older than we are, so I doubt you'd remember him."

"No, his name isn't familiar," Roulett replied.

"We were married for nine miserable years and we've been divorced for six glorious years!"

"Wow, nine years. That seems like enough time to work out your differences, but a long time to be unhappy. What went wrong? Let me guess, he was unfaithful?"

"No, I don't think so—but I could never be sure about him. Our first problems started shortly after we married and moved to El Paso, Texas. Truman started dabbling in greyhound racing. It seemed harmless enough at first, but then it became a very expensive obsession. As he so often described it, he'd 'found his calling.' Great, only his calling was eating away at our pocketbook. Our son, Darnel, was only a few months old at the time and money was so tight. I didn't think it was fair for me to sacrifice things Darnel and I needed so Truman could fulfill his dreams and have a good time doing it. So needless to say, we had arguments over his careless spending. One night it got pretty heated and he decided to slap me around a little. It was just never the same after that. I should've left him then, but I kept thinking I could change him."

"You can never change a man!"

"Well, I know that now. However, things did get better for a while. I convinced him the only way we could afford to race greyhounds was to raise them. I figured it would be something we could do as a family. So I put up with his selfishness and hateful temperament because we were always together. I always knew where he was. He was either at work or doing something with me and Darnel, which made me feel secure," Hollie said.

The waitress delivered their food. "Could I get you anything else?" she asked.

"I'd like some more tea and a double-vodka screwdriver, please. Hollie would you like a drink?" Roulett asked.

"No, iced tea is fine for me."

"Why was always knowing Truman's whereabouts so important to you?"

"Remember when I started working as a waitress at Rosie's Café when I was fourteen?"

"Yeah."

"While I worked there I met a lot of people—lots of them were married men. Most were huge flirts but some actually had the nerve to ask me out on dates and stuff. I couldn't *believe* these guys. There I was, only fourteen and they were all old enough to be my father! Anyway, I would turn them down, of course, and then the very next day they would bring in their wife and kids. It was such a turn-off. Anyway, I came to the conclusion that all men would cheat if given the right opportunity," said Hollie.

"Makes sense—keep him close all the time. What went wrong?"

"About eight years into the marriage, we had established a successful greyhound-breeding operation. We were financially better off than we'd ever been and things were really looking up for us. Then Truman quit his regular job as a mechanic. He'd quit or been fired from somewhere between sixteen and eighteen jobs over the course of our marriage. He just couldn't control his explosive temper. In addition to him never holding a job for very long, we rarely had any health insurance or other benefits. So needless to say, we barely got by. But the final 'straw that broke the camel's back' was when he decided to take a job as a delivery man for a liquor wholesaler. His job was to deliver kegs of beer to bars across six counties. He would be traveling all the time, seeing lots of other women, and sometimes staying overnight in other towns, and, I've already told you how I feel about that. To me, men are like children—if you can't see them, they may be doing something wrong. I cried all night the first time he was out of town overnight. That's when I realized the one good thing about Truman was 'gone;' he wasn't going to be right there anymore. That same morning, I decided he wasn't going to hurt me anymore and I wouldn't allow him to make me cry ever again. It was over. I didn't love him and hadn't for a long time."

"I'd have to say, if Jack ever hit me, it would definitely be over. I wouldn't tolerate physical abuse at all. If staying out of town was a reason for a divorce, we'd have been separated years ago."

"I'm sure Jack has a lot of positive things about him, but the only positive thing about Truman was that he was always with me; and when that was gone, there was nothing left. Anyway—that's enough about me and my miserable life—let's talk about you and your life. How did you meet Jack Barnes? Or better yet, how did you land such a big fish?"

"We met fifteen years ago when his mother Marie made the mistake of fly spraying a horse in a trailer. The horse spooked, stepped on Marie's foot, and broke it. She put an ad in the local paper for summer help, and I was fortunate enough to be the chosen applicant. I'd been working for Marie a little over a week when I met her sons. Jack and Kirk both showed an interest in me, but I only had eyes for Jack. We were married the next June."

Hollie asked, "How did Jack's parents react to you two getting hitched?"

"Oh, Marie has always been so sweet to me. Almost immediately after I started working for her, she's treated me like the daughter she never had. They were both very happy for us."

"What about Kirk? Was he jealous?"

"I don't know if I would call it jealousy. I think we've basically hated each other ever since. No, I take that back—I started loathing him after he arranged for his Cousin Frank to try to seduce me, so Jack and I would break up. Obviously his plan failed," Roulett said as she wiped her mouth and tossed her napkin into her salad bowl.

"Well, I guess you can't be on good terms with the whole world all the time. Anyway, thanks so much for lunch. I really enjoyed it."

"You're welcome. I've had a great time, too. Now let's go back to the ranch and I'll show you around and maybe we can walk off some of this meal."

As they reached the ranch, Hollie took in the spectacular view of the Barnes' majestic acreage. Vast open pastures in full green from cultivated winter grasses, numerous groves of tall oaks and elms, and white wooden fences seemed to go on forever. The long paved driveway circled at its end with an entrance to the Barnes' ranch-style home on one side of the circle and an entrance to the barn and clubhouse on the other side, with only a small cluster of mature trees encircled by finely manicured shrubs separating the two drives. They pulled into the entrance to the barn and clubhouse—constructed with a rustic mixture of enormous round logs, heavy steel framing, and wide wood siding. It had nearly 3,000 square feet of living space—only a small portion of the over 18,000 square-foot barn. The living space inside the barn had a hunting lodge motif, and was large enough to lodge eight to twelve people comfortably. It was bigger than Petrolia's average residential home. The huge covered balcony and large picture windows on the second level overlooked pastures in nearly every direction. As they opened the door to enter the clubhouse, a bell jingled on the door.

"What's the bell for?" asked Hollie.

"Sam doesn't like people sneaking up on him. This place is pretty big and since he's not crazy about using the intercom system, the bell lets him know when someone's here. It always reminds me of those little shops downtown."

Hollie laughed as she said, "Oh, my, it does! Where's the sale rack?"

They both giggled as they entered the mudroom—an elongated hall-type room with a floor of concrete sloping toward a middle drain. A faucet with a short hose and sprayer was conveniently located in the middle of the wall on the right side. Farther on was a large, deep sink and a sitting bench on one wall with cabinets on both sides. Extending most of the wall opposite the sink and bench was a two-tiered shoe rack with a row of coat hooks on the wall above. On the other side of the shoe rack was a door leading into a private bath with a toilet, sink, huge shower stall, but no tub. The rooms were clean, but utilitarian in style, with very little décor. After walking past the concrete area to the tiled part of the room, Hollie said, "Well, I haven't seen very much of it yet, but I like what I see. I love this tile; it's not slick like so many other tile floors."

"It's a good thing, too. Those horse-walkers and the outdoor exercise arena can cause a mud problem beyond belief, especially when it rains heavily, so this is the room where everyone washes their boots if they're muddy. Now you understand the purpose of these tiles. The shower at the end of this room is the only one in the clubhouse. There's a half-bath upstairs and one off Sam's office, but Sam didn't want but one shower in his clubhouse. He said if he added showers and tubs in every bathroom, he'd never get rid of all the company—it'd be like running a hotel. So this is it."

Hollie took another glance into the small bathroom with the shower and said, "From all I've heard about Sam that sounds like him."

"It's okay though, because the place most people congregate is right through here." She led Hollie through the door on the other side of the mudroom.

Hollie stopped in her tracks, "Wow! What a room! Darnel would go crazy in a room this big."

"This is the clubroom...the place we all come to unwind and escape from everything," Roulett said, crossing to the bar and making a screwdriver. "Would you like something to drink?"

"No thanks, I'm fine," she replied, looking around.

It was a huge room with a high vaulted ceiling, polished oak crossbeams, and four large ceiling fans. On the east side was a full kitchen with state-of-the-art appliances, including a cook-top with indoor grill, double ovens, trash compactor, side-by-side refrigerator with ice and water in the door, two dishwashers, and a fully stocked bar. The granite countertops in the kitchen, center island, and bar area were breathtakingly beautiful. In front of the island were three game tables surrounded by chairs. The game tables doubled for dining tables when needed.

On the north side of the room was an entertainment area with a huge flat screen television mounted on the wall, a tournament pool table, a shuffleboard table, foosball, videogames, and pinball machines. In the southwestern quarter of the room was a sitting area with three sofas, coffee and end tables adjoining all, and two loveseats. One of the sofas was facing the fireplace in the corner.

"Wow, they must have put a lot of thought into this place before they built it," Hollie said.

"They did. Sam designed it twelve years ago for the new barn. They'd been raising horses for years, so they knew exactly what they wanted in this building," she said, finishing off her screwdriver.

"All the furniture is a wagon-wheel design selected by Marie. Are you sure you don't want a drink? I'm going to make myself another before we see Sam's office and the loft."

Hollie looked at the three wagon-wheel couches and the matching loveseats. "I like Marie's choice in furniture—it looks like it belongs here."

Roulett said, "Follow me, and I'll show you Sam's office." She led her through the door into the northeast corner of the building, into Sam's office. "This room isn't as big as the clubroom, but it still is a very large room, with closets, bookcases, and another restroom. Those are the stairs to the loft."

Hollie followed Roulett upstairs. In her best tour guide voice, Roulett said, "As you can see, the loft is almost as large as the clubroom, with a king-size bed for overnight guests. During holidays and special parties, Sam and Marie insist that their drinking guests either have a designated driver or spend the night. There are three full-size Murphy beds in the walls and two in the walls downstairs. Folding screens provide privacy between the beds." Roulett pointed to the area in front of the big window as she continued, "This space is designed to watch mares when they foal. It has couches, recliners, coffee tables, pillows, and blankets, because foaling often takes all night."

Hollie asked, "Won't the mare become nervous seeing people watching her?"

"No. The window is a one-way mirror, so you can see the mare in the large indoor arena but she can't see you."

"That was really a smart idea."

"They drew on years of experience for the design. On the other side of the arena are twenty-two large stalls, eleven on each side. Past those there are a mouse-proof grain storage room, a breeding and examining stall, a tack room, a small hay storage area, and a horse shower stall with a specially designed heating system to dry the horses within minutes. The heated stall doubles as a place to put a wet newborn foal to dry in the cold weather. Of course, the mare stays with the foal. The clubhouse, mudroom, loft, and Sam's office have zoned central heat and air and the barn has a separate heating and air-conditioning system, but the barn temperature is kept around fifty degrees in the winter and around eighty degrees in the summer. Although a pleasant temperature for a dry horse, fifty degrees is still quite chilly to a newborn foal. The aisle between the stalls is fourteen feet wide so a truck or a tractor can maneuver through the area. On the south side of the room are closets for more storage, plus the furnace and hot water tank. There's a toilet and a sink there, but no shower. You remember the bell on the door as you come into the mudroom? Now you can see why it's necessary. Considering the size of the clubroom, Sam likes to know when someone comes in the door."

"This is such a beautiful room—I wouldn't mind staying a weekend!"

"Jack and I've spent many nights here. Marie's live-in maid, Betty, watches the children anytime we want, so staying is like having a honeymoon over and over again."

"Do Sam and Marie mind you two coming so often?"

"I'll have to explain the whole story so you'll understand. Lou is Jack's best friend and mine, too. He and his wife Joyce both work at Clayton Research Center with Jack and Kirk. Jack and I only tolerate Joyce because of Lou, but our friendship with Lou spans more than a decade. We all meet regularly at Sam and Marie's ranch to ride horses or have a few beers. We can shoot pool, play shuffleboard, throw darts, play cards, watch a movie, or sit around talking. Sam even has beer on tap in the clubhouse.

"Lou and Jack prefer Sam's place to a bar, so on Friday nights everyone gathers here. We start the evening with food—everyone brings something to eat and Marie loves to cook. We can always find something delicious in Marie's refrigerator. We decide the week before what food we want for the next Friday—Mexican is everyone's favorite. Sam furnishes most of the drinks, but Lou brings his favorite scotch.

"I don't know how well you know Marie, but she has two major idiosyncrasies. The worst one is her house rule that you never use a curse word around her, you don't say the D-word or the S-word, and I think she would faint dead-away if she heard the F-word. Her house rule has cleaned up everyone's language who's around her—so whatever you do—don't say a four letter word in front of Marie."

"She sounds like she could be related to my Grammy Nambi. More than once when I accidentally let the S-word slip, she scolded me, 'You had something in your mouth I wouldn't want in my hand,' which broke me of the cussing habit. So I won't have a problem with Marie's rule," Hollie replied.

"Marie's other oddity is giving surprise birthday parties, although the parties are never a surprise to anyone. But it makes Marie happy, so we endure them in silence.

Since I bring the children here to ride and care for their horses after school from four to six days a week, I join in the parties most of the time because I'm already here with the children and I love to party. After the partying is over, Jack and I sometimes spend the night since the children are asleep at Marie's house."

Hollie asked, "That sounds like fun. Did Sam build this barn?"

"Sam paid a contractor to build it. Now, he basically buys whatever he wants. He was poor before he married Marie. He also had polio when he was three, and he limps a little on his right side. He doesn't do much around the ranch, but we all love him. He gave my children, Michael and Tammy, their horses and provided the place to keep them on one condition—Michael and Tammy have to do most of the care for the horses. Sam said he didn't want his grandchildren to be rich, spoiled brats.

"Jack's brother, Kirk, and his wife, Pam, have only one child, Alyssa, who'll be a year old soon. Pam is the only forensic pathologist in town. Her career is very important to her, so Kirk and Pam agreed to have only one child for now. Sam doesn't think Alyssa's parents will allow her to have a horse at the ranch, but he said he'd make the offer when she's old enough.

"Sam is the one who always seems to spend the money even if it means sacrificing other things, but it's never Sam who makes the sacrifices. It's always Marie. Marie is, and always has been, very frugal even though Marie was born 'with a silver spoon in her mouth.'"

"I know the family is rich," Hollie said.

"How do you know Marie?"

"My father, Harvey Jordan, has worked for John-George Clayton for years. The rest is a very long story I'll tell some other time. I know John-George better than Marie."

"How long have you known John-George?"

"For as long as I can remember," Hollie replied.

Chapter 5 | Friday Night Get-togethers

The best a man can do is enjoy his food and drink, and his job... ECCLESIASTES 2: 24

The Friday night get-together at the ranch continued as previously planned, even though John-George remained hospitalized. Roulett, Michael, and Tammy arrived after school, but Roulett didn't wait for Jack to party. Sending the children to the house to watch a movie with Betty, she mixed herself a strong drink while putting the finishing touches on her green chile cheese dip.

Marie walked to the clubhouse about an hour later carrying a tray of ham-and-cheese sandwiches she made. Jack and Lou arrived about 6.00 p.m. Lou had followed Jack home and picked him up, so Jack could drive Roulett's car home that night, since they doubted she'd be in any condition to drive later. The children watched movies until bedtime in the house with Betty while the grownups gathered in the clubhouse. Before the meal was served, Roulett had already downed her seventh screwdriver.

Lou enjoyed a sandwich while pouring beers for everyone except Marie, who always drank unsweetened decaf tea. Lou said, "After the first, I'm going on a diet, because I'm getting too fat. I'm going to start the New Year with a resolution to lose twenty pounds, so I guess I had better eat while I can. Boy, do I love this dip! I like my food and my women the same—hot and spicy!"

"It's a good thing Joyce isn't here. If she heard you say women instead of woman, she'd box your ears," Marie said.

Darting in, Sam said, "I guess I better get some of this dip before Lou eats it all."

Jack asked, "Lou, how about a game of pool to help you burn some of those nasty old calories you just consumed?"

"Sounds great to me." The pool game was short because Jack won when Lou accidentally sank the eight ball. Lou said, "Joyce's sister-in-law, Olivia, and her husband, Garrett, are coming into town for the holidays. She's a medical research doctor, specializing in viral diseases, so she's going to apply for a job at the Center."

Marie asked, "Where do Olivia and Garrett live now?"

Lou said, "They're from Arlington, Virginia. They've had some family problems in the past year, so they thought a change would do them good."

"I didn't know there was an opening at the Center," Marie said.

"There may be. It's a long story and we don't need to go into it now. We should go by and see Grandfather soon, so I'll tell you later," replied Jack.

"Let me know how Dad is doing tonight," Marie said.

Roulett replied, "Sure, we will. The kids are going to spend the night here, if that's okay?"

"You know that's fine. We always love to have them."

"I'll pick them up sometime tomorrow afternoon, after I look for a new dress."

"You mean you haven't bought a dress yet! I thought you bought one last week," nagged Jack.

"I guess that's what you get for doing your own thinking."

Chapter 6 | The Party

Who understands the human heart? Nothing else is as deceitful — it is too ill to be healed... JEREMIAH 17: 9

On the night of the annual Christmas party, the babysitter arrived on time. As usual, Roulett was running late. Reluctantly, she perfectly did her makeup and hair then donned the exquisite burgundy-sequined dress—the same one she'd worn two years earlier. Jack didn't notice the dress wasn't new, since Roulett looked striking.

With a whistle, he said, "You clean up good for a country girl!" Jack loved to tease her about dressing like a farmhand.

Jack, who was extremely handsome, looked incredible in his black tuxedo. They made a nice looking couple although very opposite in appearance—he was tall with blond hair and blue eyes and she was a petite brunette with brown eyes.

The weather had turned much colder with strong winds from the north. The temperature was only thirty-eight degrees, but the wind chill was below twenty degrees. Jack wore his black cashmere topcoat while Roulett chose a full-length ermine coat, trimmed in blue fox.

The limousine driver patiently stood by the car for thirty minutes in complete silence waiting for his wealthy passengers to arrive. Jack and Roulett kissed the children goodnight and gave Lou and Joyce's phone number to Heather, the babysitter. As they were going out the door, Roulett ran back to her bedroom to grab her stomach medication and an extra pint of vodka to hide in her purse—just in case the drinks were too weak.

Jack asked, "Why did you go back in the house?"

"I forgot my stomach medication," she replied, omitting her real reason.

"Honey, please go easy on the drinks tonight."

"Drinking is the only way I can tolerate this horrible party."

Jack held his tongue, not wanting to start a fight.

The limousine ride was short since Lou and Joyce lived in the same neighborhood. Lou greeted Jack and Roulett at the door and asked to take their coats.

Roulett said, "The house looks beautiful," though she thought the house looked over-decorated. The Christmas tree could barely hold up the over-crowded gilded ornaments, which glittered in the glow from the numerous candles. The dining room table was spectacular, set with antique Limoges china and Waterford crystal. Joyce was showing off the set of antique Russian gold tableware they'd all heard so much about, including a service for twelve of dining utensils, wine goblets, water glasses, chargers, and two large matching candelabras. The gold tableware was gold-plated silver, which was well over a hundred years old and breathtakingly beautiful. They all knew Lou threatened to divorce Joyce over the price she'd paid for the set. Lou and Joyce wouldn't tell anyone the cost, but Lou hinted that it was almost a hundred thousand dollars.

Marie whispered to Roulett, "This table settings cost more than most people make in a year, but it's a shame the gold tableware wasn't made by my great-great-grandfather, Linford Clayton. Then the table setting would be special."

Joyce said, "We're expecting my brother and his wife from Virginia, Garrett and Olivia Aldridge. She's in town for a job interview at the Center—she has a medical degree from Harvard Medical School and specializes in research."

"I already told everyone we're expecting them," Lou said.

"I'm a little concerned about them because I thought they'd arrive about two hours ago."

"It wouldn't have taken so long if they'd flown."

Jack asked, "You mean they're *driving* all the way from Virginia?"

Lou mocked, "That's right, 'all the way from Virginia'."

"Why?" Pam asked.

Joyce replied, "Because Olivia's deathly afraid of flying."

Lou said, "How strange—a person with as much education as Olivia shouldn't be afraid of planes."

"Olivia's very sensitive about her phobia, so please don't mention it."

"I went to college with Olivia. She and Garrett were already married when Joyce asked Olivia to find her a 'sucker' from her school. She arranged a blind date for Joyce with me. I fell into their trap and it wasn't long until I was hog-tied and standing at the altar."

* * * * *

The conversation made Joyce remember her first trip to Oklahoma. It was the weekend after Lou landed the job at the Center, and she was only seventeen with a four-month-old son. Born and raised in the industrial district of Richmond, Virginia by a poor, lower-class family, Joyce was the spitting image of her father, a scrawny, shy paper mill worker. However, her personality came gift-wrapped at birth from her mother, a haughty and brash housewife who taught her how to white lie and manipulate her way through life.

At sixteen, she met Lou at an off-campus college party. She lied to him, telling him she was nineteen. Falling into her trap like a lamb going to slaughter, he asked her on a date. A few weeks later, after convincing him she was on birth control, they slept together. Since she hadn't been taking the pill in over a month, she became pregnant. Two months later, they were standing at the altar. As she had hoped, Lou insisted they marry immediately.

At seventeen, completely unashamed of the trickery behind her marriage and motherhood, and still heavily armed with cunning and complacency, she continued approaching the world as though she owned it and all its creatures. With her cute pixie looks, she managed to lie her way out of most situations, a trait that had served her well over the years.

* * * * *

Roulett was standing on the other side of the room sipping a screwdriver Jack had intentionally made with too little vodka when Garrett and Olivia arrived. She noticed that Olivia was a very petite and slim woman, probably in her late thirties. She was neither ugly nor beautiful, but appeared very pleasant.

It was Garrett who caught Roulett's attention. Her first look caused a rush of emotions so overwhelming that she didn't realize she was staring. She immediately felt the urge to kiss and hug him. She wanted to hold him close as an overpowering desire hit her. She wanted to kiss him more than she'd ever wanted to kiss anyone in her life. She thought, *Oh my God! How could I feel love for a man who I've never met before?* Not believing a stranger could have such an impact on her, she reasoned it was the vodka making her a bit crazy.

She found herself stumbling through her introduction to Garrett, trying to avoid eye contact. She didn't believe in love at first sight, but she couldn't explain her feelings. With very little chitchat, she moved to the other side of the room. Thinking 'out of sight out of mind,' she wanted to pull herself together. Her heart pounded as she realized meeting Garrett was the event she'd wanted to avoid—the reason she dreaded coming. Her 'feelings of doom' weren't about this party—they were about meeting him.

Hollie, her father Harvey Jordan, and Hollie's boyfriend, Bill, were coming in the door. As soon as Hollie finished all her introductions, Roulett motioned for Hollie to accompany her to the bathroom. Although surprised by her request, Hollie followed her.

Roulett complained, "This feeling isn't fair! It's just not fair!"

Hollie replied, "What are you talking about?"

"That man out there—I think I love him. I don't think he's extremely handsome. I've met many men who were far more handsome than he is, but I've never felt about any of them the way I do about him."

"Who? Which man?"

"Lou's brother-in-law, Garrett…I don't even remember his last name," replied Roulett as she put down the seat on the toilet and sat down.

"You must be feeling lust, although I can't understand why. He's just an ordinary guy."

"It couldn't be mere lust. I could deal with lust. I don't know if I can deal with this awful 'love' feeling. It's not fair. I don't want this attraction for him or anyone else. I simply want him to go away."

"If you think you're in love with that man, you're crazy. You have a successful, good-looking husband. This dangerous feeling could jeopardize your safe and sane life. It's insanity—you need to chalk it up as temporary insanity brought about by lust," scolded Hollie.

"I know this terrible 'love' feeling isn't reasonable. I know it's crazy."

"That's what it sounds like to me. We better get back out there or they will think there's something strange going on between us."

Less than three minutes after Roulett returned from the bathroom, Garrett managed to cross the room to stand right beside her. Now what was she to do? She was thinking, *Oh God, why me? What have I done to deserve this temptation? I've been married for almost fourteen years, and I've never so much as looked at another man.* She thought, *Why now—why me—why this temptation?* She gradually moved again, to the other side of the room. Reacting like metal to a magnet, Garrett joined her again.

Roulett asked, "Garrett, have you met Sam, my father-in-law?"

He replied, "Yes, I met him a few minutes ago."

"Did you know that he and his wife have a ranch and they raise horses?"

"No. That's very interesting."

Roulett walked toward Sam and Garrett followed her. Roulett said, "Sam, why don't you tell Garrett about your ranch?"

"I'd love to."

Sam and Garrett began talking. Maybe Sam could keep Garrett busy. She truly wanted him to go away. She didn't even know him, so how could she love him? This wasn't reasonable. This wasn't fair. She thought maybe if she ignored him, the feeling would go away. She knew she needed to play it cool or everyone in the room would know she'd fallen in love with him. Feeling paranoid, she visualized a big neon sign saying Roulett loves Garrett.

Roulett's unusual attitude worried Marie. "Roulett...is something wrong?" she asked.

"No. Why do you ask?" Roulett replied.

"You just seem agitated."

"No," she lied, "I just have a slight headache."

"Maybe you need something to eat?" asked Marie.

"I'm afraid I'll spoil my dinner if I eat now. Dinner is in less then an hour," Roulett replied nervously. She noticed Garrett hadn't followed her again. While Marie was busy talking to Joyce, she had time to think. After the party she wouldn't have to see Garrett again. Yet, if Garrett's wife accepted the job at the Center, Roulett would have to see him occasionally. Starting to pray she thought, Oh God, if this is what I'm to do, I must have a sign from you that this is what you want me to do. If I receive a positive sign then, I'll know it's your will for me to pursue this man even though we both are married. She was negotiating with God or her perception of God's will, buried deep within her subconscious.

She was trying to think of something she thought had no chance of happening, something impossible. It dawned on her—she would ask God for the sign to be that she saw Garrett at least three, no make it four times a week for a year, trying to cinch the impossible part. That's it! Garrett had to average seeing her four times a week and she couldn't go to his house to see him. She felt safe this could never happen, not in a million years. However, if the impossible happened, then her love for him was justified, and she would kiss him and tell him how she felt about him. For, like it or not, she wanted this man more than anything she'd ever wanted before in her life.

Finally, it was time to eat. As luck would have it Roulett was seated directly across from Garrett. Suddenly she was wondering how she could get him alone. She refused the wine with dinner, saying it was because of her headache. This was, in a way, the truth because she considered her attraction to Garrett as an extremely big headache. About halfway through the first course of the meal, Roulett began to fantasize about seducing Garrett in front of everyone. Because this thought wasn't practical, her wild imagination needed to think of some way to do this without everyone else in the room knowing.

Daydreaming that the soup contained a sleeping potion and everyone except her and Garrett had their heads down on the table sleeping soundly, she visualized everyone except Joyce had moved their plates before they laid their heads down. Joyce was face down in her soup, while snoring and gurgling. *Enough making fun of Joyce,* Roulett thought, *back to my seduction of Garrett.*

In her mind, Garrett stopped eating his soup and asked, "Why is everybody asleep except us?"

"I'll show you why!" Trying to decide if she should go under, over, or around the table, she wanted the fastest route to him. She imagined choosing to go over—standing and pulling her tight dress up so she could use the chair as a step to the table. She decided she'd have Garrett first see dark hose held up by a black garter-belt. Then, pulling her dress higher, she'd expose her black crotchless panties.

At this point, in her mind, he wouldn't miss she was a natural brunette. His eyes would grow bigger along with his other expandable part. Standing to help her off the table, he would forget anyone else was in the room. Again, she would pull up her dress to step onto his chair. Putting his arms around her waist to help her down—intoxicated by her charms, he would hug and passionately French kiss her.

"Sit back down!" she ordered.

He would comply without hesitation as if he was under her spell, to the point he couldn't question her.

Again, she would pull her dress higher and straddle his lap. While kissing him wildly, she would unzip his slacks. Since this was her fantasy, what she found in his pants was perfect, not too small, not too large, not too short, not too long, just right, and hard as a rock with a soft velvety cover. Feeling he was too exposed with so many people in the room, asleep or not, she'd cover him with something. Crotchless panties made this chore easy. She gently sat down on his exposed appendage similar to the way a hen sits on an egg, carefully hiding it inside her most secret and safe place so she could keep the snoring crowd from knowing what she'd found. This union made her feel as one with this stranger, but she wanted more than only a hiding place for her newfound prize. The fire she felt inside would take a great deal of effort to put out, and the confines of this dining room chair lacked the mobility needed to extinguish the flames.

Sensing her needs, Garrett would pick her up while being very careful not to become uncoupled as he carried her to the nearest sofa where they could share a few moments of ecstasy.

As she came back to reality, Roulett sighed a gentle moan, as though hearing her name being called from a distant fog was relieving.

Lou called, "Roulett, Roulett," without response. Lou finally shouted, "ROULETT!"

She said, "Yes."

"I'm glad to see you're back with us," Lou said.

"I'm sorry, I was meditating to help my headache," she lied.

"Did it help?"

"Yes, it did," she said, still thinking about the passionate adventure with Garrett.

Garrett said, "I'm prone to headaches. Maybe you can teach me your meditation method sometime."

"I'd love to," she said with a Mona Lisa smile.

Lou added, "You haven't eaten much. Would you like some tongue?"

"No, thank you, I've had plenty," said Roulett, with another mischievous smile.

Jack broke in then, insinuating, "Lou, I wish you would quit trying to slip the tongue to my wife."

"I was only offering her a slice of smoked buffalo tongue, thank you very much," said Lou. They all laughed.

Jack and Lou had a continual contest about who could serve the most exotic meat for the Christmas party and Lou had outdone himself this year.

That night, on the way home, Jack hugged Roulett and said, "I'm pleased with the way you controlled your drinking tonight. I'm really proud of you. I knew you could do it."

Roulett thought, *if he knew the whole story, he wouldn't be proud at all.*

Chapter 7 | The Box

Those seeking riches fall into temptation and are trapped by foolish and harmful desires, which lead them to ruin and destruction. 1 TIMOTHY 6:9

John-George continued to improve and by the fifth day of his hospitalization, Jack felt he could leave his ailing grandfather to attend an important meeting in Dallas with a clear conscience. That Monday afternoon Jack and Roulett visited John-George in the hospital just before she drove Jack to the Tulsa airport. His plan was to have a good night's sleep in Dallas before his 7 a.m. meeting.

While Jack was boarding his plane, his brother Kirk—who'd recently finished jogging—was on his way to see his grandfather in the hospital. Kirk hadn't showered, hoping the smell of his perspiration would overpower the antiseptic smell lurking in the hospital halls. When he arrived, he noticed the full tray of food in front of his grandfather and Kirk asked, "Aren't you hungry, Grandfather?"

"No, not really," John-George replied.

Kirk lifted the cover on the plate as he said, "Looks pretty good to me…roast beef, carrots, mashed potatoes with brown gravy, and custard for dessert."

"You can eat it if you like," offered John-George, sounding exhausted.

"It looks good but Pam would fuss at me if I didn't eat with her. Thanks anyway."

"Is Pam expecting you home right away?"

"No, she won't be home until at least 8 o'clock—maybe later."

"Would you do something for me?"

"Sure, if I can."

"I want you to go to my house and pick up a box I want to give to Roulett."

"What's in the box?"

"Just some family heirlooms, some from my father Roy, and some from my grandmother Rebecca… Oh, I almost forgot the Catholic Bible from my grandmother Caroline. It was given to her from her grandmother Flossie; it's in my will for Roulett to receive the box, but I'd like for her to have it while I'm alive—I'd like to talk to her about the contents."

"Okay. Just tell me where the box is and I'll get it for you."

"It's in my library under the large oak table that's sitting on the green Persian rug. The box is under the tile, directly below the middle of the table."

Kirk asked, "Is the tile grouted in?"

"Yes, but not as securely as the rest of the tile. Ask Ned to help you move the table. It's extremely heavy and he'll have to unlock the door for you anyway."

"Okay. I'll be back as soon as possible. You rest while I'm gone."

John-George asked, "Kirk, would you do one more thing for me before you leave?"

"Sure, if I can," said Kirk.

"Call Roulett and ask her to be here when you bring the box back."

Although Kirk hated the idea of his grandfather giving the special hidden box to Roulett, he called her, not out of loyalty—money equals power and power creates fear—but fear that John-George would change his will.

Roulett quickly answered, "Barnes' residence."

"Roulett, this is Kirk. I'm at the hospital with Grandfather. He wants you to come here tonight so he can give you a box. It's still at his house, but I'm going to pick it up for you."

"Okay. Tell him I'll be there as soon as we finish eating and I drop the children off at the ranch—about twenty to thirty minutes."

On the way to John-George's house—a fifteen-minute drive—Kirk thought how much he hated Roulett! He didn't want Roulett to have anything of his grandfather's—especially not a treasure box so cherished it was hidden under the tile. He steamed all the way there, but Kirk knew his feelings must be kept hidden.

Kirk called Ned Dobbs on his cell phone so that he could meet him at the house with the key. He knew the rest of the family disliked Ned, but he had been useful to him as a spy for many years. Kirk never focused on the Dobbs family's faults because they were his allies against Roulett, who exposed their blatant shortcomings.

When Kirk arrived, he had so much built-up anger that he wanted to rip the tile up with his bare hands. Suddenly, a wave of fear overpowered him as he drove up the long driveway. Kirk felt a sense of security seeing Ned waiting for him on the porch, not only because he needed the key, but also, because he didn't want to go into the house alone. His grandfather's house, with its old tiger, lion, bear, rhino, hippo, zebra, moose, elk, deer, and many more animals on the walls and floors, had frightened him for as long as he could remember.

Kirk said, "Ned, I may need your help, so don't leave."

"Okay. Ah'll jes foller ya," said Ned, as they walked into the library.

"I need you to help me move this table," said Kirk. The library table was a very large, extremely heavy Victorian oak.

As they strained to move the table, Ned complained, "Ah thunk ya choz th' hehvist thaing in th' hawse ta move."

"You may be right. Grandfather said I couldn't move this table alone—he wasn't kidding," said Kirk, as he rolled up the green rug.

Ned asked, "Nah whut?"

"I'll need a hammer and a chisel to remove this tile," said Kirk.

Ned lazily whined, "Why er we'uns gonna tek op thus here til? Hit luks gud ta me."

"I'm only going to take up one tile. I won't need your help any longer after you find the hammer and chisel," Kirk added, certain Ned would move faster if he knew his work was almost done. Kirk wanted to recover the treasure alone. While Ned was searching for tools, Kirk evaluated the tile. It was about thirteen by thirteen inches and thinly grouted into place.

Ned gladly left after handing Kirk the tools. He loosened the tile and slid it to the side. Under the tile was a wooden trapdoor that opened easily. A musty odor filled the room, making Kirk cough. He saw an old wooden box fitted into the space as if it were built for the space or vice versa. The box, covered with a moldy residue, had a horsehair rope tied around it, thus making lifting it out easy. A small rusty lock kept it closed. Kirk's heart pounded. He had to find a way to open the box without Roulett knowing!

His cell phone rang and he jumped, feeling guilty. Roulett was crying as she said, "He's gone."

"I was there only a few minutes ago. Did you have a chance to speak to him before he died?"

"He told me he sent you after a box he wanted me to have," she said, sobbing.

Kirk said, "I found it, but it's locked. Did he tell you what's in it?"

"Diamonds."

"Did he say how many diamonds or if the diamonds are in jewelry or not?"

"He only said diamonds, so I'm assuming there's more than one diamond. He was too weak to tell me more."

"Did he tell you where the key is?"

"Yes. It's in the top left-hand corner of the large bookcase in the den. Would you please bring it with you? We'll meet at your mother's house. We're leaving now."

"Sure, if I can find it." Kirk found a ladder so he could reach the key in the heavily carved mahogany Victorian bookcase, which was over eight feet tall. After looking for several minutes, he decided to feel for the key. "Ouch!" he yelled as a splinter of wood embedded in his finger. The next time Kirk felt, he found the key hanging on a tiny nail with a rusty cotter pin to hold it in place. Since everything was so rusty, the key was impossible to see against the dark reddish-brown mahogany patina of the bookcase.

Kirk couldn't overcome the temptation. Justifying his actions by thinking that whatever hidden treasures were inside should belong to his mother instead of Roulett, he allowed his anger and jealousy to overrule his logic. As he inserted the key into the lock and turned it, he remembered the myth of Pandora's Box. The stubborn little lock finally opened and he lifted the lid as he envisioned large stacks of cash and diamonds.

The first thing Kirk found in the box was an extremely old Catholic Bible. He didn't consider this a treasure, so he tossed it on the floor. The only other things were two burgundy velvet drawstring bags. Although disappointed by the lack of cash or gold, he remained optimistic about the diamonds.

The first bag contained two uncut diamonds—each approximately eighteen carats. The other bag contained one large uncut diamond—approximately fifty-eight carats—along with an old dried seedpod of some unrecognizable species. He took a quick look then returned them to their pouches. He needed to think fast because his mother and Roulett would be waiting for him, knowing their trip home would be shorter than his trip there.

Quickly, he unzipped the fanny pack he was wearing and dropped the contents of the bag containing the large diamond into it. Then, he took one of the smaller diamonds from the other velvet bag and put it in the empty bag. Now there was one diamond in each of the two velvet bags. Since John-George had only told Roulett about diamonds, and not a specific number of them, Kirk thought he should be able to succeed with his scheme. He first put the old Bible into the box and then added the two velvet pouches containing the smaller diamonds. All he had to do was hurry back before his mother or Roulett became suspicious.

On his way to his mother's ranch, all Kirk could think about was the gigantic diamond he'd pilfered from Roulett. Feeling a sense of justice, he thought, *what luck!* He never gave a thought to the seedpod. The pod was only along for the ride. He simply didn't have time to separate it from his huge diamond in the rough.

Kirk—overwhelmed with greed—lacked the compassion to mourn his grandfather's passing. He felt empowered and enlightened possessing the huge diamond, but in actuality, he was traveling a path of darkness. While the diamonds were family heirlooms with intriguing stories about their acquisition, it was the strange seedpod that possessed the most fascinating story of them all.

Chapter 8 | The Betrayal

Wealth does not go to the grave... PSALMS 49: 16, 17

John-George Clayton's funeral fell on a cold and damp Tuesday, only five days before Christmas. Petrolia's largest church overflowed with people who wanted to pay their last respects. Although many were friends and relatives, more than half were people who wanted to catch a final glimpse of their town's founder. The guest book could've doubled as a Who's Who of the Heartland—governors, senators, state representatives, mayors, and major company CEOs were present.

As was customary, the family occupied the first row. Marie and Sam Barnes were seated beside Jack, Roulett, Michael, Tammy, Kirk, Pam, and their daughter, Alyssa. John-George's brother, Charles Clayton, and his mother, Dorothy Clayton were on the other side of the front row. Roulett noticed an unfamiliar elderly African-American woman sitting between Charles and Dorothy. Longtime Clayton Research Center employee, Harvey Jordan, and his family occupied the entire second row. Roulett thought it surprising that Harvey and his family, including Hollie, were seated before Lou Gordon and his family. She wondered if it was because Harvey had more seniority because he'd worked at the Center longer than Lou.

While the remaining mourners were seated and the choir sang "Amazing Grace," Marie thought it wasteful to sacrifice so many beautiful flowers for her father's funeral. There were thousands of roses, mums, irises, and lilies mixed with many smaller flowers and greenery—all destroyed—for what? All the bright colors seemed so inappropriate for his funeral. She didn't consider him worthy of such natural beauty for she knew him in a way that so few did. Remembering her wedding day when John-George announced all the provisions he provided as a wedding present, which included a large house, acreage, and a steady income for as long as Sam and Marie remained married—living together as man and wife. From that day forward, Marie was no longer a Clayton, but forever a Barnes. Every person at Marie's wedding thought John-George was so wonderful, so generous, so considerate, but they didn't know the whole story.

Reverend Fields approached the podium, straightened his notes, and said, "We are here to pay our last respects to John-George Clayton. Please bow your heads in prayer, asking our Lord's blessing on this gathering." After hesitating for a few moments, he began to pray aloud, "Dear Lord we ask that you watch over our grieving crowd as we thank you for our lives. Please help me to comfort their sorrow, help me to relieve their pain, and help me to show them how to put their trust in you, knowing that you will carry the burden of pain as you have so many times in the past. In Jesus' name we pray, amen.

"We have gathered on this day to remember John-George Clayton. So many people loved, honored, and respected him that Petrolia doesn't have a building large enough to seat all who will miss him, which is a testament to his character. John-George was the first and only child born to Roy and Annabelle Clayton of New York City, New York. They had waited several years for a child and showered him with loving attention upon his arrival.

"You may ask why we should grieve for a man who had everything: power, fame, and riches. But life for John-George Clayton was not always so perfect. Like all mankind he experienced hardships. These hardships are a normal part of life. Let us read God's word in Ecclesiastes 9: 11. 'I realized another thing, that in this world fast runners do not always win the races, and the brave do not always win the battles. Wise men do not always earn a living, intelligent men do not always get rich, and capable men do not always rise to high positions. Bad luck happens to everyone.' John-George experienced such bad luck when, during his formative years, he endured the tragic deaths of his mother, his grandmother, and three of his aunts in a short period of time. Although John-George suffered these great losses, he grew to be a very intelligent man. He was a handsome man as well—tall, slender, with curly-blond hair and sparkling blue-gray eyes.

"John-George chose not to follow in his father's and grandfather's footsteps. I am told that his father was very disappointed when his son chose an agricultural career over being a jewelry maker and diamond broker, although John-George's enthusiasm for agriculture was created by his father's interest in his mysterious greenhouse. John-George did not experience the great adventures that his father and grandfather had as they traveled so many times in Africa. John-George's adventure was different, because after graduating with a Bachelor of Science degree in Agriculture, he wanted to migrate to Oklahoma, and with his father's help, John-George moved here shortly after. Petrolia is thankful that he made this choice.

"It may surprise many of you that John-George Clayton lived in a small shack for some time after moving to Oklahoma. Yes—you heard me right—a very small shack! After his first year in Oklahoma, John-George realized making a living farming—which was his way of supporting himself while trying to achieve his other agricultural goals—was more difficult than he'd expected. Desperately needing money, but refusing to ask his father for more financial help, he decided he would try to secure a loan from his bank in Bartlesville before late land payments ruined his credit. He met his first wife-to-be Josephine while applying for this loan; she was the bank president's daughter. John-George was denied an additional loan due to insufficient equity, but he fished for a way to meet the bank president's daughter, and finally attained an invitation to attend church so he could see and hear Josephine sing. With Josephine's angelic voice being the highlight of his week and the church socials' abundant food running a close second, John-George attended church every Sunday thereafter. That winter on his land was a real challenge with money in such short supply. His survival depended upon his ability to hunt and kill rabbits and squirrels to eat, which made him enjoy any opportunity to eat something besides the wild game he caught. He especially liked fried chicken, which they served frequently at church socials. Although John-George was denied the loan, he won the heart of Josephine. In time, John-George courted and married her.

As you see, John-George experienced lean times before he received his grandfather's inheritance. He and his wife then could live comfortably, but not extravagantly as he pursued his agricultural goals. Again life's obstacles prevented him from achieving his objective when he received his draft notice for the Army. He reported for duty and served in World War II bravely, receiving the Purple Heart for being shot while saving one of his platoon buddies. After the war, John-George returned home to continue working on his agricultural project. His aim was to produce a disease and insect resistant strain of corn, but to his dismay Oklahoma's weather didn't cooperate. He tried drilling a well for water, but this too, failed miserably. Frustrated by the lack of water—he began calling our area 'No Water' County instead of Nowata County."

A slight chuckle moved the crowd since many had endured Oklahoma's unpredictable weather for years.

Rev. Fields continued, "By this time, John-George's woes had reached a level that worried his wife Josephine, but no one knew the extent of his disillusionment until he shocked everyone by unexpectedly reenlisting in the Army. I am told that his actions infuriated his wife—and rightfully so—because she was expecting, with her due date being entirely too close to his departure date. Luckily for John-George, his daughter Mildred Marie was born several days early. He shipped out the day after her birth and served overseas to help rebuild and stabilize many war-torn areas.

"After his return home, John-George again tried to develop an insect-and-disease-resistant strain of corn, but his water problem proved victorious once again; so he decided to drill a deeper well. He was so exasperated from his water problems that he told the supervisor of the drilling crew, 'Drill all the way to China if you have to—just find me some water!' Keep in mind that his actual words may have been slightly more graphic, nevertheless, he didn't find water, but struck oil instead. His bad luck had turned into good luck for God had blessed him. John-George became an overnight millionaire and founded Petrolia Oil Company.

"Some may think John-George had everything because he was rich, but again tragedy began to strike his life. First, he lost his father Roy. Less than a year later his wife Josephine died, and after many years of solitude, he remarried and his new bride died on their honeymoon. Although John-George spent many years with this third wife Florence, she too, preceded him in death.

"Because of his continued interest in discovering what killed so many of his female ancestors and his own wives, John-George started Clayton Research Center. The Center, as it became known, is a pharmaceutical laboratory specializing in agricultural-related products—famous for the world's largest botanical DNA database. This database is utilized for discovering cures for the worst diseases, including cancer, heart disease, diabetes, HIV, etc. The Center has produced many beneficial pharmaceutical products.

"John-George remained a very active man for many years, always on the go, traveling the world until two years ago. Outliving three wives took a heavy toll on him, and he became a recluse, rarely leaving his house after Florence's death.

"Petrolia owes its name and economy to one man: John-George Clayton. The majority of Petrolia's residences are employed by either Petrolia Oil or Clayton Research Center. John-George is considered to be a financial genius by most who knew him and he owned the assets to prove his financial prowess.

"John-George had moved from New York to seek his fortune out west and a fortune he found. Our Lord and Savior has promised him a better eternity. Let us read our Lord's words in John 14 verse 1 and 2, 'Do not be worried and upset,' Jesus told them. 'Believe in God and believe also in me. There are many rooms in my father's house, and I am going to prepare a place for you. I would not tell you this if it were not so.'

"Please join me in the closing prayer. Dear Lord, we are gathered here as your humble servants, unworthy of your love as we ask for your forgiveness with the knowledge that our brother John-George Clayton is with you in a better place, better than we can imagine, so please forgive our selfish grief for we shall miss him. In Jesus' name we pray, amen."

After the service, Hollie said, "Roulett, I'd like you to meet my grandmother, Nambi Jordan. Grammy Nambi, this is my long-time friend, Roulett Clayton."

Nambi held out her shaky hand while smiling a big toothy grin, as she greeted, "You must be the pretty girl who married John-George's eldest grandson. Hollie has told me so much about you. In fact"—she paused a minute, trying to gather her thoughts before finishing her sentence—"I think I've heard about you from Dorothy, too. It's so good to finally meet you, and you're as pretty as they said you were."

Roulett was surprised the elderly woman was so articulate at her age. Roulett thought Nambi appeared to be close to ninety years old with her snow-white hair, eyebrows, and eyelashes. Roulett gingerly shook Nambi's hand, as she said, "It's nice to meet you, too. Do you live in town?"

"Oh no, dear, I live in New York, not too far from Charles. He brought me with him, so I could attend my brother's funeral," said Nambi.

Roulett thought Nambi must be speaking metaphorically about John-George being her brother as she asked, "Have you known John-George for a long time?"

"Oh my, yes, child, I met my brother over seventy-five years ago when Roy brought me to America. Before that, I lived with my mother in Africa, but she died when I was only thirteen-years-old. I came to America so Roy could take care of me," said Nambi.

Now Roulett thought she understood why Nambi considered John-George her brother. Roy filled the role of a father figure for her when she was growing up, thus making John-George seem like her brother. Roulett asked, "Are you going to stay in town for a while?"

"Yes, I'm going to stay until Charles is ready to go home—probably a month or more. Charles is a very good brother but not as good a brother as John-George was. He took care of my entire family. The world lost a great man when my brother died," said Nambi, as tears rolled down her cheeks and she wiped her eyes with a tissue.

"Maybe you can come with Hollie to one of our Friday night get-togethers at Marie's ranch. I think you would enjoy it," said Roulett.

"I'll try to make it one night while I'm here," Nambi replied.

* * * * *

Jack came home from work two days before Christmas, extremely agitated. He was carrying several colorfully wrapped packages, so Roulett assumed he'd been doing some frustrating last minute Christmas shopping. She kissed him on the cheek as she asked, "Bad day? You should know by now not to wait to do your shopping this close to Christmas. It's a madhouse out there."

"I wasn't shopping today. I've had these presents for weeks. I just forgot to bring them home. I'm not the one who delays my shopping to the last minute."

"Well then, why are you in such a bad mood? You don't have to go back to work until the second of January."

"I've postponed telling you about the inventory problem at the Center, thinking in vain I'd have a better solution to this perplexing dilemma. Since I don't, I guess it's time to tell you."

"Three weeks ago during inventory, the Center's board discovered four vials were missing from the biohazard level-four lab. Three of the four that were missing were Vibrio Cholerae (cholera), HIV, and Ebola. There was also a vial missing from our Grandfather's personal research lab, John-George number seventeen, we think it was some harmless vegetable-compound, but we can't be certain. We don't know how long the vials were missing because we only count the vials once a year. Only four people have the keys to that lab. Kirk and I each have one key, Grandfather John-George had one, and Dr. Cleta Worthington had two keys. To enter the level-four lab you must have two keys," Jack explained.

Roulett said, "Wow! That is a predicament. What did Dr. Worthington say?"

"We haven't asked her because she won't be back from her vacation until January 16th."

"She was at Grandfather's funeral. Why didn't you ask her then?"

"I intended to, but she left before I could speak to her."

"It would be hard for me to think Dr. Worthington would steal from the Center."

"That's the same thing Grandfather said when Kirk and I met with him several weeks ago. Kirk was adamant she'd stolen the vials because none of us had, but Grandfather said there was another explanation. He stood his ground, insisting Cleta wouldn't steal, which made Kirk furious."

"What are you going to do about it?"

"When Dr. Worthington returns, she'll be dismissed. We've hired Dr. Olivia Aldridge to replace her," said Jack.

Roulett had a sick feeling in the pit of her stomach as she realized Kirk had bullied Jack into firing Dr. Worthington without questioning her; and Kirk made certain Garrett wouldn't leave town because they'd hired Garrett's wife. She asked, "Do you think that's fair to terminate Dr. Worthington without giving her the opportunity to defend herself? Maybe she has an explanation. Are you positive Kirk didn't do it?"

Jack asked, "Why would he?"

She shrugged. "He's awfully quick to blame someone else...someone else who hasn't even had a chance to defend herself. To me that's a sign of guilt."

"Why would Kirk have wanted the vials?"

"I don't know. Why would anyone want vials of dangerous pathogens?"

"The most obvious reason would be for terrorism, but they could also be used to eliminate someone. I don't know of anyone who has died from the symptoms of any of the three diseases."

Roulett asked, "What are the symptoms of cholera?"

"Diarrhea, vomiting, dehydration, and possibly death. Those sound similar to the symptoms Florence had, but a stomach virus and cholera are similar. Since she was frail and thin, the cause of her death could've been a simple stomach virus—and Grandfather recovered from the same symptoms the week before Florence became ill."

"Could Kirk have stolen the cholera bacteria to kill Florence?"

Jack asked, "Why would he have done that?"

Roulett said quickly, "I can think of seventy million reasons why...if Florence had survived John-George's death, she would've inherited everything except Marie's trust fund."

"Don't be silly. He couldn't kill anyone. Besides I had the same amount to lose," argued Jack.

"People are crazy when it comes to money, especially when there's so much money involved."

Jack sighed. "We hired Olivia Aldridge to replace Cleta Worthington. Lou told his sister-in-law about the job opening because he knew we needed someone to fill the position. Olivia will start work on January 29th."

Roulett thought, *Oh no! Garrett is here to stay.*

* * * * *

After a rather grim Christmas, Sam and Marie planned a New Year's party to help cheer everyone. They invited a long list of friends and family. As usual, the majority of guests opted to stay at the ranch. Again, Roulett would have to deal with being in the same room as Garrett, but at least she had champagne to make it easier.

Sam tried coaxing Marie into having one glass of champagne by saying, "You tried the champagne at the millennium party. Why don't you simply have one glass with us now? You've had a rough year with your father's death and a little champagne should help you relax."

"I only tried that champagne because it was the only millennium party I would ever attend, so I had one glass. You reminded me it should be good because you paid almost a thousand dollars for the case. It was the '90 vintage touted as the best in years," replied Marie.

"That was a spectacular New Year's Eve party. I had heard rumors of a champagne shortage, so I purchased a case of '90 vintage Dom Pérignon champagne ten months before the party. I wish I'd purchased five cases since it's the best champagne we ever had!" said Sam.

Lou recalled, "I remember that special champagne. I tried coaxing Marie into giving me her part. However, she surprised everyone with her answer 'just one glass.' So she drank the expensive kind but if she doesn't want to drink the other stuff now, again I will offer to drink her part."

"You can have my champagne this year, Lou. I only drink the *good stuff* and only at millennium parties," said Marie.

They all chuckled at Marie's reply, which helped to lighten the mood and make the party a success.

* * * * *

On the following Monday, Roulett took the children to ride their horses. She was shocked to see Garrett and Sam inside the barn.

"Hi," Garrett greeted. "Long time no see."

Sam said, "Since the Center hired Olivia and I've hired Garrett to work at the ranch, he'll be here from noon to about six o'clock on Monday through Saturday. We'll be seeing a lot more of him—he'll be just like one of the family."

Pale and shocked, Roulett said, "Good," but she was really thinking, *Why me, God?* She wished he worked in the mornings so she wouldn't have to see him. Her unwelcome feelings of love for Garrett boiled, resulting in extreme rage. She wanted to be hostile, but kept her feelings in check.

Roulett said, "I thought your wife starts working here on the twenty-ninth of this month; don't you have to go back to Virginia first?"

"Olivia went back, but I'm staying with Joyce and Lou until I find us a house. Then I'll fly there to help her drive back."

Roulett simply wanted him to go away, far away and not return. Yet, she realized the first condition of her asking God to give her a sign was coming true—she would see him at the ranch at least four times a week, sometimes more.

She instantly decided to renegotiate her hypothetical sign from God, not accepting the expedient occurrence of the first sign as binding enough. After thinking for a few minutes, she thought of another perfect, improbable condition: She had to quit drinking for at least six months. Roulett's drinking problem had started years before and had steadily become more severe each year since the birth of her last child. In fact, the only time she hadn't drank heavily was during her two pregnancies. She'd struggled through the nine months, but chose only to breastfeed for two weeks before returning to the booze. She further rationalized that the anxiety from her unwanted feelings for Garrett would cause her to drink more than ever.

Garrett's interest in her appeared as only friendly, not flirty. He didn't encourage her passion for him in any way, other than by just being there; and there he constantly was! If she didn't take the children out to the ranch for some reason or another, he would stop by her house to check on them. Then, to make matters worse, he would talk to her until Jack came home.

Somehow, Garrett always managed to take his breaks at the ranch when Roulett was in the barn or clubhouse. When she let herself relax around Garrett, she really enjoyed his company. This was tormenting because she didn't *want* to like his company; she didn't want to like him, but she did, thinking she could handle loving him but liking him was even more dangerous!

On Tuesday, John-George's family members met with Vernon Bernstein, the family attorney, concerning John-George's will. Mr. Bernstein began by saying, "I'm going to tell all of you the contents of the will in plain English, but feel free to ask questions; each person will receive a copy to take home. Any questions before I begin?"

No one said a word.

Mr. Bernstein began to read, "John-George wanted Roulett Barnes to have the hidden box with its contents."

Kirk nervously interrupted, "Roulett has the box. I gave it to her after Grandfather sent me to his house to find it the night he died."

"Then we'll go on to the next item, which is Petrolia Oil Company. It'll be divided in the following manner: 50% to the Trust Fund with no voting rights and subject to the same stipulations as before; 20% to Jackson Daniel Barnes, hereafter known as Jack; 20% to Kirk Douglas Barnes, hereafter known as Kirk; and 10% to Charles Daniel Clayton, hereafter known as Charles; currently appraised value being approximately twenty-four million dollars.

"Next is Clayton Research Center, which includes John-George's home, furniture, and twelve-hundred-thirty acres. The division is in the following manner: 45% to Jack Barnes; 45% to Kirk Barnes; and 10% to Charles Clayton. Jack's employment contract will be for a guaranteed position of CEO for twenty years, with the currently appraised value of Clayton Research Center being approximately twenty-three million dollars."

"Next are the other properties, stocks, diamonds, and cash that will be divided in the following manner: 50% to the Trust Fund without voting rights and subject to the same stipulations as before; 20% to Jack Barnes; 20% to Kirk Barnes; and 10% to Charles Clayton. Currently appraised value of this portion came to approximately eleven million dollars.

"On the matter concerning the Trust Fund: Mildred Marie Clayton Barnes' weekly stipend will be doubled to equal four thousand dollars a week, with the same conditions as before.

"John-George also added all of his great-grandchildren to the trust; each one is entitled to receive two thousand dollars per week beginning at age sixteen—to receive the trust fund, three conditions must be met. First, they must stay in school until they finish college and achieve a degree in the subject of their choice. Second, they must never be arrested. And third, they must pass a monthly drug and nicotine test.

"And last, personal belongings will be divided among these family members: Marie Barnes, Jack Barnes, Kirk Barnes, and Charles Clayton.

"Any questions?" asked Vernon Bernstein as he handed out copies of John-George's last will and testament.

Kirk's heart pounded as he rapidly scanned his copy for the section regarding Roulett's box. Relief washed over him when he saw it didn't list the contents.

* * * * *

The next day at work Jack and Kirk were casually talking when Jack mistakenly mentioned that Roulett thought Kirk had stolen the cholera bacteria to murder Florence. Infuriated, he insisted that Roulett be excluded from the dividing of John-George's personal belongings. He concluded that she'd already received the box, which was all he'd wanted her to have.

When the family gathered at John-George's house, Roulett wasn't there. Jack had cowered to Kirk's wishes once again.

Chapter 9 | The Pod

Coral, crystal, rubies, the finest topaz, nor the purest gold can compare to the value of wisdom. JOB 28: 18,19

On the following Monday while admiring his diamond, Kirk wondered why his grandfather had kept the dehydrated pod. Why was it stored with the large diamond? He knew the pod must be important to warrant being stored with such a valuable stone. He picked up the pod and slowly turned it. Round like an apple, it was the size of a small plum with six distinctly uniform sections. Although old, it appeared to be a dark purplish-brown. Part of one section was missing. He didn't recognize it or know if the pod was a fruit or a vegetable. He decided to take it to the Center to have it analyzed in the drug research lab's horticulture department.

Kirk arrived the next morning with two dozen doughnuts as a bribe, hoping the girls in the horticulture lab would analyze the pod for him.

Alice asked, "Why the goodies? Do you have a crush on one of us?"

"Or maybe both of us?" Sandra laughed.

Kirk had purposely selected two girls who would've done anything for either one of the Barnes brothers. "Well, actually, I have a little favor to ask."

Alice teased, "Will I need to shower first?"

"Or should I assume that we both are included and you'll need a shower afterward?" Sandra seductively licked the sugar from a doughnut off her finger.

"Not anything like that, I only want you to analyze this," Kirk blushed, as he handed the pod to Sandra.

Sandra immediately examined it and said, "It looks very old. What in the world is this?"

"I don't know. That's why I'm here. I want to know what it is. Please don't tell anyone else about this."

"We'll see if it's in our database. We have more than 260,000 specimens for comparison. But we'll need to cut off a sample."

"Okay, but can you take the sample from the open section?" Kirk asked.

Sandra said, "I think so. We'll try to leave the other sections intact."

"Save all the seeds if they fall out."

"Why don't you let me cut a specimen now so you can take the rest with you," Sandra said.

"Great."

She found a small scalpel and carefully collected a small sample. She said, "Kirk, come look. Some seeds were exposed."

Kirk looked closely, seeing the minuscule seeds. Sandra put the pod in a small specimen bag and handed it to him as she said, "Now you won't lose any of the seeds. We'll need about three days to analyze this specimen."

* * * * *

Three days later, Kirk stopped by the lab. "Did you learn what it is?" he asked.

Alice replied, "We have a report but it's most likely not what you want to hear. So far we've only ruled out various species of plants."

"I don't understand. What are you saying?"

Sandra explained, "It's not in our database. First, we tried for an exact match with no luck. Next, we tried for the closest match, which was the DNA of *Ficus carica*, best known as the common fig."

"Maybe it's from the Garden of Eden," joked Alice.

Kirk said, "What?"

Alice answered, "I'm only kidding. You know the story about Adam, Eve, and the fig leaf in paradise."

Kirk asked, "How closely is the fruit related to the fig?"

"Not close at all, not even a distant cousin in human kinship terms. Why don't you plant a few of these seeds and see what grows? Maybe we'll be able to tell you more about a complete plant than this dried fruit. The only fact we know is your specimen is an angiosperm. That's Latin for 'enclosed seed,' which is the dominant form of plant life on earth," replied Sandra.

"Even *I* knew that. Remember I have a degree in agriculture."

Sandra said, "I'm sorry we don't know any more about this now than we did when we started."

Kirk held the pod to the light. "I'll plant some of these seeds to see if they'll germinate. Trying to identify this plant has become a rather fascinating mystery!"

"They should germinate. You know botanists have taken seeds from tombs in Egypt which were thousands of years old and often the seeds still germinated," said Sandra.

That night Kirk waited until his wife was asleep before he took the pod from his safe. He scraped out twelve tiny dark purple seeds from the open side of the pod. Kirk gingerly put the seeds in a small plastic sandwich bag.

On the next Monday, Kirk took the seeds to his mother's ranch after work and asked, "Mom, would you plant some seeds for me in your greenhouse?"

Marie asked, "What kind of seeds do you want me to plant?"

He handed her a small bag of seeds. "I don't know what they are. That's why I want you to plant them—to see what grows."

"Where did you find these?" She asked, studying the tiny seeds.

"I found them in a box Grandfather gave me before he passed away. I'm curious about their identity; surprisingly, they're not in the database at the Center."

Marie took him to her large greenhouse. When they walked inside a warm mist settled over them. Everything was green and beautiful, showing Marie's great pride and hard work.

"How many seeds do you want me to plant?" she asked.

He replied, "Twelve."

"Why so many?"

"I don't know how old the seeds are. All of them may not germinate."

Marie put the seeds in a small plastic cup with a little water. She said, "I'll plant the seeds in the morning after they've soaked overnight; they'll sprout sooner." She prepared individual peat pots for the enigmatic seeds. "Since the seeds are so small, I won't plant them very deep. I'll leave a note on this tray so Garrett will water them every day for the next week, not twice a week like the other plants."

"Call me when the seeds sprout. I'm curious to know what they are."

Six days later Marie found two of the seeds sprouting through the potting soil. Marie couldn't wait to tell him, so she called Kirk on her greenhouse phone.

"What's up, Mom?"

"I have good news! Two of your seeds sprouted," Marie excitedly reported.

"That's great. I'll stop by to see them after work."

Kirk arrived that afternoon to inspect the new sprouts. While Kirk and Marie were examining the fragile plants, they noticed four more were sprouting. Marie said, "At this rate, all your seeds could germinate."

"I hope you're right. Now, I can't wait to see what the grown plants look like," Kirk said with the enthusiasm of a child begging to open a Christmas present.

The next day, all twelve of the seeds were up and turning bright green. They grew like weeds, so rapidly that they were over six inches tall by the end of the week. At the Friday night get-together, Marie couldn't wait to tell Jack about the new plants. Marie was waiting for him when he arrived at the clubhouse and before he could take off his coat, she said, "I planted some seeds for Kirk in my greenhouse last Monday and they've sprouted and grown over six inches in only a week. Kirk doesn't know what they are, but they're extremely hardy to have grown so much in such a short time. What's strange is that he said they weren't in the horticultural database at the Center."

"Where did he find the seeds? I thought we had every known kind of plant in our database," Jack said.

"He said Dad gave them to him shortly before he died."

Jack hesitated, then shrugged. "Maybe it was some rain forest specimen Grandfather never managed to add to the database…"

* * * * *

The next day, Garrett brought Marie the bad news about a malfunction with the greenhouse furnace the night before and that, with the temperature falling well below freezing, all the plants in the greenhouse died except the twelve plants from Kirk's seeds. Although Marie was very disappointed about losing her plants, she called Kirk to tell him his sprouts withstood the cold temperatures and were extremely hardy.

Chapter 10 | Roulett & Lou

Someone who drinks too much is miserable and sorry for himself—always causing trouble, complaining, and has bruises that could have been avoided. PROVERBS 23: 29-30

Roulett arrived at the ranch at her normal time on Friday night. She was still very upset about the problem with Jack and Kirk. Lou arrived early, too, walking in the clubhouse carrying a sack containing tortilla chips, guacamole, green chilies, and sour cream. He professed, "Boy, do I love Mexican food! When will the rest be ready?"

She replied, "My part's ready—beef and cheese enchiladas. The rest is up to Marie. Why are you here so early? It isn't even four o'clock yet."

Feigning disappointment, he asked, "Aren't you pleased to see me?"

"In the mood I'm in, I don't think I'd be pleased to see anyone. Don't take it personally."

"I'm relieved to know it isn't just *me*, but, I'm sorry you're in a bad mood."

"Thanks for your concern. You still haven't told me why you're early..."

"I had to take Joyce and Garrett to the Tulsa airport so they could fly to Maryland. Their mother had emergency gallbladder surgery this morning. They won't be back until at least Monday, so tonight we can make this a late one."

"Are you prepared to spend the night here? The weather is going to be terrible. I heard on the radio a cold front will drop the temperature below freezing, with a chance of sleet."

"I don't believe everything the weather forecasters say, but I could spend the night if necessary," Lou replied as he poured himself a scotch and water. He took a sip and offered, "Can I make you another screwdriver?"

"Yes, please, and don't forget the vodka, like Jack usually does."

"He doesn't forget it. He purposely makes your screwdrivers light on the vodka."

"Okay, then please don't make it light. I don't want to drink a gallon of orange juice to feel a buzz."

"One heavy screwdriver coming up!" Carrying both drinks to the couch where Roulett was sitting, he handed her one and sat down.

She took a sip and said, "Thank you. This is good."

"You're welcome, but I need to warn you…that drink is so strong it should be called a hammer instead of a screwdriver."

"That's okay. The way I feel tonight, I like the idea of getting hammered." She sat for a moment with a puzzled look on her face, before she sniffed the air and asked, "What's that smell?"

"Mexican food."

"No!" she sniffed Lou's neck and said, "It's you!"

"That's my new aftershave. Does it smell that bad?"

"No, it smells that *good*. What is it?"

Lou said, "It's a new aftershave Garrett gave me. He doesn't wear cologne or aftershave. Someone gave it to him for Christmas. You're not going to believe what it's called!"

"Not unless it's called WOW!"

"No, it's called 4-Play!"

"Good name! I can understand why they called it that. It's the best stuff I've ever smelled," said Roulett.

"It's supposed to contain pheromones."

"I think it has horny-moans in it."

Lou corrected, "Do you mean hormones?"

"No, I meant exactly what I said—horny-moans," Roulett spouted bravely, feeling the strong drink. She thought that if Garrett had worn that aftershave when she first met him, she would've found a way to kiss him. "Lou, that stuff could be dangerous. Scent is a powerful turn on to many women."

"Are you trying to tell me this'll make the women I'm around horny?"

"I definitely think it could have that effect on some women."

"I can live with that," Lou said with a smirk.

"Remember, I told you it could be dangerous," cautioned Roulett again.

"I'm not worried about it being dangerous. I want to know if the company sells it by the gallon. I think I should buy some of their stock."

Sam and Marie walked in carrying the ingredients for tacos. Sam said, "It's sprinkling now and getting colder by the minute. I hope you're prepared to stay the night."

Lou said, "We were just discussing that."

Marie asked, "Where's Jack?"

"He'll be here at the normal time. I took off early. Garrett asked me to tell you he wouldn't be back until his mother is better. He said they'd try to be back on Monday, but he may be late for work."

Marie unloaded Lou's bag as she said, "So, you don't need to go home tonight."

"That's right, I'm a bachelor for a few days!"

Roulett laughed as she said, "You sound very happy about that—in fact, too happy. If I were your wife, I wouldn't like your reaction." Nudging him, she whispered, "Why don't you ask Marie what she thinks of your aftershave?"

Lou enthusiastically said, "Okay!" He puffed out his chest, sucking in his stomach as he walked to Marie. "What do you think of my aftershave?"

Marie sniffed his neck and replied, "That smells great! What is it? Maybe I can buy Sam some for his birthday."

Sam grumbled, "I don't want any of that stinky stuff on me. Good old soap and water's good enough for me."

Marie looked disappointedly at Sam. "It wouldn't hurt you to smell a little different for a change, you old goat!"

As Jack walked in, Lou answered Marie, "Can you believe this aftershave is called 4-Play? I wish I'd thought of that name."

"It's getting nasty out there. The rain's beginning to freeze," Jack said.

Sam added, "It'll be slicker than snot on a door knob out there by morning."

"Oh, Sam, must you be so graphic?" Marie asked.

The weather steadily became worse as the evening progressed. Soon, it was apparent to everyone they'd be spending the night. Roulett was drinking even more than her usual amount. By the time Joyce phoned, everyone except Marie was inebriated, with Roulett being the most intoxicated. The stress the family had endured in the last month had finally taken its toll on all of them. Marie graciously endured their drunkenness, then encouraged Sam to go home with her before he became too drunk to walk, which was very unusual for Sam who normally didn't drink much. Luckily, Marie had taken the time to spread ice-melt salt on their pathway home.

Once they were gone, Jack and Lou chatted while Roulett continued to drink twice as fast as anyone else. By 11:00 pm, Roulett was practically in a drunken stupor.

Lou noticed Roulett and said to Jack, "I think you need to put her in bed while she can still move."

"I may need your help getting her up the stairs. I don't think she can walk on her own."

"No problem, I'll help you as soon as I get back from the little boy's room. Try to wake her while I'm gone."

"Will do."

Jack and Lou helped Roulett up the loft stairs, Jack on one side and Lou on the other. Lou said, "I'm glad she doesn't weigh much."

"You and me both," said Jack.

Jack turned down the bed and helped her in. She didn't say a word. "Would you do one more thing for me?" Jack asked.

"Sure, what?" Lou replied.

Jack asked, "Would you stay with Roulett while I take a quick shower? I'm afraid she could choke if she rolls onto her back. She's quite drunk and if she happened to wake up, she could fall down the stairs searching for me."

"Okay, but let me make another drink to sip while I'm waiting."

Jack found his robe, a towel, and clean underwear. Lou returned with his drink and sat in the chair closest to the door. "Thanks, I don't think she'll wake before I'm back."

"I don't know why you're taking a shower. In her condition I don't think you're going to get lucky tonight."

"Maybe not for several hours, but drinking makes her a wild woman. Why do you think I tolerate it?"

"Okay. If you say so…"

"I'll be back in a few minutes."

Lou was sipping his drink and fantasizing about how all the women he met would be flirting with him because of his new after-shave when he heard a noise sounding like the bathroom door closing. He jumped up to see if Roulett was still sleeping. She wasn't in her bed. He heard the toilet flush. The bathroom door opened and Lou was shocked to see Roulett walking out of the bathroom stark naked.

Roulett asked, "Where's my nightgown?" She wasn't the least bit concerned with why Lou was in the room. She just continued to ask for her nightgown.

Lou panicked. He was afraid Jack would return and assume the wrong idea. Lou quickly rifled through the dresser drawers until he found a large T-shirt. He handed the shirt to Roulett and told her to put it on. She fumbled with the shirt until Lou had to dress her.

Befuddled, she said, "You aren't Jack. I've never thought of you in this way. Why are you in my dream, Lou?"

Lou thought for a second but he didn't know what to tell her so he blurted the first thing that popped into his head. "I'm not in your dream—you're in mine."

"Oh, if this is your dream, let's make it a spectacular one," she said, putting her arms around Lou and kissing him on the lips. He tried to back away but she held on, kissing him again. This time he mistakenly thought of her nakedness and before he realized what he was doing, he was passionately kissing her back.

"You smell so-o-o good. You smell good enough to eat," said Roulett in a sexy voice.

Lou thought, *Oh, she wouldn't do that, or would she?* He listened for the shower. It was still running. He couldn't explain this one to Jack! He'd lose his best friend, his job, his wife, or his life because Jack might just kill him. Now Roulett was rubbing his crotch and kissing him on the neck. He'd never been more aroused in his life. He didn't know if it was the booze, the danger of the moment, or possibly the fact he'd always been attracted to Roulett and he wouldn't admit it, not even to himself.

Roulett began fumbling with his zipper. Again, he listened for the shower. It was still running. Lou's heart was pounding and his penis was throbbing. He lifted her T-shirt and rubbed her breast. Roulett was moaning and breathing hard as Lou moved his hand from her breast to the hairy mound between her legs. The furnace came on, making it was more difficult to hear the shower, but it was still running. He tried to explore all her territories, which he possibly would never have the opportunity to feel again. He quickly put his finger inside her wet and willing vagina. She was still working on his zipper. He decided to help her so they could hurry. He unzipped his pants and put her hand inside. A shudder of fear and excitement shot through him at her touch. Roulett's bare hand on him was almost enough to cause ejaculation. He listened for the shower again. It was still running.

She was trying to take his engorged phallus out of his pants, so he helped. He thought this'd only take a minute if they hurried. Roulett had his penis in her hand and she sat down on the bed. Lou listened again for the shower, which had stopped! She'd started to put his penis in her mouth, but before her lips could touch him he had to make her stop.

Jack could arrive any minute, so Lou quickly put his penis back in his pants and told Roulett to lie down. He didn't want to leave her, but he knew he had to stop or risk Jack catching them in the act.

"We'll have to finish this dream later. Go back to sleep."

Roulett didn't say a word and she was asleep almost as fast as her head touched the pillow. Lou zipped his pants and grabbed a blanket from the closet to cover his lap. He heard Jack coming up the stairs as Lou sat down in the chair. He grabbed his drink and gulped the rest in a single swallow.

"The shower really felt good. I'm sorry I took so long," said Jack while towel drying his hair.

"I had nothing better to do," he replied, trying to appear calm while his pulse raced.

Jack asked, "Did she wake up?"

"Yes, she had to go to the bathroom. She asked for her nightgown, so she could change in the bathroom. I found her a long T-shirt in one of the drawers over there. While she was in the bathroom changing clothes, I decided that I might need another blanket tonight. I helped her back to bed and she was asleep as soon as her head hit the pillow. I think I'll turn in now. I'll see you in the morning. Good night." Lou was certain Jack could hear the guilt in his voice.

"Good night. Thanks for watching her and for finding her a nightgown. See you in the morning."

"You're welcome."

Lou felt very guilty as he walked down the stairs. How could he have done this to his best friend? It wasn't his idea. It was all her idea but he hadn't stopped her because he didn't want to stop her! He wondered what would happen if she remembered their tryst tomorrow. He doubted Roulett would tell Jack. Lou felt torn between wishing Jack's shower had taken five minutes longer and wishing the whole thing hadn't happened.

It was after nine when he awoke the next morning with a pounding headache and a sick feeling in the pit of his stomach. He hoped last night was a dream, but he was afraid it *wasn't* just a dream, but a real-life nightmare. He needed a cup of coffee so much that he called on the intercom to Marie's house, asking, "Is anybody up over there?"

"We're up—have been for hours. Marie has coffee made and she'll make breakfast when you all are ready," replied Sam.

"I'll be right over. The others aren't up yet."

"See you in a minute. The door's unlocked so come right in."

Lou walked to the house holding his pounding head.

Marie poured Lou a cup of coffee and asked, "Are you hungry?"

Holding his head in his hands, he replied, "Not yet, just coffee and some aspirin if you have some, please. My head's killing me."

Jack arrived a few minutes after Lou, complaining about his headache, too. Everyone was hung-over except for Marie who was bright-eyed and cheerful.

"Roulett's too sick to come to breakfast," Jack said.

Lou was relieved that he didn't have to face her.

Roulett didn't make it out of bed the entire day and she was still sick the next day. Jack persuaded Kirk's wife Pam, who was a doctor—although she was a forensic pathologist—to come to the ranch to check on Roulett.

Pam suggested Roulett go to the hospital for alcohol withdrawal treatment, warning them withdrawal can be deadly without professional help. Pam told both Jack and Roulett she had to quit drinking before it killed her, but Roulett refused to go to the hospital. Pam wrote Roulett a non-refillable prescription for strong antacid stomach medication, but told her she needed to make an appointment with her family doctor. Roulett agreed to stop drinking for the night after Jack managed to take her home. Though she was still extremely sick the next day, she failed to heed Pam's warning and she didn't contact her doctor.

That afternoon, Marie sent Garrett by Roulett's house on his way home, to take her some homemade soup. When she answered the door, her paleness and the dark circles under her eyes shocked Garrett. Before she could take the soup, she fainted, falling to the floor with a thud.

Garrett frantically called an ambulance before carrying her to a bed, where she regained consciousness for a few seconds. Then she suffered an intense pain and fainted again. Garrett thought she'd quit breathing, so he gave her mouth-to-mouth resuscitation—when he noticed the odor of vodka on her breath. She regained consciousness with his mouth on hers and was startled. He was relieved to see she was breathing.

She asked, "Am I dead?"

He took her hand. "No, why do you think that?"

She didn't answer. Instead she stared at him looking very confused.

"You're going to be fine."

"Then why were you kissing me?"

"I was trying to give you mouth-to-mouth resuscitation. I thought you'd stopped breathing."

She appeared dazed as she whimpered, "What happened?"

"You fainted. I think you're going to be okay now. You need to rest until the paramedics arrive." He sat there quietly while she appeared resting without pain. Although it seemed like a very long time, it was only minutes before the ambulance arrived.

Garrett directed the paramedics to her and told them everything that had happened.

One of the paramedics said, "Her blood pressure is low and she has a slight fever."

Another asked, "Where do you hurt?"

"Here," she replied, pointing to the middle of her chest.

The first paramedic asked, "Have you eaten anything today?"

Roulett hesitated, then softly said, "No, I haven't eaten today."

Garrett held his tongue, not adding that he'd smelled vodka on her breath. He was torn between her safety and losing her trust.

The second paramedic asked Garrett, "Do you want to ride with your wife to the hospital?"

"I'm not her husband—I'm only a friend of the family, but I'll go."

The ambulance took Roulett to the emergency room at the Bartlesville hospital. Garrett called Jack. By the time he arrived at the Bartlesville hospital the doctors had decided to transfer her by helicopter to a Tulsa hospital. Roulett arrived on the helipad at SouthCrest hospital in critical condition. They immediately performed emergency surgery for a perforated stomach ulcer. Her life teetered back and forth with uncertainty, but she pulled through…alive but weak.

Lou visited Roulett in the hospital the next day. He'd thought about her continually since the loft incident. He took her flowers and a humorous get well card. She was sleeping soundly when he entered her room. He put his gifts on the table quietly, trying not to wake her. He thought how beautiful she was, and for the first time he realized he loved her. In fact, he realized he loved her more than he loved any other woman in the world—including his wife. He loved the wife of his best friend! How was Lou going to deal with this dilemma? He wanted to kiss her on the cheek but knew that was too dangerous. He sat down to relive the night in the loft as he had done so often lately.

Jack arrived and asked, "How long have you been here?"

"Only a few minutes. The nurse told me Roulett had a shot for pain a few minutes before I arrived, so she'll probably sleep through our visit," Lou replied nervously. Jack and Lou talked for about ten minutes before Marie and Garrett arrived.

Jack asked, "Why didn't Dad come with you, Mom?"

"Sam wasn't feeling well, so Garrett said he would drive me."

Roulett began to move and mumble. The medication made her drowsy. As she looked toward Lou and Garrett, she mumbled, "He kissed me."

Lou thought how he wished the earth would open up and swallow him. He certainly didn't know how to explain this as his heart pounded and all the muscles in his chest began to tighten. Lou thought Jack would fire him…Joyce would divorce him and he would lose everything…all for a few stolen moments of pleasure!

Saving Lou from a heart attack, Garrett said, "She thought I was kissing her when

I was trying to resuscitate her. I thought she'd stopped breathing."

Lou was very relieved that she wasn't talking about him, and that she was doing well after her surgery. Although he hoped she didn't remember, he knew he'd never forget.

Chapter 11 | Vigorous Devils

After a place was cleared for it to grow, its roots grew deep and it spread over the whole land. PSALMS 80: 9

Three days after Roulett's release from the hospital, Jack and Roulett were fighting like cats and dogs. Roulett refused to forgive Jack for excluding her when the family divided Grandfather John-George's personal possessions. In addition, the weather remained bitterly cold and uncomfortable and Roulett continued to experience withdrawal symptoms. On the next day, they awoke to ten inches of snow. In spite of the extra work required to water the horses caused by freezing pipes, Garrett had visited her every day in the hospital and had stopped by her house on his way home each day since her release.

When she opened the door, she called to her son, "I thought it was somebody, but it's just Garrett."

"So now I'm a *nobody*?" Garrett asked.

"Because we see you all the time—a stranger would be *somebody*." Insulting Garrett didn't stop him from talking with her until Jack came home.

The next Friday, Roulett arrived at the ranch in a tempestuous mood. Although she had the benefits of Valium in her blood stream, it didn't take the place of the alcohol she craved. She was on the sofa when Garrett, predictably, came in for his break. They'd only exchanged a few words before Lou arrived. It was clear to both men that Roulett was more than just a little upset and they needed to spend some time trying to improve her mood before Jack arrived. Garrett was filling his coffee cup when Lou asked, "Is there enough for me to have a cup, too?"

His question surprised Garrett, for Lou normally preferred scotch. Garrett couldn't remember seeing Lou drink coffee in the afternoon, but he quickly realized Lou didn't want to drink in front of Roulett. "Sure, there's plenty," he replied, handing the hot cup to Lou.

Lou took the coffee while sitting on the sofa by Roulett. He sipped it, then placed it on a coaster on the coffee table. Turning to her, he put his arm around her as he said, "Cheer up, kid. If you don't smile, I'm going to have to hug you until you do or until Jack arrives and makes me stop."

Roulett smiled, realizing she couldn't resist Lou's charm. At that moment, she realized she loved these two men more than she did her husband—she loved Lou because he was without a doubt the most fun-loving and considerate friend she'd known in her entire life, and she loved Garrett because she didn't have a choice in the matter...she simply did.

After she smiled, Lou reluctantly removed his arm. "You're right. Jack shouldn't have cowered to Kirk's demands. You were always there for John-George and you had every right to attend the dividing of his personal belongings. But I don't want to fight with Jack, so please don't tell him that I agree with you."

Garrett said, "If it makes you feel any better, I agree with Lou. Jack and Kirk shouldn't have kept you away."

* * * * *

On the following Monday, Marie called Kirk to let him know the plants each had twelve tiny, pale lavender blooms. She said, "Come by the ranch after work. I've got something to show you."

"Sure, Mom," answered Kirk.

"I'll meet you at the greenhouse."

He arrived a few minutes late, because he stopped at a nursery on the way to purchase a flat of New Guinea impatiens to help replace the plants his mom lost when her greenhouse furnace failed. He was pleasantly surprised when he saw that she'd replaced about a fourth of her plants. His mysterious plants now resided in the prime location previously occupied by his mother's prized orchids.

She hugged and kissed her son. "Thanks for the impatiens. You know I love them. Did you see the blooms on your Vigorous Devils?"

He said, "On my what?"

"That's what I'm going to call them until we discover what they really are because your little devils were the only plants that survived the freeze."

"Ha! I'd understand the name 'devils' if they'd withstood heat but not the cold. By their location, you must not think they're too devilish."

"I won't be growing any more orchids until spring. Your Vigorous Devils are the most exciting plants in my greenhouse and will be exciting until we know what they are."

"Well, my Vigorous Devils do have beautiful purple blooms," he said.

She corrected, "Actually the blooms are lavender. Did you notice they're smart enough to count?"

He asked, "Why do you say that?"

"Because each plant has exactly twelve blooms on it, so they must be able to count."

"There's a word for that but I just can't think of it right now. I'll call you when I remember the proper term."

"Don't forget Jack's birthday party is the first Friday night get-together in March."

"I think I'll give him his gift at work and pass on the party this year. Maybe next year," Kirk said.

Marie didn't have to ask the reason. She knew the feud between Kirk and Roulett had escalated from a molehill to a full-blown erupting volcano since John-George's death.

Roulett appeared to have forgiven Jack, at least that one night for his birthday party. Lou, Joyce, Garrett, Olivia, Hollie, Bill, Vickie, and Paul attended Jack's party at the ranch, which seemed successful in spite of Kirk's absence. She told everybody about the blooms on Kirk's plants. Jack wanted to see the new blooms, so the whole party went to Marie's greenhouse to see the Vigorous Devils. When she opened the door, a burst of hot air surrounded them. Marie screeched, "Now what's wrong with that stupid furnace? Why's it still running when it's as hot as an oven in here? Jack, check the thermometer for me—all the plants are wilted."

"The thermometer says one-hundred-thirty-nine degrees now, and that's with the door open. It was probably higher before we opened the door!"

"Turn it off, please. I'm going to lose all my plants again! Tomorrow I'm going to have a new furnace and thermostat installed."

Sam said, "We'll help you water them. Maybe they all won't die."

The Vigorous Devils didn't show any signs of wilting. Marie shook her head. "The heat didn't seem to hurt Kirk's plants. I think Vigorous Devils is the perfect name for them!"

Chapter 12 | She Wants a Baby

The childless wife is honored in her home, yet children make her happy. PSALMS 113: 9

It was an unseasonably warm day for the first week of March as Roulett walked with her children on the ranch from the car to the barn to feed their horses. Of course, Michael and Tammy pleaded with Roulett to let them ride, too. The bad weather and Roulett's surgery recovery had interrupted the children's regular riding schedule. Roulett agreed, not only because of their incessant begging, but also because she wanted to spend time alone with Garrett. She sternly reminded the children to ride with caution, mentioning that horses were frisky on cool days. Both children promised to be careful.

Roulett didn't have time to fix a glass of instant tea before Garrett, true to form, arrived for his afternoon break. He removed his boots and washed his hands in the clubhouse sink instead of using the mudroom sink. He'd started this new routine two months earlier but only when Roulett was alone in the clubhouse. She felt his change of habit meant he wanted to spend as much time with her as possible.

While washing his hands, he said, "Pretty day, isn't it?"

"Yes, it is," she replied calmly.

"A nice day for the kids to ride their horses."

"Yes, but I warned them about riding on a brisk day."

"I noticed that they both had tight reins on their horses, especially Michael," said Garrett as he poured himself the last cup of coffee.

"Michael's young gelding requires a tighter rein than Tammy's calm old mare."

Garrett asked, "Speaking of tight rein, has Olivia called yet?"

"Not since I arrived," replied Roulett, "But I was only here a few minutes before you came in."

"Odds are she'll call soon to remind me to shower, change clothes, and meet her at Dr. Smith's office before five o'clock."

"Is Olivia sick?"

"No, not anything like that."

Roulett probed further, "Which Dr. Smith?"

"Ruben Smith."

"The Ruben Smith who specializes in obstetrics and gynecology?"

"Yes," Garrett said.

"Are you and Olivia expecting a baby?"

"Not exactly," he replied, suddenly unable to maintain eye contact.

"Then, *what* exactly?"

"It's a long story and I don't have time to tell you now. I have only ten minutes until I need to shower so I'll be on time."

"I could tell you my life history in ten minutes, so, if you start talking now, you should have plenty of time."

He said, "You don't give up, do you?"

"You're the one who told me about your appointment with Olivia and Dr. Smith. You broached the subject and now I want to know why. Surely you don't want me to have a sleepless night." A blush crept across her cheeks as she realized how often she'd daydreamed about an *erotic* sleepless night with him.

"I don't want to be the reason you have a sleepless night. Boy, you really know how to pour on the guilt!"

"You're wasting time. Remember you only have—" she glanced at the clock, "—nine minutes, so get to the point."

"I need you to promise me you won't discuss this with anyone, including Jack. It's very personal and difficult for me to talk about, although I guess I could use someone to talk to."

"I promise I won't say a word—just tell me."

"I'm sure you've noticed Olivia and I don't have any children after nineteen years of marriage."

She shrugged. "I didn't think anything about it. I simply thought Olivia was busy with her career."

"That was true at first. For six years she took birth control pills, but then she quit. Three years later she still hadn't conceived. Then, she blamed herself for taking birth control pills for too long. In her mind, she'd caused her infertility problem. Several years before we moved here, she decided to see a fertility specialist for a series of tests trying to diagnose her problem and to try to correct it. All her tests were completely normal—she was fertile. I dragged my feet for almost six months, before she finally lost her patience and insisted that I have a sperm-count test. I was the problem all the time. Since I have a good male hormone level with a normal sex drive, I never imagined I had a fertility problem. I'd say it's hereditary except my dad fathered eight children and all of my brothers and sisters have children. In fact, my twin brother, Jim, has four kids."

"I didn't know you have a twin brother."

"Actually, Jim was in town last weekend."

"Why didn't you bring him over so we could meet him? Does he look like you?"

"Yes, he looks exactly like me—we're identical twins. He came to give a semen specimen to Dr. Smith. So today's appointment is for Dr. Smith to artificially inseminate Olivia with my brother's sperm which means Olivia and I aren't going to have a baby…my wife and my brother are going to have a baby."

Roulett paused for a few minutes, wondering if she would react the same way to his twin brother as she had to Garrett before she said, "Since the sperm is from your *identical* twin brother with the same DNA, I think you should consider this *your* baby if you're lucky enough for Olivia to become pregnant."

"That's precisely what Dr. Smith said. After this entire insemination thing is finished, maybe I'll feel better."

"I'm sure you will."

"I didn't tell you Olivia dated Jim before she met me. The first time I met Olivia, she even thought I *was* Jim! My brother and I both worked at the stables where Olivia kept her horse. Olivia owned a beautiful, gray, hunter-jumper from the Northern Dancer bloodline. Working in the stables was the only way I would've met a rich girl like Olivia."

"Time is up—you need to hit the shower so you aren't late."

After he left, Roulett thought for a long time. Garrett's revelation hadn't changed how she felt about him. Her love couldn't be rooted in a biological urge to have another baby, since Garrett was just as sterile as her husband who'd had a vasectomy. If anything, knowing Garrett's situation made her love for him grow deeper.

Chapter 13 | Chicken Potpie

Laughter can mask a heavy heart.
When the laughter ends, grief returns. PROVERBS 14: 13

Roulett arrived at the ranch on a brisk March day the following Friday afternoon. Garrett met her at the clubhouse and opened the door for her because she was carrying a large rectangle pan covered with aluminum foil.

"You're late. I didn't know if you were coming today," he said.

"I had to take Michael and Tammy to their Aunt Vickie's house for the night," Roulett replied as she took off her gloves and coat.

"What's in the pan?"

"Homemade chicken potpie."

"That sounds great! I'm glad I don't have to leave early tonight. Olivia and Joyce have a bowling tournament, so she won't be home until after midnight. I love your chicken potpie. It's Sam's favorite, isn't it?"

"That's right. Sam's home sick with the flu, and that's the main reason why I made it. Marie's going to stay home with him, but I'll take them some as soon as it's ready." She set the oven at 400 degrees and put the pan on the top rack while Garrett washed his hands.

He said, "I fed your horses so you wouldn't have to go out in the cold, and I made a fresh pot of coffee—want a cup?"

"Sure, sounds great, maybe it'll warm me up. You know it's hard to believe, only two days ago, we had short-sleeve weather and now it's bitterly cold. I really appreciate your feeding the horses," she said. She sat on the sofa, took off her shoes, and then tucked her feet and legs under her.

He handed her the cup of steaming hot coffee and warned, "Be careful, it's really hot."

"Thanks, maybe this'll warm up my cold hands—they're like ice!"

He gently touched the back of her hand with his fingertips and said, "Boy, you're not kidding! Would you like me to grab the throw from the other sofa for you?"

"That would be nice."

Carefully placing the throw on her legs, he said, "You know the old saying, 'cold hands and a warm heart'..."

She thought he was warming more than her heart with his kindness. "I don't know if that applies when the weather is so cold."

"I've been outside but my hands are warm compared to yours. Imagine all the people who don't have the modern conveniences we take for granted. I read once that one in seven people doesn't have enough to eat and that one in six doesn't have access to clean drinking water. Considering the world population is over six billion, that's a lot of suffering people."

"It doesn't take a rocket scientist to realize there are too many people for the earth now and the population is growing at the alarming rate. In a way, the world really is shrinking," she said.

"Pretty soon there will only be room for animals that can be eaten. There won't be any room for animals we simply want to look at for their beauty," he said.

"I know you've heard how importing a new species, such as rabbits in Australia, can be disastrous to an ecological system. Sometimes I think mankind is an imported species because we are destroying the earth's ecosystem."

"I never thought of it that way, but I do think the world is overpopulated."

"Speaking of the population problem, how soon will you know if Olivia is pregnant?"

"Technically, *I* didn't contribute to the population problem, but to answer your question, not yet—I'll let you know as soon as I find out."

"Great."

Jack and Lou walked in and Lou asked, "What smells so good?"

Roulett answered, "Chicken potpie."

"The kind you make with the crescent-roll top crust?"

"That's right," she replied.

"Why isn't Sam here yet? That's his favorite."

"Sam's sick with the flu and Marie's going to stay home tonight and take care of him, so it'll only be the four of us tonight," said Roulett.

Jack sat next to Roulett and gave her a hug and a peck on the cheek. "What's wrong? Are you cold?"

"Yes. I want you to make the nice, warm weather come back that I like so much."

"Anything for you, honey, but it may take several weeks for my nice weather order to be processed. It all depends on how many weather orders are ahead of mine. You may have to endure the cold until around the middle of May."

"Thank you, dear, for ordering spring to arrive on time."

"Speaking of spring, I think now is a good time to spring this one on you. I have to go to Chicago next Monday night for a conference that starts the next morning at seven and runs through Thursday. I won't be back until late Thursday night," said Jack.

"If it makes you feel any better, I have to go, too. My wife will love having time without me!" Lou said, knowing Roulett hated when Jack was out of town.

Roulett tormented Lou, as she said, "I can understand that!"

They all laughed and enjoyed the evening.

Chapter 14 | Animal Tales

Those without regard for the law are on the side of the wicked. Those who obey it work against the wicked... PROVERBS 28: 4

The next Tuesday afternoon Marie rushed to answer the phone. "Hello?"

"Hi. It's Olivia, Garrett's wife. I hate to bother you but I have an emergency situation and I need to speak to Garrett. I tried the barn phone but he didn't answer. Could you find him for me and ask him to call me as soon as possible? I'm at home."

"Sure, I'll find him. Are you all right?"

"I'm fine, just worried about my mother. She's been rushed to the hospital with shortness of breath and possibly a heart attack," Olivia replied.

"I'll have him call you as soon as I find him."

"Thanks."

"No problem. Let us know how your mother is doing as soon as you can."

"I will. Bye!"

Marie put on her shoes and socks. She hadn't felt up to par that day and was still in her nightclothes. Fearing she was coming down with Sam's flu, she'd made a point of resting all day. Marie didn't take the time to dress, only choosing to put her coat on over her robe before venturing out in the cold to locate Garrett. She first looked for him in the barn and spotted him leading a yearling back to his stall.

He saw her and motioned for her to step back. "Be careful, Marie. Forty-five minutes on the walker didn't take the piss and vinegar out of this guy. I need to talk to Sam when he's well enough about scheduling the vet to give this big boy an attitude adjustment before he's totally out of control. He'll make a nice gelding."

"You need to call your wife at home. Don't worry, she's fine, but she needs to speak to you right away."

Garrett replied, "Okay, thanks," as he walked over to the phone cradled in a small plastic toolbox protecting it from wind, dust, and curious horses in the middle of the barn.

She stood waiting to talk to Garrett after he finished his conversation with his wife since she wanted to know if he was going to leave for the day. Then, she remembered she needed to check her overdue mare, Jill, more formally known as Marie's Wild Jill Hancock. The mare earned the Wild part of her name by being very difficult to break and the Hancock part from her breeding. Marie worried about Jill giving birth alone since it was her first pregnancy and because Marie didn't feel well enough to watch her for long. In a matter of minutes, Marie was exhausted and returned home to rest.

The next day Marie felt even worse. Garrett surprised her by arriving to work because Joyce had volunteered to drive Olivia to Colorado in his place. Since Marie was still ill, she asked Garrett to check Jill several times. He called that afternoon to report that the mare was waxing—colostrum was dripping from the ends of her teats that looked like candle-wax—which meant she could foal at any time. Marie asked Roulett if she could watch Jill until she foaled. Roulett agreed to bring her clothes and spend the night in the clubhouse loft where she could constantly monitor Jill. She called Vickie and arranged for her to keep the children, reducing their exposure to the flu. Roulett arrived only a few minutes later than normal after dropping the children off at Vickie's house. Garrett came in for his coffee break and offered to help Roulett watch Jill since he didn't need to go home.

"I'd love to have the company as long as you'll let me treat you to pizza. I'm starving."

"Sounds great—just no anchovies, please," Garrett replied.

"Don't worry. I'd never order a pizza with anchovies!"

Roulett and Garrett enjoyed their meal. When he teased her about having red sauce and cheese on her chin, she replied. "That's how you can tell it's good pizza!"

Shortly after they finished eating, Marie called. "How's Jill doing?"

Roulett replied, "No foal yet! She's just wandering around with wax about three inches long. Could be anytime or it could be tomorrow."

Marie said, "Or it could be three days from now."

"The vet book said mares normally foal within twenty-four hours after waxing begins."

"That isn't always true. Do you know why the mares don't always do what the vet book says?"

"No, I don't."

"Because they haven't read the vet book," Marie joked.

Roulett laughed, as she replied, "That's a good one. I'll tell Garrett."

Marie asked, "Are you two starving over there, or did you find something to eat?"

"We ordered pizza. Now we're so full that we may have to tell each other stories to stay awake."

"Tell him the one about Little Grey," Marie suggested.

"That's a good one—I will. And call us if you haven't heard from us in an hour or so."

"Okay."

Roulett hung up and said, "I have a story to tell you about a cat. You're probably not going to believe this one. In fact, I wouldn't believe it myself except I saw the cat. It happened about six years ago, give or take a year. One day I stopped by the ranch to see if Marie would watch the children while I went shopping. She was standing in her driveway as we pulled in. As soon as we got out of the car, she asked us to help her look for a feral gray cat that had lived in the barn for several years. We all saw the cat from time to time, but she wouldn't let anyone near her, not even Marie. When Marie would try to pet her, it would frighten the cat so badly she would hide for days. Marie named her Little Gray.

"I asked Marie why we were trying to find Little Gray and Marie explained that earlier she'd found the cat in the garage. She'd never seen her there before—it was too close to people. Marie closed the garage door before Little Gray could escape. Marie noticed the cat was so heavy with kittens that she didn't move as fast as normal and was probably too heavy to hunt. Marie decided hunger caused the fearful cat to enter the garage so she could eat dog food, so she decided to coax the cat into the house and feed her something more nutritious.

"Marie went into the house first and opened a can of tuna and poured a small shallow bowl of milk. She put them on the floor of the kitchen, opened the door to the garage, and put a large trashcan on the floor to hold it open. Marie left the house from the front door and then went back into the garage from the side door so she could herd the cat toward the open kitchen door.

"After several minutes the cat ran inside the house. Marie followed and quickly closed the door. The starving cat didn't take long to find the milk and tuna. She ate as if she hadn't eaten in days, and Marie began talking to her. She told her that she needed to come back the next day to eat and she wouldn't hurt her, only feed her.

"After Little Grey finished eating, Marie told her again to come back the next day so she could eat. Marie continued to remind the cat repeatedly to come back as she let her out the front door.

"The next day Marie was looking for the cat, afraid she'd had her kittens. So we helped Marie search, but we couldn't find her. Marie hoped the cat would be back the next day. When we arrived the next day, Marie said that when Little Gray returned to eat again it was much easier to coax her into the house. Little Gray was thin and appeared to have given birth to her kittens.

"So we searched again we didn't find her. But, after this failed attempt we went into Marie's house because she thought she could hear kittens in the attic. This was in the middle of July so the attic temperature was well over 100 degrees. Marie feared the kittens would die, but there wasn't a way to rescue them.

"We all worried about the poor little kittens. When we arrived at the ranch the next day, we went to see if there was any news. Marie took us to her pantry while telling us to be quiet so we wouldn't scare Little Gray. Marie slowly opened the pantry door—inside a small box was the cat nursing two tiny kittens. She didn't move and we kept our distance. Marie told the cat that we wouldn't hurt her, then she gently closed the door.

"I asked Marie how she'd gotten the kittens down, because I thought the opening to that part of the attic was too small for a person. She told me Little Gray had brought the kittens down. Marie said the cat had come inside to eat again that day. While she ate, Marie told the cat that she needed to bring her kittens down from the attic or they would die. She told the cat this several times, hoping the cat would understand.

"Before letting Little Gray outside, Marie showed the cat a soft bed in a cardboard box tucked in the back of the walk-in pantry. Marie told the cat to put her babies in the box or they would die. After a few minutes, Marie let Little Gray outside as usual.

"In less than ten minutes, Marie heard something banging on the front door. Marie thought someone was knocking, so she went to answer it and found Little Gray clawing the screen door with a kitten in her mouth. As soon as she let Little Grey inside, she went straight to where she'd been eating and waited until Marie opened the pantry door.

"After Marie was out of the way the cat put the kitten in the box. She waited by the front door until Marie let her out again. Little Gray repeated this feat three more times, until there were four kittens, but sadly two were already dead. That's why we believe animals understand more than we give them credit for."

Garrett smiled. "I agree. I have a story about a cow, but I don't think it can top yours."

"All you can do is try. Besides, I love animal stories."

"My father's brother, Boyd, and his wife, Opal, had a small farm in Missouri. This was back in the '50s and they were in their early sixties. They barely made ends meet by raising their own food and selling a few calves every year. Occasionally, they'd lose a calf-producing cow and have to replace her.

"Opal made most of their cow deals because she'd always been pretty clever. This time she made a major mistake by buying a cow from a notorious horse-and-cattle trader named Charlie. Even though she knew he was a scoundrel, she bought one of his cows because he guaranteed the cow was sound. To make matters worse, she paid him in full with cash.

"The next day the cow was down and she wouldn't get up. Opal called Charlie, demanding her money back because the cow was sick. Afraid the cow would die, Opal threatened to call the sheriff if he didn't give her a refund.

"That evening Charlie gave Opal a check for the cow and said he'd pick up the cow the next morning. When he arrived the next day with a trailer, the cow was dead. Charlie said he wasn't going to pay for a dead cow and he was going to stop payment on the check. Opal said she'd call the sheriff. Charlie said, 'Go ahead and call him.'

"Opal called the sheriff but there wasn't anything he could do. He felt sorry for Opal and added a bit of possibly helpful information about how it would be perfectly legal to buy something else from Charlie using his bad check as currency since it was as good as money if she could trick him into taking it.

"Opal and her son-in-law Zachary concocted a well-organized plan. Charlie was an old man whose eyesight was failing and he'd never met Zachary. The plan was for Zachary to buy a cow from Charlie and use the check Charlie had stopped payment on to pay for it.

"Zachary became friendly with Charlie while looking over Charlie's herd. Charlie appeared to really like Zachary, thinking he had a neophyte buyer in his web of deceit. Charlie continually tried to direct Zachary into considering an older cow that was supposed to produce a calf in the spring, but Zachary surprised the old man by selecting a fat Red Polled heifer to purchase.

"Opal had coached Zachary well with instructions to buy only a young, fat cow without horns. They loaded the heifer into the back of Zachary's pickup, which had Boyd and Opal's stock racks on it to contain the cow. Zachary asked Charlie if it was okay to pay him part in cash and the rest in a check. This higher priced heifer required forty dollars more than the check for the cow.

"Charlie said that would be fine so Zachary handed Charlie his bad check he had given to Opal with two twenty dollar bills on top. Charlie only looked at the dollar amount on the check and the cash, which was correct. Zachary drove off with the cow!

"Zachary arrived a few minutes later at Opal and Boyd's farm and unloaded the heifer. At this time, Opal and Boyd arrived from their house, which was about a hundred yards from the barn. Opal praised Zachary for his choice and said she'd call the heifer 'Charlie.' Less than ten minutes later Charlie arrived with the sheriff. To Charlie's surprise, the sheriff told him Opal and Boyd now owned the heifer and there was nothing that he could do about it because the transaction was perfectly legal."

"That was a great story! I would've loved to see the look on Charlie's face when the sheriff told him there was nothing that he could do!" Roulett laughed.

Time had flown because they enjoyed each other's company so much. Roulett thought how glad she was that she wasn't drinking tonight, knowing the temptation of being alone with Garrett would be more than she could handle in any condition other than sober.

Shortly after midnight, Jill became agitated and started looking at her stomach. "It won't be long, she's having contractions," said Garrett.

"We'll wait here until we see the feet coming out. She'll be too busy after that to worry about us being there."

The mare pawed at the ground and paced. After several minutes, she sprawled on the straw-covered ground and continued to look at her stomach while straining. "It's time to go help. I see something coming out. Let's hope it's the front feet," said Roulett.

When they arrived in the foaling pen, they could see two feet and a nose through the emerging membrane bag—it was a normal birth. Roulett tore the bag surrounding the foal and wiped the nostrils.

The foal didn't move and its tongue was hanging out. After the next contraction, the foal snorted and moved its head. One more push and the shoulders came out, so the hardest part was over for the mare. She rested a minute before the last push and the foal was born.

Roulett squealed with joy as she saw the huge white blanket on what appeared to be a black foal. Garrett helped her remove the membrane bag covering the foal, putting the scent of the foal on them. The protective new mother wouldn't show any animosity toward them while they smelled like her foal. "Marie will be thrilled. I hope it's a filly, but I bet this is a stud. You can't get better Appaloosa color than this and the loud colored ones are normally studs," she said.

Garrett checked to see if Roulett was right by raising the tail of the foal. "You're wrong. It's a filly."

The mare stood, breaking the umbilical cord. Jill licked her baby, trying to stimulate circulation and encouraging her newborn to stand. The filly tried to move but couldn't manage to stand on her long spindle legs. She wobbled for several more minutes before finally standing.

Her triumph was short-lived as she fell on her nose, but she quickly sprang up again. Her legs were getting stronger by the minute. Roulett felt the filly was strong enough to dip the umbilical cord stump in a jar of iodine to prevent infection. Jill was encouraging her filly to nurse by using her nose to push her in the right direction. The newborn quickly suckled and after a few swallows of her mother's sweet colostrum she began jumping around.

"She's doing fine so I'm going home now to feed my dog. I'll see you tomorrow," Garrett said.

"Thanks and good night!"

"You are welcome. I had a great time." Watching him leave, Roulett smiled.

Marie was overjoyed with her black filly, which had a white blanket and large halo spots. She named the foal Jill's Cloudy Midnight.

* * * * *

On March 27th, Marie called Kirk to tell him there were twenty-four new blooms and twelve green fruit about the size of quarters on each of the plants. Each bush had grown about two f eet in the last month. That evening after work, Kirk dropped by the ranch to see his plants and was happy with the results.

Six days later, the phone rang in the clubhouse while Garrett and Roulett were having coffee and talking. Roulett answered the phone, "Hello."

"Hello, this is Olivia. Is Garrett there?"

"Yes, he is."

Garrett took the phone. "What's up, honey?...That's great news, dear. We'll celebrate tonight, but you can't drink champagne—not now!"

Even though Roulett couldn't hear Olivia, she knew she was pregnant. Garrett's terms of endearment for his wife infuriated Roulett, though she hid her feelings, pretending to be happy about his news.

Chapter 15 | Rainbow Fruit

I had a vision while I slept of a huge tree at the center of the earth. It grew until it reached the sky and everyone in the world could see it. Its leaves were beautiful and it was loaded with enough fruit to feed everyone... DANIEL 4: 10, 11, 12

The next week, Kirk was at the ranch checking his plants. The first fruit were about the size of silver dollars and beginning to show a variety of colors. A week later, Marie called Kirk to tell him the first fruit were ripe. They were the size of a small orange with six distinctive sections of different colors: purple, blue, green, yellow, orange, and red. Marie said the fruit was as beautiful as a rainbow.

When Kirk came to the ranch to see it, their beauty astonished him. "I'm calling them rainbow fruit." Like a small child, he said, "Mom, I'm going to give you four of these plants since you grew them for me. You can have all the fruit from those four plants, but I want all the seeds."

"Thank you. They're such beautiful plants and fruit. When will you learn if they're edible?" Marie asked.

"I'll take one to the Center tomorrow, so we should know soon."

On a glorious spring morning, a chipper Kirk carried one of the fruit in a small brown paper bag into the Center for examination. He could have the fruit analyzed without secrecy because Jack knew about Kirk's prized fruit and shared his enthusiasm. He whistled all the way to Sandra Evans' desk.

She smiled as he handed her the fruit, and asked, "What's this?"

Kirk replied, "Do you remember the dried-up pod that I brought in for you and Alice to analyze several months ago?"

"Yes."

"This is one of the fruit produced by the seed from that pod. You said plant some seed and see what it produces, so I did," said Kirk proudly.

"Wow, it's beautiful. It doesn't look anything like that dried-up creepy thing you brought to us. I've never seen a fruit or a vegetable this colorful. It looks too pretty to be real."

"It's real all right and I have 143 more exactly like that one at home."

Sandra asked, "Wow! How many seeds did you plant?"

"Twelve seeds produced twelve plants, which each produced twelve fruit."

"Both you and the plants seem to like the number twelve. Maybe you should call them zodiac fruit. Have you decided on a name?"

"They're rainbow fruit," said Kirk, beaming with pride.

"That's appropriate if this is a fruit. You know, it might be a vegetable."

"That's what I want you to tell me. I want a complete analysis, including vitamins, minerals, trace minerals, proteins, carbohydrates, fats, and antioxidants. Oh yeah, and the most important thing to analyze is if this fruit is poisonous or not. In fact, that should be the first issue you address."

Sandra asked, "How'd you say you obtained the original fruit?"

"My grandfather, John-George, gave me the original fruit shortly before he passed away," said Kirk.

She probed deeper, "Did he tell you how he came to possess it?"

Annoyed by her prying into his business, he snapped, "No, he didn't say and I didn't ask. Why?"

"Well, I was just wondering if this could've been a gene-splicing project of your grandfather's. It looks like six different fruits and vegetables spliced together," she said.

"I don't think so…remember how old the original fruit pod looked? Gene-splicing technology isn't that old," argued Kirk.

"You're probably right—but I have an eerie feeling about this," she said, staring at the fruit in her hand.

"Let me know as soon as you have the test results. I'll be in my office until noon if you need me."

"I will, but don't expect the test results for a few days."

Two days later, Kirk returned to his office after lunch precisely as his phone rang. The Center's receptionist said, "Your mother is on line 2, Mr. Barnes."

Kirk said, "Thanks, Vonda." He sat in his burgundy leather chair before answering, "What's up, Mom?"

Marie asked, "Are you busy?"

"No, I just returned from lunch so I haven't started doing anything yet."

"I have some good news. I just came back from the greenhouse where I found thirty-six new lavender blooms on each of the Vigorous Devils."

"That's great! From now on I'd like you to call them rainbow plants, not Vigorous Devils. That name makes the plants sound so sinister," scolded Kirk.

"I'm sorry. I was so excited about the new blooms that I forgot you named them rainbow fruit."

"I have good news, too, Mom. I brought one of the rainbow fruit in two days ago to be analyzed, and we should know all the details soon."

Marie asked, "That's great. Would you tell Jack about the new blooms?"

"Sure, Mom, I'll tell him and I'll come by tonight to see them."

"I don't want to keep you from your work, so I'll let you go and talk to you tonight."

"Okay. I'll see you tonight."

He and Jack both were ecstatic about the fruit, which was the main topic of conversation that evening. Roulett said she had a bad feeling about the fruit, but the only person to agree with her was Garrett.

On Wednesday, Sandra called to tell Kirk the analysis of the fruit was complete. He agreed to meet with her in her office to discuss the details of the laboratory analysis.

A minute later, Kirk eagerly listened as Sandra explained, "Our tests show that it's something between a fruit and a vegetable, but we'll call it a fruit. The fruit isn't poisonous and it has the right amount of protein, carbohydrates, and fats for a balanced diet, containing all known amino acids. This makes it the only known plant to produce complete proteins like animal protein. With the fruit's six different colors, it's extremely high in vitamins and minerals including many rare trace minerals. The fat in it is polyunsaturated and rich in omega-3, omega-6, and omega-9 acids. It's also very high in antioxidants such as allicin, lutein, lycopene, quercetin, flavonoids, genistein, and many more. Another interesting fact is that its carbohydrates are digested slowly, which gives them a long-term benefit in the bloodstream rather than short-term like most carbs and sugars. This will be very beneficial for people who are diabetic or on weight-reducing diets. This is, without a doubt, the healthiest food I've ever seen. You could live on nothing but this fruit and water. It's the discovery of a lifetime! I think it's the missing link between plant and animal."

"Is that why the juice from the center of the fruit looks like blood?" he asked.

"The juice looks like blood because it contains molecules of haemin. That's what gives the juice its color, exactly like haemin molecules make blood red. In plants, only the nitrogen-fixing nodules in the roots of peas contain it."

"Does the juice taste like blood?" he asked.

"Not at all, the juice tastes sweet. If this fruit is easy to grow, world hunger could end. Where has this been all these years?" she asked enthusiastically.

"I don't know where it has been, but all I want to know is—what is the first step to marketing it?"

"Although the fruit doesn't need FDA approval, we'll feed it to some rats and monkeys for sixty days, so we can show the fruit has been lab-tested. I'll get back to you with the results after that."

Kirk timidly asked, "Is it safe to taste?"

"Sure," she said, laughing. "I've tasted it and I've been feeding it to the animals for several days. The lab animals enjoy the fruit and they don't appear to have any adverse side effects from eating it. Remember, it's not poisonous."

Kirk asked, "You didn't lose any of the seed, did you?"

"No, of course not, and just to show you how competent I am, I counted all the seeds. There are 24 in each section which makes a total of 144 seeds in each fruit."

"Thank you for your help, I'll see you tomorrow."

"You're welcome."

Kirk was so excited that he decided to leave work early so he could count the seeds from more fruit to see if they all contained 144 seeds. He counted the seeds from four more fruit and found each had 144 seeds—which meant he would have a total of 20,736 seeds.

That night at the ranch, Jack and Kirk decided to taste the fruit. It was mild in flavor, good, but undeniably different from anything they had ever tasted. It didn't seem high in acid. The syrupy-sweet fluid around the seeds, which was dark blood red in all the sections, tasted precisely as Sandra had described.

The next day Kirk and Jack discussed a partnership in a "Feed-the-World" plan. They arranged to lease a half-acre from their dad and decided to have four different greenhouses built so Kirk and Jack could test the plants in four different climates. Setting up a corporation named Famine Free Future, they agreed on a partnership agreement, with Jack owning 40% and Kirk owning 60%. Roulett was upset with Jack about his new corporation, knowing he would be away from home even more than usual.

Kirk didn't waste any time waiting for the results from the lab animals. He hired Quinn Jordan to oversee the construction of the planned greenhouses and a building for processing the fruit. Quinn was Hollie's brother and the eldest son of

Harvey Jordan—the only employee who'd worked for the Clayton family for over forty years. Kirk wanted the greenhouses finished by the first of June, thus putting a lot of pressure on Quinn.

That night Roulett was still angry with Jack. She didn't enjoy the weekly Friday night get-together where Jack had rainbow fruit for everyone to taste. Roulett chose not to taste the fruit, not only because of her ominous feeling about it, but also as a silent protest to Jack's latest business venture with Kirk.

On Saturday, Kirk and Jack stopped by the greenhouse project to see how Quinn was doing. He and his crew were hard at work and near completion. While they were there, they decided to look at the fruit in their mother's greenhouse. They were both ecstatic when they found forty-eight new blooms on each of their rainbow fruit plants.

The following Monday, Quinn completed the outsides of the four greenhouses several days ahead of schedule. He hired thirty men from the H.O.W. Foundation to build the raised beds and plant 2,500 seeds in each greenhouse. The completion of the whole project by the first day of June earned Quinn a thousand dollar bonus. A few days after the seeds were planted, Jack and Kirk abandoned the idea of having different temperatures in the four houses because Marie's furnace fiasco proved the rainbow plant's cold and heat tolerance.

That night Roulett had her second dream. She saw a large group of people, predominately women, waiting in a very long line, so long that she couldn't see the end on either side. Everyone was wearing ankle length white robes tied in the middle with cumbersome gold ropes. They were groaning and wringing their hands. The sky was full of dark clouds. Lightning and thunder accompanied the pouring rain, soaking everyone to the skin. She heard screams, but they were too far away to see where they originated. The rain suddenly turned to blood. As it flowed over the people, the thunder became deafening. They crouched in terror, covering their ears and weeping. The blood ran in rivers down the dirt road.

Roulett awoke in a cold sweat, screaming and trembling with fear. It took Jack several minutes to calm her.

Chapter 16 | Family Lies

We are suffering for the sins of our ancestors. LAMENTATIONS 5: 7

Thursday, June 1st, was a beautiful spring morning. The sun beamed and the birds sang as Marie, Vickie and Roulett took cards, presents, and a white cake with pink frosting and pink flowers to Dorothy Clayton in Our Lady of Grace Nursing Home to celebrate Dorothy's 91st birthday.

Since mornings were the best time of day for Dorothy, they arrived early. She was extremely happy to see them but was a little upset that her son, Charles, was out of town. She hadn't seen him since John-George's funeral in December and was disappointed. He'd called her that morning to wish her a happy birthday and to tell her he was sorry he couldn't make it to her party.

Dorothy happily opened her presents. Vickie had crocheted pink booties because Dorothy's circulation wasn't good, so her feet were always cold. She thanked Vickie and gave her a hug, claiming that she liked any color as long as it was pink.

Marie had made her a fluffy pink lap blanket that was only a little larger than a baby blanket. Roy and Dorothy's house in New York, except for Charles's room, had been almost entirely pink.

Marie remembered her mother saying that Marie's grandfather had let Dorothy do anything she wanted because Roy was twenty-one years Dorothy's senior. Marie was only five when her family had visited, yet she recalled every detail.

She didn't know if she'd forged her heightened memory because of the hostility between her grandfather and her dad, or because it was the only time they had visited them before the family went to New York for Roy's funeral.

Today, Dorothy showed her delight with the blanket. Roulett's present was a pink floral print flannel bed jacket, which pleased Dorothy, too. She laughed and said, "You'd think it was winter in June with all these gifts to keep me warm."

Marie laughed as she said, "It's always cold in here."

After they had finished their cake, Dorothy said, "I have something to tell all of you—especially Marie. Brace yourself Marie, this is going to be a major shock."

"Are you getting married again?" Roulett joked.

"No, it's not anything like that," replied Dorothy. "I'm concerned this could be my last birthday and this story needs to be told while I'm still alive. The only other person who could tell you was John-George and since he's gone, it's up to me. This happened over sixty years ago and I've never told a soul."

They all listened intently.

"It was the second week of April. John-George had stopped in New York to see his father before John-George was to travel overseas. He'd joined the Army to help fight in the war. He arrived a day before Roy actually expected him.

"You see, I told Roy the wrong arrival date on purpose. Roy had expected John-George to arrive on the fifteenth, and he arrived on the fourteenth instead. Because Roy had an overnight business trip he needed to take care of soon, I suggested he get it over with so he could enjoy his son's visit without the obligation hanging over his head. Roy agreed and left early the morning of the 14th. I wanted to spend that first night alone with John-George.

"I wanted a baby desperately. I'd been married to Roy for more than six years and I wasn't pregnant yet. I rationalized the baby would be a Clayton and Roy would never know. I made John-George an innocent victim of my plot to become pregnant. I gave him lots of wine with dinner to make the seduction easier. Even with the wine, he resisted."

Marie broke in, "It was a good thing your plan didn't work."

"I didn't say my plan didn't work. I only said he resisted. He finally surrendered to my advances."

Looking as if she'd been shot, Marie turned as pale as a ghost.

Dorothy looked Marie in the eyes. "Charles isn't your half-uncle—he's your half-brother!"

Roulett and Vickie feared Marie would faint. She felt cold and clammy and her heart was pounding. Vickie wet a washcloth for Marie to put on her forehead.

"I'm sorry I've taken me so long to tell you. It was entirely my fault. Your father was a good man. My seduction of him and the resulting pregnancy wasn't his idea."

This statement didn't seem to make Marie feel any better. Neither Roulett nor

Vickie understood Marie's extreme reaction.

Roulett suggested to Dorothy, "We should go and let you rest before lunch."

When they all arrived back at the ranch, Marie went into the house to rest, claiming her head ached from too much sugar in the cake. However, Roulett and Vickie knew that it wasn't the cake that had upset Marie.

Chapter 17 | Brown Bread

...Man cannot live by bread alone. LUKE 4:4

Marie saved a gallon of the blood-red syrupy juice taken from the center of her rainbow fruit to experiment with new uses for it. She used it to sweeten the bread made in her bread machine, giving it a beautiful medium brown color with a great flavor. Sam loved it so much he said, "You need to make a loaf of this for Kirk's birthday. It'll please him, seeing you've thought of such a clever, tasty way to use the juice."

"That's a wonderful idea. I'll make a loaf in the morning for him. We are supposed to take him and Pam for dinner tomorrow night."

"Why tomorrow night?"

"Because it's his birthday," replied Marie.

The next night, Marie, Sam, Pam and Kirk celebrated his birthday as planned. While waiting for their food to arrive, Marie gave him the loaf of brown bread she'd brought in with his birthday present.

"Mom, you didn't have to bring your own bread. We could've ordered a loaf," teased Kirk.

"I wanted you to see how I used rainbow fruit juice to make this bread."

"It's pretty, but does it taste as good as it looks?"

"Have a bite and see," Sam suggested.

Kirk opened the bread and tore off a small piece, putting a little butter on it from the dish on the table. He popped it in his mouth and chewed for a few seconds before he said, "This is really good."

"I told you. I have a toasted slice of this bread every morning now," said Sam.

"You know the rainbow fruit produces a lot of sweet juice from around the seeds, so I think you should try to sell the juice to bakeries to use for baking. It tastes great and has a beautiful color," said Marie.

"That's an excellent idea. I'll talk to Jack about it—but we have to wait until the sixty days are up on the lab animal tests."

By the end of June, 432 rainbow fruit ripened and each plant had sixty new blooms. The test results were all positive with no adverse side effects noted.

Kirk started working on his mother's idea of selling his fruit juice to a bakery. Kirk remembered an old friend from college who was now vice-president of his father's tri-state bakery. Although he wasn't the sharpest knife in the drawer, Kirk would need some compelling evidence to convince him to change their time-tested recipes. He again asked his co-worker from the Center, Sandra, for help. She compiled a list of reasons that Kirk was certain would impress anyone. Kirk read Sandra's sales pitch:

*Rainbow juice costs less than sugar, is sweeter per ounce, and metabolizes slower which results in less blood sugar fluctuation.

*Rainbow juice increases the protein level while lowering the sugar and carbohydrate level.

*Rainbow juice requires less yeast because of the higher protein level, which increases the yeast's ability to leaven bread.

*Rainbow juice raises the vitamin, mineral, and antioxidant levels without additional cost.

*Rainbow juice saves the cost of caramel coloring due to the juice's natural color.

Choose rainbow juice for higher profits and healthier bread products!

Kirk thanked Sandra for her impressive work. With these statements, he easily convinced his friend to try the fruit juice, and after a brief trial period, Kirk acquired a contract to sell all the juice they could produce to his friend's tri-state bakery.

Chapter 18 | Wrong Horse

Stupid people are certain they are always right. The wise heed advice. PROVERBS 12: 15

The annual Clayton Research Center Fourth-of-July picnic at Clayton Park was uneventful for everyone except Lou. Since Lou's feelings for Roulett had blossomed since the incident in the loft, he had noticed a bond between Roulett and Garrett and it disturbed him. After the picnic, all the Friday night regulars traveled from the park to the ranch to escape the July heat. At the ranch, they all chose to go into the cool of the clubroom to hear one of Sam's horse tales.

Sam said, "This happened years ago when our stallion, Petrolia Pete, was a young horse. Thinking we needed to find out if he was potent enough to settle a mare before offering his stud service, we decided to buy a test mare."

Marie added, "We had geldings for riding, but this was our first experience with breeding horses."

Sam continued, "We decided to go to the Thursday night horse auction in Chandler, which is about halfway between Tulsa and Oklahoma City, planning to buy a good looking young mare broke to ride—reasoning if she didn't produce a foal, we could always use her for another riding horse.

"It was a long trip pulling a horse-trailer but we arrived in time to look over the horses before the auction started at 7:00 p.m. We found a small sorrel mare and Marie wrote down the numbers from the sticker on the top of the mare's tail, so we'd bid on the right one."

Marie interrupted, "We chose this particular mare because she looked like our gelding, Sox. Being a double-bred Leo gelding, he was a bulldog-built sorrel with four white socks and a blaze face and really flashy. We talked about how it was a shame Sox was a gelding instead of a mare, because he'd be a perfect cross for Petrolia Pete. Pete's sixteen hands height with long muscle made him a very good athlete."

"I wanted more than just a good athlete—I wanted a halter foal so I could show at halter and win the trophies and the blue ribbons," Sam said.

"To produce the bulgy, short muscle for halter, we needed a stocky bulldog type mare. Pete was a dark bay but Sam wanted a black foal and I'd read that crossing a sorrel with a dark bay was one of the best ways to produce a black foal," explained Marie.

Sam said, "That's what I wanted, a black halter-built show foal with a big white blanket and spots on his rump. I wanted a winner."

Roulett interrupted by asking, "You mean like Jill's Cloudy Midnight?"

"Well, she has the flashy color, but we'll have to see if she'll be a halter winner," answered Sam.

Marie mused with sarcasm, "You can tell he didn't want much—just everything."

Everyone in the room except Sam chuckled. He continued, "We needed to know if Pete could produce Appaloosa color with a solid color mare. This was another reason to buy a test mare. Pete didn't show a lot of Appaloosa color when he was young even though both his parents had large white blankets with spots. Marie was convinced he would produce Appaloosa color with a solid mare because of his background, but I had my doubts."

"But I was right," gloated Marie.

"Yeah, yeah, but let's not get into all that now. I am trying to tell them the auction story. So, we bid on the little sorrel mare and ended up buying her," continued Sam.

"You forgot to tell how it was almost midnight when we bid on the mare because the tack sale was first and the little mare was one of the last horses to sell," said Marie.

"That's right and we still had to make that long, boring trip home, and we both were so tired we were a little cranky," said Sam.

Jack said, "Dad, you are always a little cranky. Are you sure you didn't mean a whole-bunch cranky?"

"I wish you all would just shut up and let me tell my story!"

"I've proven my point—go on with your story, Dad."

Sam continued, "I went to the office to pay for the little mare, and they gave me a ticket so I could pick her up in the back. Having the ticket numbered 218 on it with 'Sorrel Mare' written below, I didn't think we'd have a problem. That was the same number I had Marie write down before the auction began. I took the ticket with a halter and lead rope back to pick up my mare.

"When we reached the back, a skinny young man chewing tobacco and spitting frequently on the ground, took our ticket, halter, and lead. He then handed everything to another young man with stringy blond hair who proceeded to fetch a sorrel horse. As I watched him lead the horse toward me, I could tell something was wrong. Even in the dim lights of the horse pens, I could see this horse was bigger than the mare I bid on. I said to the first young man, this isn't the horse I bought, while the second young man was about to hand me the lead.

"Then, looking closer, I could see this wasn't a mare and my ticket said a mare. The problem was this horse did have the number 218 on him, and he was sorrel. I tried desperately to convince them this wasn't the horse I bid on. I said how I was buying a test mare for my young stallion, and this wasn't a mare.

"The first young man lifted the horse's tail and said with tobacco juice trickling down his chin, 'He's right—this ain't no mare.' The second young man looked between the horse's hind legs with a flashlight he'd taken out of his back pocket and said, 'He's been cut, so he's not all horse.'

"I told them again I didn't want a gelding. I had two geldings at home already, and I wanted a test mare for my young stallion. The first young man's mouth was so full that I thought he was going to drown before he finally spit a large wad of tobacco on the ground. Although the young men seemed very concerned about our problem, they didn't have the authority to do anything except match horse-sticker-number with ticket-number. Sticker-number and horse-number matched, so all they could do was send us back to the office to talk to the main guy.

"The main guy wasn't any more help than they were. Telling us the same thing over and over again, he said, 'You bought the horse that has the same number on it as your ticket.' He asked us, 'Does that gelding have the same number on him as the number on your ticket?' I said he did have the same number but he wasn't the horse I bid on. I showed him my ticket and knew he could see written in plain English were the words 'Sorrel Mare.'

"He said it was possible for them to make a mistake on the sex of a horse that late in the night and it was my responsibility to look over what I bid on. I told him this gelding was larger and probably worth more money than the small mare. Horses always have a value by the pound and, at the current rate, the gelding was worth at least a hundred dollars more than the little mare—by weight alone.

"Trying to give me a horse worth more money didn't make sense, but it did seem like they were trying to switch horses on me. The whole thing would've made more sense if they were trying to switch to a cheaper horse. The fact this horse was worth more than the mare I'd bid on didn't impress the main guy one little bit. He said, 'You should be happy you got such a bargain.' I told him my young stallion wouldn't think his new mate was such a bargain."

Marie said, "The main guy told us it wasn't his problem and he wasn't going to give us our money back. He said, 'You bought the horse with number 218 on it, and it doesn't matter how much it's worth. Your ticket and the number on the gelding match, so that's what you own. It doesn't matter to me if this is the buy of your lifetime, or if it's the worst deal you've ever made. Your only choice is the horse with your number on him or nothing.'

"Sam and I both were so tired and frustrated when he wouldn't listen to us that I told Sam we should take the gelding tonight because I was too tired to argue anymore. We reasoned that we could sell the gelding as soon as possible and we could buy another mare. The difference in the value of the mare we'd bid on and the gelding the main guy insisted was ours should pay for our time and trouble to buy another mare."

Sam said, "I finally agreed because I didn't have a choice—leaving the gelding just because I was angry would only hurt us. I knew the main guy would surely sell the gelding again and pocket the money. I was mad as a wet hornet as I stormed out of there in a huff. The kid at the gate could see I was fit-to-be-tied, so he didn't ask for my ticket. Failing to tear off the bottom stub, he didn't have proof showing I'd picked up the horse. I was furious all the way home."

Marie said, "It was a long trip. We didn't arrive until almost three in the morning. Sam unloaded the unwanted gelding and put him in a stall in the barn. We drug ourselves to bed so tired and disgusted, vowing we'd never go back to that auction again."

Sam interrupted, "If Marie hadn't figured out what happened that would've been the end of that story..."

Marie said, "I woke about an hour after we went to sleep, remembering there was a lot of glue on the gelding's tail. Adding up all the facts, I concluded our gelding was auctioned before this one. Starting the auction with more than one number sticker glued on his tail, he'd lost the top ticket sometime after he was auctioned but before we picked him up. The only number he still had showing was the number from the previous auction—the same number as our mare. He wasn't the horse we'd bid on, so our mare was still there!

"Waking Sam, I told him what I thought had happened. He agreed with me that our mare was still there, and he helped me make plans to pick her up. We clearly remembered reading the sign posted at the cashier's window: 'All sale items must be picked up within twenty-four hours after auction,' so we still had time to claim our mare. Since we had a complete ticket for her, we decided Sam could take the ticket and pick her up in the morning.

"Sam got up in spite of his fatigue. Our plan was to pick up the mare when a different crew would be at the horse auction. Deciding it wouldn't be practical to take the gelding back to those jerks, we considered him payment for our time and trouble. The main guy insisted we owned whatever sported number 218 on its sticker. Playing by his rules, we owned both horses. Sam took the ticket and picked up the mare we'd originally bought. He didn't have any trouble claming her because the day crew knew nothing about the previous night."

Roulett asked, "Didn't you feel like a horse thief?"

Marie said, "No, we were only doing what he told us to do. We tried our best to tell him that the gelding wasn't the horse that we'd bought. He finally convinced us, no matter what...we now owned the horse having the number 218 on it. It wasn't *our* fault both horses had the same number on them."

Sam said, "I sold the gelding at the Collinsville sale the next Saturday—and he sold for twice the amount I paid for the little mare."

Lou asked, "Did Pete like the mare better than the gelding?"

Sam replied, "He liked her *too* much. As luck would have it, the mare was in heat when we brought her to the ranch. I let Pete get acquainted with her through the fence long enough to know that she was ready to breed, so I turned her in with him."

Marie said, "I thought the fool was going to kill himself."

Garrett asked, "Sam?"

"No, Pete!"

Sam laughed. "He bred that mare ten times before we could catch him."

Marie said, "I think it was closer to eight times he actually bred her, but I'm sure he mounted her at least forty times to do so. The ten acres where we turned her loose was all new territory for her, so she couldn't choose between her new suitor and her new home. Exploring her new pasture, she wouldn't stand still; he was breeding her on the run. I thought the fool was going to kill himself before we could catch him. When we finally caught him, he was soaking wet with sweat. The fool had enough lather on him to have run in a ten-mile race."

Lou asked, "How long did it take to catch him?"

Sam replied, "About twenty minutes."

Roulett asked, "Eight times in twenty minutes?"

All the men in the room became very quiet.

Marie said, "Why do you think they call them stallions?"

Sam replied, "Wait just a minute. You need to tell everybody the rest of the story before you brag on his stamina. Tell them how too much of a good thing isn't always good for a rambunctious young stallion."

Marie chuckled as she continued, "Pete could barely move the next day. He had used muscles he'd never used before with such gusto that he was sore all over. He was in so much pain that he didn't show any interest in the mare. We had to call the vet to give him medication so he could move enough to work the soreness out."

Everyone laughed.

Chapter 19 | Cousin Gillian

To stay out of trouble, always be careful what you say.
PROVERBS 21: 23

Several days later, Marie received a phone call from Gillian Holt, a distant cousin on Marie's great-grandfather Edward's side of the family. Although from Great Britain, she was visiting relatives in the United States and would be in Tulsa on Friday. Marie invited Gillian and her family to stay at the ranch. Roulett volunteered to drive Marie to the airport to pick up Gillian and her family since Marie hated driving in the city.

Everyone was fascinated by Gillian and her daughter's British accents. Her daughter, Tiffany, was surprised that Oklahoma was modern, although she seemed disappointed that Roulett and Marie hadn't picked them up in a stagecoach.

Marie said, "I wish you had visited before my father died last December. He would've been eighty-nine if he'd lived to his birthday, which was last Sunday."

"It's a shame I missed him by such a short period of time," replied Gillian.

Roulett noticed that her son, Michael, was smitten with Tiffany, who was a very pretty twelve-year-old.

Roulett said, "If Michael had his way, he and Tiffany would become kissing cousins."

"That sort of behavior may run in our family," said Gillian.

"What are you talking about?" Marie asked.

"You mean you haven't heard the story about our great-grandfather Edward?"

"I've heard how he became rich as a diamond broker and that he loved big game hunting in Africa."

"You mean you've never heard the story of Edward and Vanora?"

"No, I don't remember hearing anything about them."

Gillian continued, "Vanora was Edward's sister, the sister who was only a year-and-a-half older than he was. Have you heard about our great-great grandmother who died with four of her daughters, including Vanora?"

"No."

"Vanora was only a teenager when she died. My great-grandmother Gladys—Gladys was one of Edward's sisters—told my mother the reason they all died was they'd taken Vanora to see the doctor in London where they were exposed to cholera."

"So what does their dying from cholera have to do with Edward?" asked Marie, still on the defensive.

"Great-grandmother said that Vanora was pregnant when she died and that Edward was the father of his own sister's baby."

Marie asked, "Why did they think that Edward was the father? He was the youngest, wasn't he?"

"Yes, he was almost fifteen and Vanora was sixteen, almost seventeen, when she became pregnant. They'd slept together when they were very young and it was a habit that they didn't want to give up when they reached puberty."

"I find that story hard to believe," said Marie.

"Believe what you want to…but he came to America to forget his shameful past," said Gillian.

"Are you certain they weren't simply telling you tall-tales about my great grandfather to see how gullible you were?"

"I don't think they'd fabricate such a story. Edward was the last of nine children and the only boy, living in a secluded area—so secluded that they only attended church twice a year on Christmas and Easter making the children closer than those who had other friends. Edward and Vanora became intimate."

"I have a difficult time thinking of my great grandfather as a pervert."

"Actually, I think Vanora seduced Edward. Vanora had a distorted fascination for Edward's private parts. She frequently asked her mother why she'd been cheated out of a tassel. Apparently, all the girls knew about Vanora's fascination with Edward's so-called tassel, making her do almost anything to see and touch it. Of course, this easily could've led to Vanora's pregnancy."

"Do you have any proof of this story other than hearsay?" asked Marie.

"No, but I'm telling you this is a true story," said Gillian.

Roulett stepped in because she didn't want them to fight about something which may or may not have happened many years ago. She asked Gillian, "Would you like to see the greenhouses?"

Gillian said, "Yes, that sounds very interesting. What do you have growing in them?"

"I'll be happy to show you," Roulett replied.

Gillian was very impressed with the fruit, suggesting they should dehydrate it after they removed the seeds. It would be easy to ship worldwide without losing any seeds, and a good way to carry fruit samples when selling the seeds.

Kirk and Jack were very impressed with Gillian's idea. They met with Quinn the next day to describe what they wanted. They next week Quinn purchased several large dehydrators to add to the fruit processing building. The dried fruit kept well, which made distributing it an easier task to accomplish in a timely manner. Kirk came by to see the dehydrators and told Quinn he could eat all the rainbow fruit he wanted, but to save every seed.

Chapter 20 | Roulett's Handsome Neighbor

Gossip is sinfully delicious—we love to swallow it! PROVERBS 18: 8

On the next Friday, Hollie and her boyfriend Bill came over for the weekly ranch get-together. Hollie noticed the same spark between Roulett and Garrett that Lou had observed earlier.

When Hollie and Roulett had lunch on the following Wednesday, Hollie asked, "What's the deal with you and this Garrett guy? I thought after our talk at the Christmas party you'd realized that falling for him was crazy!"

"What do you mean?"

Hollie said, "You can fool some of the people some of the time, and Hollie none of the time! I want to know how involved you are with Garrett."

Roulett asked, "Why? Is it that obvious?"

"Oh yeah, it's obvious! With a husband like Jack, how you could even consider messing around with a bum like Garrett?"

"We haven't messed around!"

"If you haven't yet, you will soon, unless one or both of you change direction. I don't think that's a wise idea."

"Hollie, I can't seem to help myself. It was love at first sight."

"I know that love is blind, but in your case, love is blind, deaf, and really stupid!"

"Believe me...I didn't want to feel this way about him. I've fought it for a long time."

"Keep fighting it. He's a bum compared to Jack."

"He isn't a bum. He's really a wonderful person."

Hollie shook her head. "Without his doctor wife, he would be a bum. Look at what you have! Garrett's not worth losing all you have—a rich, handsome husband and a loving family. Keep fighting the urges, Roulett."

"I didn't choose to feel this way," said Roulett.

"I don't find him attractive, but you must. You claim to have loved him at first sight, which means you found him pleasing to your *sight* not your heartstrings. I think you're in lust, not love."

"I guess I think he's more attractive than I previously said, but I still don't think what I feel for him is mere lust. Lust I could deal with and, believe me, I know the difference."

"So you admit to feeling lust before? Tell me more…"

"It was when Tammy was a baby. I was in my early twenties and the Smith family lived across the street from us. They had a very handsome young son who was studying to become a missionary, no less."

"Oh! You were lusting after a preacher man! How much worse could this be! Was he underage *and* a preacher? Tell me more…please tell me more!"

"I think he was about seventeen and a real hunk. He was so handsome…he was pretty. Oh, yes, and he was so innocent—that's a very big turn-on for me. I would watch him as he left every day and think about how handsome he was."

"There has to be more to this story…tell me what *really* happened," said Hollie.

"One day while I was watching him, his car wouldn't start. He'd locked his house but didn't have a house key so he started walking toward my house. I had all these fantasies running through my mind of how he was coming to tell me he wanted to make passionate love to me. I felt pure lust as I watched him cross the street. He had broad shoulders with narrow hips. His brown, curly hair blew gently in the wind while his chiseled face, bronzed from the sun, made his blue-green eyes sparkle. He was so handsome and he was at my door!" said Roulett, and then paused for a moment to think about him.

"Tell me more—what happened?" asked Hollie.

"His mother told me he was once a male model."

"I get the idea…he was gorgeous…"

"He rang the doorbell and asked to use my phone. First, he called his work to tell them he couldn't be there that day because of car trouble. Then, he called his mother and she said she couldn't come home until lunchtime. It was only 9:30 a.m., so that was over two and a half hours away. He asked me if he could stay at my house until his mother returned. Of course, I said yes. Marie had my children and she wouldn't be back until about four, so I spent several hours alone with the most handsome young hunk I'd ever seen," confessed Roulett.

Hollie pressured, "Must I beg you to tell me what happened?"

"I offered to take him to work, but he said they wouldn't need him until after noon. Did I tell you that he was big flirt?"

"No! What happened?"

"I made the mistake of asking him what he wanted to do while he was waiting. He smiled and said, 'Anything you want to do.' I thought my heart would stop beating then," said Roulett.

Hollie asked, "Do you think he really meant 'anything'?"

"You would've thought so if you could've seen the look on his face."

Hollie asked, "And..."

"We played cards."

"What a disappointment!" Hollie groaned.

"That's exactly what he said halfway through our third game of Old Maid. He said disappointedly how I was acting like an "Old Maid" and if I thought about it, I should be able to imagine something more exciting and more pleasurable to do."

"Do you really think he was coming on to you?"

"I'm *sure* he was coming on to me!"

Hollie asked, "What about his religious training? Didn't he think that was sinning?"

"I think...for the moment...he'd forgotten his religious training."

"So nothing happened?"

"No, I told you I could handle lust. What I feel for Garrett is different than ordinary lust."

"That was an anticlimactic story."

"I agree. And I'm sure my handsome neighbor would agree, too!"

Chapter 21 | Lou's Concern

Peace of mind reaps a healthy body, but jealousy consumes us like a cancer. PROVERBS 14: 30

The next Friday, Lou arrived early at the ranch for the get-together hoping he'd have an opportunity to speak alone with Roulett about Garrett before he took his break. Lou wondered why she'd never shown an interest in him as she did for Garrett, with the exception of the one time in the barn loft, which she was too drunk to remember. When Lou walked into the clubhouse at 3:50 p.m., he noticed Garrett washing his hands.

Garrett looked up to ask, "What brings you here so early?"

Lou walked toward the sink as he replied, "I decided to take off early to renew my driver's license today, instead of waiting until the end of the month when the tag agency is busy. Sure enough, it only took a few minutes, so here I am." Since Roulett was busy at the other side of the sink, he asked, "What are you making?"

She replied, "Iced tea. Do you want some?"

"I'd love some."

Roulett put ice in three large glasses and filled them with freshly brewed tea.

"Garrett, I'm surprised you're not having coffee," Lou said.

"I've had about eight cups today, so iced tea sounded good for a change."

Roulett sliced a lemon, put wedges on the rims of the glasses, and then asked, "Do either of you want sugar or sweetener in your tea?"

Lou teased, "Just stir mine with your finger—that'll make it sweet enough."

"Oh, no—he's buttering me up for something!" she said.

Garrett said, "Just tea for me."

Lou asked Roulett, "Can't I be nice without wanting something?"

"Have you been out in the heat too long or what?" she replied as she carried two of the glasses of tea to the table.

"You would make a good waitress, Roulett," Lou commented.

Roulett snarled, "Don't get used to it or next time you'll be pouring your own tea!"

"You know how Okies are about their iced tea," said Lou, trying to pick a fight.

"Boy, you're in an ornery mood today."

"I'm just trying to enjoy my last few days of being thirty-nine," said Lou.

"That's right, you'll be forty on the tenth," she said, suddenly grinning.

"Oh yeah! You're going to be over-the-hill on Monday. I guess you better enjoy this last weekend before you're old!" Garrett added.

"While you still have the energy to enjoy life!"

Lou said, "I know Roulett has several years to go before reaching forty, but Garrett…I think you're only a few years behind me, right?"

"Don't remind me!" Garrett cringed.

"Roulett, would you please pour these two old men a refill of your wonderful tea?"

"Okay, this time but don't make a habit of *me* waiting on either of *you*."

"And please stir mine with your finger again—the other was just right," Lou added.

"Okay, but you don't know where I've had my finger last. I could've had it up a horse's butt for all you know," she said, then grinned as she handed Lou his tea.

"What I don't know won't hurt me. Besides, I didn't think equine proctology was your thing," said Lou.

Garrett drank his tea and stood. "It's getting too deep in here for me—I'm only glad I'm wearing boots. I'm going to do some work. I'll see you two later."

Lou said, "Don't work too hard."

Garrett answered as he walked toward the door, "You've known me long enough to know I won't do that."

Roulett said to Lou, "We all have fun together, don't we?"

"Yes, we do. And speaking of fun…I noticed you and Garrett were having a great time at the ranch picnic."

She nodded. "You know Garrett and I enjoy each other's company. So what…?"

"There's no other way than just to tell you."

"Tell me what?"

"I think you and Garrett have a thing for each other and you two could be much more than platonic friends if you continue to spend so much time together."

"Why do you think that?"

"Lots of reasons…the way you look at each other. How he always takes his break when you arrive. If you're in the clubhouse he's there, too. He follows you around like a little lost puppy. Are you going to tell me you never noticed?"

"Apparently not the way you have," said Roulett defensively.

"I'm telling you from a man's point of view—Garrett has a thing for you. Do you have a thing for him?"

"Lou, I'm a married woman!"

"I didn't ask your martial status! Do you have a thing for him?"

"If I tell you something, will you promise never to tell anyone?"

"Yeah…Yeah…What?"

"You have to promise me you'll never, never…tell anyone, and especially not Jack!"

"Okay, I promise I'll never tell anyone and especially not Jack. What?"

"The first time I met Garrett at your Christmas party, I had an overwhelming desire to kiss him, even though I didn't *want* to be attracted to him."

"Do you still have that desire?"

"Yes. It never goes away—no matter how much I want it to."

Lou's mind drifted back to the night in the loft with her. "Have you ever had the desire to kiss any other man besides Garrett, other than your husband?"

"No, never!"

Lou smiled. "Not even me, as handsome and charming as I am?"

"No, Lou, I've never had the desire to kiss you, as handsome and charming as you are."

"Do you think Garrett is more handsome than I am?"

"I don't think you understand. My feelings of love for Garrett have nothing to do with how handsome I think he is or isn't. My feelings are not simply lust. I could deal with my feelings for him a lot easier if only it were lust—I'd have gotten over it by now."

"You still haven't answered my question—do you think Garrett is more handsome than I am?"

"I never really thought about it before, but I see you're going to insist on an answer." Roulett paused for a few minutes as she looked at Lou and thought before she expressed her feelings…"I'd say you're equally as handsome as Garrett. You have beautiful eyes and a great personality."

"So why did you have a desire to kiss Garrett instead of me? What's wrong with me? Am I chopped liver?"

"You absolutely don't get it, do you? This feeling wasn't solely a physical attraction. I didn't *choose* to desire Garrett because I thought he was handsome. I didn't have a choice. This feeling was constantly there from the very first moment

I saw him."

"Does he know how you feel about him?"

"No, and I don't plan to tell him."

"If you two don't cool it, everyone will know."

Before they could finish their conversation, everyone began arriving for Lou's surprise birthday party. Although everyone appeared to have a great time, both Lou and Roulett had a lot on their minds.

* * * * *

By the middle of July, Kirk's ten thousand rainbow fruit plants bloomed, so there were 120,000 blooms on the new plants. Kirk and Jack bought four beehives, with bees to help pollinate the blooms. The next week 576 fruit ripened on the first plants. That Friday, seventy-two new blooms appeared on the old plants.

* * * * *

On Monday, Roulett and Hollie were having lunch at their usual restaurant when Roulett confessed, "I'm going to kiss Garrett when I'm alone with him."

"You're making a major mistake," Hollie said.

"I promised myself…if I stopped drinking for six months…I'd kiss Garrett. Maybe I won't like kissing him, and I'll finally rid my system of this awful feeling."

"But what if you like it more than you can imagine?" Hollie's eyes opened wide as she glared at Roulett.

"I'm going to take that chance—the desire to kiss him is driving me crazy."

"I think you're already *crazy.*"

"Maybe I am…" Roulett replied.

* * * * *

Jack, Kirk, and Quinn met at the newly constructed greenhouse project office for the August monthly meeting. They discussed the 240,000 new blooms and agreed that they needed to order more bees to keep up with the pollination. After the meeting, Jack and Kirk had lunch at their mother's house. With the increase in fruit production, Marie suggested they acquire another bakery contract. Kirk liked the idea and said he would contact a national bakery.

Marie said, "Don't forget that we're going to celebrate your Uncle Paul's birthday next Friday. I expect both of you to be there. Dorothy's coming over with Charles and we may not have her with us much longer."

"We'll be there, Mom," said Jack, knowing that birthday parties were important to her.

"You're not the son I thought wouldn't be there!" replied Marie, staring at Kirk.

"We'll be there, too, if Pam can leave work in time," said Kirk.

"I thought you would use Pam for an excuse, so I called her and she said she'd be there—so I expect you both to arrive on time!"

Pam and Kirk kept their promise, and Marie enjoyed giving Paul's party even more than normal.

Charles arrived with Dorothy. She'd told him that John-George was his biological father. Since Charles loved to irritate Marie, he made a point of hugging her as he boasted, "Well, I always wanted to have a sister and now I do!"

Marie ignored him. Hatred for him radiated from her, which only encouraged his taunting.

Roulett noticed Marie's discomfort and asked Charles, "Would you mind appraising the diamonds John-George gave me?"

"Sure. Can we meet tomorrow at my hotel room so I can examine them?"

"Why don't you meet here for lunch instead—this would be a safer place to bring the diamonds, don't you think?" Marie said, casting Roulett a stern look.

"I think that's a great idea," Roulett replied.

Charles said, "That sounds good to me. What's for lunch, sis?"

"I promise it'll be delicious. Roulett, would you walk to the house with me and we'll take something out of the freezer for tomorrow?"

"Sure."

On the way to her house, Marie warned, "Never be alone with that man!"

Roulett asked, "Charles, your brother?"

"He may be my brother, but he's still a womanizer."

"I'm sorry. I didn't know that about him."

"Why do you think he's been married five times? I was concerned about *your* safety more than the safety of the diamonds."

"Thanks for the warning. I'll be careful."

*****

The next week, Kirk acquired a contract with a nationwide bakery for his rainbow fruit juice. This particular bakery distributed food additives, resulting in rainbow fruit juice being used in the majority of processed food products from soup to nuts—including baby food.

*****

The following Monday, Marie called Kirk to inform him that the original fruit blossomed eighty-four new blooms each on Sunday.

That same day, Marie, Vickie, and Roulett visited Dorothy at the nursing home. Marie took one of the rainbow fruit plants she'd grown in her greenhouse to show Dorothy.

"I can't leave this plant with you, because Kirk would be upset," Marie said.

Dorothy replied, "I've seen one of these before, but I can't remember where."

"Dad gave the seed to Kirk shortly before he died," Marie said, hoping to help Dorothy remember.

"Oh, yes…that's Roy's special tea plant. The one I gave to John-George after Roy passed away, but I never saw it bear flowers or fruit."

"Is it the terrible smelling tea that Dad drank for all those years?" Marie asked.

Dorothy replied, "Well, I only know it was the tea Roy drank for years and after Roy died, I gave the plants to John-George." It puzzled everyone why she'd never seen the blooms or the fruit.

The next day, Marie called Kirk to tell him what Dorothy had revealed about Roy and the tea. Kirk assured her the leaves weren't poisonous, but that he wasn't certain Dorothy knew what she was saying about the plant.

At the next Friday night ranch get-together, Marie made tea from the leaves of the rainbow fruit plant. She told everyone about Dorothy's memory of the plant. "Kirk assured me the tea isn't poisonous, so I think we should all taste it," she said.

The tea smelled so horrific that only two people tried it—Lou and Garrett. Garrett didn't like it, so he took only one sip before spitting it in the sink. "That stuff is disgusting," he said.

Lou placated, "Oh, it's not so bad with an extra spoonful of sugar in it."

"I think you'd drink horse urine if it had sugar in it," said Garrett.

Jack refused the tea after smelling it, saying, "Sorry, Mom, I'll drink the fruit juice instead. I think Grandfather Roy consumed the wrong part of the plant. Speaking of the fruit, we harvested 864 today from the original plants. Our projections show that by next December we'll have harvested over a billion seeds. It's time for us to collect the contracts for the seeds from all the foreign countries Kirk and I visited earlier."

"I guess that means that soon you're going to have more rainbow puree than the bread companies can handle?" asked Marie.

Sam sipped his Guinness stout beer, then said, "Maybe you should try making a dark beer with the puree. If the beer is half as good as the bread, it'll be a winner!"

Thinking it was a good idea, Jack suggested, "Dad, if you wouldn't mind—why don't you make some home-brew, so we'll know if the fruit makes good beer?" He knew that Sam had dabbled with different home-brew recipes before and seemed to enjoy it.

Sam smiled. "I'll get out my book on zymurgy—the chemistry of fermentation." He loved to use big words and relished the idea of being involved in Jack and Kirk's work.

Later, Marie remembered everyone's reaction to the tea and wondered if Dorothy might be mistaken about the source of grandfather's Roy tea.

Chapter 22 | Roy Clayton in Africa, 1924

...They broke our agreement
...They took things condemned to destruction
...They stole, lied about it, and kept the things... JOSHUA 7:11

The golden sun hung low in the vivid African sky. In a little less than one hour, the glowing sphere would hide behind the horizon. Time being ever significant on these journeys, making camp was the weary group's first priority. Any delay would put Roy Clayton, his two native guides, and the four native porters in danger of being at the mercy of the nocturnal insects and other predators. Roy stopped in an open grassy area where he enjoyed a clear view in every direction.

Careful calculations with his well-worn map led him to believe they were approximately four miles south of the Kenya-Tanganyika border in Eastern Africa. Rotating slowly, he looked through his binoculars for animals that could be easy prey. He didn't want to see herds of antelope, wildebeest, or any other abundant species in the savanna, for killing prey wasn't his intent. Easy prey often meant the presence of predatory animals. He didn't want to be dinner for a hungry lion—one of his worst fears, which frequented his nightmares all too often.

On his right, he saw a troop of clamorous monkeys in a clump of acacia trees. The monkeys were screaming an alarm because of the presence of humans, the worst predators of all. Roy hoped the monkeys would settle down and stay in the trees for the night to serve as an alert system against possible danger.

He scanned everything within range several times. The only remaining animals were a herd of elephants foraging about a quarter of a mile away—with Mt. Kilimanjaro as their background. The elephants didn't worry him at all since man was their primary predator.

Roy walked a few yards in the direction of the monkeys, stopped and said, "I think we should camp here tonight."

Yowana, one of Roy's native guides, said, "Yes, Bwana, good place."

Dropping his heavy backpack while staring at the majestic Mt. Kilimanjaro, Roy marveled at the imposing smoky-gray leviathan with its snow-covered peaks. *What a magnificent sight,* he thought.

Although Roy Clayton resided in New York City, he wasn't a stranger to Africa. He'd traveled there many times for business and pleasure and he loved Africa in spite of the obnoxious insects and the volatile weather.

The presence of a blue sky with only a few white puffy clouds was enough to make the entire group rejoice, since it had rained for ten of the last fourteen days. It was extremely sultry, but tolerating the relentless heat and humidity was not nearly as challenging for the group as traversing the land in the rain.

Roy was the tallest and appeared to be the most athletic of the group, but he was probably the weakest. At thirty, he stood a little more than six feet tall in his boots and had a slender but muscular physique with very broad shoulders. Unfortunately, his upper-class urban background meant he wasn't accustomed to hard work.

Only a few years older than Roy, Yowana and Rupia sported much rougher appearances, a direct result from the unforgiving environment in which they'd lived. Brothers from the Luo tribe, they had the same father, but different mothers. Yowana—the oldest and the tallest of the two guides—was five-foot-nine, with a bony frame, scrawny limbs, and skin as dark as stove-black. Their frail appearance was deceptive, for they were both extremely strong and agile. Their tree-climbing skills put Roy's to shame.

Yowana dominated Rupia by giving all of the orders, which made Rupia grumble at times but, despite his discontent, he rarely challenged his brother's authority. Rupia was an inch shorter and about ten pounds heavier than Yowana. Both brothers' skin color and facial features were almost identical, with their large black eyes with tea-stained whites, their bumpy complexion, and wide, flat noses. The few remaining teeth in their mouths were dark and decaying, a result of not only poor hygiene, but also bad dietary habits. Their short fuzzy hair was half-gray and half-black with obvious balding spots.

Roy didn't have even one gray hair mixed with his curly, thick, brown, shoulder-length locks in dire need of a trim. Although Roy visited the jungle from time to time, he didn't have to endure its brutality on a daily basis; which only heightened the age contrast between him and his two native guides.

The four native porters weren't from the Luo tribe, but came from a small, secluded tribe called the Nakizara. Rarely leaving their village, they were an enigmatic tribe. Yowana hired the young Nakizara natives to carry the heavy gear and to accomplish the hard work, which they did very well. In their early twenties and about the same size as Yowana and Rupia, the Nakizara displayed a healthier appearance than Yowana and Rupia. They all maintained beautiful smooth skin, which looked like the skin that forms on dark chocolate pudding when it cools. Their eyes and teeth were healthy and pure, presumably because of a more protected youth within the Nakizara village compound.

Over the years, Roy had learned some Swahili, but he couldn't understand the dialect spoken by the Nakizara natives. He grasped the majority of Yowana and Rupia's conversations, partly because they kept it very simple for him. Yowana and Rupia could speak and understand enough English and many other African dialects to communicate. But they, too, were unable to decipher the dialect of the Nakizara natives.

Two of the Nakizara natives could speak some very simple Swahili. Okech, their leader, did most of the talking while his brother, Masaba, would only take part in the conversations occasionally. The two youngest Nakizara natives, Joni and Semu, could only speak their native tongue. Yowana continually reminded Okech and Masaba to speak Swahili so he could understand them. When he didn't understand them, he became paranoid and thought they must be saying something bad about him.

Roy helped the native porters unpack his tent since his was always the first tent erected. Once it was up, he routinely took a nap before the evening meal while the natives continued setting up the other tents and preparing the camp for the night.

It had been six months since he'd seen his wife and son. This trip had become longer than usual because, after he'd taken care of his usual business of buying diamonds and other precious stones in Johannesburg and then spending a week in Yowana and Rupia's village, he'd spent more than a week looking for a zebra to kill. His wife, Annabelle, desperately wanted a zebra skin rug for her bedroom, because her mother-in-law Rebecca owned one. A zebra skin seemed a small price to pay for Annabelle tolerating his absence. He knew she didn't want him to be away from home as much as he was and he knew she tried her best to be understanding of his long trips away, despite her disapproval.

Roy was a very sensitive and gentle man who didn't find killing animals amusing in the least, so he looked for almost a week to find the right zebra. Ten days earlier, he'd found a zebra stallion limping on one hind hoof. Knowing death would inevitably come soon to this weakened animal in his vulnerable condition, Roy mercifully shot and killed the lame stallion with one bullet.

That same night, Roy and the natives ate roasted zebra and baked sweet potatoes. The meat had a good flavor, but was very tough. The zebra was old. Yowana and Rupia made about twenty pounds of zebra jerky, giving the group ample meat for the remainder of their journey.

Roy told Yowana and Rupia to offer the rest of the tough zebra to some of the nearby natives who were very grateful to have any meat. Roy didn't like the idea of leaving the meat to scavengers while people went hungry.

He completed his trip with the zebra skin for Annabelle. The group would then travel on to Nairobi so Roy could catch a train to the coast. At the coast, he would book passage on a ship to New York. If all went as planned, he would be back before John-George's eighth birthday.

The natives had finished setting up camp and were beginning to prepare for the evening meal when Yowana told Rupia to build a fire. Rupia was concerned that there wasn't enough wood to keep it going all night, so Yowana ordered the young Nakizara natives to gather a fresh supply. Since there were so few trees on the savanna, it could take a while to find enough, so the natives set out immediately.

In his tent Roy fought sleep. Dark was quickly settling in and Roy realized napping would make sleeping later impossible, so he decided to write in his journal instead, a routine he'd maintained for many years. He adjusted himself in his bedroll and reached for his lantern. Opening his journal, he began reflecting on the day's events. He'd just finished writing the date, Thursday, April 17, 1924, when he heard a loud ruckus. Quickly grabbing his rifle, he rushed out of his tent to find the source of the disturbing noise. About two hundred feet away against the faintly lit horizon, he saw the young Nakizara natives shouting in their native tongue at the top of their lungs. Yowana and Rupia were running toward them, too.

Moving closer, Roy realized it was something the young Nakizara natives had found on the ground while looking for firewood, which was causing their excitement. Very close to the young natives Roy saw what looked like a small bush that was apparently causing all the commotion. Two of the Nakizara natives were frantically slashing at the defenseless bush with their pangas—similar to machetes—as if the bush were a mortal enemy, while the other two natives were beating loudly on their drums.

Less than two feet high, with what looked like Christmas tree ornaments on it, the tiny bush appeared to be anything but a threat. Walking closer, Roy saw bright multi-colored fruit about the size of small apples and shaped like tiny pumpkins, hanging from the delicate bush. Having never seen the bush or any other like it, Roy was immediately curious to learn more about the peculiar plant.

Slashing the bush to bits, the same two Nakizara natives pulled up its roots and picked up all the limbs, leaves, roots, and fruit including the fruit on the ground. While still shouting wildly and beating their drums with a fury, the natives carried all the pieces back to the campfire.

Yowana, Rupia, and Roy followed the Nakizara natives back to the camp. On the way Roy asked, "What's going on, Yowana?"

"I know not, Bwana. I know not what they say," said Yowana.

"Tell them to speak in Swahili."

Yowana told the Nakizara natives to tell him the problem in Swahili. While Yowana was talking to the Nakizara natives, they were busy throwing the broken remains of the bush into the fire.

Okech said, "*Matunda ya mungu!*"

Roy shouted, "I hope they don't think that bush is firewood."

"No, Bwana," Yowana translated, "God's fruit."

Masaba said, "*Mtu kula, wanawake kufa, hapana watu!*"

Again, Yowana translated, "*Men eat, women die, no people!*"

Roy asked, "Are you sure you understood them? That doesn't make any sense."

Yowana asked them again and their answer came again, the same as before.

"Ask them if the fruit is poisonous."

"*Ni—sumu?*" Yowana asked.

Okech replied, "*Hapana sumu, tamu chaukula, chaukula ya mungu. Mtu hapana kula chaukla ya mungu.*"

Yowana translated, "No poison, sweet food, God's food. Man no eat God's food."

The Nakizara natives continued throwing the roots into the fire, and appeared to be counting the fruit before tossing them into the sizzling flames.

Okech counted, "*Matunda kumi na mbili.*"

Yowana translated, "Twelve fruit."

In their mad frenzy, the distracted natives overlooked one of the fruit, which had ricocheted off a burning limb and fell beside Roy's right foot. Pretending not to notice the fruit by his foot, he tried to think of some way to divert their attention so he could pick it up without their knowledge.

Roy said, "Yowana, tell them to go back and make sure they found all of it."

Yowana ordered, "*Upesi upesi, kuna ingine matunda!*"

Distracted, the natives scrambled in the direction from which they'd come and Roy quickly shoved the fruit into his pocket. He didn't believe their ridiculous superstitions.

A few minutes later, they returned, and Yowana told Roy that the natives had gotten the entire bush and its fruit the first time. Then Yowana asked, "Bwana, they miss any here?"

"No, they put it all into the fire," lied Roy.

"Good," said Yowana.

Roy asked Yowana, "Have you ever seen this bush before?"

"No, Bwana."

"Are you positive that on all the safaris with my father, you've never seen that bush before today?"

"No, Bwana, never," replied Yowana.

Roy decided this was too good to be true. He could possibly hold in his pocket something his father had never seen or even heard about. His father was an intelligent, well-traveled man who never missed an opportunity to show-up those around him, especially his son. He was forever boasting of his exotic findings and newfound knowledge. Roy felt triumphant knowing he possessed something his father had never even seen.

The next morning the rain poured again. Roy didn't want to get up. He'd only been awake a few moments when he heard Yowana outside his tent.

Yowana asked, "Bwana, you awake?"

"Yes, come inside, Yowana. You're getting soaked."

"Bwana, Masaba bad sick…very sick, big headache, no travel."

"Okay, Yowana. We'll stay here today. I didn't want to travel in the rain anyhow. Maybe Masaba will feel better tomorrow, and the rain will stop."

Roy didn't go into the tent to check on Masaba because he was afraid Masaba suffered from something contagious. He didn't want to risk catching anything that could keep him from going home in time for his son's birthday. Instead, he instructed Yowana to report to him about Masaba's condition. Late that same afternoon, Yowana told Roy that Masaba had gotten worse.

The next morning the rain had stopped. Roy hadn't heard from Yowana so he stepped out of his tent and called, "Yowana, Rupia—are you awake yet?" He didn't hear an answer and didn't see anyone around. This had never happened before—one of the natives had always remained in the camp. He tried again, "Yowana, Rupia, Okech—is anybody here?"

Again, no one answered. He looked around for anything out of the ordinary that could've caused them all to leave. He noticed the remains of a fire apparently built earlier that morning after the rain had stopped, so he knew they couldn't have been gone long. Looking around, nothing seemed unusual or out of order. Perplexed, he sat on a stool by the campfire and scratched his head. Suddenly, he heard a noise behind him. Quickly turning, he saw Yowana, Rupia, Okech, and Joni coming toward the camp.

"Where have you been?" Roy looked at Yowana with disapproval.

"Sorry, Bwana—Masaba, and Semu die in morning before sun up."

Roy asked, "Did you know Semu was sick?"

Yowana said, "Little time, he die. He have big headache."

Roy was puzzled, but he didn't tell them how afraid the sudden deaths made him. Even though he feared it was something highly contagious, he wanted to see the bodies for himself. He'd never heard of an illness killing someone so quickly. He asked Yowana, "Where are the bodies?"

Yowana said, "Nakizara tribal law, bury dead before body cold, so we help Nakizara bury bodies."

"Tell the Nakizara I'm sorry about their brothers," said Roy.

Yowana told Okech and Joni that Roy was sorry for their loss.

Okech translated, "*Asante sana.*"

Yowana didn't translate for he knew Roy understood, "Thank you."

"We need to move out as soon as possible. I want to be in Nairobi before Wednesday," said Roy. He was afraid he or one of the other natives would become ill. His urge to go home was even stronger.

That night after they made camp, Roy insisted that Yowana come into his tent and tell him the details about Masaba and Semu's deaths. "Did they appear to have a high fever or any other symptoms besides a bad headache?"

"Very hot when we bury bodies," said Yowana.

"I guess you mean they had a fever. Anything else?" asked Roy, although he couldn't be certain they had fevers since to Yowana anything that wasn't cold was described as hot.

Yowana said, "*Kutoka damu puani, tapika, kuharisha!*"

"English, Yowana! My Swahili isn't that good," scolded Roy.

Yowana translated, "Nose blood, vomit, and diarrhea."

This news troubled Roy but he didn't tell Yowana because he was worrying enough for all of them. They arrived in Nairobi Tuesday afternoon, with Roy feeling fine and all of the other natives appearing to be healthy. Roy paid Yowana and Rupia first, and then he counted out the money for Okech and Joni.

Yowana objected, "Bwana, that two moneys—I not tell them two moneys."

"I know. I'm paying them their brothers' pay, too. Please explain that to them."

His generosity came as a pleasant surprise for the Nakizara natives, and they thanked him several times.

Waving to them from the train, he felt relieved they'd arrived without any more sickness or death. As soon as he was out of their sight, he wanted to look at the mysterious fruit hidden in his knapsack, but there were too many people on the passenger car for him safely to see his prize. With the fear of one of the natives catching him with it, he had left the stolen fruit in its hiding place since the evening he'd put it there. Then, for a moment, Roy experienced a pang of guilt. In his entire life, he'd never stolen anything...but the Nakizara were burning the fruit. If he hadn't taken it, it would've been destroyed. *It isn't exactly stealing*, he thought, *or is it?*

Thinking about using the fruit to better the life of his wife and child quieted his distraught sense of right and wrong. He considered moving to a house with some acreage adjacent to the city, yet enough in the country to be a better place to raise John-George. If this fruit really was something special, he could possibly become famous for discovering it. Then, back to reality, he remembered he didn't even know if the fruit was edible or not. It could be poisonous or very bitter. The Nakizara natives said it was sweet and not poisonous, but he couldn't trust the judgment of people so superstitious.

Roy couldn't make sense out of the men eating the fruit and the women dying. Could it contain some kind of hallucinogenic, making the men crazy enough to murder the women? However, that didn't make sense either, if the men were crazy enough to kill their women, surely they would be crazy enough to kill each other, too. He contemplated—and what about Masaba and Semu? They'd slashed the bush to bits and handled the roots, limbs and fruit, but they never ate it. Yet they both died within hours of the incident. It simply didn't add up. He decided it was all an old tribal myth, passed down from generation to generation. After all, the Nakizara were an unusual tribe, unlike most others he'd encountered.

Chapter 23 | Seeds for the World

...Like a tree thriving upon a riverbank with roots reaching deep into fresh water—a tree that withstands heat and long droughts. Its leaves stay green and it keeps producing succulent fruit. JEREMIAH 17: 8

After the September greenhouse meeting, Jack and Kirk went to the ranch for lunch. While Marie fixed the food, Kirk and Jack sat at their mother's kitchen table discussing the report Quinn had given them. "I have wonderful news, Mom. We have 120,000 more ripe fruit, ready to be dehydrated and shipped all over the world!" Jack said. After a quick calculation, he added, "We'll harvest over 17 million seeds from the fruit this month alone."

"That's great!" said Marie, before adding, "What are you going to do with so many seeds?"

"We're going to sell them and make a fortune," boasted Kirk enthusiastically.

"Why are you waiting to sell them?" asked Marie.

"Mom, these are heirloom seeds, meaning that as soon as the buyers of these seeds plant them and grow their own plants and their plants produce mature fruit on them, —which takes approximately three months—they will have their own seeds. Most of the plants we buy today are hybrid plants, which means if you plant a seed from the produce harvested from the hybrid plant, it won't be the same variety as the original plant you bought," Jack explained.

Kirk continued, "You see Mom, we'll only have a little over three months to control the market—after that there'll be an abundance of seeds. Our monopoly will be short-lived."

"So how much will one of those tiny seeds be worth?" asked Marie.

"It depends on how many seeds they order, but each seed will never be priced less than ten dollars and that's the price if they buy more than 10,000 seeds at once," Jack said.

"Now you see Mom why this is so exciting. I hear the *ka-ching ka-ching* of a cash register when I think of 360,000 new blooms!"

"I'm disappointed that you seem so concerned about money, since you've always had plenty," replied Marie.

Jack tried to alleviate his mother's concerns by adding, "Mom, the seeds will make us billionaires, but the fruit will also feed a multitude of starving people. To you this may only seem like greed, but actually we're accomplishing a humanitarian endeavor."

The greenhouse project continued to prosper and by the end of September, each of the original plants added 96 new blooms and produced 864 ripe fruit.

* * * * *

The next month Marie, following her normal ritual, planned the first Friday night get-together in October as a party to celebrate Garrett's birthday. Lou arrived at the ranch a few minutes later than normal, but he was still the first to arrive from work. Roulett and Garrett were having coffee and talking when Lou walked through the clubhouse door carrying two large bottles of scotch.

Roulett mused, "Are you planning some heavy drinking tonight or what?"

Lou complained, "No, I just don't enjoy stopping at the liquor store, so I thought I'd stock up on Chivas before the price goes up for Christmas. I always need more scotch during the holidays to give me the courage to open Joyce's credit card bills. She thinks I'm made of money."

"Since you bought your own scotch, I won't know what to buy you for Christmas," griped Roulett.

Lou looked at Garrett and said, "Speaking of gifts, would you like a drink, birthday boy?"

"No, thank you, I'll stick to coffee"

Lou said, "You'd better enjoy this weekend while you can, because on Sunday you'll be fairly close to being over the hill. Are you *sure* you don't want a drink?"

Garrett looked at Lou with a big grin and said, "I guess *you* would know about being over the hill. I'll just stick with coffee."

Roulett said, "You know how much fun these so-called 'surprise' birthday parties are for Marie, so we need to tolerate them for her sake even though we think they're hokey. We're going to have another party in three weeks for Vickie."

"Well, at least I have plenty of scotch to endure them," said Lou.

"I have to endure them sober and without my husband," complained Roulett. "During the month of October, Jack and Kirk have trips scheduled all over the world to sell contracts for their precious seeds. The scheduled delivery of the first seeds is for the first week in January. Jack complained about only having a little over three months after the delivery of the first seeds to control the market, because the buyers of the seeds will be able to produce their own seed from their plants. So he and Kirk will be away from home twenty-two of October's thirty-one days."

"Before Jack left this time, he told me some interesting statistics on the rainbow fruit. At the end of last month, each original plant will have increased its production by twelve each month for seven months straight in a row, putting on 108 blooms per plant last month alone. Those 108 blooms will produce 15,552 seeds. The plants continue to grow larger—they're almost seven feet tall. Kirk and Jack were selling the plant as an annual because they thought the plant would stop production soon like a tomato plant does, but so far none have stopped producing," said Lou.

After Joyce and Olivia arrived, Lou and Joyce barely spoke to each other at the party. They were fighting a lot more than usual because Lou was more concerned with Roulett than he was with Joyce.

* * * * *

All that month, with Jack away from home so much, Roulett was champing at the bit to kiss Garrett, but it hadn't been a good month for her to find time alone with him. Olivia was in her eighth month of pregnancy, and it had been a dangerous month for her because she had symptoms of an early delivery several times.

Chapter 24 | The Kiss

His mouth is wonderful to kiss—I am enchanted by everything about him... THE SONG OF SOLOMON 5: 16

The next Wednesday, Marie harvested so much fruit from her four rainbow fruit plants that she decided to make jelly. She was desperately trying to find uses for her quarter of the original rainbow plants' production for the month of October. Sam loved it with the homemade brown bread, which Marie also made with rainbow fruit puree, but making bread couldn't use all of her continuous supply of fruit. She made forty-eight pints of jelly. Afterward, she called Kirk to tell him that she could no longer use her entire supply of fruit each month since her freezer was full, she had three gallons of syrup, and enough jelly to last a year.

Nine days later, Marie invited Vickie and Paul to the weekly Friday night ranch get-together. Jack went out of town with Kirk, selling contracts for rainbow fruit seeds. Garrett stayed longer than normal since his mother-in-law was staying with Olivia until the baby arrived.

Marie gave Vickie two jars of jelly and said, "I made this about a week ago, and I want you to have some. It's really delicious."

"Thank you, it's beautiful jelly. What flavor is it?" asked Vickie.

"I made it from rainbow fruit. My plants are producing so much now that I'm trying to find new ways to use them. I really hate to waste anything."

"That jelly is great on homemade bread. I really like it, so I think you will," said Sam.

"I had some this morning on toast and I was surprised how good it was, considering a tablespoon of that jelly has your daily vitamin and minerals in it plus antioxidants," Lou added.

"They should hire you to sell the jelly," Paul said.

Marie asked Vickie and Paul, "Would you like to try the rainbow tea?"

"Sure," said Vickie, before Paul could answer. Marie carried a tray with a teapot, cups, spoons, cream, and sugar over from the clubhouse's center island. She poured them steaming cups of rainbow tea.

Vickie put the cup of steaming tea up to her lips to take a sip. She yelped, "Wow, how do you get past the smell?"

"It tastes better than it smells," Marie claimed.

"That's her opinion—I think the stinky stuff smells too nasty to drink," grumbled Sam.

"You don't know—you've never even tasted it," griped Marie.

"I'm afraid I'm going to agree with Sam. I'm sorry Marie, but I don't want to taste this nasty-smelling concoction, either," declined Paul.

"This tea has to have health benefits or my father and grandfather wouldn't have consumed so much of it," Marie said.

"I believe you, Marie, so I'll take a cup. I'll probably outlive the whole bunch of you simply because I'm willing to drink the tea," Lou claimed.

"None for me," Garrett said.

Marie asked, "Garrett, when is your baby due?"

"The doctor said any day now. She's hoping on her birthday, the 28th, but as miserable as she is, I don't think that she'd mind delivering before then."

"Wow, that's only four days away! Do you think we should have a birthday party for her at the ranch?"

"I don't think so—she's too miserable to enjoy a party. In fact we're both too miserable to enjoy it."

"Why are you too miserable to enjoy a party? You're not pregnant!"

"My mother-in-law is staying with us and will be here until the baby is about a month old," Garrett explained.

"I was wondering why you're here tonight with your baby due any time," Marie said.

"Believe me, they'll call if her labor starts…"

*****

On the next Tuesday, Marie and Roulett went to Garrett and Olivia's house to take her a birthday present and wish her well. They met Olivia's mother, Kathy, when she answered the door. Olivia waddled out of the bedroom to greet them, immediately telling them she'd been at the doctor's that morning, and he didn't think it would be today. She gingerly sat in a large recliner and looked at her presents. She opened Roulett's first because it was the smallest. The beautifully wrapped box contained a bottle of expensive perfume. Olivia liked the perfume, but she didn't know Roulett had an ulterior motive for her gift. She had given Olivia the same perfume that she wore so that when she kissed Garrett, Olivia wouldn't notice a strange perfume on him.

* * * * *

The first Friday night get-together in December, Jack and Kirk were only home for one night, but they were celebrating that the original fruit had added 120 new blooms and produced 1152 ripe fruit. Roulett was not pleased with the news. Jack boasted that the fruit was the most prolific of any known plant.

* * * * *

On Saturday, December 2nd, Olivia gave birth to a 7 lb. 10 oz. baby girl. Both Olivia and Garrett were delighted with their new baby and they named her Nicole.

* * * * *

Five days later while Quinn was working at the greenhouse, he received a phone call from the hospital notifying him that his wife, Donna, was en route to Petrolia's emergency room—hemorrhaging profusely from an apparent miscarriage. Donna received two units of O-negative on the way to the hospital but had bled more than she'd received. Her doctor needed Quinn's permission to do an emergency hysterectomy.

Quinn rushed to the hospital and paced as he waited to hear from the surgeon. When the doctor finally emerged from the operating room, Quinn knew the unthinkable had happened—Donna had died on the operating table. Her doctor couldn't explain why her uterus had bled internally and externally, causing her sudden death.

Four days later, the entire families of Clayton and Barnes joined the Jordan family to mourn the loss of their loved one. Roulett sat with Hollie who took the sudden death of her sister-in-law very hard. As Hollie cried, she told Roulett how Donna had always been like a sister to her and how Hollie couldn't comprehend Quinn surviving without her.

They all met at Harvey's house for a meal furnished by Donna and Quinn's church. Many were concerned how Quinn would care for three children without his wife. Hollie volunteered to watch the children while Quinn was at work. He agreed to it, only if he could pay her. Marie took Jack and Kirk aside insisting they increase Quinn's salary so he could afford the unexpected childcare expense. They agreed, not wanting anything to upset their greenhouse project, which prospered with 480,000 ripe fruit and 727,000 new blooms.

* * * * *

On Thursday, December 14th, it rained all day, not hard but steadily. The temperature wasn't cold enough to freeze and the wind chill made it feel like ten degrees instead of thirty-eight degrees. Roulett and the children arrived at the ranch at their normal time.

Earlier that afternoon, Marie called Roulett, requesting that they come by even though the weather was too bad for the children to ride their horses. Roulett and the children went directly into the house instead of the barn. Marie asked, "I guess you'd like to know why I wanted you here on an afternoon like this?"

"Yes, I did wonder why. It's a miserable day," Roulett replied.

Marie said, "We want to take the children to the mall in Tulsa so they can buy their Christmas presents for you and Jack. We promised them a week ago that we'd go one day this week. We'll eat out so we should be back about 9:00 p.m. Do you mind staying here to watch the ranch while we're gone?"

"I don't mind. With Jack out of town, I don't have anything better to do. You all go and have a good time, but be careful," cautioned Roulett.

"It's not supposed to freeze tonight," Marie said.

Sam added, "When you see Garrett, tell him where we've gone and tell him that he can go home early. It's too cold to work outside. We'll pay him for a full day."

Roulett said, "Okay." She realized that her opportunity to be alone with Garrett had finally arrived. She had waited so long. She tried to think if anyone could interfere with her plans. Lou and Joyce were leaving town for a four-day trip to Virginia. Jack and Kirk were gone and Sam and Marie would be in Tulsa, which left the coast clear. She kissed the children goodbye and said, "You be good for your grandma and grandpa."

"Maybe the mall won't be too crowded because of the bad weather," Sam said.

Roulett added, "This close to Christmas, the mall will probably be a madhouse."

Roulett was so nervous about kissing Garrett that her hands began to tremble as she walked to the clubhouse. She made a pot of coffee since it was time for Garrett's break and she was certain he'd like a fresh, hot cup.

She thought that a drink might help stop her nervous shaky feeling. No, she couldn't do that. She'd managed her sobriety for over six months—and kissing Garrett was her reward! Feeling intense trepidation for a brief moment, she wished the 'kissing thing' were over. She stopped, trying to remind herself that this was a moment she'd dreamed about, planned, and desired for almost a year. Why was she dreading it so much? Was she really more apprehensive about *kissing* him or *telling* him? She rationalized that this kiss could be a life-changing situation, which caused her great fear. As she thought about her fears, they seemed to multiply. She worried about being rejected and about him responding favorably. Fear or not, she wanted her kiss, rationalizing that she deserved it.

Trying hard to relax and be ready to enjoy the moment, she looked in the refrigerator for something to snack on, thinking that eating something would relieve her shakes. She looked first in the freezer where she found frozen pizza breads—no, she didn't want garlic breath.

She looked in the refrigerator but only found sodas plus small cans of fruit: peaches, pears, pineapple, and fruit cocktail. She decided to have a can of peaches. She pulled the tab on the can before getting a spoon, remembering when this would've been a peach daiquiri. She'd taken three bites when Garrett came in the door.

He stuck his head through the doorway between the mudroom and the clubhouse to see if anyone was there. He said to her, "I'll be in there in just a few minutes. I have to take off my wet coat and wash my hands."

A lump in her throat kept her from eating the peaches as she waited.

He finally came in and said, "I'm surprised to see you here today. Where is everyone?"

"Sam and Marie took Tammy and Michael to Tulsa to shop for Christmas."

"Why on a day like this?"

"Sam thought it wouldn't be as busy. Oh, coffee will be ready in a few minutes," she said, almost trembling with anticipation.

"That sounds good. It's really cold."

"Sam said you could go home early if you want to. He'll still pay you for a full day."

"Are you going to wait until they come back?"

"Marie asked me to watch the ranch while they're gone, so I'll be here until at least nine or maybe longer."

"I probably won't accomplish any more work, but I'm not in a hurry to leave either. It'll take me at least an hour to warm up enough to even think about going out in the cold again, even if it's to go home."

"Marie said it's not supposed to freeze tonight."

"You can't believe everything those weathermen say. The coffee is ready. Do you want me to pour you a cup? It's just me, you, and the coffee today."

She blurted, "Just me, you, the coffee, and the mistletoe."

He looked at the mistletoe hanging above the clubhouse doorway. Then he looked back at the wicked little grin on her face. Obviously trying to avoid the subject, he said, "Boy, this coffee's hot. Did you say you want a cup?"

Her heart pounded, as she continued, "No, thank you. Did you hear what I said about the mistletoe?"

"Yes, but I think it's safer to avoid the mistletoe subject now," he said sternly.

"Lou and Hollie think we have a thing for each other."

"Why do they think that?" This time he was the one with a wicked little grin.

"Maybe because, from the first moment we met, you've followed me around like a little lost puppy dog. You always manage to be on my side of the room, and today, you decided to stay because I'm staying."

"That only proves I like your company. And besides, I'm not the one who brought up the mistletoe," Garrett replied defensively.

"The reason I mentioned the mistletoe was that I've wanted to kiss you from the very first moment we met, and that feeling has continued right up until now."

His eyes opened wide as he looked at her. He was overwhelmed. "I'm not sure we should travel down that road. I think I should go home after I finish my coffee and we should think about this first. We have other people's feelings to consider, not just ours." He spoke with sternness in his voice as though empowered for the first time.

Nevertheless, she took the power back. "You can go home after I kiss you, if you still want to..."

While gripping his coffee cup as if it would run away, he asked, "Why have you waited so long to tell me this?"

"We needed to be alone."

"We've been alone lots of times."

"Not like this...we have plenty of time...not just minutes."

"How long did you plan this kiss to last?" he asked, smiling, with both anticipation and fear in his voice. He was standing in front of the fake fireplace, as if it produced heat.

She started walking toward him as she said, "I guess we'll have to find out."

Before she reached him, he asked, "Is that all, just a kiss?"

She stopped and thought for a moment. She hadn't considered beyond a kiss. She answered, "That's all for now." Taking the coffee cup from him, she sat it on the table. He didn't resist any more. They embraced and shared a very passionate kiss. Because of his initial resistance, his obvious enthusiasm amazed her. For someone who thought this wasn't a good idea, he certainly seemed to be enjoying it! Roulett couldn't remember ever being kissed so passionately.

After their second kiss, she said, "If I'd have known your response would've been this good, I'd have kissed you sooner." He didn't say anything—he only kissed her again.

He then pulled back from their embrace and said, "Wait a minute, we were alone in the loft the night that we waited for Jill to give birth. Why didn't you tell me then?"

"I guess I just didn't feel it was the right time."

At that moment, they heard the door to the mudroom open and close as someone called, "Is anybody in here?"

Recognizing Lou's voice, Roulett whispered to Garrett, "It's Lou! He's supposed to be on an airplane to Virginia."

Garrett panicked but managed to wipe Roulett's lipstick off his lips.

Lou walked in the door and yelled, "Where's everyone?" He poured himself a scotch-and-water as he observed Roulett and Garrett acting like children caught with their hands in the cookie jar, appearing to have guilt written all over their faces.

Roulett said, "Sam and Marie have taken my children to Tulsa to do their Christmas shopping. I thought you were leaving for Virginia today."

"I had an emergency at work and, with Jack not here, I had to handle it myself. Joyce went on without me and I'll leave Saturday morning—no Friday night flights were available."

"I'm sorry your plans had to change," said Roulett.

Lou sat by Roulett and said, "That's all right. I kinda' like being here with you two." Looking at Roulett with a smile on his round boyish face, he said, "So what have you two been up to?"

"Nothing," said Roulett, "Simply trying to warm up."

"It's terrible out there—but you two look like you've done a good job of warming up," mocked Lou.

Garrett drank the last of his cup of coffee and said, "I think that I'm warm enough to face the cold, so I'm going home now. I'll see you later."

Lou asked, "How're Olivia and your new baby?"

"They're both fine. Olivia is tired because of the night feedings. Otherwise, everything's fine."

"I remember how much attention a newborn needs. It can make a new father feel neglected."

Garrett nodded and said, "Good night, I'll see you two tomorrow."

"Be careful going home," said Roulett.

"I will," he said, while trying not to make eye contact.

Lou and Roulett were silent for a few minutes after Garrett left. Roulett was afraid that Lou knew about the kisses and that if she tried to carry on a conversation, she too would arm him with more information.

Lou felt the tension in the room. "I think I better go home, too. Before I go, I want to remind you of an old saying."

Roulett asked, "What's that?"

"'While the cat is away, the mouse will play.' You may fool the cat but you don't fool me," he said as he walked out the door.

*****

At the next week's Friday night get-together, Garrett and Roulett were making eyes at each other and sending out little coded messages. He grew nervous when he suspected Lou knew about them, so Garrett went home earlier than normal. Then, Roulett was upset Garrett had left early, so she sulked the rest of the evening. Since Lou had noticed them flirting, he warned her to cool it or soon everyone would be wise to them!

*****

The next day, Roulett awoke knowing she had to pick up Jack at the airport and attend Sam and Marie's Christmas party later that evening. She wondered how she'd react to him after she'd kissed Garrett, the love of her life! How could she let Jack's lips touch hers again? She waited for Jack's plane to land, nervously pacing and trying to wipe the guilt off her face. His plane finally landed and she saw him walking toward her. As he gently kissed her, she wondered if Garrett felt the same way when he kissed Olivia.

Chapter 25 | The Bad & the Good

One day there will be an abundance of crops—the harvest will scarcely end before the next crop begins to grow... AMOS 9:13

Marie chose the last Saturday before Christmas, which was the day before Christmas Eve, to host the annual Christmas party. Since Roulett had to spend time with Kirk, she was miserable until Garrett arrived. She was happy to see him even though he was with Olivia, her mother, and their new baby. The large crowd included Sam's sister Vickie and her husband Paul; Hollie and her boyfriend Bill; Lou, Joyce, and their two boys; Dorothy and her son Charles; Hollie's brother Quinn, their father Harvey, and Quinn's three children; Kirk, Pam, and their daughter Alyssa; and Jack, Roulett, and their two children. Betty watched all the children in the house while the adults celebrated in the clubhouse.

Joyce and Quinn showed an immediate interest in each other, but Lou was so busy monitoring Roulett and Garrett that he didn't notice his wife flirting with another man.

Kirk and Jack were talking about the trucks scheduled to pick up the rainbow fruit seeds on January 3rd. Famine Free Future had obtained sales contracts for rainbow fruit seeds all over the world because of Jack and Kirk's exhaustive efforts.

Joyce said, "I would like to see one of the fruits that everyone has been talking about."

"I can't believe you haven't seen one yet," said Lou with amazement. He didn't want to leave Roulett in the same room with Garrett without his supervision, so he waited for another volunteer to show her.

"I'll show you one. It'll be easier for me, because I already have the keys. Besides, I like someone showing an interest in my work," said Quinn.

Quinn and Joyce were hoping to go alone, so they both were pleased when nobody else showed any interest in accompanying them. The greenhouses weren't interesting anymore to everybody else.

On the way to the greenhouse, Quinn asked, "Am I receiving the vibes from you that I think I'm receiving?"

Joyce said coyly, "That depends on what vibes you're receiving."

"I don't want you to slap me, but I'm getting the feeling that you're hitting on me," said Quinn cautiously.

"Yeah, and I'm getting the feeling you're putting the moves on me, too," said Joyce, realizing they were at the door of the first greenhouse.

Quinn inserted the cardkey, the red light turned green and a computer voice asked for his right thumbprint for verification on the small screen. Quinn followed the computer's instructions and the mechanized voice said, "Thank you, Mr. Jordan," while the other light turned green and the door unlocked. He opened the door for Joyce and politely said, "Ladies first."

Joyce immediately was overwhelmed by the amount of plants inside. "Wow! What a jungle."

"You need to decide if you want me to kiss you, or are you here just to see fruit?"

"I didn't come all the way out here just to stare at the vegetation!"

Quinn moved closer and hugged her before he kissed her. His six-foot height towered over her petite frame. He stopped after the second kiss and said, "As much as I'd like to continue, we can only sample the good stuff now—we can't go further. This is where I work, you know, sweet thing."

"Maybe we can meet one day soon for lunch?"

"That'll work for me. Just call. We'd better not stay too long in here, or someone will become suspicious," cautioned Quinn before adding, "You really better look at the fruit because you may be asked what you thought about it."

Joyce was surprised at how colorful it was. "They are so beautiful. They look almost like Christmas trees or like fig trees with Christmas ornaments on them," she said.

When Quinn and Joyce returned from the greenhouse, Kirk asked, "What did you think about the fruit?"

Quinn smiled at her, as she replied, "They're beautiful."

Before everyone left the party that night, Sam and Marie invited everybody to their New Year's Eve Party. The same crowd who attended the Christmas party came for New Year's, too, with the exception of Garrett and Olivia because her father had joined her mother and they both were staying in town until after the first of the year. As usual, the majority of guests opted to stay at the ranch, since Sam and Marie had plenty of room.

The evening was uneventful, lacking the excitement of the Christmas party. A few sparks came from Quinn and Joyce who hadn't managed their rendezvous yet.

Again, the main topic of conversation that night was the fruit, as Jack revealed that the original fruit had put on 122 blooms and produced a total of 1296 ripe fruit. Roulett found all discussion of the fruit boring, plus she missed Garrett and yearned for a stiff drink. Jack and Roulett didn't stay overnight because she was sober and capable of driving them home.

* * * * *

That same week, Roulett met Hollie for lunch. Roulett contained her eagerness, waiting until after they were seated and had ordered their food before she blurted, "I did it!"

Hollie was stirring the sugar in her iced tea as she asked, "You did *what?*"

"I kissed Garrett," whispered Roulett.

"You did what?" exclaimed Hollie in a voice that everyone in the restaurant could hear.

"Not so loud!"

"I'm sorry, but you shocked me..."

"I told you I was going to kiss him."

"I know, but I didn't really think you had the nerve to do it."

"Well, I did!"

Although Hollie had strongly disapproved of Roulett kissing Garrett, she couldn't wait to hear all the juicy details as she tenaciously asked, "Tell me what happened. When did you kiss him? How did he react?"

"We were alone at the ranch clubhouse when I told him that it was just me, him, the coffee, and the mistletoe. He objected at first, trying his best to avoid the subject. But I was determined to kiss him. And it was worth it—I've never been kissed so passionately!"

"So I guess this means that you're not going to rid your system of him as you'd hoped kissing him would do."

"I think you're right about that."

"When did this happen? Is that all, just a kiss?"

"That's strange that you used the same phrase that Garrett did before I kissed him. He asked me if that was all, just a kiss. I think he was wondering if he was going to get laid or not."

"Maybe you're reading more into it than was there because you said he objected at first. Maybe he's just like the rest of us and he had holes in his underwear that he didn't want you to see."

"I never thought of that, but you're right. I wear my underwear until they fall apart."

"Now that you've tasted the forbidden fruit, will you continue eating until you're thrown out of paradise?" asked Hollie.

Roulett thought deeply about Hollie's provocative question. Finally, she said, "I don't know."

* * * * *

That evening at home, Jack failed to see Roulett's agitation for he was too busy telling her that the original fruit had 1296 ripe fruit and 144 new blooms on each. He also reminded her that the fruit had increased in increments of 12 for the past 12 months.

She was not impressed.

Chapter 26 | The Market

When there are many years, the price will be high, but when there are only a few years, the price will lower... LEVITICUS 25: 16

On the next Wednesday, mid-afternoon, Roulett arrived at the ranch while the rainbow fruit seeds were being loaded into four Cowboy Trucking Lines semi's with different colored horses on each one: palomino bucking-bronco; sorrel calf-roping horse; gray-white bulldogging horse; and a black cattle-cutting horse. While Roulett watched, the truck drivers prepared to transport the seeds to four different airports, two to the East Coast, and two to the West Coast. The seeds would reach their final destination to all parts of the world via cargo ships. An ominous feeling overcame her as she watched the trucks leave. Jack had boasted many times that just six shipments would distribute almost two billion seeds worldwide. Shaking off her bad feelings, she realized that Garrett was gone for the day. She wanted desperately to talk to him; but he was avoiding her.

That same night Roulett had another nightmare: She saw a large group of people, predominately women, waiting in a very long line—so long that Roulett couldn't see either end. Everyone wore long bulky white robes tied in the middle with cumbersome gold ropes. They were groaning and wringing their hands. The sky was full of greenish black clouds, and it thundered loudly. Then, big bolts of red-orange lightning flashed violently while the rain poured in heavy sheets.

Soon, everyone was soaked to the skin. In addition, Roulett could hear screams that were too far away to know where they originated. The rainwater suddenly became blood and everyone was drenched in it. They held their ears while the thunder boomed loudly. Why was there so much blood and thunder? By then, the road that they were traveling held blood about a foot deep. Their gold ropes turned into large dark snakes with green eyes, while the people turned into rotting corpses guarded by big black rottweiler dogs with red eyes.

Again, Roulett awoke from her nightmare in a cold sweat, trembling with fear.

* * * * *

Weeks later on an exceptionally warm February day, Joyce called Quinn, arranging a time that they both could be absent from work. They met at Clayton Park and Quinn took her to an abandoned, dilapidated shack hidden in a thicket—completely lacking any romantic ambiance. However, he attempted to make it tolerable by spreading a blanket over the dirty, insect-infested plank floors.

"I know, sweet thing, that this place doesn't look like much, but it's actually an historical landmark that very few people know about," Quinn said.

She looked around. "Are you sure? It doesn't look like any landmark that I've ever seen…"

"I'm telling you the truth. This is where John-George Clayton first lived when he moved to Oklahoma from New York."

"I would never have guessed John-George Clayton ever stayed in a place like this."

Purposely mixing his words, he replied, "It just shows to go you that he wasn't always rich."

Although Joyce was not impressed by the surroundings, they proceeded to enjoy a "quickie" on the blanket. Afterward, he offered her one of the two greasy cheeseburgers he'd brought for lunch. Even under these less-than-perfect circumstances, her conscience didn't bother her because she'd already had several extra-martial affairs.

She felt some cramps shortly after she returned to work, which surprised her because her period wasn't due for a week. About thirty minutes later, she noticed a trickle of blood, which didn't alarm her, thinking she'd just started her period early.

After another fifteen minutes passed, she was cramping so severely that she had to go home, take some pain medication and go to bed. Within a few minutes, the pain medication began to work, and her cramps felt better. She thought how she really was paying for her two minutes of illicit, wild, passionate lovemaking with Quinn! She was feeling no pain, but bleeding profusely by three o'clock. At four, she tried to get out of bed to get a drink but was too weak. By five o'clock, the bed was soaked with her blood.

When Lou returned from work shortly after five, he found her so weak that she was fading in and out of consciousness. He quickly used his cell phone to call 911, screaming at the operator, "My wife needs an ambulance now! She's dying! Hurry!"

"Calm down and tell me your name and address," said the 911 operator.

"My name's Lou Gordon and my address is 742 South Walnut Street. My wife is dying!"

"I have an ambulance and the police on their way, Mr. Gordon, but don't hang up. Do you know what's wrong with your wife?"

"No. The bed is covered with blood. I think she's bleeding to death."

"Is she still breathing?"

"Barely."

"She could be in shock due to blood loss. You need to elevate her feet."

As Lou was doing so, Joyce mumbled the word, "Water."

"I elevated her feet, and she asked for water. Should I give it to her?"

"Yes, it's okay to give her water."

"She feels extremely cold," said Lou.

"Cover her with blankets. You need to keep her warm."

"Okay."

"Can you tell what's causing the bleeding?"

"No, I don't know…"

"Is there any sign of an intruder or a burglary? Could she have a stab wound or a bullet wound?"

"When I found her, I didn't look around. Everything looked fine when I came in the house," Lou said as he tried to find the source of the blood. "There's no apparent wound, but there's blood all over the bed. I think that the blood is coming from inside."

The operator asked, "Why do you think that?"

"Because when I removed her panties I found a soaked sanitary pad," said Lou.

"Do you know if she was pregnant?"

"I don't think so. I hear the ambulance now."

"Let them in and they'll take over."

Lou hung up and ran downstairs. The paramedics rushed upstairs, checked her vitals quickly, and took Joyce out on a stretcher.

"Is she going to be all right?" Lou asked.

"All we can tell you now is she's still alive, but it doesn't look good," said the older paramedic as they loaded her in the ambulance.

Lou asked, "Can I ride with her?"

"Sure, but hurry and let us do what we need to do to try to save your wife," said the younger paramedic. Lou climbed in and tried to stay out of their way.

The older paramedic asked, "Do you know her blood type?"

"No, I don't remember," said Lou while thinking he should know his wife's blood type, feeling inadequate as her husband.

"Let's give her two units of O-negative, than we'll check her type when we arrive at the hospital," said the younger paramedic. Suddenly Joyce's blood pressure fell and her heart stopped.

The younger paramedic put the paddles on her chest and yelled, "Clear."

One shock and her heart started beating again. The younger paramedic said, "Hang in there, girl. Hand me a bag of Plasmatein and an eighteen-gauge needle. I'll put this on the other side." After a few minutes, her heart stopped again. They tried shocking her several times, but it didn't work. She was dead by the time they reached the hospital and in spite of their best efforts, the ER team couldn't revive her.

* * * * *

The next morning, Lou called Pam at work. He asked, "Will you do the autopsy on Joyce? I would feel so much better if you did it."

"Of course, I will. I want you to know I'm so sorry about her sudden death. Please let Kirk and I know if there's anything we can do for you."

"Thanks. How long will the autopsy take?"

"I'll start on it this afternoon and I'll make sure I'm through by late Wednesday afternoon. You can plan her funeral any day after Wednesday."

On Wednesday afternoon, Pam called Lou at work. "Could you come by my office at four today?" she asked.

Lou said, "Yes. Do you have the autopsy results?"

"Yes, we'll discuss them when we meet this afternoon. Why are you working today? I think you should have some time off, after all you've gone through."

"I tried staying at home but I feel better working. It takes my mind off Joyce. I'll see you at four."

When Lou arrived, her secretary showed him to Pam's office and said, "Have a seat, Mr. Gordon. Dr. Barnes will be here in a few minutes. Can I offer you something to drink?"

"No, thank you," replied Lou. He sat on one of the hunter-green leather chairs and read the plaque on her desk, "Pamela Barnes, MD, Medical Examiner." He thought how cheerful her office was for her to deal with the grim reality of forensic pathology. He wondered how many other people had thought the same thing while waiting to hear their loved one's cause of death.

Lou knew it took a special person to do Pam's work. Doctors whose patients are alive experience the reward of saving lives or at least trying their best to do so. But what reward is there in working with the dead? He couldn't think of a more difficult task than to cut up a dead body to harvest tissue samples for analysis, although it was certainly a job that needed to be done.

Pam entered her office carrying a chart. She said, "Again, Lou, I want to say how sorry I am for your loss."

"Thank you," he replied.

"I'll try to make this as brief as possible. The cause of your wife's death was massive uterine bleeding causing exsanguination. I haven't diagnosed the cause of the bleeding yet. I need to know if Joyce could have had an abortion recently."

"I don't think that's possible. I had a vasectomy more than ten years ago."

"That would explain the seminal fluid without active sperm."

Lou thought for a moment before he said, "But we hadn't been intimate for at least ten days, maybe longer."

Pam looked disturbed. "I'm sorry to have to add insult to injury, but your wife experienced sexual intercourse with somebody in the last twelve hours before her death. I mistakenly assumed it was you. Again, I'm sorry."

"Do you have any idea what caused the bleeding?"

"I can't explain it. My primary focus was a botched abortion, but that would've had to be weeks ago because her progesterone and estriol tests showed that she wasn't pregnant near the time of her death. I've seen two similar cases in the last few months. I'm going to fax my finding to the Center for Disease Control in Atlanta and to the Department of Public Health to see if they have any similar cases on record."

"Thanks, Pam, for doing this for me. Would you do one more thing?"

"Sure, if I can."

"Would you mind keeping the part about her being unfaithful a secret?"

"Of course. All my findings are confidential."

As Lou left the building, he blamed himself for Joyce's death, certain it was somehow because of his romantic encounter with Roulett in the loft and his resulting preoccupation with her.

Lou tried scheduling Joyce's funeral on Thursday, but he couldn't find a coffin for her until Friday, since all the local funeral homes' supply had been depleted by the past months higher than normal death rate. Friday was a damp and dreary day—

appropriate for a funeral. Although the majority of people who attended her funeral didn't love Joyce, everyone there felt compassion for her loved ones—Lou, her sons, her mother and father, and her brother Garrett.

* * * * *

Two weeks later at the Friday night get-together, Roulett was almost bored to tears as she listened to Jack and Lou's conversation.

"Kirk and I are a little disappointed about the original fruit ceasing blooming after its 12 months of continually increasing by 12 each month, but the plants are still thriving. They seem to be experiencing a growth spurt and we still have 1584 fruit that will ripen soon, with an additional 1728 that will ripen by the end of next month...

* * * * *

Less than two weeks later, Sam was rushed to the hospital complaining of a severe headache. During one of her frequent nighttime bathroom trips, Marie had found him moaning in pain. He slipped into unconsciousness en route to the hospital. The ER doctor told Marie that he thought Sam may have had a stroke.

Vickie and Paul rushed to the hospital to be with Marie after they received the news of Sam's condition. Shortly before dawn, Sam died without regaining consciousness. Pam didn't perform an autopsy on Sam because she considered his death was from natural causes.

Marie was traditionally old-fashioned, normally wearing her black dress to funerals. Since she'd recently attended two other funerals wearing it, she changed to her navy suit to honor Sam.

While she waited for the family car to arrive, she thought how disappointed she was that her father hadn't lived to see her fulfill her "until death do we part" wedding vows with Sam. This fulfillment had taken over forty-four years of her life, but she'd won. She'd finally beaten her powerful father who'd played God with her life, sentencing her to a life of his choosing and she'd served her sentence in silence to protect her family's inheritance.

The victory was hers, but it was an empty victory because of the enormous number of years she'd invested to win.

Chapter 27 | Close Call

Another man's wife may have lips as sweet as honey and kisses as smooth as olive oil, but... PROVERBS 5: 3

Roulett rushed to answer the phone before she left to pick up her children from school.

Marie asked, "Are you coming by the ranch today?"

"I'll be there," Roulett replied. Even though it was Friday, she wasn't excited about going to the ranch since Garrett kept avoiding her.

"The head of the nursing home called a few minutes ago to tell me she'd called an ambulance for Dorothy since she's having trouble breathing. I need to go be with her, but my overdue pregnant mare, Moon, is waxing. She could be showing minor symptoms of labor. I would appreciate it if you'd stay and watch her until I'm back, if you have time."

"Sure, I don't mind. With Jack traveling with Kirk all over the world, I have plenty of time on my hands. I should be used to him being gone by now, but I still don't like it. Just let me know how Dorothy is doing when you get a chance."

"I'll let you know as soon as I find out, and thanks for doing this for me," said Marie.

"Sure, no problem," replied Roulett, who suddenly realized she could possibly be alone with Garrett. She barely had enough time to change into a denim blouse that snapped down the front, no bra, a long denim skirt, thigh-high black stockings, garter belt, and black crotch-less panties. Because the weather was cold, she put on socks over her stockings before she put on soft black ostrich quill boots. Marie met Roulett and the children as they were exiting their car. Marie said that Garrett was watching the mare now and Betty would watch the children.

Marie asked, "I guess you were wondering why I didn't simply ask Betty to watch the mare?"

"Well, yes..."

"I tried asking her before I called you, but she screeched...she *didn't know nothing about birthing no horses*," said Marie, as they both chuckled.

Since it was too cold for Michael and Tammy to ride their horses, Roulett took the children directly inside the house where Betty was waiting for them.

"I'll be in the barn loft watching room if you need me. I'll spend the night there if I don't call you by nine. I'm going to watch Moon until she foals or until I fall asleep from boredom because 'I'm experienced at birthing horses,'" teased Roulett, smiling.

"Better you than me. I'll have the children in bed by nine, if I haven't heard from you."

Roulett picked up a couple of sodas from the refrigerator as she walked through the clubhouse and carried them to the loft. She sat on the sofa beside Garrett, not sure if he'd be pleased to see her or not. "Marie's gone and she probably won't be back for hours. How's the mare doing?" Before she gave him time to answer, she asked, "Does it look like she's close to time?"

"I can't see any symptoms other than she's waxing. We know from past experience the birth could be soon or days from now," he said, staring at the mare as if she was going to run away.

He doesn't even want to make eye contact, Roulett thought. "Do you think Marie was exaggerating the mare's symptoms?"

"Isn't it exactly like a woman to overreact in any situation?" he asked, finally looking at her and smiling.

"I'll show you a *woman overreacting*!" She stood and climbed on his lap facing him, glad she'd worn a dress and crotchless panties in case they found time alone.

He asked, "Where are your kids?"

"They're inside, watching movies with Betty. I told Betty to call me if she needed me," answered Roulett.

Garrett asked, "Where's Jack?"

"He's out of town. He won't be back until Wednesday. We're alone again."

"You thought we were alone the last time, but we were almost caught. Where is Lou? He seems to watch you closer than your husband."

"Lou normally doesn't come on Thursdays because he'll be here tomorrow night. But, if he happens to drop by tonight, it should be after five—and that's almost an hour away. We shouldn't be caught this time. I want to make love to you."

He put his arms around her and embraced her as he said, "If you're positive we won't be interrupted. I want this just as much as you do—but I don't want to be caught in the act."

"I don't think anyone will catch us this time. We'll hear the bell on the door if anyone comes in—we've got the intercom to monitor the clubhouse."

He kissed her very passionately and stood, carrying her to the tall table close to the stairs leading to the clubhouse. He sat her on the table only a little shorter than a countertop and right next to the intercom, not wanting the heat of the moment to keep him from hearing if someone came into the clubhouse.

She spread her legs so he saw her garter belt, hose and crotchless panties. He exclaimed, "Wow! You are serious about this," while moving his hand up her thigh.

"I wanted to make it easy and exciting for you," she said playfully.

"Actually, you are making it hard for me." He unsnapped her blouse and saw that she wasn't wearing a bra. She had beautiful firm breasts that looked like the breasts of an eighteen-year-old girl. As he felt them, he said, "These are really beautiful!"

"Would you believe that I grew them just for you?"

"No, but it sounds good," he said, smiling with delight. She unzipped his jeans and felt his erect penis still inside his jockey-type underwear. He unbuttoned the top of his jeans and pulled down his underwear so he could feel her hand on his bare skin. She was gently rubbing his engorged penis when he cautioned her, "As much as I like that, you better stop rubbing or it'll all be over before we start."

She charmed him by adding, "Are you trying to say you're like a steaming volcano ready to erupt?"

"That's right and you'll have lava all over your hand if you keep rubbing," he said. They both chuckled as she put her arms around his neck and kissed him, while pulling him closer. With her crotchless panties, he was only seconds away from penetration when at the most inopportune time they heard the little bell on the front door of the clubhouse.

"You're going to get me killed," said Garrett.

Roulett snapped her blouse as she whispered, "I'll see who it is."

"I bet I can *guess* who it is!" grumbled Garrett with a tone that showed his frustration from their interruption.

Lou yelled from the clubhouse, "Anybody here?"

Roulett replied as she came down the stairs, "We're up in the loft watching Marie's mare, Moon—she's showing foaling symptoms."

"Who's with you?" asked Lou.

"Garrett," she said, trying to look innocent.

He rolled his eyes, and then suddenly, provocatively pinched one of her erect nipples easily seen through her denim shirt, committing the brazen indiscretion based on her compromised situation. He said, "You're playing with fire and your life could go up in smoke."

Shocked by his forwardness, she jerked back as she said, "I don't know what you're talking about. We're only watching Moon."

He said, "Let's go see how the mare's doing."

Garrett was sitting on the couch trying to look calm with a pillow in his lap to cover his aroused state, but it was obvious that he didn't fool Lou.

Lou asked, "When will Jack be back from Africa?"

Roulett answered quickly, trying not to appear nervous, "He's supposed to return on Wednesday. Why…is there a problem?"

Lou took another drink before solemnly answering, "One of the girls from work was rushed to the hospital in hemorrhagic shock. She died less than twenty minutes after her arrival. I followed the ambulance to the hospital, and just left there—so I stopped here to have a drink, which I really needed after all that blood. It was too close to what happened with Joyce."

"Who was the girl?" asked Roulett.

With a worried look on his face, he said, "Sandra Evans. She dated Larry Stevenson, Vickie and Paul's son. Don't you think it's strange how so many people have died recently from hemorrhaging?"

She thought for a moment, then said, "Three women since December…" She remembered her dreams about the women and the blood, but decided not to share the details with them.

"All of them had some connection to the greenhouse or to the Center, in one way or another."

"I need to talk to Jack about this when he returns from Africa," Lou said. He sat on the couch, looking out at the mare. She was standing very still in the arena so relaxed that her lower lip was hanging down. "She doesn't appear to be close to foaling. I think she's sleeping," he said smugly.

Garrett took the cue to leave, and said, "Then I'm not needed here anymore, so I'll go home. If you need any help with the mare, just let me know." He looked at Roulett as he said, "Before I leave, I'll feed your horses so you don't have to go out in the cold."

Roulett said, "Thanks. I'll see you tomorrow." She misread his words to mean that he would be back and that she shouldn't let the passion cool.

Lou was quiet for a few minutes as he waited to be certain Garrett was gone. Once they heard the sound of his truck fade, Lou scolded, "As I told you before, you two are playing with fire and you're going to get burned. This is the second time I've rescued you from making the biggest mistake of your life. If he hadn't been trying to hide his arousal, I could've only guessed if I stopped you in time."

He paused a minute to take another drink before asking, "Have you done the deed with him yet? Maybe...some other time when I wasn't there," he pressured almost shouting, "*Have you*? I'm not leaving here until you tell me! Well, *have* you?"

She whimpered, almost in tears, "No, we haven't yet! I don't know why knowing this is so important to you—it's none of your *business* what we do!"

Lou said, "For your sake, I hope the 'yet' never comes! Look around you! I don't think you want to trade all you have for a strange dick. I'm making this my business. And, as for the reason I want to know, well...maybe someday you'll figure that out for yourself!

"I'm going back to the office. We have more important concerns than your silly puppy love. People all around us are dropping dead and we could be next. I think you should concentrate your thoughts on our life-and-death situations," he said, slamming the door as he left.

She sat alone, deep in thought. Tears threatened, but she held them back. She hadn't wanted to love Garrett, but she did. Yet, Lou was right about one thing—she didn't want to trade all she had for a fling with Garrett. She didn't want to give up her family.

Since the death of her own mother, Marie had filled an enormous void. In addition, Roulett didn't want to lose her husband and her children—she wanted both Garrett *and* her husband!

Garrett wasn't supposed to be so willing, once she'd cornered him. He should've resisted more! This was his fault! She remembered their first kiss...she was only concerned with just kissing him, while he wondered if he was going to get laid.

What was she to expect from him? He thought like all men, with his penis instead of his head...but she was the one wearing the hose, garter belt, and crotchless panties. She wanted to keep his interest, but things hadn't progressed as she'd thought. She craved the thrill, the danger, but didn't want to face the consequences of her actions.

In her mind, they could simply steal a few kisses from each other and that would be it. But that was solely her fantasy—to have a man who loved her and kissed her on a regular basis, without requiring sex early in the relationship. She remembered how much that she wanted to consummate her relationship with him that day, more than she'd ever wanted any man in her life. And, if Lou hadn't interrupted them, they would've made love.

She thought, *What then? What could be next?* Would it have been the best moment of her life—making everything after seem dull? Her spirits fell. Yet, she didn't want to give up the intoxicating high feelings of pursuing Garrett. He made her feel so alive! She was a little like a dog chasing a car, loving the chase but not knowing what to do with Garrett if she caught him. Yet, to continue the chase, she must never let him know her doubts. Or could it be that she couldn't lose what she never had...him?

The phone rang and Roulett answered, hoping it was Garrett. It was Marie. She said, "Dorothy has bacterial pneumonia. The ER doctor said that it wasn't an antibiotic resistant strain of bacteria, so she should be fine. He admitted her to the hospital and she's resting now."

Roulett replied, "Thank goodness it's something they can treat. When are you coming home?"

"As soon as I can get there. Has Moon showed any other foaling symptoms?"

"No. In fact, I haven't seen any symptoms other than the waxing."

"Well, I always say *better safe than sorry.* I'll see you in a few minutes."

Safe than sorry echoed in Roulett's mind as she sat in the dark waiting for Garrett to call, but it didn't happen.

Marie arrived about fifteen minutes later.

Chapter 28 | Death Angels

Angels stood at the corners of the earth holding back the winds so that no wind could blow... REVELATION 7: 1

A few days later when the hospital released Dorothy, Marie and Roulett drove her back to the nursing home. When Roulett and Marie finally returned to the ranch, it was after five o'clock and Garrett had gone for the day. In spite of her mixed emotions about their last encounter, Roulett was very disappointed that she didn't have another opportunity to see him.

That same day, Lou called Dr. Pam Barnes from his office and asked, "Did you do the autopsy on Sandra Evans?"

Pam replied, "Yes, I did."

"Was the cause of her death similar to Joyce's?"

"Yes, exactly the same."

"Are you going to send tissue samples from Sandra Evans to the CDC?"

"I already did. Again, I didn't find anything, but I'm concerned because they both worked at the same facility."

"That concerns me, too."

* * * * *

On Wednesday, Kirk and Jack came home from Africa. When Jack returned to work at the Center that afternoon, Lou confronted him about his concerns with the gruesomely similar deaths. He said, "You and Kirk could've been exposed to some new virus such as HIV, Ebola, or hemorrhagic fever and possibly spread it around in your travels."

Jack replied, "Don't panic. Let's wait and see what the CDC says about the samples." He asked Pam to let him know as soon as she heard something.

That afternoon, Pam called. "All these deaths are scary, and there are too many people dying for it simply to be a coincidence. The CDC hasn't been able to find anything yet. Strange deaths are occurring all over the central United States—the majority are women of childbearing age who've died from uterine and vaginal hemorrhaging. A smaller percentage are men of all adult ages dying from what appears as a strange type of stroke—again, a hemorrhage. Since there doesn't appear to be any known pathological cause, I wonder if I should've done an autopsy on your dad. The CDC is calling it the Heartland Plague because of the locale."

Jack knew that her observation wouldn't alleviate Lou's concerns.

* * * * *

The next Monday, Kirk stopped by to see his mother on the way to work. Marie insisted they share some of his grandfather's tea. They'd had it several times before, so he indulged his mother. Although he never enjoyed the tea, it was more palatable with a couple of spoonfuls of sugar.

* * * * *

That same day Roulett and Hollie met for lunch. Once their food arrived, Hollie said, "Okay, let's weigh the evidence. Women all want three things from our men. We want physical, emotional, and financial support. I'm going to use these sugar packets to represent these three qualities in Jack and Garrett. First, I'll give Jack's side one sugar packet for the physical relationship that you share with him. Second, I'll give Jack's side another sugar packet for his ample financial support. I'll assume because of your crazy infatuation with Garrett that Jack doesn't give you the emotional support you require. Nevertheless, he has two packets on his side. Garrett doesn't receive any sugar packets on his side because he doesn't provide you with sex, money, or emotional security—no sugar packets!"

"I know loving Garrett is irrational. My brain tells me this while my mindless heart yearns for him."

"You need to listen to your brain!"

"What my heart wants doesn't matter because Garrett is avoiding me."

"Are you sure that he's avoiding you?" Hollie asked.

"I'm sure. I'm not imagining his rejection."

"Maybe it's time that you gave up on this Garrett bum, because if he's avoiding you now, it is a sure sign that he wants to end your relationship. Most likely, the only way he knows how to end it with you is to avoid you. Garrett is doing you a favor by avoiding you. Maybe he does love you! I can't think of any better way for him to show you that he really, really does love you, than to leave you alone!"

After their conversation, Roulett decided to cool it with Garrett for a while.

* * * * *

The following week around noon, Vickie, hemorrhaging profusely, called an ambulance. Paul called Marie and asked her to meet him at the hospital. Shortly after Vickie's admission to intensive care, she died. Marie arrived to console Paul as they received the news of Vickie's death. The Friday night get-together was cancelled.

Marie insisted that Paul go with her to the ranch for a while. She tried her best to console him after they arrived. She fixed him a cup of hot tea and said, "This'll make you feel better. I think that this tea has something in it that calms your nerves—or at least it seemed to help me when Sam died."

Paul was so distraught that he didn't refuse the nasty-smelling tea, which tasted much better than the odor it emanated. He said, "I guess this tea is like Limburger cheese. It's not so bad once you get past the smell."

"I hope my grandfather's tea makes you feel better."

"I need to tell you something that's very embarrassing for me."

"You know you can tell me anything. As long as we've known each other, you have no reason to be embarrassed."

Paul hung his head as he said, "I don't have the money for Vickie's funeral."

Marie hugged him. "Don't worry—I'll be happy to pay for it. It'll make me feel good, knowing I can help you and for Vickie's memory. Money isn't an issue. After Sam's death my lawyer notified me that my stipend from Dad's trust would double to eight thousand dollars per week."

The next morning, Pam called Jack to schedule a meeting for that afternoon in Jack's office. She'd invited Kirk and Lou. After everyone arrived, Pam started by saying, "I have the report back from the CDC. No *known* cause of death killed your employees. We're not dealing with a pathogen as easily identified as AIDS or SARS because the CDC can't find a viral, bacterial, or parasitical pathogen—making these strange hemorrhagic symptoms hard to explain since the clotting factors in the blood were satisfactory. The only connecting fact is that they both experienced sexual intercourse within twenty-four hours of death. However, the seminal fluid didn't contain sperm or any deadly pathogen. We all know sex doesn't kill women, or most of the women on earth would be dead.

"I called the CDC today and told them another woman died from what appeared to be the same symptoms. The CDC is flying in a team of people to pick up Vickie's body. They want to double check to make sure that we haven't overlooked something."

Later that same afternoon, the CDC team arrived at the Center wearing full HAZMAT gear. Pam immediately called Dr. Worthington. "Why is your collection team wearing Biohazard level four suits? They're making our employees nervous. I thought this plague wasn't contagious," Pam said.

"The suits are to prevent our team from contaminating the body, not vice versa. If this plague was contagious, we'd both be dead," said Dr. Worthington.

On the next Thursday, Dr. Worthington informed Pam that Vickie's body would be returned the next day, and that two people needed to talk to her as soon as possible. That afternoon, Dr. Cleta Worthington from the CDC and Dr. Alex Mueller from the health department arrived for the meeting. Dr. Worthington showed Dr. Mueller around the Center. She knew most of the employees and the layout of the Center since she'd worked there for years before accepting a position with the CDC.

Jack shook hands with Dr. Worthington and greeted her. "It's good to see you again, Cleta. I didn't know the CDC was sending *you* here."

"I'm in charge of this project. I want to introduce you to my friend and colleague, Dr. Alex Mueller, head of the Atlanta Department of Health." In the past, she'd liked Jack better than Kirk, but since her dismissal from the Center, she didn't trust either one. Her quest was to prove that the Center was the source of the mysterious deaths. Jack walked with them to the conference room where Pam, Olivia, Lou, and other prominent employees of the Center were waiting.

Dr. Worthington said, "The test results are the same as before. We still don't know the cause of death. We have created and sent a bulletin to all the doctors and health care workers in the United States, starting with this state, requesting that they report any and all deaths caused by hemorrhaging, other than gunshot and stab wounds, and that they report all stroke-type deaths."

CHAPTER 28

* * * * *

The following Monday, they held Vickie's funeral. Paul wanted to have a graveside funeral to save money, but Marie insisted that Vickie have a church funeral, complete with lots of beautiful flowers, reminding Paul that money wasn't a problem. All through Vickie's funeral, Marie and Paul clung to each other. They'd shared many years together and had both lost their mates recently.

Several weeks later, when Roulett arrived at the ranch, she wasn't surprised to see that Garrett's pickup was gone. He'd missed most of the weekly Friday night get-togethers since the afternoon in the barn when Lou had caught them. Roulett had no doubt that Garrett was avoiding her.

Chapter 29 | To Run or not to Run

**Guard your affections above all else—
they influence everything in life.** PROVERBS 5: 23

Roulett brought the children to ride their horses at the ranch as Marie walked toward them saying, "Isn't it a beautiful day!" Her mood had greatly improved over the past few weeks. She also was heading to the barn, so she walked with them and added, "Tammy and Michael, I baked chocolate chip cookies this morning and you two can have some when you return from your ride."

Roulett spotted Garrett in one of the stud exercise pens trying to fix the automatic horse watering system. The valve wasn't working right and it kept overflowing, which made a very muddy pen, plus it wasted water.

She yelled, "Can you come inside when you reach a stopping point? I need to talk to you for a few minutes."

Garrett called back, "Okay!"

Marie said to Roulett, "Come in the clubhouse after the children leave for their ride."

"Okay," she replied as she helped the children put saddles and bridles on their horses.

As they were riding off, Michael said, "We'll be back in about an hour. Save me some of Grandma's cookies!"

Garrett took several more minutes to pry off the faulty part, trying to avoid getting muddy again. When Roulett and Garrett arrived at the mudroom door at the same time, she opened the door for him since his hands were filthy. He said, "Thank you. Would you tell Marie I'll be there in a minute? I need to wash up." He sat on the bench in the mudroom, took off his messy boots, and hosed them down.

Roulett said, "Sure," noticing the tension between her and Garrett that was never-ending since their first kiss. Before the kiss, they had always been relaxed around each other.

When she reached the clubhouse, Marie said, "I heard him."

Roulett walked to the refrigerator, grabbed an orange soda and offered it to Marie, "Do you want one?"

Marie replied, "No, thanks. I just had a big glass of iced tea."

Garrett came through the door and poured himself a cup of stale coffee. He asked, "Anyone else want a cup?"

They both answered simultaneously, "No, thank you," laughing together as Roulett added, "Great minds think alike."

Marie said to Garrett, "I'm going to have the vet out one day next week. What day and time would be best for you? Since you've needed to leave early several times recently, I wanted to make sure that you'd be here. The vet will need your help worming and vaccinating the herd."

Garrett thought for a minute. "It doesn't matter to me. You schedule him and I'll be here. Just let me know which day to expect him. I can save the vet some time by having the halters and leads on the horses when he arrives."

"Great, I'll call the vet tomorrow to see when he's available, and then I'll let you know when he'll be here."

Garrett asked, "Is that all you wanted to talk to me about?"

She said, "No, I need to tell you both that I'm leaving for the rest of the day. Paul's picking me up in a few minutes. We're going to Tulsa to the mall on a shopping spree. After we're tired of shopping, we'll find somewhere to eat dinner before we return home. We may not be back until nine or so."

Roulett hugged Marie. "I think that's great. You need to stop hibernating here. There's no need to hurry back—relax and have a good time."

Garrett and Roulett followed Marie outside as they spoke. Garrett said, "That'll be good for both of you."

Marie headed toward the house to wait for Paul. It was less than a minute before Garrett and Roulett heard his car. Marie wasn't even inside the house yet. She yelled to Paul, "Just a minute, I need to grab my purse and sweater." Soon, they drove off.

When Marie left, Roulett and Garrett looked at each other for a few moments. As they want back to the clubhouse, they chitchatted about how happy and surprised they were that Marie and Paul were going on a date.

Roulett abruptly asked, "Why have you been avoiding me?"

He gave her a serious look. "Because I don't want to walk around with an obvious boner all the time, since that's how you affect me now."

She was both relieved and flattered by his answer. "I thought you didn't like me anymore."

"If only I *just* liked you."

She realized that he was telling her in his own way that he loved her. She walked over to him and put her arms around him. He embraced her and they kissed.

He asked, "Are we going to try this again? First, we better call and see where Lou is."

"Sorry, not this time. I'm on my period."

"Let's sit and talk about our situation for a moment."

"All right." They both sat on the couch.

"We have to discuss if we really want to end up together, because if we are caught, that's most likely what'll happen. I need to know if you want to risk all you have only to be with me. I need to know before I can even consider if I want to risk all I have to be with you."

Roulett thought how she'd underestimated him as she hastily blurted, "I love you more than anyone in the world, and I always will."

"That doesn't tell me if you're willing to risk all you have for me. We can't continue our relationship unless we're willing to give up everything to have each other. Eventually we'll be caught by someone who won't keep as quiet as Lou has."

Without thinking, she said, "I would give up all I have for you."

"Now I have to make my decision, but I'll need some time to think about it. I can't think rationally while sitting beside you. I'll give you my answer in a week or so."

She said, "Okay."

"If my answer is yes, then we'll have another decision to make. Do we simply fool around until we're caught, or do we tell everyone that we want to be together?"

She nodded.

He kissed her lightly on the lips. "We need to cool it until I've made my decision, so I'm going back to work now. We'll talk about this soon."

* * * * *

The next day Roulett invited Hollie to lunch at their usual restaurant so Roulett could talk to her about the latest events with Garrett.

"I told Garrett that I would leave Jack for him," said Roulett.

"I can't believe it! You're willing to give up paradise to run away with a bum!"

"He hasn't told me if he's willing to leave Olivia for me."

Hollie thought for a few moments before stating her opinion. "Well, I don't think he'll be leaving his financially successful wife for you, since your husband, not you, has the money."

"In some ways I hope you're right. Surprisingly, I don't know which I fear the worst—the possible 'yes' or the possible 'no.'"

More than two weeks had passed since Garrett talked to Roulett about their possible life-changing decision, and Roulett was anxiously waiting his answer. Garrett came in for his break shortly after Roulett arrived at the ranch. The children were riding their horses and Marie was at the grocery store, which gave Garrett and Roulett a chance to talk alone. He poured himself a cup of coffee and asked, "Would you like a cup?"

"Sure, that sounds good," said Roulett, nervously.

He handed her the coffee as he said, "I bet you're wondering about it…Yes, I've made my decision." He sat beside her on the sofa, pausing a moment, trying to choose his words carefully. "You know I love you, but I want to stay where I am, because I really can't leave my wife. I love you and, if I had met you before I met her, I know I'd be with you instead.

"Olivia experienced so much pain in the past years. First, she had to make it through medical school. Second, she wanted a baby so badly. She went through a whole battery of fertility tests, to realize finally that *I* was the problem. After a miscarriage and giving birth to a stillborn baby boy, I can't abandon her. I made a promise that I must keep even if I do love you. I don't want to leave her, not even for you. I'm sorry."

Roulett didn't know if she was disappointed or relieved. "You wouldn't be the man that I love so much if you could leave your wife," she said smiling, with tears in her eyes.

They hugged. "Because I've made my decision, we have to stop this today."

She said, "Okay," then asked, "What if there was no possible way for anyone to catch us?"

"I'd be all yours, but it couldn't be here."

"Well, at least I have some *hope* of time alone with you."

After her conversation with Garrett, Roulett felt a little down, so she went to the house to talk to Marie, which didn't improve Roulett's mood. Marie had recently returned from the grocery store and all she could talk about was how the fresh rainbow fruit was available everywhere. Roulett wasn't impressed with Marie's enthusiasm for the strange fruit because Roulett knew how Jack would be equally excited, and she'd hear all about it again from him that night.

Jack arrived home late; he'd met Kirk at the ranch. Marie had called both of them on their way home with exciting news about the original fruit. To everyone's surprise, the original fruit appeared to be starting its cycle over again with 12 new blooms on each of them. Roulette sadly endured Jack's enthusiasm for the news.

* * * * *

Almost three weeks later, Jack and Roulett arranged for their children to spend the night at the ranch with their grandparents. Jack and Roulett wanted to celebrate their anniversary alone. They ate at a nice restaurant before returning home to a long night of lovemaking.

Roulett awoke early the next morning, too early for her feelings of fatigue. She felt wetness between her legs, rationalizing that so much sex caused the unwanted feeling of dampness. She was overly protective of her mattress and had wisely chosen to lie on a thick towel folded over to add extra absorbency. She rolled out of bed and grabbed the towel, noticing it had a tinge of blood in the middle. She wondered if her period had started over a week early. She ran to the bathroom and turned the shower on, wanting to warm up as soon as possible. As she stood in the shower, she noticed drops of blood falling from her body to the shower floor, while remembering her dream with the women being drenched in blood. She watched the blood drops fall—drip, drip, drip. The crimson drops fell to the shower floor and mingled with the water before swirling down the drain. She crouched down on the shower floor holding her knees tight against her cramping abdomen while the water drops splattered over her body. She felt achy, tired, and out of sorts while remembering about several women who'd recently died from hemorrhaging.

She chose to wear both a tampon with a sanitary napkin because her blood flow was so heavy before slipping on a fresh nightgown and going back to bed. Continuing to feel wetness as if her lifeblood was oozing out of her body, she tried to lie still, hoping it would slow the flow. She felt strange and still sleepy but couldn't fall back to sleep. Trying to analyze why she felt so restless, she realized that her problem could be her feelings for Garrett—the same feelings that caused her to fantasize about Garrett, while making love to her husband. She wondered how she would survive without him in her life. She remembered in the restaurant that Jack had told her how proud he was of her, proud she'd stopped drinking. She was relieved that he didn't know the real reason why she'd quit drinking. She felt weak and sad as she put her arm around her husband while the situation took a few minutes to register in Roulett's fatigued brain—Jack was cold! She frantically checked for a pulse, but found none. She shook him vigorously, hysterically trying to revive him. Jack was dead! The only person Roulett thought to call so early in the morning was Lou.

The first question Lou asked was, "Where are the children?"

She sobbed, "They're at their grandma's house. They stayed all night because Jack and I were celebrating our anniversary."

Lou said, "I'll be right over. I'll call an ambulance and Pam from my car since she needs to know, but don't call Marie yet." He arrived a few minutes later. He hugged Roulett and asked her how Jack died.

She barely could talk as she said, "He complained of a headache. I didn't have a headache, which I thought was because I didn't drink any of the champagne that he did. We were celebrating our anniversary; Jack died on our fifteenth anniversary," Roulett sobbed, thinking his death was her punishment for loving Garrett.

Lou asked, "Did he take anything for his headache?"

Roulett struggled to answer, "Yes, about three in the morning. I gave him a couple aspirin. I thought that he went back to sleep, but this morning I realized he wasn't breathing. He was so healthy! What could have caused this?"

"Pam will discover the reason for his death," Lou said.

The ambulance arrived a few minutes later. The paramedics were bringing out Jack's body when Pam arrived. She followed them to the ambulance while writing down some details. She then instructed one of the paramedics to take Jack's body temperature as she checked his body for rigor mortis, which had barely started in the small muscles.

"Temperature is 93. 7 degrees," he said.

"Thanks," said Pam. She looked at her watch—it was seven forty-five. "I would guess that he died about four this morning. What do you think?"

"That sounds right to me. What a waste! The guy had everything. He was handsome, smart, rich, had a pretty wife, and beautiful children. Even with all that, he couldn't escape death!"

Pam said, "You can take him in now but don't put him in the cooler. I'll be there to do the autopsy in less than an hour. I'm going to talk to Roulett for a few minutes."

She walked into the house and saw Roulett sobbing on the sofa. Lou had his arm around her, trying his best to console her.

Chapter 30 | Desperation

Man is frail, with few days filled with trouble! He only blossoms for a moment—then withers. Like the shadow of a passing cloud, he soon fades. JOB 14: 1-2

The local and national news were full of stories about the strange deaths. Because so many were in Petrolia, the annual Fourth of July celebration picnic seemed somber. The Center's board considered canceling the picnic, but chose not to because the annual event was something the employees eagerly anticipated every year.

Marie, Roulett, and Lou were all sitting together. Of course, they always had a good seat at Clayton Park. In spite of their recent losses, they struggled to be positive.

Lou said, "Beautiful day isn't it?"

"Perfect day, hot but not windy or too humid," Marie said.

Paul arrived and Marie waved to him. He joined them and said, "Great weather, isn't it?"

Roulett said, "We were just talking about how nice it is today."

Marie asked, "Paul, will you go with me to tell Ella Mae how sorry we are to hear about her husband's death? He died only last week from this plague. It hit her so hard because she'd lost both her daughter and daughter-in-law that same week to this awful thing!"

"Sure, it's good that she's out with people. We all know how important that is," said Paul.

Lou said, "That's right, I don't know what we would've done without each other. Looking around, I would say that at least a third of the people here have recently lost a spouse or other relative."

Marie said, "I hope they find a cure soon. Paul and I'll be back in a few minutes."

Lou looked at Roulett and said, "Alone at last."

Roulett ignored his flirtation, thinking he was only trying to be funny. Her thoughts wandered as she noticed Garrett and Olivia arrive, so she waved at them. They acknowledged by waving back but didn't come over.

Lou noticed and said, "He's avoiding you, isn't he?"

Roulett asked, "Why do you say that?"

"Because with Jack gone, you're no longer safe."

"I don't think he would say I was ever safe."

"Now you're much more dangerous."

"Why?"

"Because, if you decide that you want him bad enough, all you have to do is destroy his marriage by letting Olivia learn about the two of you."

"I wouldn't do that!"

"Everything has changed. Before, you risked losing your money, power, children, or even Marie. Now, you have nothing to lose by Olivia finding out about you and Garrett, but he's still in the same situation. He's terrified of you."

Roulett repeated, "I would never do that to him!"

"He doesn't know that for certain. In fact, I'm not sure you won't eventually do it out of desperation."

"What part of me-loving-him do you *not* understand?"

"You don't know what you would do in the heat of passion. Besides, he's doing you a favor by leaving you alone," said Lou.

Roulett sarcastically said, "Yeah, sure!"

"That leaves you more time for sincere suitors like me," Lou said with a smile.

That night after the picnic, Garrett started pressuring Olivia to change jobs, because being around Roulett was too difficult. He told Olivia that he wanted a change of scenery and that he was tired of Oklahoma. She thought he was unhappy because of the recent deaths, so she agreed to consider his request.

* * * * *

Seven weeks later, Pam and Olivia attended a two day conference on the plague in Atlanta. Garrett arranged for time off from the ranch and volunteered to accompany them. The first day of the conference was for the press. Alex Mueller introduced the main speaker, Dr. Worthington. After her speech, she fielded questions and did her best to convey the limited information available. Although Dr. Worthington couldn't answer the reporters' questions about the plague, she mentioned it had been called the "Spouse Killer" and the new term immediately gained widespread popularity.

The next day's conference was easier for Dr. Worthington because she was dealing with people from the scientific community instead of reporters. She said, "I'm sorry to have to report that the CDC is receiving reports of deaths all over the United States. More than 230,000 women and approximately 80,000 men have died in the last month, with over forty million confirmed deaths in the world—78% women. HIV kills in years, Ebola kills in days, but this kills in hours. We hope we never see the plague that kills in minutes. The CDC is working on where the deaths started, and we've sent out the same bulletin all over the world. The only thing that we can find in common in these deaths is sexual activity."

Olivia whispered to Pam, "This sure would lend credence to the religious belief that sex was the original sin."

Pam softly replied, "Or it could explain where the silly idea that sex could be the original sin came from."

After Dr. Cleta Worthington's speech there was a question-and-answer forum. Cleta acknowledged the CDC staff's conclusion about the Spouse Killer possibly starting in the central United States. Cleta failed to tell the group her suspicions. She felt that Kirk, Jack, or one of their traveling companions might have inadvertently brought something contagious into the country.

Unbeknownst to Olivia, the day before their trip, Garrett had faxed her résumé to Dr. Worthington with a note stating he would like to live in Georgia. He asked that Dr. Worthington keep their correspondence a secret, which resulted in a job offer for Olivia at the CDC while she was there. Garrett encouraged her to accept by telling her how much he'd always wanted to live in Atlanta. She accepted the job and the CDC expected her to start work on October 8th.

Several days later at the ranch, Lou arrived as Garrett was leaving. Lou walked into the clubhouse to find Roulett calmly reclining on the sofa. Lou tried to analyze her mood, wondering if she knew that Garrett was leaving town. Lou had heard the news two days earlier. Roulett appeared too calm to know, so Lou poured a drink to help calm his nerves. "Have you heard the latest news?"

She snapped, "No. Who died?"

"I'm afraid it could be me for being the one to tell you…"

"Tell me what?"

"Garrett and Olivia are moving. Olivia is taking a job in Atlanta in October."

Roulett thought that her heart would stop beating. Her first reaction erupted as hostility. She glared at Lou and asked, "How long have you known?"

"I heard two days ago."

"What! Am I the last person to hear about it? I own 45% percent of Clayton Research Center…yet, I'm not important enough to know about this? Does Kirk know?"

Lou sheepishly said, "Yes, but Kirk works at the Center. He's basically the head honcho and will be until Jack's position is filled."

"Well, I need to do something about that!"

Lou asked, "Which 'that?' Garrett leaving town or Kirk being the head honcho of the Center?"

"Maybe both!"

"How do you plan to do that?"

"I think I'll trade my Famine Free Future stock for Kirk and Charles's Clayton Research Center stock," said Roulett.

"Your Famine Free Future stock is worth a great deal more than your the Center stock. I hope you're not planning to propose an even trade!"

"I'm not concerned with the value—I simply want to own controlling interest in the Center."

"Famine Free Future is projected to net over six billion dollars by the end of this year. The Center's total value pales in comparison."

"This isn't a matter of money. I've always had a bad feeling about Kirk's devilish fruit and I want to put as much distance as possible between Kirk's whole fruity project and me. I may lose money but the trade will make me feel safer," said Roulett.

"I hate to see you lose a fortune because you're obsessively trying to keep Garrett here."

"I'll call my stock broker tomorrow and arrange for him to make the trade. And if it makes you feel any better, I'll make Charles and Kirk pay the broker's fee."

Roulett desperately wanted to keep Garrett in town. She called Hollie the next day and invited her to lunch, needing someone more objective to talk to about Garrett leaving.

They met at their usual restaurant and before they sat down, Roulett said, "Garrett is leaving town—Olivia accepted a job at the CDC in Atlanta."

Hollie replied, "Maybe now you'll get over that loser!"

"You know I don't want him to leave. I don't know if I'll survive without him in my life."

"You'll be fine without him. Besides, you don't really have him in your life now, not the way you really want him."

"I've traded my Famine Free Future stock for all the Center stock so I can offer the CEO position to Olivia. Maybe that'll keep them here."

"I hope you made a lot of money on your stock trade—the Famine Free Future stock is extremely valuable."

"You sound exactly like Lou," said Roulett.

Although both Hollie and Lou opposed the idea, the next Monday Roulett met with the board and voted to offer the CEO position to Olivia.

Olivia replied, "Thanks for the offer, but we're looking forward to living in Atlanta; and I think I'm needed more at the CDC because of the research on the Spouse Killer."

A few days later, Roulett was depressed but still desperate to spend some time alone with Garrett, so she tried finding a reason for traveling to Africa and a way to take Garrett with her. She called Hollie and asked, "Will you go with me to New York, all expenses paid, to visit Charles? I want to ask him if he knows where his father...no, I forgot...I mean his grandfather Roy found the original plant."

Hollie said, "Sure, sounds like fun, will we see my Grammy Nambi?"

"Yes, we can. I'd love to see your Grammy Nambi again. I'll arrange for our flights tomorrow," said Roulett.

Hollie and Roulett arrived in New York City the next afternoon. Hollie visited her Grammy Nambi while Roulett kept her appointment with Charles. Failing to heed Marie's former warning about Charles, she met him alone in his office.

Charles appeared overjoyed by her visit. As she walked into his office he gave her a tight hug, which was far too familiar. Roulett sat across from his desk and began questioning him. "Do you know anything about Roy's tea plant?" She felt awkward by not referring to Roy as Charles's dad but Roy wasn't Charles's dad, he was technically Charles's biological grandfather.

Charles sat in his chair while putting his feet up on his cherry desk and scratched his head. He recalled, "He caught me taking a sip of his tea when I was sixteen and I got such a scolding that I'll never forget it. For years after that, I stole the tea leaves from a large metal can where Dad kept them. Stealing those leaves was a real challenge because he kept the tea in his locked greenhouse.

"Dad would add the dried leaves several times a week, and I would take some about once a month, which I hid in a bag in my room for years. After I was away from home, I still would occasionally drink the tea made from those stolen leaves. Somehow, it wasn't a big deal, not like I thought it would be. The tea never made me high or even addicted to the damn stuff, unlike these darn cigarettes that Dad had also caught me smoking," he said, lighting a cigarette.

Charles continued, "I remember him telling me that he'd picked up the tea plant near Magandi in Kenya. I used a permanent marker to highlight it with a red circle on my globe of the world. I saw that spot on the globe all the time."

Roulett asked, "Is that all you know about the tea?"

"Yeah, that's it. I could show you the old globe if you would like to go with me to my apartment. I'll take you out to eat afterward," said Charles. He had moved closer and she could feel his breath. She thought Charles was handsome for his age, but he was old and had bad breath. The very thought of him touching her was repulsive. She realized that he was hitting on her, and she remembered Marie's warning. Roulett replied, "I'm sorry—maybe next time. I'm expected at Nambi's house tonight."

That night at Nambi's house, Roulett mentioned needing to go to Magandi, Africa, to try to discover something about the fruit.

"I have a younger brother in Nairobi, and I'm sure he would show you around," said Nambi.

"That would be great. Nairobi is the closest place to stay in a decent hotel," said Roulett.

Hollie and Roulett returned home the next day, and Roulett planned a trip to Africa for the tenth day of October.

She called Olivia at home that same night. Roulett said enthusiastically, "I'm going to Africa because I've found the location were the rainbow fruit originated. Hollie's uncle lives in Nairobi, which is close. Nambi called him last night and he said he'd be happy to show me around after I arrive in Africa. I'll try to learn more about the fruit and maybe find a clue connecting the fruit to the Spouse Killer." Since Olivia was deathly afraid of flying, Roulett asked, "Is there any way you could go with me? I don't feel safe going to Africa alone."

Olivia replied, "I'm obligated to start work at the CDC on October 8th. Could Lou go with you?"

Roulett said, "He's needed at the Center because you're leaving. I must have someone who I trust in charge of the Center while I'm gone."

"What about Kirk? He's experienced at running the Center."

"He's not speaking to me since I bought controlling interest."

"I heard that he's celebrating because of the trade."

"Well, celebrating or not…I wouldn't have him guard a dead dog if he volunteered."

Olivia paused for a moment before she asked, "How about Garrett going with you? He has given notice at Marie's ranch. He would love to travel, but can't because of my fear of flying. Would that be all right with you?"

Roulett thought, *Yes...pay dirt!* She composed herself before she calmly said, "That would be fine."

"First, we have to see if it's all right with him. I'll let you speak to him," said Olivia. She put Garrett on the phone.

He asked, "What's up?"

Roulett said, "I've located the place where Roy found the fruit. It's in Africa and I'll need someone to go with me. The trip should take about two weeks. We may find a cure for the strange deaths. Will you go with me?"

"Hold on for just a minute." He covered the phone receiver with his hand as he asked Olivia if this was okay with her.

Olivia said to him, "You need to go and assist Roulett's efforts. Everybody needs to do anything possible to learn more about the fruit, which may be the source of the plague. Time is of the utmost importance."

He said, "All right. When do we leave?"

"I've planned to leave on the tenth of October, and we should be back some time within two weeks. You'll need your passport," said Roulett.

"That won't be a problem. I'll get it tomorrow."

The next day, Roulett was busy most of the morning arranging hotel and flight reservations, requesting adjoining rooms with a door in between so he could answer his phone from her room. She was so excited about this trip; but when she arrived at the ranch that afternoon, she was disappointed that Garrett's truck was already gone. Marie told her he left early to do something concerning his passport, which alleviated her concerns.

That night, Olivia called Roulett at home to relate the latest news. "I talked to my supervisor at the CDC today. I asked if there was any new information concerning the cause of these deaths, and he said they haven't learned anything new. I mentioned that some people think there may be a connection between the deaths and the rainbow fruit, although no one has any proof. I told him about your trip to Africa—the origin of the rainbow fruit—hoping to attain more information which could prove or disprove the theory. He approved, asking if he could offer assistance. I said that my husband was going with you since Dr. Louis Gordon couldn't leave the Center once I was gone. My supervisor suggested it would be advantageous for you to take Dr. Gordon, rather than Garrett, since he has more expertise. He said he'd postpone my starting date, so I can tend the Center while you and Lou travel to Africa. I really think it's a great plan."

Roulett said, "Me, too," although she was so disappointed she had to fight back tears.

Olivia said, "I called Lou first, and he agreed to go with you, so now you'll have almost a month if needed, in Africa. That should give you plenty of time, just in case you need it."

Chapter 31 | Africa, O Africa

The sound of your name recalls your fragrance.
No woman can help but love you. THE SONG OF SOLOMON 1: 3

On the flight to New York, Lou realized that Roulett was upset that he had taken Garrett's place. Her spirits were so low, Lou said, "I had nothing to do with the change of plans."

"I don't blame you. It may have been Garrett's idea," she grumbled, thinking she needed to be careful not to take her frustrations out on Lou. She didn't know what she would've done without his loyal and loving friendship after she lost Jack.

"You can look at it this way—if we crash and die, your beloved Garrett will still be safe and sound back on land."

She smiled. "To live a very long life with his beloved wife—for some strange reason that scenario is not very comforting."

"If you'll cheer up, I promise you I'll do everything that's humanly possible to make this a pleasant trip."

"Thanks."

That afternoon when they arrived at their hotel room, Roulett locked the door between their adjoining rooms. They ate together that night in the hotel restaurant and talked. He asked, "Do you really think we'll discover something important in Magandi?"

She thought for a minute and realized there was no point lying to him. "No."

"You may be wrong. We may find something helpful."

* * * * *

On the airplane to London, Roulett whispered, "Thanks, Lou, for being so understanding yesterday."

He put his hand on hers and replied, "I'm thankful you're in a better mood today. I was afraid that you thought the change of plans was my fault since I was the one who was always interrupting you and Garrett."

"I never blamed you." After hesitating a few seconds she added, "Did you know Garrett and I were considering running away together?"

"No, I didn't know your relationship was that serious. What happened?"

"Back in June he told me we were going to be caught by someone other than you if we didn't stop trying to be together."

"He was right. I think I told you the same thing."

"Garrett told me that he loved me, but he couldn't leave Olivia because he still loved her, too. I felt I couldn't hold on to the feelings of euphoria that I experienced when I was with him, so I asked how he would react to a situation together with no possibility of anyone catching us. He said under those conditions he would enjoy the time he could spend with me."

"And Africa would be so far away that no one would catch you—not even me," said Lou.

"That was the plan. Now you know why I was so down yesterday."

"You seemed more disappointed about Garrett not going to Africa with you than you were about him deciding to stay with Olivia."

"I know this is going to sound crazy, but I didn't know which I feared more, Garrett choosing Olivia over me or him choosing me over Olivia."

"It sounds to me like you may've wanted him to stay right where he was but you didn't want to stop seeing him. The old *have your cake and eat it too.*"

"That's *exactly* what I wanted, but we don't always get what we want. I didn't want to love Garrett, but I do. At first, I didn't want him to stay in my life, but he did. And now...when I want him to stay in my life, he'll leave. We don't always get what we want. When it comes to Garrett I don't think I'll ever get what I want."

"This was what I was afraid would happen. He would hurt you. He has a pattern of doing that," said Lou.

Roulett asked, "What do you mean?"

"Nothing, just forget I said anything."

"Are you trying to tell me there've been other women in his life, before me?"

"I didn't mean to tell you. But, if you remember, I said they were having some family problems before they moved to Oklahoma."

"Yes, I remember—but you didn't say anything about Garrett seeing another woman. Did Olivia know?"

"I don't think she knew, but I could be wrong. I wasn't going to ask her."

"How did you find out?"

"Since Joyce was Garrett's sister, he would tell her things he wouldn't tell anyone else. She told me about a woman from work who'd developed a crush on him and how he and Olivia needed to move away from the woman because he was afraid that Olivia would learn about her. He didn't want to give up his wealthy wife for a poor girl who *thought* she loved him."

"I guess I can understand that, because of all that Garrett gave up so Olivia could finish college."

"What did Garrett tell you he gave up for Olivia?"

"He said he'd given up his plan to finish college and earn a degree in business management. He said he needed to work then, so Olivia could afford to finish college."

Lou angrily said, "I can't believe he had the balls to say that!"

"Are you trying to tell me it wasn't true?"

"It couldn't be any farther from the truth. Olivia's parents are wealthy and they paid for all her college plus Olivia and Garrett's living expenses. Her parents offered to pay for Garrett's college, too, but he obviously wasn't interested in acquiring an education, so he turned down their offer."

Roulett felt like a wilted flower. Her beloved Garrett wasn't at all as he'd appeared. Could Lou be lying about Garrett? No, she thought, Lou wouldn't lie about Garrett. In all the years she'd known Lou, he'd never lied about anything.

"I'm sorry—I didn't mean to depress you again, but I thought you should know the facts."

"I do need to know the facts even if they hurt. Did I ever tell you how meeting Garrett for the first time made me so angry I could've chewed nails and spit bullets? I felt this overpowering love for him from the first moment I met him, yet I had a large void in my heart. I think from the beginning I knew he wouldn't end up satisfying me," she said.

Lou took her hand. "I'm sorry I told you. I would never intentionally do anything to hurt you." He gently kissed her hand and held it.

"If only you understood how it feels to love someone you don't want to love. Unconditional love is so unfair."

Lou didn't say anything but he knew how she felt. He didn't want to love her but he did and, loving her so far had been anything but fulfilling. He said, "Have you ever considered you may've needed someone different to love and that if Garrett hadn't come along, it could've been someone else? Maybe you needed the thrill and excitement of forbidden lust or maybe, subconsciously, you selected a man who you wouldn't end up having. Maybe, deep down, you sensed that he wouldn't make you happy because you weren't his first extramarital involvement."

Sadly, Roulett knew that nothing short of her last breath would stop her from loving him. She regretted kissing him—if she hadn't kissed him, he wouldn't have needed to move away.

Lou was a very good friend who was here with her now, and he was holding her hand. She wished a fairy godmother would wave a magic wand and transfer the love Roulett felt for Garrett to Lou. She needed Lou to help her escape her biggest fear—that once Garrett was gone she'd sink into a pit of despair that she couldn't lift herself out of.

She remembered how dead she'd felt inside when she met Garrett and how alive she'd felt after their first kiss. That kiss was the most wonderful moment of her life, and she wished it could've lasted forever.

Lou was still holding her hand when they arrived in London. In the cab on the way to the hotel, he asked, "Would you like to go to a fancy restaurant tonight?"

"No, I'm so tired that I'd prefer eating in the hotel. Maybe we'll have something to celebrate on the trip home and we can go out then. We should be back in about two weeks."

"That sounds good to me. We're not in London very often, so we need to make the most of it," he said.

They arrived at the hotel and Lou paid the cab driver while the porter loaded their luggage on a cart. They checked in and were quiet all the way to their rooms. "I'm going to freshen up and change my clothes. I'll meet you in the restaurant in about thirty minutes," Roulett said as she opened her door.

"Okay, but don't get lost," he joked.

Lou decided that he would take a quick shower, shave, and change his clothes before dinner. He selected his best smelling after-shave, which he thought was so accurately named 4-PLAY. He couldn't forget the night in the loft, and he hoped she would react the same way she had that night. She had said that smell was a very important sense to women, and that it could affect a woman's reaction to a man.

Since that night his desire and love for her had steadily increased. His advances on this trip hadn't materialized as he'd hoped, making him think he needed all the help he could muster in his attempt to woo Roulett. He knew that he must be patient and not rush her; but he'd probably never have a chance like this again. The trip hadn't transpired as Roulett's fantasy trip, but it had the slightest possibility of being his. He dressed and then put on his after-shave, trying not to apply too much.

He arrived at the restaurant before Roulett and requested a romantically secluded table with a view of London. He ordered a scotch and water to drink while he waited.

Roulett arrived about ten minutes later. He stood and held her chair as she sat. She said, "You really smell good. Did you take a shower or just a French shower?"

Lou said, "Even though I'm in Europe, I didn't just put on perfume. I thought a shower would make me feel better and it did. Do I have on too much after-shave?"

"No, you smell great."

Lou asked, "Are you hungry yet?"

"Yes, I'm starving. I didn't care for the food on the plane. Maybe we could eat here in the morning, before we board the plane for Africa."

"That sounds like a great idea—I can have my coffee earlier," he said.

"Which means I won't have to deal with the *big bad bear* in the morning!"

"I thought that *big bad* was a wolf," he said.

Roulett laughed as she said, "You are so funny."

They enjoyed a wonderful meal, then turned in early.

The next morning at 4:00 a.m., Roulett received a wake-up call. She called Lou at 5:00 a.m. and asked, "How did you sleep?"

"With my eyes closed," he joked.

She chuckled. "No, I mean did you have trouble sleeping?"

"Not until you woke me up."

She laughed. "With the joking mood that you're in maybe the *bear* won't come out this morning."

"Don't count on it. I think the *bear* isn't awake yet. In just a few minutes, I'll be in dire need of a cup of coffee. Did *you* have any problem sleeping?" he asked.

"I don't think I got more than an hour of sleep the entire night. I'll tell you all about it while we're eating breakfast. We'll meet at the restaurant about 5:30. If you arrive before I do, please order our coffee."

"I think you're trying to avoid the *bear*."

"Actually you may be right. I'll see you in a few minutes."

When Roulett arrived, Lou had her coffee waiting. He'd finished his first cup and was starting to drink his second.

She said, "I'm sorry I'm late but I had to push myself to be here by now, since I'm so tired."

"I understand. I move slowly when I haven't gotten a good night's sleep." Lou handed her a menu and said, "I know what I want."

As she looked at the menu she asked, "What are you going to order?"

"A ham-and-mushroom omelet. What sounds good to you?"

"I want something light. I believe the rich meal that we ate last night was the main reason I couldn't sleep. I think I'll have a poached egg, wheat toast, and a fruit cup."

Lou gave the waitress their order, then said, "I'm sorry you didn't sleep well last night because I slept like a baby. Maybe you were in the wrong bed. I'm sure you would've slept better in *my* bed."

"I didn't know trading beds was an option. I'll try to sleep some on the plane."

"I don't think you understood what I meant by in *my bed*."

"I understood. I'm simply ignoring you."

* * * * *

On the airplane to Nairobi, Roulett slept most of the trip. Lou took several catnaps because she wasn't awake to talk with him. They arrived at the Nairobi Hilton and checked into a suite with two bedrooms, a sitting room with a balcony, but only one bathroom. Lou told Roulett to take the larger bedroom, so she couldn't lock her door because Lou needed access to their shared bathroom.

Both Roulett and Lou wanted to take a shower before dinner. They decided that Roulett should shower first because she needed the most grooming time. She finished a quick shower and shampoo. Lou was in the sitting room on the couch reading a magazine when she came out wearing a pink terry robe and a large white towel around her wet hair.

She said, "Your turn—don't forget your robe."

"What robe?" he joked.

Roulett didn't answer but noticed he was carrying his robe as he walked past. She said, "That robe." She was still doing her hair when Lou finished his shower. He walked past her with his robe on, but he'd tucked the back under his belt to expose his bare butt. Roulett didn't say a word—she just smiled.

Lou wanted more reaction from Roulett, so he complained, "I feel a little draft in here. Are you cold or is it just me?"

Roulett couldn't contain herself any longer. She burst out laughing as she said, "I don't know what I'm going to do with you!"

He stuck his head around the doorsill from his room and said, "I'll give you a few ideas if you can't think of any on your own."

Roulett couldn't help but notice Lou's very handsome, smiling face. She thought for a moment how thankful she was to have him in her life—he always made her laugh. Without thinking, she said, "I don't know if anyone has told you this or not, but your face is more handsome to look at than your butt."

"Is that supposed to be a compliment?"

"That's what you get for showing your butt!"

After they were ready to go, they decided that they would eat in the hotel's restaurant. It was very romantic with dim lights and candles on the tables. In fact, it was surprisingly like most American restaurants.

Lou asked, "Would you like wine with dinner?"

"I don't think I should. You know I stopped drinking over a year ago."

"I just thought a little wine could help you relax so you can sleep tonight," he said.

"All right, on one condition—this is the only time you offer me something to drink. I don't want to get started drinking too much again."

"That's a deal. This'll be the only night," he said.

They looked at the menu for several minutes before he asked, "How about ostrich steaks with a bottle of Cabernet Sauvignon?"

"Sounds different, but interesting. I've read ostrich tastes more like beefsteak than like chicken, so now we can learn if it's true," she said.

"Will the rice and steamed vegetables be light enough?" he asked.

"They sound great."

They were having their second glass of wine when their dinners arrived. Roulett looked at her plate and said, "This looks fantastic."

"Just like you," he said.

The food was delicious. Roulett relaxed so much that they had a great time together. They'd finished the first bottle of wine when Lou suggested they order another bottle to take back to their room and said, "We can have this one on the balcony and see the night lights."

"Sounds good to me. I'm not sleepy now because I slept so much today on the plane," she said.

Lou told the waiter that they wanted a bottle of wine to take to their rooms. The waiter said he'd have one sent to them with glasses in a few minutes. He held her hand as they walked upstairs. Later, they were sitting on the balcony when the wine arrived—open and perfectly chilled in a wine bucket. Lou poured a glass and handed it to Roulett. She sipped wine while looking over the balcony at the clear night sky, as she said, "This place is so beautiful. I've heard so often how much Roy Clayton loved Africa, and now I can see why."

"Speaking of being beautiful, have I told you yet how beautiful you look tonight?" Lou asked.

"Flattery will get you everywhere, so keep talking."

"I wasn't trying to flatter you. I mean it."

"Have I told you yet how great you smell? I really love that after-shave," she replied.

"Not today," he said as he poured them another glass of wine.

Roulett stood shivering from the cool night breeze with her arms resting on the balcony. Sitting on a wicker loveseat out of the wind, Lou said, "Sit down here and I'll keep you warm."

She sat as far away from him as possible. She said, "I don't feel the wind as much here."

Lou poured the last of the wine and asked, "Do you think I should order another bottle? The night is young."

"No. I don't want to have a hangover tomorrow. We have a lot to do. We need to make a genuine attempt to find something that could stop the deaths."

"I hope we find the answer."

She took another sip of her wine and said, "I don't know what I'd do without you."

He put his arm around her as she moved closer and put her head on his chest. They both were quiet for a few minutes as they finished the wine. "Are you sure you don't want me to order another bottle? I'm enjoying tonight so much I don't want it to end," he said.

"No. The last glass hit me like a ton of bricks. Another glass and I would be out cold."

"I wouldn't want that since you're the reason I'm enjoying the night so much."

Roulett raised her head to look at him. He leaned in and kissed her and she kissed him back. After the kiss, she got up suddenly and said, "I'll be back in a few minutes."

Lou waited for what seemed like an hour although it was only fifteen minutes. He decided that he should check on her. He found her in her bed sound asleep. The toilet was running in the bathroom so she'd been in there. He didn't know if she'd been sick or the wine hit her so hard that she had to go to bed. He was surprised to see she'd changed into her nightgown. He covered her with a sheet and kissed her on the cheek. So much for their romantic night.

Although she'd kissed him back, he didn't know if she'd ever respond to him the way he wanted. He fixed the chain on the toilet and went to his bed, very disappointed.

About three hours later, Lou needed to go through her room to use the bathroom. He was trying to be quiet but he thought he could hear her whimpering. He could still hear her when he came out of the bathroom.

He asked, "Roulett, are you all right? Are you sick?" He walked to the side of her bed. "Are you crying?"

"I just feel so alone," she said, softly sobbing.

"Why didn't you come tell me you didn't want to sleep alone? You know I would stay with you here or you could've joined me in my bed. Why didn't you tell me?" he asked.

"When I went to bed, I told you to join me," she said.

"I didn't hear you. Why didn't you wake me when you woke up?" he asked.

"I was afraid."

"You have no reason to be afraid of me. We've known each other too long for you to react this way."

She sat up in the bed as she said, "I'm not afraid of you."

"Then what are you afraid of?"

"I'm afraid if we become involved it'll put a strain on our friendship."

"Why would you think that?"

"Because my involvement with *Garrett* put a strain on that friendship! We were relaxed around each other 'till the day we kissed. After that, it was never the same."

"Let's examine the differences in the relationship you and Garrett tried to have and the one you and I can have. You and Garrett were both married, but not to each other and that caused a lot of tension. You two wanted to spend time with each other yet tried to keep it secret, which also caused a strain. The two of you never had a satisfying sexual encounter, which equaled a lot of sexual tension.

"Now, if we were going to have a relationship, we wouldn't have the same problems because our mates have died. We wouldn't be afraid that someone could catch us together. We'd have a satisfying sexual relationship because we could be together anytime that we wanted. Do you see the differences?"

She nodded. Then, he held her face in his hands he vowed, "I've loved you for such a long time as a friend. Making love to you won't change that. I know I'll definitely love you more than ever as time goes on." He put his arms around her and gently kissed her. She put her arms around him, and their next kiss was more passionate than the first. She was sitting on a tall Victorian-style bed with her legs crossed beneath her. She could feel his bare skin rubbing on her leg, felt the bare skin that was poking her, and found his hard penis protruding out of his robe.

For a moment, she pushed him back. He panicked and his heart pounded, fearing that she'd changed her mind. He thought that he'd moved too fast and that she was afraid again. He was pleasantly surprised to see she was only trying to uncross her legs.

She pulled him closer and kissed him again. He was relieved that his momentary panic hadn't caused him to lose his enthusiasm. She felt him again and boldly directed his penis to the spot where she wanted it to be. This time he felt bare skin because she wasn't wearing panties. He stopped long enough to pull the nightshirt that she was wearing over her head and dropped it onto the floor.

She untied the belt on his robe first, then put her hands on his shoulders, letting the robe fall to the floor. He kissed her erect nipples while caressing her breasts as she put her hands on his buttocks and pulled him closer. He followed her cue and penetration was easy. Yet, he pulled out after only a few strokes to begin kissing her again, first on the lips and then on the back of the neck.

He whispered in her ear, "You know that I love you."

She was breathing hard and pulling him closer. She wasn't timid about letting him know that she wanted more.

And more he gave her! They made love three times that night. She'd never experienced a lover like Lou. She'd only read about multiple organisms before that magical night. During their lovemaking, he told her how much he loved her over and over again, but his words were unnecessary for she felt with every ounce of her being how much he truly loved her. He loved her in ways mere words couldn't describe.

She was so thankful she'd not known his lovemaking skill before now because, even with her marriage to Jack and her insane love for Garrett, she would've made love to Lou at every opportunity, simply because making love with him was a breathtaking experience. His touch was intoxicating and his caress was the most addictive feeling she'd ever known, except for Garrett's kiss. Regrettably for Roulett, Garrett's kiss still captivated her the most.

Chapter 32 | In Search of the Truth

...The Lord will strike you with every sickness and plague...

DEUTERONOMY 28: 61

The next morning Roulett awoke with a throbbing headache, remembering the sulfites in wine always triggered the same affliction.

Lou hugged her and asked, “Would you like to have breakfast in bed or do you feel like going downstairs to eat?”

“Just give me a few more minutes, then we’ll go eat.”

“I’ll give you anything you want that’s within my powers,” he said, hugging her.

“I guess it wouldn’t surprise you to know that I have a pounding headache,” she said as she pulled him closer and kissed him.

“I’m sorry I coaxed you into drinking wine. It’s my fault you’re suffering.”

“If a headache is the price I have to pay for last night—it was well worth it!”

After her headache improved, she joined him on the balcony. “I think I feel well enough to go eat. Maybe some food in my stomach will help me feel better.” While he hugged her, she looked around, noticing that Nairobi looked more dangerous in the daylight than it had the night before—but she felt safe in Lou’s arms, the safest she’d felt since Jack’s death.

After breakfast, they returned to their rooms and decided to spend the day there for an encore of last night’s excitement. They discussed how they would start searching for clues the next day.

That afternoon Lou couldn’t suppress the urge to confess the loft story to Roulett. He broached the subject by asking, “Do you remember the first night you noticed my after-shave?”

"I remember smelling it and liking it, but I can't tell you the night it happened. I think I was still drinking heavily then, so the details are fuzzy."

"So you don't recall the night in the ranch loft?"

"I remember lots of nights in the ranch loft."

"So you don't remember our first kiss?"

"Of course I remember our first kiss—it was just last night!"

"That wasn't our *first* kiss..."

"I don't know what you're talking about."

"We kissed the night you first noticed my after-shave in the ranch loft."

"Where was Jack during this alleged kiss—watching?"

"No. He was taking a shower and I was watching you. You were extremely intoxicated and passed out in bed. Jack asked me to watch you while he showered because he was afraid you could fall down the stairs looking for him," said Lou.

"If I was passed out—how'd we kiss?"

"We thought you were, but you managed to go to the bathroom and remove all your clothes. You walked out stark naked and asked me for your nightgown," he said, turning red with embarrassment.

"I can't believe I did that. Are you sure you're not just making this up?" asked Roulett.

"I swear it happened. I was so afraid Jack would walk in. If he had, I would've needed a shower or at least a change of underwear," said Lou.

She laughed. "I still can't believe I did that. I don't remember any of it."

"Oh, there's more," he continued.

"It couldn't be much more embarrassing...Could it?"

"I panicked and thought the best thing to do was cover you up, so I frantically searched for a nightgown in the dresser drawers. I found a long T-shirt, but you were too drunk to dress yourself. I slipped it over your head as fast as I could."

"Well either you were being the perfect gentleman, or I didn't look good nude!"

"No, you looked great! But, Jack could've caught us at any moment."

"But you hadn't done anything wrong."

"Well...there's more."

"Oh no! You sound guilty!"

"I'm desperately trying to confess...After I put the T-shirt on you, you became aware that I was in the room. Realizing I wasn't Jack, you asked me why was I in your dream. I'd been drinking heavily, too, so I didn't know what to tell you. I said the first thing that popped into my head—I'm not in your dream, you're in mine."

"You know I think you're a warm, loving, gentle person but that was a dumb thing to say."

"I know that now, but then I wasn't thinking straight and what you said next didn't help matters at all. You shocked me by saying if this was my dream then we should make it a good one. You put your arms around me and kissed me on the lips. I tried to remove your arms but you only kissed me again," said Lou.

"Should I feel bad for sexually assaulting you? So far, I haven't heard anything *you* did wrong! Jack was stupid to leave you guarding me, knowing I was drunk and horny. He knew being drunk affected me that way, so you have no reason to feel guilty."

"But there's more...I was really aroused, and before I realized what I was doing, I was enjoying being so close to you way too much. To make matters worse, you told me that I smelled good enough to eat..."

"Oh, I didn't—did I...?"

"I thought oh, you wouldn't do that, or would you? I listened for Jack's shower, and it was still running. I knew I couldn't explain it to Jack. For the heated moment of passion, I was willing to risk losing my best friend, my job, my wife, or my life because Jack could've just killed me. You were rubbing my crotch and kissing me on the neck. I'd never been more aroused in my life! I didn't know if it was the booze, the danger of the moment, or the fact that I'd always been attracted to you but just wouldn't admit it, not even to myself.

"We felt and caressed everywhere possible, and you were just about to polish my knob when I realized Jack was out of the shower. I had to make you stop since he could've caught us in the act. I told you we'd finish the dream later, and you were asleep almost as fast as your head touched the pillow. I felt guilty when Jack returned because I wanted to make love to you so much that I ached all over! I knew then that I loved you and I have ever since."

"Wow! I'm sorry I don't remember any of that, but I still don't think it was your fault. Now I understand why you wanted me to drink last night!"

* * * * *

The next morning, Roulett and Lou were up early to have breakfast before going to Nambi's brother's house. They were surprised how many people in Nairobi spoke enough English to communicate with them.

Lou and Roulett were welcomed into Wangambi's small one-room shack. He was very old and extremely shaky. Roulett guessed he was almost eighty. She asked, "How did you learn to speak English so well?"

"I learned from my father. When I was younger I was an English teacher," Wangambi replied, trying his best to use the correct words.

Roulett asked, "Do you remember Roy Clayton?

"Yes, I remember Roy Clayton—he's Nambi's daddy," said Wangambi.

"Do you mean that Roy was Nambi's adopted daddy?"

"Roy bedded my mama to get Nambi, so I don't call that adopted!"

"Is Roy Clayton your daddy, too?"

"No. Mama married my daddy after Roy traveled back to America. My daddy died when I was young. Roy come here again and bedded my mother shortly before she died," said Wangambi with sadness in his voice.

"Do you have a wife or children?" she asked.

"I had several wives and bedded many women, but I don't have any children."

"How did Roy know your mama?" asked Roulett.

"My mama, Yowani, was the daughter of Yowana. Yowana was one of Roy's guides. My granddaddy's daddy worked for Roy's daddy," said Wangambi.

Roulett realized that Nambi was right when she called John-George her brother. "How did Nambi go to America?" asked Roulett.

"Roy arranged for Nambi to go to America in a boat when she was thirteen, and he then paid for her education and employment. She met Isaiah Jordan when she was in college and married him that same year. As Nambi's daddy, Roy and his son John-George have always taken care of Nambi's family," answered Wangambi.

Harvey was Roy's grandson, so now the family connection to Harvey Jordan and his family made sense to Roulett. She remembered that they'd sat in the family section at John-George's funeral. Hollie was not only Roulett's best friend but also a cousin of her late husband, Jack.

Roulett asked, "Why didn't you go to America with Nambi?"

"Most of my family is still here in Africa. Nambi has always sent me money, which greatly improved my life as well as the life of my family," said Wangambi.

Roulett looked around to see the state of poverty in which he lived. She couldn't imagine how bad his livelihood would've been without Nambi's help.

He said, "I've never gone without food like so many people that I know. With my generous sister's help, I've always been able to have health care, which I believe is the reason that I've outlived all my wives."

Roulett asked, "Do you remember anything about Roy finding the fruit—the same fruit that is growing everywhere now?"

"I remember a conversation I'd overheard between my granddaddy and Roy, about how Roy had taken the plant from a tribe that my granddaddy had hired as porters on one of Roy's safaris. I don't recollect the tribe's name, I only remember the tribe came from somewhere between Axum and Lalibela in Ethiopia, a sacred place where legends claim are where Adam's tomb and the Ark of the Covenant are located.

"My granddaddy told Roy that the fruit was 'God's fruit,' it was forbidden fruit, and it would bring death until it was returned to the natives—the natives who Roy stole the fruit from. My granddaddy and Roy tried to find the natives, but they seemed to have vanished from the face of the earth. No one even remembered them except for my granddaddy and Roy."

"We need to go to Magandi, which is supposed to be near where Roy found the fruit," said Roulett.

"You won't find any information there that you don't already know. My granddaddy and Roy searched the entire area for many months, but found nothing and neither will you. But I've arranged for someone to take you. This is my aunt's great-grandson Andy. He will take you anywhere you want to go for gas money."

Andy smiled and asked, "Where you wanta go?"

Roulett showed Andy the location on the map, "Here, please."

As they departed in his dilapidated Jeep, Wangambi yelled, "Take care of them Andy, they are family!"

Roulett and Lou spent a miserable day, jostled around from trail to trail, trying desperately without luck to glean information about the fruit. The fruit seemed to be growing everywhere! They returned to Wangambi's home shortly before sunset—tired, dirty, and completely frustrated from the wasted trip.

"Did you find anything?" Wangambi asked.

"No. The trip was just as you said it would be," replied Roulett.

"Wangambi, do you think the Spouse Killer plague is caused by the rainbow fruit?" asked Lou.

"I don't think it. I *know* it is!" he declared.

"Do you have any suggestions how we can stop the plague or even prove that the cause is the fruit?" asked Roulett.

"You can't find the natives! You can't give back the fruit. You can't stop the deaths! But sometimes, the answer is right under our noses and we just don't see it..." Wangambi replied.

Roulett handed Andy and Wangambi each a hundred-dollar bill, insisting they take it for their time and trouble. Although reluctant at first, Wangambi finally agreed and thanked her repeatedly. Andy thanked them for the money and the tank of gas, then offered to take them on another tour tomorrow. They declined and headed back to the hotel.

Chapter 33 | Green-Eyed Monster

Cruel, destructive anger is nothing compared to jealousy.

PROVERBS 27:4

Marie had just finished breakfast when she heard a knock at the door. After looking through the peephole, she saw Garrett and opened the door with a cheerful, "Good morning!"

Garrett said, "You're in an exceptionally good mood, for so early in the morning. Did I barely miss Paul?"

"No," Marie answered, as her cheeks turned a rosy-pink.

Garrett asked, "What do you want me to do today?"

"I got a letter from Roulett yesterday and I thought you might want to read it first."

"Why don't you just tell me what she said?" Garrett unenthusiastically replied.

Marie asked, "Are you disappointed that you didn't get to go to Africa?"

Garrett thought for a few seconds. "Yes, I guess so. I think it'd be an interesting place to see. This was probably the only chance I'd ever have to see Africa, because you know how Olivia feels about flying, and you can't *drive* to Africa."

"Have you thought about a cruise? You could travel to Africa by boat."

"No, Olivia has a problem with seasickness, too."

"I'm sorry you weren't able to go, but in some ways I'm glad that Lou went with Roulett."

"Yes. His education would be more help in her quest."

"That's not the main reason I'm glad he went."

"Then why?" Garrett asked with a puzzled look on his face.

"Well, I don't know if you've thought about this or not, but Roulett and Lou are both single now. I think it's good for both of them to escape all their sad memories by spending more time together."

"You're right. I'd never thought of that," Garrett said.

"I know from experience that it isn't easy losing a long-time spouse, but a widow or widower's happier going on with their life by loving those who remain rather than fretting over lost loved ones. I would like to see Lou and Roulett together because I've noticed for a long time how Lou looks at Roulett...as if he's loved her for years."

"Do you think he's ever told Roulett how he feels?"

"I'm almost positive that he hasn't said a word to her."

Garrett remembered how Lou always seemed to catch Garrett and Roulett at the wrong time. He'd thought Lou was only trying to protect his best friend's wife, but Lou may've been motivated by jealousy. Garrett never thought about the possibility of Roulett and Lou having a romantic interest in each other until now and he didn't like the idea.

"Haven't you ever noticed how Lou looks at her?"

"No, I never paid any attention. Do you think the feeling's mutual?" he asked.

"I don't believe she's thought about him in any way other than as a friend. Maybe that'll change after this trip because they'll be alone day and night for almost two weeks."

"I never thought about that," Garrett said, deep in thought.

Marie asked, "Now do you want me to tell you what Roulett said in her letter?"

"Maybe it'd be easier if I just read it," Garrett said, wanting to see if he could glean a clue about how things were going between Lou and Roulett in Africa. Garrett took the letter and read it carefully.

October 15

Dear Marie,

Unfortunately, there's no great news to write about yet. We haven't found anything important, but we'll keep looking. The hotel here is nice. We're doing some sightseeing while we search for clues.

The rainbow fruit is everywhere here. Jack and Kirk did such a good job of spreading the seeds that we can only hope that the fruit's not the cause of the Spouse Killer.

Kiss Michael and Tammy for me and tell them I love them.

I'll call you before we travel home.

Love, Roulett

Garrett didn't pick up the slightest clue about how Roulett and Lou's present relationship. Uncertainty weighed heavily on his mind as he wondered if he'd made the right choice.

*****

On the Friday after Roulett and Lou's return, Marie invited Kirk and Pam to the ranch get-together so that Lou and Roulett could talk to Pam about the trip to Africa. In addition, Paul was there with Marie. That night, Olivia and Garrett attended their last ranch get-together before they were to leave for Atlanta. Garrett noticed Lou sitting by Roulett with his arm around her—an unwelcome surprise. Although he tried not to stare, he couldn't keep himself from wondering what had happened in Africa.

Lou said, "We were disappointed when we didn't determine more usable information about the fruit, but being in Africa certainly made us appreciate the good old USA."

Garrett's curiosity was overwhelming. He wanted to ask Roulett about Lou and her, but Garrett didn't think he'd have an opportunity to talk to her alone. Therefore, he tried something he and Roulett had accomplished in the past. The bond between them was so close that they could talk with subliminal messages, which only they understood while the rest of the people in the room were clueless to their conversation. In his agitated state, he would have to proceed cautiously or everyone would see his feelings for her.

He asked, "Roulett—was Africa all you expected it to be—or were you extremely disappointed?"

She replied, "It was almost exactly what I expected it to be. I was only disappointed when we didn't discover more about the fruit."

Garrett remembered her asking him in the ranch loft if he felt like an erupting volcano and came back with, "It's a shame how the fruit didn't come from Hawaii. The islands are so beautiful with the beaches, the palm trees, and the gigantic volcanoes that could erupt at anytime. I think you would've enjoyed Hawaii more than Africa."

She answered quickly, before anyone else could speak, "If people can't go to Hawaii, they cope with where they are and try their best to enjoy it. They may not like where they are at first, but they can grow to love it."

Although stung by her words, he still asked, "Did you like it enough to go back there on vacation, instead of somewhere like Hawaii?"

She snapped back, "I would consider it because *I know what to expect* in Africa but I don't know what to expect in Hawaii and I may never know."

No one else in the room could understand why Garrett and Roulett were having this strange conversation, but Lou was catching the underlying message.

Garrett pressed his luck. "I'm surprised that you would consider going back."

Before Roulett could answer, Lou said, "The trip wasn't all bad. We had many good moments." He smiled as he looked at Roulett, remembering to be careful, trying not to let Marie know the closeness he and Roulett had developed in Africa. She felt it was too soon after Jack's death for Marie to accept her daughter-in-law with another man.

Roulett said, "It may surprise you, but you weren't there to know why I'd go back."

Lou interrupted, "That's enough about Africa. We need to talk about what we can do next to find the underlying cause of the plague."

Marie came in from the kitchen carrying a tray of snacks. Garrett spent the rest of the evening silently pondering the possibilities—most of which he didn't like.

Chapter 34 | Dealing with Death

The Lord showed Amos a basket of fruit and told him there would be dead bodies everywhere. AMOS 8: 1-3

The next week, Pam sadly sent brain and tissue samples to the CDC from Dr. Warren Long, her long time friend who'd died suddenly while on duty that morning at the hospital. Pam had called his wife minutes after his death, not only to report the terrible news about her husband, but also to request permission to perform an immediate autopsy on him. His wife, Ling, who'd been a nurse for many years, allowed the rapid autopsy because she knew that's what he'd have wanted. Pam sent the tissue samples overnight air to Dr. Worthington at the CDC.

Dr. Cleta Worthington called Pam the next afternoon. Obviously concerned, she asked, "Did Willie collect these samples for you?"

Pam replied, "Yes, why?"

"You need to fire that necrophilia pervert. He's screwing the corpses again, or he's masturbating while collecting the samples. I found live sperm in the brain tissue. I assumed he preferred women but this sample was from a man," Cleta said.

"Yes, I know. It's from my friend, Dr. Long," said Pam.

"I'm sorry about your friend, but we're desperately trying to uncover the details to help us understand what we're dealing with, and I can't tolerate adulterated samples."

"I'm sorry, I'll have a talk with Willie."

"If I were you, I'd do more than talk to him! You should immediately terminate the disgusting pervert."

"I promise, it won't happen again."

"I am sorry about your colleague. I'm so busy that I can't even manage to e-mail all of my grieving friends sympathy notes."

"Is there any news on the plague from the CDC?" asked Pam.

"The CDC has a theory that someone from the Famine Free Future organization may've picked up some strange bug, which we haven't been able to identify yet. Because they traveled to many remote areas of the world while spreading the seed of the rainbow fruit, they may've also spread this unknown bug. Right now, that's the best theory we have."

That afternoon, Roulett took the children by the ranch to ride their horses. When they arrived, Roulett was surprised to see Garrett's truck. She helped the children saddle their horses, then watched them ride down the trail. When she entered the barn, she saw Garrett coming down the opposite hall leading an overexcited yearling. She asked, "I'm surprised to see you here today. What happened to Frank?" In the last week, Marie had hired Frank Probus to replace Garrett as the ranch hand.

Garrett stopped and tried to talk to Roulett, but the yearling didn't want to stop—she nervously pawed the ground and fidgeted. Garrett said, "Wait here. I want to talk to you. I'll be back in just a minute."

"Okay," said Roulett, pacing back and forth waiting for Garrett to return. She was afraid he'd ask her something about her trip to Africa with Lou.

Garrett returned in a few minutes. He pulled off his leather gloves as he said, "I had to put that filly on a walker before I could talk to you. Frank's mother died on Saturday, so I agreed to work for him until Friday."

Roulett asked, "What caused his mother's death?"

"The Spouse Killer. I read in the paper this morning that the most booming businesses in the last four months were funeral homes, casket manufacturers, crematories, and cemeteries."

"I know—it's scary," she said.

Marie had walked from her house to the clubhouse and then into the barn loft. She was checking to see if she needed to order more Christmas cards. Since the intercom from the mare foaling pen was on, she overheard Roulett and Garrett's conversation as she searched the cabinets.

Roulett asked, "What did you want to talk to me about?"

"Will you answer one question for me?"

"If I can."

"Did you sleep with Lou on your trip to Africa?"

Marie hadn't been paying attention to their conversation until then, but she put down the Christmas cards and turned up the volume on the intercom as loud as it would go while she watched them through the one-way glass.

Roulett thought for a few moments before she replied, "I'll answer your question if you'll answer one for me first?"

"All right. What?"

"Did you suggest that Olivia call the CDC to see if she could start work a month later?"

It was his turn to pause. "Yes, but I wasn't trying to avoid going with you. I was only trying to make Olivia think I wasn't eager to go to Africa with you. I didn't think the CDC would agree to Olivia starting work later. I wanted to go with you, but at the same time, I didn't want Olivia to be suspicious."

"I knew you had sabotaged our trip!"

"I didn't do it on purpose! I really wanted to go with you. Did you sleep with Lou to punish me?"

"No, I didn't sleep with Lou to punish you..."

"I'm glad that you didn't sleep with him."

"I didn't say I didn't sleep with him."

"I can't believe you did that!" he seethed as he took off his gloves and threw them on the ground.

His reaction infuriated her. "I guess you're all alone every night so you expect the same of me!"

"That's not the point—I was married to Olivia before we met. I never complained about Jack—did I?" he asked.

"But now, with Jack dead, I'm to remain alone for the rest of my life waiting for a crumb from you? Maybe I want more than a crumb; maybe I want a whole cake. I don't even have the memories of being with you because you messed up our trip to Africa. I can't help thinking that you did it on purpose. The trip that I carefully planned, scheduled, and arranged for adjoining rooms just so that *we* could finally be *alone*, where we could make love! I won't wait around for the occasional bit of affection that I might receive from you. Loving you is the most unfulfilled thing that has ever happened to me."

"I told you that I wanted to go with you," he replied, reaching for her hand.

Roulett began to cry. "I never wanted to love you, but I still do. *Wanting* something doesn't make it happen. I *wanted* you with me in Africa, but wanting it didn't make it happen. You weren't there when I needed you. We've wanted to make love for almost a year, but it hasn't happened. Now, I don't think it'll ever happen. I don't want to spend my nights alone! The last two years while Jack was alive, I spent so much time alone I was miserable. He was gone so many nights. I don't ever want to feel that lonely again.

Lou can give me what you can't or won't. He loves me. He wants to marry me. He'll spend time with me, and he'll spend all his *nights* with me."

"Are you going to marry him?" Garrett asked.

"I don't know," she cried. "I didn't want to love you, but I do. Nevertheless, nothing short of taking my last breath will stop me from loving you. I wish I could transfer all the feelings I have for you to Lou, which would make my life so much simpler."

Garrett was almost in tears too, as he put his arms around her and said, "I'm sorry, I don't have the right to question what you do. But because I love you, I don't like to think of you being with him. I feel he's taking something that's mine."

"I feel I *should* be yours, but you're the one who won't let it happen, not me," she said.

"I don't want us to part angry with each other," he said while comforting her. He kissed and hugged her while she sobbed like a little girl.

As she listened on the intercom, Marie was almost in shock.

Roulett and Garrett continued to hug each other for a long time before they heard the children coming back from their ride. Roulett said, "Maybe someday?"

Marie was very quiet going down the steps and through the clubhouse to the barn. The children came back from their ride as she walked up to them, pretending to have just arrived at the barn. Since Jack's death, it was common for Roulett to cry, so nobody mentioned her eyes being red.

Marie asked, "Why don't you and the kids come inside for something to eat and drink?"

"Maybe tomorrow night, I'm tired and I have a lot of things to do," declined Roulett.

"Okay, I'll see you tomorrow."

Roulett stopped for a minute, thinking something was wrong with Marie, before Roulett asked, "You aren't going to be alone tonight—are you?"

"No, Paul will be here in a few minutes—I'll be fine. Go on home and rest. I'll talk to you tomorrow," said Marie.

Paul pulled in the driveway as Roulett and the children were leaving. Roulett waved but she didn't stop. She was in a hurry, knowing Lou would be waiting at home since they were going out to eat and to a movie.

They hadn't been together since Africa, but after her upsetting day Roulett planned to ask Lou to spend the night at her house. She desperately needed his reassurance and to be reminded that he loved her with all his heart.

Chapter 35 | Revelation

...And there will be enmity between you and the woman and between your seeds... GENESIS 3: 15

As the only medical examiner in the town of Petrolia, Dr. Pam Barnes was overwhelmed as the death toll continued to rise. She called Dr. Cleta Worthington at the CDC often to hear a sympathetic voice and to have a sounding board for her thoughts. One such conversation began, "Cleta, have you noticed more and more of our colleagues are dying?"

"Yes. We've lost two people this week. We should be thankful it's not us," replied Cleta.

"I know I should be thankful, but I feel so helpless. There must be something we've missed. Maybe we're not doing the autopsies soon enough."

"Since your office and lab are in the Petrolia hospital, I don't know how you could accomplish it any faster unless you started before the person died."

"Actually, many of the men are brain-dead before their hearts stop," Pam replied.

"Are you suggesting you start cutting on them before they flat line?" Cleta asked.

"No! I know I can't do that, but I would like to start as soon as possible. Now I have to wait until the corpse arrives and then obtain written permission before I begin. I feel in my gut that I could understand the Spouse Killer plague better if I could start sooner," said Pam.

"Why don't you obtain written permission from the hospital staff now for an autopsy in case one of the hospital personnel suddenly dies at work? That should speed things up."

"That's a great idea, but it seems a little morbid to wait for a colleague to die."

"Remember, you're trying to save many lives. Right now we can't save *any* and they would die anyway."

The next week, a long-time hospital employee who had just signed his release form died shortly after he arrived to start his shift. Because Pam had obtained prior consent, she had Lester on the autopsy table only minutes after his last breath. She quickly gathered the specimens, packed them in dry ice, and sent them by air express to Cleta at the CDC.

The next afternoon, Cleta called Pam, who was napping on the couch in her office. "I told you that you should do more than *talk* to Willie. I found live sperm again, in the brain specimen you sent me yesterday!"

Pam replied, "That's not possible. Are you sure you have the right specimen?"

"I'm sure! Pam, I told you talking to that necrophilia pervert wouldn't work. He's still masturbating while collecting the specimens."

"Well, that can't be right. Willie got so angry when I talked to him about the last specimen that he quit last week."

"Willie didn't collect these specimens?"

"No! I collected and packaged them myself."

The phone line went silent while Cleta thought about the revelation. Cleta realized what she'd found, as she said, "I think I know what's causing the deaths!"

Pam asked, "What?"

"Let me get back to you after I do some more research to make certain I'm right. Is Roulett Barnes running the Center?"

"Yes, why?"

"I'll tell you later."

"Okay, but call me as soon as you know something...Hello, Cleta—Cleta, are you still there?" Pam asked, realizing Cleta had hung up. Pam wondered if Cleta were losing her mind, but she had too much respect for her to call her back and say so.

Three days later, Cleta called Pam at home. "Pam, I want you on the next available flight to Atlanta. I've found the cause of the Spouse Killer!"

Pam wasn't alert enough to be cooperative. "What? Oh, Cleta, it's..." she paused while squinting at the clock on her nightstand, "It's four o'clock in the morning. Can't you tell me on the phone?"

"No, you wouldn't believe me if I told you. This is so outrageous that you'll have to see it in person. Bring Roulett and Dr. Gordon with you. They need to see this, and Dr. Aldridge will be here."

Pam asked, "Should I bring Kirk?"

"No, but I'll warn you ahead of time, he's not going to like my research findings."

Cleta thought for a moment before adding, "But Pam, the more I think about it, the more I realize that he should be here. You need to bring him with you."

Kirk was lying beside Pam and he complained as she hung up the phone, "Why did she call so early in the morning?"

"I don't think she was aware of the time. She was so excited because she said that she's found the cause of the Spouse Killer plague. She wants Lou, Roulett, and the two of us in Atlanta as soon as possible. So do me a favor and make coffee while I call Roulett and Lou so we can make arrangements for our trip."

After she booked the flights, she called Cleta to inform her that the four of them would arrive at 12:40 p.m. at the Atlanta airport.

Cleta said, "I'll send a driver to pick you up at the airport and I'll schedule a 3:00 meeting at the CDC. After I bring everyone up to date, we'll decide how to report the news to the press."

When Pam, Kirk, Roulett, and Lou arrived that afternoon, Cleta met them at the airport herself. She said, "I thought we'd all have lunch before the meeting." They all agreed, and by a majority vote, they decided on Mexican food.

On their way to the restaurant, Cleta instructed, "Please don't ask me questions about my research findings until the meeting. I promise you, after the meeting, all these strange deaths will make sense for the first time."

Everyone respected Cleta's request. After the waiter handed them menus, the group spent considerable time mulling over the cuisine possibilities and making small talk until Kirk noticed the rainbow fruit appeared on the menu complete with a colorful photo. Excited, he said, "I can't believe my rainbow fruit is on a Mexican restaurant menu in Atlanta, Georgia!"

Pam replied, "I'm not surprised. Your fruit's very colorful and festive, and this is a very festive place."

Lou added, "I think your fruit is everywhere now, or at least, it was everywhere that Roulett and I traveled in Africa."

"That proves that you and Jack did a fantastic job of spreading the fruit all over the world."

Cleta snapped, "That's right, the fruit is everywhere, exactly like the plague it's all over the world!"

Kirk instantly tensed. "Are you implying that my fruit has something to do with the deaths?"

"I said I'm not going to talk about my research findings until the meeting, and that includes questions about your fruit," Cleta replied.

Pam asked Cleta, "Is your friend Alex Mueller attending this meeting today?"

"No, he won't…he passed away over a month ago."

"I'm sorry I upset you, I didn't know he was dead. How did he die?" asked Pam.

"He was another victim of the Spouse Killer. If I'd known then what I know now, I could've possibly saved his life," said Cleta, trying to hold back tears.

"I'm sorry to hear about Alex. He seemed like such a nice man," said Pam.

"He was a wonderful man and I loved him very much. Thanks for your concern."

When they finished the meal, everyone loaded into Cleta's van for the tense trip to the CDC. After arriving, Cleta led them to the reserved conference room. She instructed them to take seats facing the large white board, which had an eraser and multi-colored erasable markers in the tray. The large clock on the sea-foam green wall showed only seven minutes remained before the start of the meeting as Cleta handed each person a white legal pad and a pencil.

Lou joked, "Are we going to have a test later, or are we required to sketch you?"

She chuckled. "Neither—I thought you might want to take notes."

Dr. Olivia Aldridge, two of her colleagues, and two armed CDC security guards entered the conference room. Everyone, including Kirk, knew the armed guards were there to ensure Kirk remained civil.

After a brief round of introductions, Cleta began, "I'll write the six findings concerning the Spouse Killer on the board—some facts you already know, others will be new. Please wait until I'm through before asking questions."

Choosing a red marker, she wrote as she explained, "Number one is that *all* the victims of the Spouse Killer have experienced *sex*ual intercourse within twenty-four hours or less of their deaths." She underlined the words "all" and "sex."

"Number two is that all the male victims were either homosexuals or men with vasectomies."

"Third, my findings show lesbians never die from the Spouse Killer unless they were bi-sexual."

"Fourth, women who die from the Spouse Killer are those whose sexual partner hasn't had a vasectomy. In all cases, seminal fluid was present in the vagina even in the cases where condoms were used. This strange phenomenon is a puzzling part of this mystery, but the most baffling part is that this seminal fluid, which should contain sperm—does not! Be patient—I realize this is not logical, but allow me to finish."

"Fifth, the killer is *sperm*!" She underlined the word sperm.

"And last—but certainly not least—the *killer-sperm* is caused by the rainbow *fruit*!" She underlined the words "killer-sperm" and "fruit."

The only thing keeping Kirk from taking a swing at Cleta were the guards. He exploded, "You dumb dyke, my fruit isn't the cause!"

"One more outburst like that and you'll be escorted out of here and we'll finish the conference without you. Kirk, do you understand?" Cleta asked.

Kirk managed an angry nod.

"Now, if you have a question, please raise your hand. I'll answer your questions or I'll show some video of experiments that prove what I've just revealed." Pam raised her hand and Cleta pointed to her. "Yes, Pam, what's your question?"

"How can sperm be the killer if you never find any sperm in the women victims?"

"I know it sounds like something from a B-rated horror movie, but the sperm traveled out of the body. The damage inflicted as the sperm escape the body is the cause of death. I'll show you on the video." Cleta touched the sophisticated control panel and the first images appeared. "This is a human stomach taken from a fresh cadaver, cleansed on the inside to eliminate the contents as well as the acids. As you can see, I inserted a specimen of the killer sperm into the uncontaminated stomach. I've both glued and surgically stapled the ends shut to form an impenetrable seal. Normal sperm wouldn't be able to penetrate the stomach and escape—but for these Houdini-type sperm, it isn't a difficult feat.

"I'll show you first with the regular time-lapse camera. Now, if you'll notice on the screen, small holes are appearing on the outside of the stomach. We can't see the cause with the naked eye, but now I'll show you with a magnified time-lapse camera. I'll warn you though—don't watch if you're squeamish."

One woman screeched as the heads of the determined sperm made holes in the human-stomach specimen. The holes become larger and larger as more and more sperm squeezed through where their predecessors had escaped. The numbers increased each time the holes enlarged. The killer-sperm resembled tiny maggots eating through the tissue incredibly fast.

Cleta said, "Now, imagine a uterus or a brain being attacked by these killer-sperm, which are at least a thousand times stronger than normal sperm. These mutated sperm are programmed to travel and penetrate like normal sperm, but at an alarming higher level.

"The second video shows how this killer-sperm reacts to a human egg." Again, she narrated while the tape ran, "This a human egg in a petri dish. Notice that the sperm continue to penetrate the egg until it is torn into a million parts, leaving it incapable of being fertilized."

Cleta pointed to the board as she said, "Let's go back over the six facts I stated earlier. All the victims of the Spouse Killer have experienced sexual intercourse within twenty-four hours or less of their deaths. Now my statement makes sense! If this plant was on the earth years ago, we can understand how the religious concept started that sex was the original sin—sex caused death, therefore sex must be a sin!

"Second, all male victims were either homosexuals or men who'd had vasectomies. The sperm of other men caused the deaths of the homosexual men, and their own sperm killed the men with vasectomies. This also explains the one-or-the-other deaths—male or female—but not both. Again, I think this fruit was on the earth years ago at the beginning of civilization, and, because men who experienced sex with men died after consuming this fruit, their deaths were considered God's punishment for homosexuality, therefore, perceived as a sin.

"Third, lesbians never die from the Spouse Killer unless they are bi-sexual because they aren't exposed to sperm. The Bible doesn't mention women who lie with women being a sin—no sperm, no death, therefore no sin.

"Fourth, the women who died had a sexual partner who hadn't had a vasectomy because sperm equals death. Worldwide, more women have died from this plague than men have. Which leads me to remember a story about a woman, a forbidden fruit, and a sinful act that required God's punishment—does this scenario ring a bell for anyone? I believe many years ago, when everything that caused death, from earthquakes to floods, was perceived as punishment from God, and before the medical technology of vasectomies, mostly women died from consuming this fruit. Therefore, women needed punishment for a sinful act involving a woman and a fruit. All we need is the serpent to understand the whole Garden of Eden scenario. This explains volumes more than the plague we're aware of now.

"Fifth, I've proven that sperm is the killer.

"Sixth, I've analyzed the rainbow fruit, which contains a unique type of protein. This new protein is complete protein, which resembles animal protein more than plant protein and thus, possibly forms the missing link between plant and animal. This protein contains a prion, not the same prion that produces Mad-Cow or Creutzfeldt-Jakob disease, but a prion that creates genetic changes in the sperm of men and a hardening of uterine walls in women making the completion of a pregnancy impossible. The world pregnancy rate has dropped eighty-seven percent in the last three months and is still declining.

"Another interesting fact is the rainbow plant contains minute amounts of iridium, which is a rare trace element. Iridium is normally associated with meteorites, but it's my speculation that this plant could explain why dinosaurs became extinct."

Kirk couldn't hold his tongue any longer. "Is there any world disaster that you can't attribute to my rainbow fruit?"

Cleta replied, "We're not here to discuss all the past disasters of our planet—only the one we're dealing with now. For all of you from Petrolia, I know your return flight is scheduled for tomorrow afternoon, so I'll give you more information in the morning meeting I've scheduled for nine o'clock. I promise that I'll have some enlightening details, which I expect you all will want to hear. Please feel free to take the pencils and paper with you so you can jot down any questions you might think of later."

* * * * *

That evening in the Atlanta hotel, Pam tried to calm Kirk by saying, "When we return home, I'll do some experiments of my own. I'll try my best to disprove Cleta's theory. She must be wrong because we did extensive testing on the fruit before we fed it to humans. I think it's only a coincidence that the fruit and the Spouse Killer both spread all over the world at the same time. You know after the animal tests, we fed the rainbow fruit to ten well-paid volunteers who now, to the best of my knowledge, haven't died or caused the death of their significant others from the killer-sperm. There has to be another explanation because each volunteer ate a fruit a day for thirty days. We need to test the sperm of the male volunteers when we return. The cause has to be something other than your fruit, and I'll do everything that I can to prove it."

"I wish we could go home tonight. I don't want to stay here another minute," whined Kirk.

Meanwhile, in the hotel room next door Lou said to Roulett, "I think you made a wise decision to trade your Famine Free Future stock for Kirk and Charles's Clayton Research Center stock. At the time you did it, I thought it was an enormous mistake!"

"I definitely had a feeling I should rid myself of anything connected with the fruit. Although Charles accepted the trade as I proposed, I would've included the two large diamonds that John-George gave me if Charles hadn't immediately agreed to trade."

Lou kissed her on the cheek. "I'm glad you managed to keep your diamonds. I'd add diamonds to my marriage proposal to you if it'd make you accept."

"We'll talk about setting a wedding date when we return home."

Lou couldn't believe his ears—Roulett had agreed to marry him! He said, "You've made me the happiest man in the world!"

"I hate to disappoint you—we can't celebrate by making love until we learn more about this killer-sperm thing."

"I'm thrilled with being near you, knowing you'll be my wife."

The next morning, Kirk reluctantly attended the meeting at the CDC with the same group who attended the prior day—including the armed security guards. Dr. Cleta Worthington began, "Today, I'll finish my explanation of my research findings concerning the Spouse Killer." The facts she'd written on the erasable board were still there, so she used the bottom of the board to highlight the points of her speech.

"Condoms don't work because the killer-sperm can easily penetrate ten condoms at one time. Spermacides don't work on the killer-sperm, because the chemicals strong enough to destroy them damage other human tissue as well. Acid and alkaline do not work on the killer-sperm unless the substances are strong enough to burn human tissue because the killer-sperm have transformed into tiny prion particles that cannot be killed with boiling water, chemical disinfectants, or radiation. The primary solution at this time is for men to abstain from sex. While this will protect most men, it could be dangerous for those with vasectomies since a nocturnal emission could kill them. For those men, the only safest procedure at this time would be for them to be castrated and begin male hormone-replacement therapy."

This was more than Kirk could tolerate. "You dumb-dyke bitch! That's your lifelong-dream, to cut the balls off of all mankind!"

Cleta motioned for one of the armed guards to move closer to Kirk, who immediately sat down. She picked up one of the many files in front of her as she said, "Kirk, I have your medical records here, which shows me you've had a vasectomy. So, by all means, keep your testicles, because, if you have the killer-sperm, the only person that'll die will be you!"

Pam immediately asked, "Is Kirk in any danger now?"

"No, only if he has the killer-sperm and experiences ejaculation! I know Kirk loves to hear me talk—but I don't think my speech will have that effect on him," Cleta said smugly, then asked, "Any other questions or comments?"

Roulett asked, "Why does the sperm kill men differently than women?"

"The killer-sperm appears to recognize hormone differences in males and females. In men, the sperm travels up through the bloodstream to their brains and in women, the killer-sperm travels from their uterus or vaginal cavity downward into the bloodstream to their heels. I've found many exit points in the heels of the deceased women, which were previously mistaken for normal lividity marks. Men have shown some visible signs of bleeding from their ears, nose, eyes, or mouth. Their cause of death is normally massive cerebral hemorrhage, while women show signs of vaginal hemorrhage or massive internal and external uterine bleeding. I'm doing more research on these phenomena, and I'll inform you later of the results," said Cleta.

Lou said, "I think we should work on a better solution than castration, which seems rather drastic."

Cleta reminded him, "*Death* is far more drastic! I'm open to any solution that could prove effective. I'm trying to obtain more information about the fruit. The U.S. Attorney General signed a search warrant for Clayton Research Center, Famine Free Future offices, Petrolia Oil, John-George Clayton's property, Marie Barnes' property, Roulett Barnes' property, and Pam and Kirk Barnes' property, which were searched yesterday for anything that could assist us with our research of the Spouse Killer.

"Something of interest that may or may not have a connection to the Spouse Killer is, during the searches, the authorities found the missing vials from the Center. The HIV, Ebola, and John-George number seventeen vials were full while the cholera vial was empty: John-George number seventeen tested as an altered version of the rainbow fruit plant extract."

Kirk blurted, "That's a harmless plant extract!"

Cleta said, "If it's a harmless plant extract, why did your grandfather keep it in the Biohazard level-four lab at the Center?"

Kirk couldn't answer her incriminating question, but if looks could kill, Cleta would've died from his disturbing stare.

She asked, "How did you obtain these vials that were kept in the Biohazard level-four lab? You know, I was wrongfully accused of taking the vials that were found yesterday in your personal vault! The authorities also found an enormous diamond in a small Crown Royal bag with what apparently is the original rainbow fruit. Can you explain how you acquired these?"

"My grandfather gave them to me before he died," lied Kirk.

"Are you telling me John-George gave you the fruit, the large diamond, and the missing vials before he died?" pressured Cleta Worthington.

Kirk replied, "Yes, he did. Why?"

"I acquired the original copy of John-George's last will and testament, which lists the contents of a box allotted to Roulett Barnes upon John-George's death. The contents of this box didn't appear on the distributed copies of John-George's will to keep the contents a private matter between John-George's attorney and Roulett. I'm going to read you the list of all the contents in that box—an heirloom Catholic Bible, three diamonds (one approximately fifty-eight carats and two approximately eighteen carats), and the fruit! Can you explain to me and to Roulett, why the large diamond and the fruit that were supposed to be Roulett's were found in your personal vault?"

"I told you, Grandfather changed his mind and gave them to me instead of Roulett!"

"How did you acquire the missing vials I was accused of stealing?" drilled Cleta.

"Grandfather gave them to me, too, but I don't know why he had them!" Kirk lied.

"Didn't you question why he gave you vials, which were originally kept in the Biohazard lab?" asked Cleta.

"No, he was dying so I only did as he said," answered Kirk.

"Was the cholera vial full or empty when he gave it to you?" said Cleta.

Kirk hesitated, thinking hard before he answered, "It was empty."

"Did he hand them to you or did you have to retrieve them?" asked Cleta.

"He sent me to his house to pick up the box for Roulett and a box he had for me," answered Kirk.

"So you are telling me John-George Clayton gave the fruit and large diamond to you, and that when John-George died he didn't intend for Roulett Barnes to receive the fruit and large diamond as his last will said?"

"Yes, that's right!"

"Don't you think you should've called to apologize to me for wrongfully accusing me of stealing the vials when John-George gave them to you?"

"Yes…I should've called you, but I couldn't explain why he had them. That's why I didn't call. I'm sorry."

"You'll have to explain to your local authorities why you also had in your possession the biohazard vials of HIV and Ebola. And, because John-George's will wasn't legally changed before his death, I'm sure that Roulett's attorney will be contacting you concerning the rightful ownership of the fruit and the enormous diamond! I think Dr. Olivia Aldridge has something to say before I dismiss this meeting," Cleta said.

Olivia stood and began, "Now that we know the cause, a worldwide effort will start today to stop the ever-increasing deaths caused by the Spouse Killer. News sources all over the world will carry warnings suggesting sex may be hazardous to people's health. A panel of the world's leading prion researchers will meet for a conference next week at the CDC. The state's health departments and many hospitals will offer free sperm checks. The World Health Organization has offered a three-million-dollar reward to any person or group of people who finds a cure to the Spouse Killer. This effort will be funded by the generosity of many of the world's largest companies in a united effort to stop this scourge."

"Thank you, Olivia, for your input. I know some of you have to catch a plane in less than two hours, so I'll adjourn this meeting."

Roulett asked, "Dr. Worthington, could Lou and I have a word with you in private?"

"Certainly. We'll talk in my office and I'd be happy to drive everyone to the airport afterward."

"We'd love a ride to the airport," replied Roulett. She and Lou followed Cleta to her office where she invited them to have a seat.

Cleta asked, "What did you want to talk to me about?"

"I think Kirk used the cholera vial to kill his step-grandmother Florence. You see, if Florence had outlived John-George, Kirk would not have inherited anything," said Roulett.

Cleta calmly answered, "That doesn't surprise me, but I don't know if there's any way to prove it now."

"Can't you have Florence's body exhumed and tested for cholera?" asked Roulett.

"I can do that, but testing Florence's body will only tell us if she died from cholera. It won't prove who killed her with the virus. Although, I agree he had motive and probably did steal the vials and use the cholera to kill her, he'll just blame John-George since he can't defend himself."

"Kirk seems capable of getting away with anything, including murder," complained Roulett.

"If it's any consolation, I agree that Kirk most likely committed both grand larceny and murder. There will be a worldwide wrongful-death class action suit filed against him, which should leave him a pauper, eliminating the wealth he has loved all his life."

"You mean he'll end up broke?" asked Roulett.

"And possibly in jail. It's reassuring that there's some justice in this world—isn't it?" Cleta said with a smug smile.

Later, on the airplane trip home, Kirk and Roulett didn't even look at each other for fear they'd fight. Pam wasn't happy with Kirk because he'd kept so many secrets from her. She scolded him, "How could you keep vials of dangerous pathogens without telling me? I'm the local medical examiner! My husband keeping biohazard vials in his personal vault will probably damage my career and ruin my credibility!"

"I'm sorry. I know I should've told you, but I couldn't explain why my grandfather had the vials."

"You know that when we arrive home, I'm going to have to schedule you to have a vasectomy reversal so we can check your sperm because, although I'd like to believe Cleta is wrong about the killer-sperm, I can't take that chance."

"Will that hurt?" whined Kirk.

"You won't feel a thing. Dr. Green will perform an end-to-end suture anastomosis of the cut ends with splinting, using internal polyethylene tubing, preceded by resection of the fibrosed vas on each side. If successful, the re-establishment of the ducts should occur in seven to ten days, soon enough that they can be checked with a tiny camera threaded through your urethra. Then we can determine if your sperm is lethal. Pam was enjoying her husband's obvious discomfort—just the beginning of the paybacks for his recently revealed deceptions.

Chapter 36 | Pam's Mistake

...People doomed to die of disease will die of disease...

JEREMIAH 43: 11

The next day when Pam returned to work, she instructed her secretary to call the spouses of Pam's female autopsy patients who'd died from the Spouse Killer, scheduling the men who hadn't had vasectomies to have sperm tests done over the next few days. Pam also told her secretary to warn all these men to abstain from sex until after their test.

Later, after many of the men's tests were complete, she decided to try her own experiments with the killer-sperm that she was finding over and over again in the patients who'd lost a significant other to the Spouse Killer.

First, she put a human egg cell in a petri dish and added a sperm sample from a donor with the killer-sperm. The sperm traveled through the egg splitting it into many parts.

Next, she put a piece of human tissue in a petri dish and added the killer-sperm; and the sperm traveled right through the tissue. This is what sperm are programmed to accomplish, traveling and penetrating the egg cell—but these sperm were thousands of times stronger than normal sperm, exactly as Cleta had said. She called Olivia to find out if anything new had been learned.

"I'm afraid I don't have any news, but I'm going to be in Petrolia next month for Paul and Marie's wedding. We can meet at the Center to discuss our collective research when I arrive," Olivia said.

"I didn't know Marie and Paul were getting married. I've been so busy since we returned from Atlanta that I haven't seen or talked to Marie. Where are they going to have the wedding?" asked Pam.

"At Marie's house. It's going to be a small service with only family and a few friends invited. I think Marie agreed to marry Paul when his sperm tested dead. Having a safe-sex man made him a hot item, which Marie didn't want available on the open market. I understand how she feels, being married to one of the only two safe-sex men found in the world so far," said Olivia.

"Kirk's recovering from a vasectomy reversal so his sperm can be tested."

"There are a lot of reversal procedures going on now, since most men want to know if they have the killer-sperm before even considering castration."

"Men are such babies about the whole thing—women have been dealing with sterilization procedures for years with minimal side effects. Hormone replacement therapy can work for either sex."

"I guess it's different for women because we've never scratched our ovaries or adjusted our tubes," said Olivia. They both laughed.

On Friday January 4th, the day of Marie and Paul's wedding, the newspaper reported that millions more people had died all over the world because they hadn't heeded the warnings about abstaining from sex. Since it'd been more than six months since Jack's death, Roulett was becoming more involved with the Center. That morning, she had scheduled a meeting with Lou, Pam, and Olivia to discuss the latest news on the sperm tests of the forty-six men who Pam had originally tested.

Pam was the last to arrive at the meeting because she didn't work at the Center. To Roulett's dismay, Kirk was with her. Pam was carrying a large brown leather briefcase, which she opened before she said, "I wish I had more to tell you. We've done two more sperm tests besides the forty-six men that we originally tested, and so far, Lou and Kirk have dead sperm. If we could determine why some men have dead sperm, we would probably think it's the fruit, but this clearly doesn't make sense."

Kirk said, "I told you it's not the fruit. It may be some kind of bug we picked up in another country and it's feasible that we spread it around as we were selling the seed, but it's not my fruit. I think terrorists caused this plague. Doesn't anybody remember 9-11? It has to be caused by something other than my fruit and I don't care what Dr. Worthington claims!"

Pam said, "Well, we better find an answer soon, because the death toll is well over eighty million and rising every second!"

"Paul, Garrett, Kirk, and Lou have dead sperm, but all the others have killer-sperm, so there's no change in any of these tests. The strange thing is that we've completed sperm tests from all over the world and, so far, none tested have dead sperm, but the majority test positive for the killer-sperm. There may be something local that prompts the killer-sperm to die. If we could discover the reason for this difference, we could stop the deaths," said Olivia.

"If all men had dead sperm, reproduction as we know it would cease," Lou commented.

Pam replied, "There has been some discussion that this may be an evolutionary step toward a different form of reproduction. The only problem with that theory is that evolution normally progresses very slowly."

Roulett said, "I still think there's some connection to the rainbow fruit and the deaths. I believe that Dr. Worthington is right."

"It's strange the deaths appeared to start in this area and this is the only area in the world where we find the dead sperm. It's too large of a coincidence to simply accept," Lou added.

"I know Kirk isn't going to like this, but I'm beginning to believe that Dr. Worthington is right and the Spouse Killer is caused by the rainbow fruit," Pam replied.

* * * * *

That afternoon at Paul and Marie's wedding, Kirk was still angry with Pam for taking Dr. Worthington's side. After the ceremony, Marie insisted everyone go to the clubhouse for a toast. Everyone was expecting champagne to toast with, but Marie came out carrying a tray of her grandfather's special tea. She cheerfully said, "Tea time!"

"Oh no, not that nasty-smelling stuff!" griped Roulett.

"I may be strange—but I've learned to like it," Lou said.

"It's not that bad, once you get past the smell," Paul agreed.

"I had to put extra sugar in mine," Kirk admitted.

"Trying it once was enough for me," said Garrett.

"I expect everyone to have a sip of tea as a wedding toast," Marie announced.

As Roulett held the cup of steaming hot tea under her nose, she remembered what Wangambi had said to her in Africa. His words 'right under your noses' echoed in her mind as she said, "Marie, can I ask you a question before we toast?"

"Okay," said Marie.

"Have you ever given this special tea to anyone at the greenhouses?"

"No, Kirk wouldn't want me to bother his workers," said Marie.

"That's it! It's the tea! The men who have the dead sperm are the men who've consumed the tea. The tea's what neutralizes the killer-sperm!" said Roulett.

Lou hugged Roulett and said, "I hope you're right!"

Pam said, "That could mean the cure will cause all men to be sterile."

"Being sterile is better than being dead!" said Lou.

Chapter 37 | Marie's Confession

Your descendants will confess their sins and the sins of their ancestors... LEVITICUS 26: 40

Three weeks later, Roulett was having a conversation with Marie while the children were riding their horses. Marie said, "Roulett, I have something I need to confess to you."

"Are you going to tell me you slept with Paul before you two were married?" Roulett joked.

"No, I'm talking about a *real* confession. Several months ago, I overheard you and Garrett fighting and then kissing in the barn. I was up in the loft checking my Christmas card inventory when I saw the two of you through the one-way mirror. I had no intention of spying, I just happened to be there..."

Roulett sat quietly, too overwhelmed to speak.

Marie asked, "Do you think you're the first married woman to fall in love with a man who's not your husband?"

"I didn't think about it that way. I really thought you would hate me if you knew."

"I don't hate you but I'm glad Jack never knew. He didn't know—did he?"

"No, and I'm glad he didn't. You realize that I didn't want to have those feelings for Garrett. I just couldn't help myself."

"Believe me, I know you didn't have any choice in the matter," sympathized Marie.

"You sound like you are speaking from personal experience."

She nodded. "The same thing happened to me shortly after I married Sam."

Roulett didn't know if she should believe her ears—could Marie really be saying this? "Are you sure you aren't just telling me that to make me feel better?"

"No, it happened to me, too, the first time Vickie brought Paul over to meet Sam. One look at Paul and I fell in love with him."

Roulett asked, "Did you ever tell him?"

"No, but I feared everyone knew after a while."

"Why did you think that?"

"After years of our families being close, they quit visiting very often. I thought they all knew how I felt about Paul."

"Did Paul ever show any interest in you?"

"Just as a friend, but we were never alone because Sam didn't work. He was *always* there," said Marie.

"Do you think Sam knew?"

"I don't think so, because he never said anything to me about it—and you know Sam, if he'd known about it, he would've mentioned it. He was never tight-lipped. I was always so afraid Vickie knew, but I only hope her mother Bertha never knew."

"I guess you do understand why I never confided in you."

"Yes, I spent many days wondering if Vickie knew how I felt about Paul, and if she'd told Bertha," said Marie.

"You may've been surprised by Bertha's reaction if she'd known—I was surprised by yours!"

"Remember I understand because the same thing happened to me. I know you've punished yourself over and over—like I punished myself—so I don't need to punish you, too."

"Marie, I have one question for you, but you don't have to answer if you don't want to," asked Roulett.

"What's that?"

"How could you fall in love with someone else when you were a newlywed?"

"It's a long story but I guess it's time you knew. My dad, John-George, was always in a bad mood after the death of my mother. Dad met and married the sister of my best friend—Lillian Jacobs—two years later. His mood improved while he was dating her. I didn't really approve of him marrying her because of the differences in their ages, but I was happy that he was more content. I decided to try my best to accept her as my stepmother, but there wasn't really time for us to become close because she died the day after their wedding from what was diagnosed as a spontaneous abortion. Dad said he didn't know she was pregnant and the baby couldn't be his. He said she was obviously pregnant when he met her. We always thought the Clayton men were hard on their women, but now we know the fruit was the reason for their wives' deaths.

"To my chagrin, Dad's bad mood returned immediately and lasted until he became very busy the next year. He started the Clayton Research Center and buried himself in his work. I couldn't understand why he started another business then because he didn't need any more money. I guess he thought that if he stayed busy he wouldn't have time to think about the two wives he'd buried.

"The next year, I got my driver's license in April when I turned sixteen. Dad bought me a car the same week, so I was usually on the go. That fall while I was riding around in my car, I decided to go by one day and see Dorothy, my grandfather Roy's widow. It was in the first year after Dorothy and her son Charles moved to Oklahoma. Dorothy hired a manager to run the diamond broker business. The Barnes family had been living on the ranch and taking care of the place since Roy bought it. I hadn't seen Dorothy or Charles in years. I'd forgotten how beautiful she was—she had long, curly blonde hair and striking green eyes. She looked like a movie star but had the personality of an angel. She wanted me to see her son Charles because she was always so proud of him. When he came through the door, I couldn't take my eyes off him."

Roulett asked, "Charles?"

"No, not Charles, Daniel—Daniel Barnes, he was Sam's younger brother. I probably had seen him before when we were younger, but we hadn't paid any attention to each other until that day when Daniel showed an interest in me.

"He asked me if I could go horseback riding someday with him. I told him I would go if Dorothy approved. She said it was fine as long as we rode gentle horses and were careful.

"I visited Daniel's house almost every day, but we could never be alone because Charles was jealous of Daniel. Charles wanted my attention, but I mistakenly thought this was because he was an only child and spoiled rotten. I didn't tell Dad the reason I was over there all the time, so he thought I was only visiting Dorothy or Vickie.

"Daniel was drafted in the Army in March of the next year. I was so happy to see him when he came home for a two-week leave after boot camp. That was my last chance to see Daniel for a long time because he had orders to go overseas.

"Dorothy had to go back to New York City to take care of some business. She didn't want to take Charles with her because she was afraid she wouldn't be able to return before his school started. Dorothy asked Dad if he would keep Charles for her. We now know Dad was obligated to keep Charles because he was his son.

"The first day Charles stayed overnight at our house, I devised a plan so I could see Daniel alone. The next morning I got up early so I could leave the house before Charles was out of bed. I left immediately after Dad went to work. I drove around until after nine, then I went to Daniel's house. Vickie asked where my "shadow" was, which was what she called Charles. Proud of accomplishing my goal, I bragged about leaving him at home in bed.

"I asked Vickie, 'Where's Daniel?'

"She replied, 'He's still in bed, but if you want I can wake him. I'm sure he would want to know you're here.' Daniel came out of the back of the house and said, 'Actually, I've been up for a while.' We saddled the horses, then rode to a wooded area that had a homemade picnic table. That was the first time he kissed me. I loved him so much. We talked about getting married some day. I knew he was serious about our marriage because he never tried to go any further than kissing. The entire week, I would sneak out as often as I could to spend time with Daniel and to avoid Charles.

"The weekend before Daniel was scheduled to go overseas, I asked my dad if Daniel and I could have a real date on Saturday night. I pleaded with Dad that Daniel was to leave on Tuesday. Dad got angry and told me I was too young to date. He said, when I was old enough to date, I needed to date someone other than the hired help. I went to bed that night crying.

"I couldn't sleep, so I got up about midnight. I got the key to Dad's liquor cabinet, opened it, and took a nearly full fifth of Jack Daniels to my room. Charles, who watched every move I made, saw me take it. I was afraid he would tell Dad or maybe blackmail me, so there was another thing to upset me. I drank so much that I passed out.

"The next morning I was so sick I thought I was going to die. In fact, I was so sick that I wished I could die and be out of my misery. After my third trip to the bathroom to vomit, I noticed a small amount of blood on my sheets. I thought it was very early for me to start my period, but I was too ill to care.

"I stayed in bed all that day, too sick to hold my head up. I remembered having some strange dreams the night before, but since this was the first and last time I was drunk, I thought those dreams were simply a side effect from the liquor. I remember calling out Daniel's name and faintly seeing someone, but I assumed my intoxication made me hallucinate the strange dreams.

"I didn't say anything to Dad about what I'd done, and he never paid any attention to the disappearance of his liquor. Dad wasn't a drinker, so the variety of liquors was only in the house for guests. Dad and I didn't do much more than speak to each other for the next few months.

"About three months after that night, I realized that what I thought was a dream turned into a real nightmare. I had a problem and I didn't know what to do. After several days of worrying, I went to Dorothy crying. She took me to her doctor—a nice woman. That day I received the news that I was pregnant, but I didn't dare tell anyone who'd fathered the child I carried. Dorothy assumed the father was Daniel and she felt partially to blame for allowing me to spend so much time alone with him. She volunteered to tell Dad for me.

"I didn't know until that day in the nursing home, when Dorothy told us why she and Dad were so close. She had a way of talking to Dad that no one else had. I know now this closeness was because they'd been lovers!

"Dorothy told Dad about my pregnancy. Needless to say, he was furious. I could hear him all the way up in my room. Dorothy called Henry and Bertha Barnes. She asked that they come over right away because Dad needed to talk to them. They arrived at the house less than fifteen minutes after Dorothy called them. Dorothy told them we had a serious problem because I was pregnant with Daniel's baby. Dorothy decided to do most of the talking because Dad was still too angry to talk.

"Henry told Dad they would get Daniel back to marry me. Henry said that he was sorry and he would make Daniel do the right thing. I think this news petrified Henry who feared Dorothy would fire him because of what they thought Daniel had done. I didn't know what to do then because I wanted to marry Daniel, but I didn't know how I was going to explain to him I was pregnant. Even as naive as I was then, I knew I didn't become pregnant from his kisses.

"Several days passed and Henry and Bertha hadn't been able to contact Daniel. This turn of events put a damper on Henry and Bertha's plans to bring him home and make him marry me. After the week of trying to make contact with Daniel, they received the devastating news about Daniel's death—he died in an airplane crash traveling to a base overseas. I thought I would die then, too, from a broken heart.

"After several weeks of adjusting to the fact that Daniel was dead and that they didn't even have his body to bury, everyone resumed dealing with my problem. Dad and Henry talked again and they left me completely out of the decision.

"Dad told me that he and Henry had arranged for me to marry Sam. He said that I should be thankful Sam was willing to marry me because the baby wasn't his and I was 'damaged goods.' Dad said he would set up a trust fund for Sam and me and we'd have a good income if we stayed together. He made it clear that we'd have nothing if we didn't.

"Dad chastised me with a harsh tone by saying, 'You fool around with the hired help and shame your family, and you end up with what you deserve, stuck with the hired help. The baby will have the correct family name this way, Barnes.'

"I cried then because I was a scared young girl. However, if I'd known then what I know now, I would've told him the only way for the baby to have the correct name was for it to have my last name since the father of the baby was a Clayton. Charles Clayton had raped me while I was drunk. This whole tragedy resulted from the illegitimate son *my father* produced by having sex with his own stepmother, Dorothy.

"How do you know for certain Charles raped you?"

"Because Charles and Dad were the only males in the house and it couldn't have been my overly modest dad—who I'd never even seen in his underwear. It was Charles all right—he lurked in the shadows, watching me, waiting to pounce on me when I was vulnerable! Now you can understand why I was so upset when I realized Charles was my half-brother. The rape was bad enough when I thought he was my half-uncle," said Marie.

"Jack's biological father was Charles—your half-brother?" asked Roulett, amazed.

"That's right but, as with most family secrets they are kept under the covers—which is where most of them start anyway! It's been a rough few years for everyone. I've lost my dad, my husband and my son, besides finding out that my great-grandfather impregnated his sister, which indirectly resulted in the death of his mother and four sisters; and my father impregnated his stepmother, which produced my half-brother, who raped and impregnated me! If all families are like ours, I don't think we have to wonder why the whole world is falling apart!"

Roulett paused, trying to digest everything that Marie had told her. Finally, she asked, "Did Jack ever know this?"

"No, you're the first person I've told. But I didn't know most of it myself until recently. I'm surprised nobody ever asked why I named Jack, 'Jackson Daniel'—he was named after the bottle of Jack Daniels whiskey I drank that night!"

"I never noticed the connection to his name before. Now I know why you have an aversion to drinking liquor. So, I guess you didn't love Sam when you married him?"

"That's an understatement. We were married for almost a year before I would sleep with him."

"How did he feel about that?"

"He was a very patient and gentle man. I remember thinking about the fairy-tale stories of the princess who kissed the frog and turned him into a prince. I kept trying to turn Sam into a prince—but every time I kissed him, he only turned into a horny-toad instead!"

Roulett laughed. "Did you fall in love with Paul before, or after, you and Sam had slept together?"

"Before, thinking about Paul was the only thing that got me through the first few times with Sam. Even though I didn't really ever love Sam in the romantic way, I did love him and I've missed him since his death. I was married to that man for almost forty-four years, and you'd miss a sore thumb if you had one that long."

"Do you regret not telling Paul you loved him when you were both young?"

"No, because Dad had the trust fund arranged so my heirs and I would forfeit everything if I didn't stay with Sam. Dad controlled his money, money is power, and power corrupts. I married and stayed with Sam for my children and their descendants. Besides, it's just as Bertha always said, 'there's a time for everything,' and undoubtedly, it wasn't the right time. Paul and I are together now because I waited until we both were free before I let him know how I felt. I now know I would've had a much better love life if I'd married Paul when we were both young."

"So I guess that means you're enjoying married life with Paul?" asked Roulett.

"Yes, I am...speaking of married life, how're things going between you and Lou with Garrett out of the picture?" asked Marie.

"I've agreed to marry Lou and we're considering an April wedding. Does that surprise you?"

"No, remember—I saw you talking to Garrett in the barn when you told him about marrying Lou."

Later that night, Roulett and Lou met at her house for dinner. After dinner, the children went upstairs to do their homework before getting ready for bed. Lou helped Roulett load the dishwasher before they sat in the den to talk. "I told Marie today that we were getting married," said Roulett.

"Great! Now I can kiss you in front of her."

"So you'll like our relationship being out in the open?" she teased.

"Yes, just not too far out in the open or we won't be allowed to dine at restaurants any more."

"You are such fun! That's why I love you so much," she said.

"I guess you know we're going to have to invite Olivia and Garrett to our wedding and I'll be kissing you in front of him."

"Yes, I know."

"After you're a married woman, you'll be more interesting to Garrett again."

Roulett said, "I don't think it will make any difference."

Lou sighed. "Only time will tell if I'm right..."

Chapter 38 | The Wedding

Servants delivered the message to the guests: "Come to the wedding feast!" MATTHEW 22: 4

Roulett wore an exquisite ivory wedding gown covered with hand-sewn ivory pearls and lace. The gown's fitted bodice and low cut neckline accentuated her bosom. During the ceremony, when the minister asked if anyone objected to the marriage, everyone tensed. As silence filled the room, everyone breathed a sigh of relief.

At the reception after the ceremony, Lou noticed that Garrett couldn't take his eyes off Roulett. Approaching him, Lou softly said, "I want you to know I'll be good to her because I really love her. You know, I've loved her longer than you've even known her."

Garrett sadly replied, "I know you do." He cast Lou a long, serious look and added, "But it's not difficult to love Roulett."

Lou thought for a moment and replied, "I'm going to tell you something that may surprise you."

Garrett muttered, "What?"

"I want you to go dance with her and, if you have the opportunity to give her a last kiss, you have my permission. I want you to know I expect that to be the last time your lips touch hers as long as I'm alive. Do I make myself clear?"

"Yes, Lou, you've made your point. Even though it's very generous of you to allow me to kiss your bride, I don't think it's a good idea for me to kiss her in front of all these people—including my wife, who by the way, hasn't given me *her* permission. And I'm not dumb enough to ask for it!"

"I can't change the fact that she will probably always love you in some ways more than me—that's obviously something I'll have to live with. Yet, because I love her so much, I have come to grips with it. I think she would love to have a *last* kiss from you on her wedding day, so I'll keep Olivia busy if she comes down the stairs.

"While you are dancing, you can tell her to meet you in the dressing room. I'll be timing you. Not more than five minutes and only a goodbye kiss! I just hope this is the closure your relationship needs."

Garrett danced with Roulett and whispered in her ear. "Don't forget we have some unfinished business to take care of before we're too old."

Roulett replied, "I could never forget that."

"Meet me in the dressing room in five minutes."

"Are you crazy? *Here*—at my wedding!"

"No, that's not what I meant. I just want to give you a goodbye kiss."

"I can't do that! Lou could catch us. Have you forgotten this is our wedding day?"

Garrett grinned. "It was his idea."

"I hope you're kidding me—right?"

"No, I'm serious. He said he'd keep Olivia busy if she came down the stairs. He thought we needed closure."

"That was generous of him," snapped Roulett, unsure if she approved of his generosity or not.

Garrett said, "He wasn't that generous—he only gave us five minutes."

"That was reasonable," said Roulett. "I'll meet you in the dressing room in a few minutes."

Garrett nodded.

Roulett waited only moments before Garrett managed to slip into the dressing room to meet her. He hugged her and said, "You're a beautiful bride."

"I hope you know I'll always love you," she replied with tears in her eyes. They shared a long passionate kiss.

"I want to believe you, but time changes everything."

"Time won't change the way I feel about you."

"Speaking of time," he said, glancing at his watch. "Lou only gave us five minutes—I'm sure he's afraid we'll be humping like bunnies."

Roulett smiled. "If we were bunnies, five minutes would be more than enough."

"The way you excite me, I have to confess that three minutes would be more than enough."

"It's strange—in spite of all the time we've spent together, we couldn't seem to find that three minutes…"

Chapter 39 | Roulett & Garrett

While sleeping, my heart stayed awake.
I dreamed my lover was at the door... THE SONG OF SOLOMON 5:2

While waiting for the ambulance to arrive Roulett wondered where the time had gone. She'd known for some time this day would come, but knowing didn't make giving up her husband of nearly fifteen years any easier.

Although Lou wasn't her first choice at the time, they married and he was—and had always been—an extremely obliging husband. To even have to think about giving up such a remarkable man seemed almost more than she could bear. Although it'd only been minutes since she'd called 911, it seemed like forever, because she sensed that this time he wouldn't be coming back.

The liver and pancreas transplants had given him some extra time, but medical science could only delay the inevitable. Stress made everything seem unreal, as though she'd stepped into an imaginary world.

For three days, Roulett only left Lou's side to bathe and change her clothes. That evening her stepson, Shawn, and his wife arrived from Colorado. Shawn insisted Roulett go home to sleep for the night. Since his dad had been unconscious for the last two days, Shawn promised to call her if Lou's situation changed.

"Dad would want you to get some rest. Go home and get a good night's sleep in your own bed, and I'll see you in the morning," said Shawn.

Fearing Lou would expire while she was away, she didn't want to leave. Finally, she reluctantly agreed to go because the thought of a peaceful night's sleep was so appealing.

Roulett was deep in thought, trying to remember if there was anything she'd forgotten to tell Shawn, so she didn't notice the young woman accompanying her in the elevator. When it stopped at the ground floor, Roulett noticed the young woman looked familiar. She looked at Roulett as if she recognized her, too.

The young woman said, "I know you—don't I? Are you my aunt? Aunt Roulett?"

Even with her hazy mind, she remembered the only person who'd ever called her Aunt Roulett was Garrett and Olivia's daughter, Nicole. Recognizing Nicole after all these years wasn't easy, but Roulett could see the resemblance to the little girl she hadn't seen for ten years. She said, "Yes, that's right, you must be Nicole. Why are you here?"

"Mom's upstairs. We brought her here five days ago. She's in a coma and I'm afraid she's barely holding on," said Nicole as tears rolled down her cheeks from her bright blue eyes.

"I'm sorry to hear about your mother. I'm afraid your uncle, Lou, is in the same shape. He's been unconscious for two days and his doctors tell us he's living on borrowed time."

Nicole said, "I'm sorry to hear about Uncle Lou, but I know how you feel. Mom has terminal cancer. They found it three years ago—first in her ovaries, which were removed then, but the cancer had spread to her liver and bones. She's had radiation and chemotherapy, but nothing's stopped it. What's wrong with Uncle Lou?"

"He's been sick for several years. He's had two liver and pancreas transplants. He was healthy for a while after each surgery, but the anti-rejection drugs finally took their toll on his system."

"I'm sorry that he's so ill. Do you think it would help if I visited him?"

"No dear, I don't think he would know you were there," answered Roulett.

"Do you still live in Petrolia?" asked Nicole.

"No, we moved to Tulsa a few years ago to be closer to this hospital. I'm surprised to see you in Tulsa. I thought you still lived in Atlanta," said Roulett.

"Mom and Dad moved here three years ago when Mom became ill. She wanted to live closer to Grandma after Grandpa Aldridge died. They live in Okmulgee now," Nicole replied.

"Is your grandma still living?" asked Roulett.

Nicole shook her head. "She died last July."

Roulett's heart pounded and the palms of her hands became sweaty. She asked, "Is your father here?" She'd tried to wait until Nicole mentioned Garrett, but she couldn't wait any longer, because she had to know if he was in the hospital right now.

Nicole nodded. "He's here. Would you like see him?"

"Yes, for a few minutes. I was just leaving to go home to sleep tonight. Your cousin,

Shawn, is going to stay the night with Uncle Lou. He insisted that I go home for the night."

They returned to the elevator and Nicole pressed the button for Lou's floor. "I'm surprised we haven't run into each other sooner since we're on the same floor," Roulett said.

"Dad rarely leaves Mom's room so I'm not surprised you haven't seen him. Do you live nearby?" asked Nicole.

"Yes—only five minutes away."

"Would you object to taking Dad home with you for the night if I can talk him into going? He could really use a good night's sleep. He's been here for five nights straight."

"I wouldn't mind at all, but why do you think you can talk him into going?'

"Dad said the reason why he doesn't go home is that it'll only remind him more of Mom and it's too far away from the hospital. Your house is close and it won't remind him of Mom."

"It's fine with me, if you can convince him," offered Roulett, thinking that if Nicole knew their history she wouldn't suggest they be left alone. She suddenly felt shaky at the prospect of seeing him again after so many years.

Garrett was sitting in a recliner with his eyes closed when they walked into the room. He had less hair and more wrinkles than he did when she last saw him. His five-day growth of beard made him look rough, but he still made Roulett's heart flutter.

"Dad, look who I ran into," Nicole said.

Garrett must have thought he was dreaming when he opened his eyes. When he realized he was awake, a big smile lit his haggard face. He stood and hugged Roulett while asking, "How did you hear about Olivia?"

"I didn't know about Olivia until Nicole told me. I'm here with Lou. He's in a coma, too," said Roulett as her whole body tingled from his touch. She wanted to hold him forever.

"It's great to see you, but it's too bad it's under these circumstances," he said.

"It's good to see you, too." His words were so soothing to her frayed spirit, making her feel like melting into a pool of total surrender.

"Roulett, I'm so tired that I'm almost crazy. I've been here for five nights."

"I know. I've spent the last two nights with Lou. Shawn and his wife are going to stay with Lou tonight. Shawn insisted I go home tonight because I need some rest, and I'm too tired to argue with him. I was on my way out when I met Nicole in the elevator," said Roulett, who couldn't believe that she was still feeling the thrill from Garrett's touch.

Nicole said, "Dad, I have a great idea. Why don't you go home with Aunt Roulett so you can sleep tonight? I'll stay with Mom."

Garrett asked Roulett, "Do you still live in Petrolia?"

"No, I live about a mile from here. You're welcome to go with me. I have a guest suite and there's plenty of room. I'll be coming back in the morning anyway," Roulett said, desperately hoping he would agree to go with her. She needed to be close to him so much her whole body ached with desire.

"I could sure use a real shower and I haven't shaved in almost a week."

"Oh, Dad, now I don't know if Aunt Roulett will let you ride home in her car after telling her that," fussed Nicole.

Roulett said, "Not a problem, the guest bathroom has a very relaxing Jacuzzi in it, which should soak you clean and help you relax so you'll sleep well. We can go somewhere in the morning to have a nice breakfast before we come back. I know you must be tired of hospital food, because I know I am."

"Dad, you need to go with Aunt Roulett for the night and I'll not take 'no' for an answer. You go. I'll call you if there's any change."

"Roulett, I see what you mean by being too tired to argue. Okay, I'll go. I certainly need some rest," said Garrett.

Roulett wrote her phone number for Nicole and said, "Call if you need us." She thought this was too good to be true—time alone with Garrett!

"Should I take my car? If Nicole phones me in the night, I don't want Roulett to have to bring me back."

"That's not a problem. I have three vehicles and you can use one of them if need be," offered Roulett.

"Okay, now that's all settled, I'll see you both in the morning." Nicole replied, kissing her dad on the cheek. "You both try to rest tonight."

In the elevator, Garrett said, "I wanted to go with you from the start, but I had to make it appear that she'd talked me into going."

"If she'd known our past, I don't think she would've been so eager for us to spend the night in the same house."

"I hope you don't expect too much from me tonight. You know I'm worn to a frazzle."

"Garrett, I learned a long time ago not to expect too much from you!" She smiled as she added, "Besides, I'm tired, too."

They left the elevator and Garrett followed Roulett to her car. "I'm surprised to see you're still driving your red Cadillac after all these years."

"I have a new one, but if you have to leave a car parked in a parking lot overnight, it had better be an older one—less likely to be stolen, you know."

"It's strange for us to meet like this, after all these years," Garrett said while buckling his seat belt.

"It does seem that it's meant to be."

"You're probably the only person in the world who can take my mind off my troubles for a while."

"I feel the same way about you."

"I was afraid, as bad as I look, you wouldn't want to take me home with you," he said.

"It wouldn't have mattered if you were bald, toothless, a hundred pounds overweight, and had fallen in a sewer—I would still want you."

"Wow, even if I'd fallen in a sewer?" he asked.

"You're forgetting—the sewer part would be the easiest and the fastest condition to remedy from *my* scenario."

Garrett chuckled as he said, "I guess so, but it really sounds so terrible."

Roulett pulled into a large gated entrance. She inserted a card into a box on the driver's side, punched in the security code and put the palm of her left hand on a smooth scanner surface. The box beeped once and said, "Good evening, Ms. Gordon. You may enter now." The massive gates slowly opened. From the entry gate they drove almost a city block before pulling up to a three-story English Tudor house majestically nestled in a grove of mature oaks and maple trees. She parked in the five-car garage.

"I can see why you said you have plenty of room for me. Just how big is this place?" he asked.

"Would you believe a little over ten thousand square feet?"

"Do you ever get lost in there?" he asked.

"Funny you mentioned that, because Lou and I used to lose each other all the time. We quickly learned to use the intercom."

Roulett put her purse and keys on a small desk in the kitchen. "Garrett, would you like something to eat or drink before your bath?" she offered.

"No, thank you, maybe later. I'm hoping a bath will revive me some so I'll feel like being better company."

"Okay, follow me and I'll show you to the guestroom."

The guestroom was actually a guest suite complete with sitting room and bar. "This is beautiful," he said.

"Thank you, call me on the intercom as soon as you're done. I'll have set out some food and drinks downstairs," she said.

"Okay."

"Don't worry about cleaning up. The maid will be back tomorrow. If you need anything, look in the drawers, cabinets, and in the closet—they're very well stocked. Have a nice bath," she said as she approached the door.

"Any tricks to operating the Jacuzzi tub?" he asked.

"There's an instruction sheet for the Jacuzzi and an inventory list of the guestroom in the drawer below the guest towels," she said while pointing to a large linen closet directly behind Garrett.

"Thanks, I'll see you in a little while," he replied.

After Roulett left the room, he remembered he didn't have any clean clothes, but she told him to look for anything he might need, so he checked the closet. To his amazement, he found both new underwear and new casual clothes in a splendid array of sizes that would accommodate almost anybody. The huge walk-in closet measured about twelve feet deep and twenty feet long, and it was clearly marked "male" on one side and "female" on the other side.

He selected his clothes and underwear first and then noticed there were men's casual shoes from size six to fourteen. His shoes were fine, but it was nice to have an option. He laid the clothes on the beautiful antique four-poster bed. He didn't know if Roulett intended for him to sleep in this room alone, if she would join him, or vice versa. Looking in the bathroom, he saw that Roulett was right—he found everything he needed and more. He realized Roulett and Lou's billion dollar net worth made it easy to accommodate houseguests.

After his bath, he called Roulett on the intercom and she gave him instructions to find the sunroom. On his way, he walked through her bedroom lit only by the glow of a glass-covered fireplace. Even in that dim light, the room was breathtakingly beautiful. Double French doors opened to a spacious sunroom with another fireplace. The flames magically flickered, casting dancing shadows on the walls.

Roulett was lounging on a sofa surrounded by scented candlelight. He could tell by the smell of shampoo and light perfume that she'd showered. On the coffee table was a tray of cold cuts, cheese, crackers, and fresh fruit. Roulett had poured two glasses of red wine, which glimmered in the mesmerizing atmosphere. Garrett sat beside her and looked up through the glass roof at the puffy clouds and the stars in the nighttime sky.

"Would you like a glass of wine?" she offered softly.

"You know I'm not much of a drinker."

"I know, neither am I anymore. I thought, under the circumstances, a small glass could help us relax," she said enticingly.

He took a deep breath before he answered, "Why not? Maybe it'll help me cope with the feeling that this is too good to be true!" He reached for the glass and took a sip.

"If not for Lou and Olivia both being at death's door, this would be my ultimate fantasy," she said.

He took another sip of wine and said, "I know. I'm no wine connoisseur but this is really good wine."

"Lou and I don't drink often, but when we do, we prefer the best."

"The bath made me feel so much better, and you weren't kidding about the guestroom having everything I would need. This is an unbelievably beautiful house from what I've seen so far."

"I would offer to show you the rest of the house, but I think we're both too tired tonight."

"Maybe in the morning," he said, suppressing a yawn.

"You really should eat something before you fall asleep."

"I'm sorry—the bath and the wine have relaxed me."

"Don't apologize. I want you to be comfortable, but I also want you to eat before you fall asleep," she said.

"Okay, but I know you own a pharmaceutical lab—so which food did you hide the generic Viagra in?" he said with a grin.

"I wouldn't do something like that—but are you trying to tell me you're too old to complete our unfinished business?" she asked, smiling.

He took another sip of wine and gently placed the glass on the coffee table before he answered, "I didn't say that!" He put his arm around her and pulled her close enough to kiss.

"Why did you take so long to do that? I've wanted to kiss you from the first moment I saw you."

"Be thankful I waited until after my bath. Besides, I'm so tired I had to gather the strength to kiss you," he said before starting to nibble on the food.

"I'm glad to see you eating. The food will give you more energy."

"Speaking of energy, where did you plan on me sleeping tonight?"

"Well, you should know where I *want* you to sleep. However, where you sleep is entirely up to you," she said.

"How would it be if I sleep in the guestroom upstairs—" he saw a look of disappointment flash across her face before he could finish saying, "—and you can join me there? I don't think that I'd be comfortable sleeping with you in Lou's bed."

"That sounds good to me. I'm going to put this food in the refrigerator, freshen up, and I'll join you upstairs."

He drank the last of his wine before saying, "Okay!"

He was in the bed waiting for her when she entered the room. "I'm sorry it took me so long. Perfection takes time, you know." She pushed the straps of her teddy over her shoulders so it slid to the floor, then slipped under the covers.

"You gave me more time to rest," he said as he caressed her. They reveled in the feel of their bodies together for the first time. In spite of the circumstances, they made passionate love, resulting in a mutual climax, built up for almost two decades of fantasizing about each other. She felt her severed soul was whole for the first time in her life. Hot, sweaty, and out of breath, he declared, "That was even better than I ever imagined!"

"I know!" For several minutes they enjoyed the afterglow. She was about to say that loving him had caused her to suffer both the most tremendous pleasure and pain, when the phone rang. Roulett reached for the phone beside the guestroom bed and picked it up, expecting the worse.

"Hello." She paused for a moment then said, "I'll need to put you on hold while I go to the guestroom to tell your dad." She put the phone on hold, and said, "Nicole needs to speak to you, but you need to wait a minute before you pick up this phone, so she won't know we're in the same room."

Garrett failed to heed her warning. He leaped out of bed and tugged on his underwear as he hurried around the bed to grab the phone. "What's wrong, Nicole?" he asked in a panic. Roulett put on her teddy and stood next to him. She couldn't hear the other side of the conversation, but knew what Nicole was telling him by the look on his face.

He asked frantically, "When?" He repeated the words that he'd heard, "About three minutes ago! I'll be there as soon as possible." Tears were rolling down his face as he said, "Olivia just died! And another call is coming in…"

Roulett took the phone and answered, "Hello." It was Shawn telling her Lou had passed away only a few minutes ago. She repeated Garrett's word, "I'll be there as soon as possible."

Roulett and Garrett glared at each other, each waiting for the other to speak. They both felt horrible. Finally, Garrett broke the silence. "We should've waited…thirty more minutes and we would not have been committing adultery while our loved ones took their dying breaths. I think they knew somehow! That's why they *died* at the very same time!" His voice carried every ounce of his fury.

How could such a kind and gentle man change so quickly? Roulett remembered how his testosterone had kicked in after she'd kissed him the first time. Now he was empowered with a testosterone jolt, jumping to an off-the-charts level. She realized living with a man who possessed such a volatile personality couldn't be easy. She tried to reason with him by saying, "Maybe they were holding on until we found each other? Maybe they wanted us together?"

Justifying their actions was not going to console Garrett. The fire in his eyes showed her his true feelings. "This is entirely your fault! You shouldn't have agreed to bring me home with you. You knew what we would do when you brought me here... you Jezebel!"

His accusing words caused tears to roll down her cheeks as she wondered how she could've loved such a cruel man. "I know you're hurting because your wife just died, but I just lost my husband, too. I don't think you have the right to take your pain out on me."

"This would've never happened if you hadn't lured me to your adulteress bed... You adulterous whore!" he shouted.

"How could you accuse me of luring you here when you came on your daughter's request? I didn't ask you to come home with me nor did I drag you here, kicking and screaming. You initiated our first kiss tonight and I gave you the choice of where you wanted to sleep. *You* invited *me* to join you!"

"It's entirely your fault because you kissed me years ago and started this ungodly passion between us. You knew when you brought me here I couldn't resist you. Your plan was to tempt me. Somehow, Olivia and Lou saw or sensed us together. They knew we were unfaithful to them and it's your fault."

"I thought you loved me. How could you talk to me like this if you love me? You willingly shared the pleasure from our lovemaking, but don't want any of the blame from the repercussions."

"You Jezebel whore—you cost me the last moments with the woman I loved. You lured me to your adulterous bed where you finally stole my soul...by having your way with me. Now would you cover up your nakedness and drive me to the hospital? No, better yet, I'll call a cab. I don't want to ride in the same car with a trashy slut like you!"

Garrett's last words were more than Roulett could endure. She felt blackness overcome her as Garrett lunged toward her. She fell to the floor with a thud.

Roulett tried to move, but couldn't. She tried to open her eyes, but couldn't. Her brain and her body were not communicating. She felt the fear, but didn't know why—except that she wasn't able to move. Her thoughts were hazy. She tried to sense her surroundings with closed eyes; they remained closed no matter how hard she tried to open them. She felt she was in her own bed, in her own house, but didn't know if it was day or night. She felt a sense of belonging from the low hum of the ceiling fan and the faint odor from her familiar fabric softener; but couldn't be sure if she could trust her senses. If she couldn't move, or open her eyes, how could she trust her sense of hearing or smell?

She felt so exhausted from trying to move that she seemed to drift in and out of sleep. In one of these naps, she felt she was holding hands with a baby boy whose hand felt soft and pudgy as he held tightly onto her finger. Now the hand seemed to change, it was no longer soft and pudgy, but was now rigid and firm. She seemed to visualize the person that was holding her hand as a body made out of red-hot coals, but the touch was neither cold nor hot. His image was the rough image of a man but appearing more like a monster. Red to her meant anger, so this was an angry monster, she reasoned. The top of this monster-like image's head was the most interesting—with no hair, but what appeared as peaks and valleys made of the hot coals. Again, the hand changed. Now the hand became warm and familiar, it was Garrett's hand. She was rubbing his hand while he gently held hers, when again it changed, now it wasn't his hand she was rubbing because her hand was in his underwear. She became very aroused before she remembered that they'd finally made love and it was wonderful. Now she remembered that she needed to go to the hospital and she'd been fighting with Garrett. She wondered if he'd hit her…remembering his angry words and him lunging toward her…was she unconscious or dead? Fear overtook her as she thought the worse…maybe she was alive, but paralyzed; she couldn't move nor open her eyes! She felt a chill of fear travel up her spine. Relieved to feel any sensation in her body, she struggled harder to move her limbs, but still couldn't. Her thoughts drifted again, to why she couldn't move. She thought—I couldn't be dead because I can think. Nevertheless, she found fault in her theory, realizing that she didn't know if one could think after death. Maybe she was in a coma, knowing that some people have reported an ability to hear while comatose. With her energy drained again, she began to fade away…

Time passed before Roulett slowly opened her eyes to see it was night. She was lying on her side, in a bed, facing the edge. Her face was wet with tears. She wiped her eyes while realizing she was in her own bed and she wasn't alone—someone was beside her. She breathed very shallow, trying to be quiet, afraid of what could happen next. Instead of turning over to see who was beside her, she chose to slip quietly out of bed while her heart pounded so hard that it seemed as if it would jump out of her chest. Fearfully she turned to face the unknown. What she saw made her shriek with terror. She saw the body of a man in her bed. At that moment, the man sprang out and rushed toward her.

"What's wrong?" asked Lou, as he stood there, startled by her scream.

She felt so relieved—he wasn't dead! Reality rushed back and she realized they'd only been married for two weeks. "I had a bad dream," she said. As he hugged her, she was thankfully secure in his loving arms.

Epilogue | The Journals

The four angels were released...to kill a third of all mankind. REVELATION 9: 15

Two Years Later

One-third of the childbearing population was dead and the world was a much different place. The Spouse Killer resulted in a metamorphosis of the remaining inhabitants of the earth. With every human life so precious, violence faded from society. The result was a quieter and gentler world, a new world order that had an uncertain future.

On a splendid April morning, Lou and Roulett were celebrating their second anniversary, which they chose to continue for the entire week. After eating out, they stopped by John-George's abandoned mansion, which they'd owned for some time. They were considering moving there to enjoy the amenities of country living with the conveniences of close proximity to town. Their final decision depended on how much restoration and updating the enormous house would require. The 16,000 square feet house was so huge they could renovate it in stages by living in one area, while redecorating the other areas. The monetary cost was not a consideration, but they were uncertain if they wanted to live with the constant chaos caused by dealing with contractors. For now, they were only looking at the possibilities.

While there, they decided to check the old greenhouse, which hadn't been visited by a human for many years. For several years before John-George's death, his failing health prevented him from enjoying his greenhouse. The door was locked with a padlock that'd rusted with time. Lou and Roulett didn't have the key nor did they have a clue where it was.

Lou said, "I'll be right back." He returned in a few minutes with a tire tool and said, "I should be able to open it with this." The old lock easily snapped apart.

The first glimpse inside the greenhouse was a somber sight. Row after row of large clay pots with parched soil and brittle brown stalks sat on the shelves. Lou and Roulett had seen enough of these in the past to know that these stalks were the dead remains of rainbow fruit plants. The fruit and leaves were stripped from the plants leaving only the bare, lifeless stalks.

She said, "Do you think John-George knew what he had? Or would it be a surprise to him to know that now almost one-sixth of the world's population has died from the same kind of fruit that'd once been carefully cultivated and nurtured in this room?"

Lou replied, "We'll never know for certain, but I doubt he could've foreseen all the consequences."

"He knew about the tea!" recalled Roulett.

"Yes, but I think if he'd known all the consequences, he would've totally destroyed the fruit, the leaves, the plants, and the seeds," replied Lou.

"You're probably right."

"It's ironic these plants are almost in the same condition the world's inhabitants are in now, unable to reproduce."

"It gives me chills to think about all that's happened."

"I think what seemed even worse than all the deaths to me, was the thought that nobody on earth could ever reproduce. I wanted grandchildren."

"Theoretically, we were wrong before. We might be wrong again."

"I hope you're right, but you have to admit we had every reason in the world to believe the theory about no one reproducing. There'd not been one single birth reported on the entire earth for over a year, which put the fear of God in everybody," said Lou.

Roulett said, "Yes, but we *were* wrong. Because last year, as if by some miracle, there were twenty-four babies born, with each one born in a different part of the world and to mothers from different races, nationalities, and religions!"

"It makes me feel good to be related to one of them."

Roulett corrected, "Well, not by blood kin."

Lou said, "Garrett is my children's blood-uncle, and he was my brother in-law for years. Therefore, I consider Garrett and Olivia's son to be my relative. He carries some of the same blood as my children; therefore, I feel I'm the baby's relative. I've known people who say if they are lucky enough just to know one of the parents of the twenty-four babies, they feel related to the baby."

"Yes, I guess you have a point. I think in some strange way that I feel I'm related to Garrett and Olivia's son, too."

Lou couldn't avoid the temptation to torment Roulett about her answer, so he said, "Why? Because you tried to steal his daddy away from his mommy?"

"That happened a long time ago, and I thought we'd agreed not to mention it again."

"I'm sorry, honey. I really couldn't resist teasing you."

For a few minutes, Roulett was lost in thought as she wondered if Garrett's reward for staying with his wife was having what he'd always wanted—a natural son—not just a child from the donated sperm of his brother, as with their daughter Nicole, but also his own child.

Roulett felt good about him having the son he'd wanted. She would always have a soft spot in her heart for Garrett. She remembered Garrett hadn't totally resisted her, so the baby was most likely a blessing given to Garrett and Olivia, due to Olivia's consistent goodness. For whatever reason, they were blessed.

When they stepped through a door at the south end of the greenhouse into the potting shed, Roulett noticed a table with a rug under it in the potting shed. She asked, "Why would Grandfather put a rug on the floor of the potting shed?"

Lou replied, "I don't know—but it does seem strange, as much dirt as would always be on this floor. I could understand if the rug was in front of the table for standing comfort, but not under it."

"Do you remember where John-George hid the box with the Bible, the fruit, and the diamonds in it?"

"No."

"The box was under a rug beneath a large table in the library, hidden in a compartment under a tile."

"What does that have to do with this?"

"I think something is hidden there. Help me move the table." Beneath the rug was a wooden trap door. Lou slowly lifted it.

"I was right," she said as she pulled an old journal out of a hole in the floor. From the overpowering stale odor they knew the book had been hidden for a very long time. They walked outside to escape the musty scent and to have better light. They sat in the shade of an old pecan tree on a cast-iron bench in dire need of a paint job, and Roulett began to read the journal aloud.

The Story of the Fruit

By John-George Clayton

I received the plant, which produced the fruit after the death of my father, Roy Clayton. My stepmother Dorothy gave me all the plants from my father's greenhouse while I was in New York attending his funeral. She'd not found his journal yet, so the fruit caused the death of two of my wives before I knew the cause or the cure.

Dorothy gave me my father's journal at the funeral of my second wife. She said she'd not read the journal because it contained material about my father's previous wives.

I read in my father's journal about the tea. The tea was made from the leaves of the same plant that produced the fruit. The tea would stop the deaths of our wives, but had the strange side effect of causing sterility.

I started Clayton Research Center the next year. The main reason I started the research center was so I could secretly do experiments with the fruit and the leaves. I found the fruit caused men to produce deadly sperm. First, I did extensive research concerning the time required for the fruit to cause the deadly sperm. I did this research on a variety of lab animals but found only humans were susceptible. My human tests were limited to several volunteers from an African tribe and myself. I also analyzed the deaths of both my wives and the deaths of my father's wives. I came to the same conclusion on all—it takes from three to six months to produce the deadly sperm in men after they have regularly consumed the fruit. By regularly, I mean at least once a month. I studied various amounts from a minimum of one drop of the juice surrounding the seeds of the fruit to a maximum of six fruit a day. This juice was the most concentrated part and looked like blood because it contained molecules of haemin, which gave the fruit's juice its color, precisely as these same haemin molecules made blood red. The three-to-six month's variance depended upon the amount consumed and the individual's body consuming it. Once to this level, the deadly sperm continued production even when discontinuing the fruit.

On the other hand, the tea would stop the mobility of the sperm within twenty-four hours after consuming it and would continue to do so for months and even years in some cases. I studied the amount of tea consumed from one sip to one cup, brewed from two medium-sized leaves. For my wife's safety, I consumed a cup of tea at least once a month. Apparently, my father didn't know this and he consumed more tea than was necessary. When I turned eighty, I decided I didn't want to mess with the plants anymore so I stripped the leaves from my greenhouse plants, dried, powdered, and made them into capsules that I could take once a month.

I'm not certain of the biological cause for both abnormalities, but I would guess it was caused in some way by the fact the fruit contained complete protein similar to that found in meat. This was strange that this plant appeared to make animal protein.

My father and I both felt the need to keep the fruit a secret, but we continued to consume this tempting treat not only for the flavor, but also, because of the invigorating feeling it produced. It was not addictive but the rejuvenation of health and stamina made consuming it impossible to stop. We both felt we'd found the fountain of youth and planned to prosper from our treasure; but alas, our plans were foiled—for there were side effects.

From reading my father's journal, I found that he also had lost two wives, with the first being my mother, before he discovered the tea was the cure. He also knew the tea caused sterility. I never knew why he appeared to know I was the biological father of Charles, instead of him, until I read his journal.

Before he knew about the tea, but after my father caused the death of two wives, he returned to Africa to what he thought was the source of his grief in a futile attempt to gain some knowledge of why his wives had died. He found the Nakizara natives (from whom he'd stolen the fruit) had vanished from the face of the earth. No person alive, young or old had ever heard of them (with the exception of his native guides who were with him when he stole the fruit).

He spent week after week traveling from village to village, trying to find information about the fruit or the natives from whom he'd stolen it. His desperate journeys were to no avail.

Lou interrupted by saying, "That sounds familiar."

"Yes, it does," Roulett replied, then continued to read.

Roy returned to America in such agony that he considered committing suicide. He felt first he must ask for God's forgiveness for stealing the fruit from the Nakizara, so he prayed for hours, trying to relieve the guilt he felt. The pain didn't stop. He realized he must become familiar with God first, then plead for God's forgiveness. Roy decided the best way to know God was to read his word. Roy spent several months reading and studying the Bible. His goal was to read the entire Bible. He found the answer less than a full page from completing his task. In the last chapter of Revelation and the second verse he read:

"On both sides of the river was the tree of life, bearing twelve fruits, yielding its fruits every month: and the leaves of the tree are for the healing of the nations."

He knew the plant he had wasn't the tree of life because it brought death, but the description was so close to his plant— it produced fruit in increments of twelve and it produced every month—could it be "the other plant" mentioned in Genesis? The other plant was the plant Adam and Eve were told not to eat because it would cause their deaths. Maybe it was the forbidden fruit. At that time, he thought he knew the cure was the tea made from the leaves of the plant, which produced the fruit. And he was right! The Nakizara were apparently the only people who ever knew about the fruit, so Dad assumed the four Nakizara natives were really angels sent by God and returned to heaven after accomplishing their task.

I'm an educated man, a scientist. Therefore, I was reluctant to believe the Biblical story of the Garden of Eden. But today I'm sure of one fact: the fruit my father and I both have possessed was the forbidden fruit mentioned in the Bible. If not for God's divine forgiveness, Adam would've continued to eat the fruit and mankind, as we know it, would never have existed.

Humanity's survival doesn't depend on the occasional sin that we all commit but on the practice of sin; and this practice of sin will eventually produce our destruction.

Today we're a world where the majority of people practice sin. They practice sin so often, making them skilled at sinning. For many, the pleasure of the flesh is the main objective in life; therefore, I fear the end of humanity, as we know it could be near. Although I have been guilty of these same sins, I only hope this doesn't occur in my lifetime.

You possibly will ask why I didn't destroy the fruit, the plants, and all the seeds. Because I know this plant was a part of God's ultimate plan. I cannot destroy it, but I can only guard it. I've hidden the original fruit taken from Africa with its remaining seeds in a box under a large oak table in my library, under the rug, under the middle loose tile. Lifting up the tile reveals a hidden storage area where there is an old wooden box with an heirloom Bible, two velvet bags that contain three diamonds, and the fruit.

Because it'll take a person of enormous greed and power to spread the seeds all over the world, I've willed the fruit to the least greedy person in my family. I couldn't will it to my daughter Marie, although I've never seen any signs of greed in her, because I fear that, if the fruit belonged to her, it would most likely end up in the hands of one or both of her sons Jack or Kirk. I feel greed should be her sons' middle names. I'm not leaving it to my biological son, Charles for that same reason.

I've willed the box and its contents to my granddaughter-in-law, Roulett. She has a strong will and a mind of her own; therefore, I don't think Jack or Kirk could persuade her to do anything other than what is right for all. Roulett has been a sweet song in my golden years, and I trust with all my heart that she'll make the right decision concerning the fruit.

I've willed to her the old Bible that belonged to my grandmother, Caroline, which was an heirloom from her grandmother, Flossie, and the original stolen fruit. The three diamonds—highly prized gifts from my grandfather Edward Clayton, to my grandmother Rebecca—are actually bonuses from me. The Bible contains some highlighted scriptures that could be a hint about what the fruit is, but I can't simply tell her about the fruit. She must face the test of temptation concerning the fruit, the same test as all others before her, so I've hidden the journal separately from the fruit. Nevertheless, I hope someday one of my relatives will find it.

You may think this is a heavy burden to put on any one person; but, in the end, it won't be Roulett's decision about what happens with the fruit. If it's God's will, she'll guard it, as has been done in the past. However, when God selects the time to use the fruit, no man or woman can stop it.

I don't know when, or to what extent, the fruit will be used to cleanse the earth. Only time will tell if it'll be only some of mankind, the most of mankind, or all of mankind. Only God can judge the sins of mankind and only He'll know when it is time to fulfill the prophecy Revelation 11: 18—"It is time to destroy those who destroy the earth!"

Roulett stopped reading as she contemplated John-George's profound words. After a few moments, she said, "I'm not certain that he knew the whole story. I think there's a lot more to the Garden of Eden story than we may ever understand! I don't think God would destroy mankind in this manner…but it certainly is food for thought."

Lou was beyond answering her as he watched Roulett look down at John-George's final words. "This is an interesting finish," Roulett said before continuing to read.

In the end, I don't know if it was a curse or a blessing to possess the Seeds of Temptation.

Acknowledgments

To everyone who helped and encouraged me...I thank you. There are too many friends, family, and of course, editors to list but you know who you are. This was a daunting task for me. Although I graduated from the 8th grade from Tiawah School as their valedictorian, it was not because of my English and spelling skills. While I excel at math and science, I ain't no good at grammar. I cannot spell well enough to type more than about three words per minute, and sometimes a simple word will stump me for as much as an hour. I use voice type but since I speak fluent Okie and the voice type does not always understand me, that is not a fast solution either. Nevertheless, I thank everyone who helped me finish this first book—there are more to come!